SWEET ANTICIPATION

Kate put on her nightgown and sat down to brush
her hair, but she had completed no more than half a
dozen strokes when Brett entered the cabin quietly.
She heard a click as he turned the key in the lock
and her heart nearly stopped beating. Now there
was no hope of escape. *You're a fool*, she told herself.
There never was.

Brett came to stand behind her; without a word he
took the brush from her hands and began to stroke
her hair expertly. He's probably brushed more hair
than half the ladies' maids in London, Kate thought.
There's no telling *what* this man has done.

Kate started to tie up her hair, but Brett pulled it
loose again. "I don't want it in a knot. I want to be
able to run my fingers through it," he said softly.

For one moment, she thought wildly of throwing
herself on the captain's mercy or leaping into the
sea, but she couldn't even get out of the cabin. She
trembled inside. She could think of nothing to do,
so she got up and walked over to the narrow bed.
"Which side do you prefer?" she asked in what she
hoped was a calm voice.

"It doesn't matter tonight," he said with a smile
that promised pleasures she could not even imagine
...or resist....

Leigh Greenwood

Seductive Wager

LOVE SPELL NEW YORK CITY

LOVE SPELL®

February 2009

Published by

Dorchester Publishing Co., Inc.
200 Madison Avenue
New York, NY 10016

ISBN 10: 0-505-52529-1
ISBN 13: 978-0-505-52529-1

The name "Love Spell" and its logo are trademarks of Dorchester Publishing Co., Inc.

Printed in the United States of America.

10 9 8 7 6 5 4 3 2 1

Visit us on the web at www.dorchesterpub.com.

Chapter 1

The large room lay shrouded in shadows except for two points of feeble light coming from near-guttered candles, their pale glow casting into relief the motionless figures seated at opposite ends of a massive oaken table strewn with scraps of paper and empty glasses. Black with age and use, the table so dominated the room it threatened to reduce its inhabitants to mere trappings.

"I'm ruined," Martin Vareyan declared with a sharp eruption of contained breath that fell into the silence of the room like drops of water into a hot fire. "You've won everything." He stared with a fixed gaze at his antagonist, his blazing eyes a window to the turbulence raging within him; he longed to spring up and close his hands around Brett Westbrook's throat, to crush the beautifully tied cravat until those masterful eyes were filled with fear, a sensation Brett had never experienced.

"You shouldn't have raised the stakes when the cards were against you," Brett said, his tone matter-of-fact.

"Shut up, dammit!" Martin shouted, unable to contain a spurting flame of wild anger. "I don't need anybody to tell me how to play cards."

"I suppose your game tonight is proof?" Brett questioned, bald contempt in his nearly black eyes.

5

Martin choked back an intemperate reply as his rapt gaze focused on a single scrap of paper, larger than all the rest, whereon was listed his house, his lands, his money, his *entire inheritance!* Now it belonged to Brett Westbrook. There was no question but that he had to get it back. What taxed his mind was how.

Martin looked around at the other players, desperately seeking a way out, but they had come to the end of their luck long ago and were scattered about the room like pieces of discarded clothing. Edward Hunglesby slept upright in his chair without sound or motion; Peter Feathers, too drunk to know he was near suffocation, lay with his head hanging over the arm of his chair; Barnaby Rudge, sprawled half on and half off the sofa where he lay, snored with huge, gusty sobs that rasped Martin's badly frayed nerves. A small water spaniel lying on a grimy rug underneath her owner's chair shifted position then was quiet once more.

Martin's hooded gaze returned to his opponent for a long moment. Unmoved by the scrutiny, Brett leaned back in his chair and returned Martin's stare with unflinching *sang-froid;* he had lost interest in this interminable game long ago, but his sable eyes were watchful and his mind alert.

Martin swallowed convulsively several times, causing the muscles around his mouth to tighten. "No," his hissed reply came at last. "Not tonight."

"I didn't think so," Brett returned in icy affirmation. His own temper had flared dangerously; he was a proud man who rarely suffered even his best friends to speak to him as Martin had just done. "What you needed was better cards and more luck. You were completely out of both."

"I suppose you'll be willing to wait longer than the usual fortnight?" Martin temporized, trying to gain time, trying to think. "There's a good deal more than

6

can be done in two weeks." He reached for the brandy, poured the remaining drops into his glass, and drained them off in a single gulp. He then looked around for more, but there was nothing left save empty bottles; he would have to summon Ned. His legs threatened to buckle under him as he rose to his feet, but by concentrating with savage intensity, he forced them to bear him across the room. Even three-parts drunk, his pride wouldn't allow him to stagger in front of Brett.

Martin gave the bell rope a sharp jerk. "That ought to raise the old miscreant from his slumbers," he announced morosely, but Brett ignored his remark and Martin was forced to turn on Barnaby Rudge to vent his fury. "Lawyers take forever to do a thing and then make a mystery about it. Don't know why I invited the bloodsucker," he growled, giving Barnaby such a vicious kick he awoke, cursing and bellowing, with a startled howl.

"Who in the bloody hell kicked me?"

"I did," Martin snarled. "You've been snoring all night."

"That's no reason to kick a man in his sleep," Barnaby groaned, still only half awake. "If you wanted me to stop, all you had to do was ask."

"Ask!" Martin snorted indignantly. "I might as well talk to this bitch spaniel," he stormed, pointing to the dog still slumbering under his chair. "I never heard such a filthy racket. I don't know how *you* can sleep through it." He stomped back to his chair, forgetting to conceal the drunken lurch in his stride, and sank down, cold rage threatening to destroy the last remnants of his restraint.

He was losing control of the situation, and now Brett was smiling at him. Damn the supercilious bastard! He would be revenged on him if it took every cent he possessed, but first he had to think of some way to win back his fortune. If only his head didn't

7

feel like solid wood.

"Gawd!" Peter Feathers groaned piteously as he raised his head and opened his bloodshot eyes. "How much brandy did I drink?" Putting his fingers to his temples, he shut his eyes with a grimace. "Never had such a head in my life. Your wine merchant must be cheating you, old man. Couldn't be so burnt in the socket otherwise."

"Bloody hell," Martin cursed. "Now we'll have the whole room up."

Feathers attempted to sit up, but that was beyond him, and he slumped forward on the table. He was very drunk, but he didn't care; he had lost a great deal of money, but he didn't care about that, either. All he could think of now was how to get more brandy. "The hair of the dog that bites you," he muttered obscurely. He picked up the bottle Martin had just emptied, peered at it closely, then rolled it from side to side.

"It's empty," he said in the voice of one making a surprising discovery. "Must get more. Tell your man to bustle about, Martin. Can't have your guests going thirsty."

"You ought to have your head shoved under a pump," Brett snapped, glowering coldly at Peter. He wasn't in the habit of consorting with green boys, and he resented having to put up with a stripling who should have been in bed hours ago.

It was a badly mismatched party. There was only one guest for whom Brett felt any liking, and that one had just opened his eyes. Edward Hunglesby didn't move at first but allowed his gaze, clear and unclouded by sleep or alcoholic fumes, to slowly inventory the room and its occupants. Then, with a quintessential sigh of world-weariness, he sat up.

"I suppose you're wondering why I don't take myself off to bed rather than loll about in the middle of your game," he said, directing his remarks to no one

8

in particular. "Actually, I don't know myself. My cards didn't offer me sufficient reason. And as I remember it, if I *must* remember it," he said, staring accusingly at Feathers's vacuous face, "the conversation didn't, either. Considering the service in this ill-run establishment has rendered my stay as close to a sojourn in purgatory as I ever hope to experience, I'm surprised I haven't removed to the nearest inn, no matter how bucolic its proprietor." These remarks caused Martin to swell with fury, but Edward felt so much better for having rid himself of some of his spleen, he actually smiled at his host.

"Might I be allowed to ring for water?" he inquired with bland innocence. "I doubt this beverage has ever graced your table, either in a glass *or* a cleaning pail," he said, eyeing the wine stains with disgust, "but when I drink bad brandy, I get a noble headache, and the only thing that seems to help is water." He leaned back, closed his eyes to underline the exquisite nature of his agony, and prepared to wait for Martin to summon his servant.

"I know how you feel," Feathers informed him, full of sympathy for a fellow sufferer but aghast at such a notion. "I feel pretty grim myself, but you can't mean to actually *drink* water. I promise you won't like it. Have some more brandy. Or maybe you ought to try some beer."

Edward sat up very straight, opened his eyes, and fixed Feathers with a deadly gaze. "I do not know why you should think you know better than I what will best suit my constitution," he said in a voice that had abashed more than one seasoned aristocrat, "but I can assure you that you do *not!*" Feathers blinked at the reproof. "I should feel much more hopeful of your being safely restored to the bosom of your family if *you* would forego the brandy decanter as well."

Making a heroic recovery, Peter smiled brightly at

9

Edward. "There's no call for you to fall into a worry about me."

"I wasn't aware that I had," Edward replied, appalled at the thought of so uncharacteristic an action.

"I'll be in fine shape as soon as this head goes off a bit," Peter continued. "Never considered anything like water, though. I'm surprised you keep the stuff about, Martin."

"Shut up, you fool," Martin growled before turning to Edward with an ugly glare. "Ned'll be here with some more brandy any minute now. You can tell him about your water then. If anybody wants anything different, speak up. I don't keep a bunch of fancy servants to eat their heads off and fall over themselves with nothing to do," he announced belligerently. "And I get what I want, when I want it, just the same." The last remark was directed at Edward, but that gentleman had once more closed his eyes. It was beneath his dignity to bandy words with Martin.

"Take a damper," Peter intervened, dead to the heated emotions that swirled about him. "No sense in getting excited over something as silly as water." Smothering a huge yawn, he stood up to stretch his long, lithe body; his eyes fell on Martin's cards, and his interest was caught immediately. "What a rotten hand. You were getting some pretty good cards before I fell asleep."

Noticing neither Martin's clenched teeth nor his hard eyes, Feathers leaned over to glance at Brett's hand. "Scalped him again, did you?" he announced merrily. "Damn, you do have all the luck."

"You're not playing, so sit down and be quiet," Brett commanded with barely contained annoyance.

"No need to get upset," Peter said, as oblivious to the red glow in Martin's eyes as he was impervious to insult. "Damned fool thing for Martin to do, betting on a hand like that, but it's his money and he can do anything he likes with it."

Martin started up with murder in his eyes, but Edward forestalled him. "Unless my ears deceive me," he said, cocking his head in the direction of the door, "that is the deathlike tread of the faithful Ned." Martin sank back into his chair, his eyes still burning dangerously.

"I have suffered much from you," Edward said to Feathers with stinging contempt, "but the fatuous mumblings of a hairless stripling I will *not* endure with this vile brandy hammering in my head."

Feathers's easy temper remained unimpaired for the simple reason he could not believe such a reprimand was meant for him.

"What took you so long?" Martin demanded as an aging retainer entered the room. "I was hoping you were dead."

"I will be if I keep running up and down these halls," his grizzled servant replied as he pushed the empty bottles aside and sat the brandy and glasses down in front of Martin. "The corridors to hell can't be any colder than this old castle." He dodged Martin's halfhearted attempt to cuff him. "Would your honors be wanting anything else tonight?"

"Mr. Hunglesby wants some water. And you needn't stare at me like that," Martin snapped in surly response to Ned's gawking disbelief. "I'm not going to drink any."

"My desperation is undoubtedly a testament to the quality of your brandy," Edward purred. The quiet voice coming so unexpectedly from behind him caused Ned to spin around too quickly, and he stumbled over Martin's spaniel. She responded with a yelp and a snap at his ankle; Ned turned on her with curse and an upraised hand.

"Touch that dog, and it'll be your blood that's spilt," Martin warned.

"That old bitch is gonna take a chunk out of me one of these days," Ned protested.

"She won't get much for her pains."

"Loath as I am to interrupt this exchange of pleasantries, I must entreat you to fetch my water with all possible dispatch," Edward murmured in dulcet tones. "This vile potion has so battered my sensibilities, each minute seems destined to be my last." Ned's incredulous look brought a thin smile to Edward's lips. "You need not worry. I am not a lunatic, nor will you be required to summon aid to subdue me."

"It may take a little while," Ned mumbled peevishly. "We don't keep water inside at night."

"Then have done with your complaining and be gone," Martin ordered.

Ned had almost reached the door when Martin called after him, his voice a little edgy and overloud. "Tell my sister I want her to come down as soon as she can get dressed."

Ned whirled around, too surprised to remember his rheumatism. "But she's sound asleep," he stammered. "She's been in bed for hours."

"Then wake her," Martin snarled. "I want her down in fifteen minutes, or I'll come up and get her myself."

Ned had never been one to endanger his own hide for anybody else, but he made one last attempt to protect his mistress. "You know she won't come down, not when you're having company."

"Get her down here inside of fifteen minutes, or I'll sic the dog on you," Martin threatened.

Martin knew Kate had refused to leave her bedchamber the moment Ned stuck his head in the door without entering the room.

"Miss Kate says she's not coming down in her robes or any other kind of dress," he disclosed hurriedly. "She says you're to send for your tavern trollops if you want female company." Ned snapped the door

12

shut just before an empty brandy bottle smashed against it, scattering dangerous shards of broken glass over the flagstone floor.

Martin could see the corners of Brett's mouth quiver, and his anger exploded like a volcano. This hated man had humiliated him at cards and stripped him of his possessions; now he was actually laughing at him. It was more than Martin's fevered brain could bear, and he rose to his feet in an almost blinding red haze of fury.

"You goddamn worthless son of a bitch!" he bellowed after his servant as he ran unsteadily toward the door. But Ned's tottering form had already disappeared through the archway at the back of the great hall. "I'll break every bone in your maggot-infested body if my sister's not down in five minutes," Martin shouted after the hollow echo of Ned's retreating footsteps; then he stomped back into the room, snatched the brandy bottle from Feathers's hands, raised it to his lips, threw back his head, and drank deeply from its contents.

Brett reacted with disgust, but Peter said in a hollow voice, "Really, old fellow, that's not the done thing. Been happy to give you the whole bottle if I'd known you wanted it. Didn't know hollering could make a man so thirsty."

Martin slammed the bottle down on the table and his large fist snaked out to grasp Peter by his neckcloth.

"Shut your mouth, you jabbering fool," he roared. "If I don't have at least five minutes without the sound of your voice, I'm going to hang you on a nail by your fancy cravat." Peter struggled to free himself, his breath coming in gasps, but he was too drunk and Martin was too strong.

"You have my sympathy," intruded Brett's cold, flinty voice, "but I shouldn't think it would be necessary to resort to such extremes." He eyed Martin with increasing dislike. "Neither would I like for you to mishandle poor Feathers. He's the last of his name, and his family still holds out some hope for him." Brett's eyes no longer smiled and his body was tense, ready to spring.

"He's already a horse's ass," Martin choked, furious at Brett's intervention.

"Possibly, but he's not *your* horse's ass. I'm sure you can leave him safely disposed in his chair. I can't imagine he'll be very comfortable there, but he's bound to feel better once he can breathe." Feathers's struggles were growing more frantic, and Brett continued to regard Martin with the unmistakable bearing of a man who expected to be obeyed, one who was prepared to *see* that he was obeyed. Martin's courage faltered before the keen-edged lance of Brett's gaze, and nearly choking with fury, he released Feathers; that bewildered gentleman staggered backward to the safety of his chair.

"I never meant to hurt the young cockerel," Martin growled. "It's my bitch of a sister I want to get my hands on. Tavern trollops, says she. I'll have her down here if I have to drag her by her hair, half naked and screaming all the way."

"I can't imagine how I can bear to tear myself away from this enthralling melodrama," Edward intoned in a blighting voice, "but I believe I shall go to bed. I wonder why I came? Whatever the reason, it was not sufficient. I feel positively *soiled.*"

The last word was weighted with enough contempt to penetrate a hide far thicker than Martin's, and he quailed inwardly under the lash of that silken tongue.

"You shouldn't expect drawing-room manners from Martin," Brett said, disregarding Martin's gobbling fury. "Didn't you hear him say he preferred his horse to his mistress?" Martin brought his fist down on the table so hard the brandy bottle jumped and two of the glasses spilled their contents.

14

"You can't goad me with your insults," he roared, hate nearly choking the words in his throat. "I've never cared what you thought of me, and it's not going to worry me now." He turned on Edward, thrusting his face so close their noses nearly touched. "And you, my ever so fine and particular gentleman, can sit back down. I haven't finished with you yet."

"Possibly," Edward said, drawing his face back from Martin's nearly purple visage with obvious distaste, "but I see no reason why I should be expected to inhale the air you have just fouled with your breath." With deliberate insolence, he placed the carefully manicured index finger of his right hand squarely in the middle of Martin's nose and slowly pushed his face away from him.

"I can see no purpose in pursuing this disastrous game," Brett interrupted, out of patience with Martin's ill humor. "I suggest we retire to our respective chambers. Rest may bring council, and a change in your luck."

"I don't want your advice, damn your eyes," Martin screamed, a wild and uncomprehending look in his eyes. "I don't want *anybody's* advice. I want to play another game, and I'm *going* to play another game. You can't refuse me the chance to recover my losses." He banged his fist on the table again. "Hell and damnation, man, you've *got* to keep on playing."

Brett glanced at the pile of coins and pieces of paper littering the table before him. It galled him to admit Martin was right, but he'd won so heavily there was no way he could honorably refuse.

"It was never my intention to strip you of your possessions," he said contemptuously. "I have enough for my own needs, and suitable charities are hard to find."

"You don't have to be so high and mighty just because the cards have been running your way," Martin stormed. "I'm not done up yet." Brett was

15

annoyed at the slight to his skill, but he held his peace. Martin took another deep drink from the bottle and leaned down the table, his breath labored and his eyes wide.

"You haven't beaten me yet," he rasped, his words beginning to slur. "I'll come about. He stood up on unsteady legs and whirled around like he was looking for something. "Where's that whoring sister of mine?" he yelled. "I sent for her ages ago." There was a hint of querulousness in his voice. He staggered over to the bell rope and began to pull on it like a steeple bell ringer.

"You know *I* find your company quite delightful," Edward murmured in an expressionless voice, "but it is entirely possible your sister has no liking for you in your present condition."

An unusually violent pull on the bell rope caused it to come away in Martin's hands, and he threw it from him in a flurry of virulent curses on the nature of Edward's conception and the manner of his birth. The rope glanced off his spaniel's hip, and she leaped up with a protesting howl that turned into a menacing growl. In his wild fury, Martin charged his dog, kicking drunkenly at her age-thickened body, and she sank her teeth into his leg with a snap. Exploding with a roar of pain, Martin gave her such a savage blow upon the nose that she released her grip on his calf, whined, and cowered under his raining blows.

"Stupid bitch!" Martin thundered, stumbling over to the door and dragging the yelping animal behind him. "No female is going to flout my orders. She'll learn to her sorrow who's master in this house." He opened the door and flung the whimpering animal into the hall without a glance. "Don't any of you leave this room. I'll be back with that black-hearted wench, and then we'll see if you can keep on winning."

He turned so swiftly he rocked on his heels, but he

recovered his balance quickly and strode out of the room, slamming the door behind him with a loud crack.

Edward raised his eyes from their contemplation of his impeccable nails and addressed the room with an unruffled calm. "I wonder which bitch he was referring to? If he treats one like the other, I shouldn't be surprised if we see Miss Vareyan sink *her* teeth into his flesh. I can't help but think it a suitable response to the tender regard he so touchingly expressed for her. You're a clever man," he said turning to Brett. "Isn't there some way you can accidentally discharge a pistol in his direction? Actually, a sword would serve just as well. I'm persuaded if you cleaned the blade very carefully afterward, there would be no lingering effects." Brett refused to be drawn, but Peter more than made up for his restraint.

"The fellow's loco. Had a filly once acted like that. Couldn't do a thing with her. Attacked her groom. Even tried to climb a tree. Nothing for it but to put her down. Shame, too. She had the finest shoulder of any horse I ever owned."

"I'm sorry about your filly, Peter," Brett remarked, unable to keep his voice entirely steady, "but Martin is our host, and we can't put a bullet through him no matter how much he may remind you of a horse's shoulder."

"On the contrary," Edward remarked, taking a small enameled snuff box from his pocket, "I think it's an excellent suggestion. I suspect the justice of the peace would take exception if we were to make a *practice* of it, but one small shooting might very well go unnoticed. If we were to offer his remains to his misused spaniel or that pitifully abused hunter I saw him hacking this afternoon, I'm convinced little evidence of our misconduct would remain."

"For God's sake, be quiet," Brett begged. "Everyone knows you have no conscience. The only guilt

17

you can feel is over a poorly chosen waistcoat, or a drawing room hung in crimson velvet." Edward winced palpably, but his eyes twinkled.

"I should think he would," the forever gullible Feathers declared. "It's enough to give a fellow the shakes. Not that I ever had much use for drawing rooms myself," he added thoughtfully. "Can't stand them actually. Always full of frightful females trying to get your ring on their finger and their hand in your pocket."

"If you could still your tongue for even a short while," Brett snapped, unable to contain himself, "it is just possible your eyes and ears might be able to deposit some small amount of knowledge in your pitifully empty head."

"If you mean to try and rectify all of Mother Nature's oversights, dear boy, you're in for a wearisome existence," Edward drawled. "For all her accomplishments, the old girl is remarkably careless sometimes." He rose to his feet and stretched his stiff limbs. "I really must have something to drink. I don't suppose Ned will hazard a return to this room tonight, nor can I blame him, but I wish he had thought to furnish me with directions to the kitchen. In my desperation I considered brandy, but after the manner in which our host slaked his thirst, I would prefer the stable pump."

"Shut up about your water," Brett ordered. "You're getting to be as long-winded as Feathers. When a man makes a mistress of his housekeeper, there's no chance of being properly attended to in his house. Now sit down and stop prowling about the room. I don't know what Martin means to do, but I fear you'll need all your strength before this interminable night is over."

"He does seem determined to play out his final dissolution before our very eyes," Edward complained. "If the sister is anything like the brother, the

18

final scene should be ghastly." With a shrug of resignation, he settled back in his chair to await the inevitable dénouement.

Chapter 2

The door burst open and a girl catapulted into the room with such momentum she tripped over the bell rope and tumbled into Feathers's lap. Before the astonished onlookers could do more than gasp in unison, she looked about in utter terror and retreated as far as possible from the strangers who goggled at her as they scrambled to their feet. She was nearly fainting from shame, but the passionate rage blazing in her eyes refused to acknowledge that her whole body quivered with mortification.

Even in the dim candlelight, it was obvious that Kate Vareyan was stunningly beautiful. The perfect oval of her face, the shining halo of her golden hair, the delicate loveliness of her features, and the creamy peachlike softness of her skin combined to strike her audience mute. But it was her form, imperfectly concealed by the threadbare nightgown, that set Brett's pulses racing and caused his breath to catch in his throat. Hers was not the body of a girl, but that of a young woman, a titillating combination of youthful innocence and full-blown sensuality. Brett could easily see the shape of her breasts where they thrust out against the fabric of her gown, her nipples forming small points of desire, and it caused a pulsating ache to arc through his whole body. From the narrow tapering waist to the long, slim limbs and the dainty ankles, she was a vision certain to arouse the demon of desire in any man. When she faced her beholders with flashing blue eyes and the blush of roses in her cheeks, the effect was breathtaking.

It was left to Feathers, rooted to the floor like a biblical pillar of salt, to sum up the group's collective opinion. "Gawd Almighty," he stammered in awed tones. "She's perfect. Like a goddamned Greek statue."

In the agony of her shame, Kate turned on Martin like a cornered creature. "How dare you expose me to the leering gaze of your drunken companions?" she blazed at him. "Are you completely without a sense of decency?"

Martin's slap caused her to stagger against the massive carved stone mantel, but before his hand could return to his side, Brett had sprung from his chair and sent him crashing to the floor.

"A gentleman does not strike a lady, not even when he's drunk," Brett said in a voice tight with rage, his eyes like onyx. "Get up and beg her pardon."

"Hell and be damned," Martin blustered. "I'll be more likely to raise another welt on her face." Brett dragged Martin to his feet and sent him sprawling against the legs of the table with a second blow.

"Apologize, or I'll choke it out of you," he declared with lethal menace. Feeling his jaw to make sure it wasn't broken, Martin collected his numbed wits, swallowed his pride, and mumbled something that could be taken for an apology. Then he crawled into his chair and reached for the brandy bottle.

Brett turned to Kate, his heated gaze traveling slowly over her body from head to foot; his inflamed senses turned his usually well-ordered thoughts into a chaotic jumble, and he felt desire spring up like a raging bull. He knew the danger of continuing to stare at her, but she was undoubtedly the most beautiful creature he had ever seen, and he was unable to turn his gaze.

Kate was infuriated by Brett's probing eyes, but

she refused to cringe before his brazen scrutiny even though it covered her with fresh embarrassment. Why didn't he have the decency to look away instead of boring through her with those coal black eyes? *I hate him,* she thought to herself. *I hate all men.*

"Thank you, sir," she said, speaking the words in a sweetly ironic voice, "but forgive me if I seem astonished at your concern for a lowly female. I've not been accustomed to look for consideration from one of your sex."

Brett didn't answer immediately, and Kate thought she saw something flicker in his eyes—a softness or a feeling of sympathy—but it was quickly gone. "I don't imagine you were ever a *lowly female,*" he stated bluntly, "but if you continue to stand about bandying words with me in your present state of undress, I shall be forced to take you at your own estimation."

Kate swelled with such indignation she momentarily forgot her outraged modesty. "It may have escaped your brandy-clouded notice, but I did not come into this room by choice," she raged, her eyes flashing blue fire. "It has never been an object with me to pander to the low passions of the male sex. I loathe and despise the lot of you." Her hand brushed her face to dash away the tears of hot humiliation flowing down her cheeks. "Even you must perceive the difficulty of covering one's self with a robe one does not possess." She clenched her fists in frustration and stamped her slipper-clad feet on the stone floor.

Brett was not accustomed to females who stamped their feet at him or tore his character to shreds. He had the distinct feeling that getting to know her would be an enlivening experience, but it was not an acquaintance, he decided on reflection, he wished to pursue. Nevertheless, a curious smile broke the solemnity of his expression and he sat down slowly, continuing to stare at her in an oddly abstract manner.

"All this is most entertaining, but highly improper," Edward observed dryly. "Miss Vareyan, I fear nothing short of blinding will stop these normally courteous men from staring at you in this blatant manner. I also expect Martin would resist any effort of mine to assist you to leave this room. That, I'm afraid, leaves us very little choice as to how to resolve this embarrassing situation." He retrieved his driving cloak from where it had been tossed over a chair and draped the large, heavy garment over Kate's shoulders. She was too angry with Brett to do more than offer Edward a nod of her head in gratitude.

"She may return to her bedchamber," Brett said, his quietly spoken words directed to Edward but his eyes on Martin. Edward's eyes traveled quickly from Brett to Martin and then back to Kate.

"She's my sister, and she'll do what *I* say," Martin shouted.

"Not unless she wishes," Brett countered, his unbending gaze shutting off Martin's protest. "Do you wish to retire, Miss Vareyan?"

Kate didn't know what to say. That anyone would help her was unexpected, that anyone would defend her hard to believe, but that this stranger would defy Martin just to spare her embarrassment was inconceivable. She glanced up at her brother and quailed inwardly at the venom in his eyes. This stranger might protect her now, but he wouldn't be here tomorrow, or the next day, in case Martin decided to take out his anger on her. Besides, what harm could there be in staying a few moments more? She couldn't be any more embarrassed than she already was.

"Thank you," she said finally, "but I'll stay a little

23

longer. Martin must have wanted me for something, and I'm warm enough with this cloak." She pulled the garment tightly around her shoulders. It didn't reach her ankles, but she was hardly aware of that.

Brett nodded curtly and sat down, a fierce scowl on his face. He could guess the reason behind Kate's answer, and the thought that she might be mistreated in his absence angered him.

After gulping down another glass of brandy to help him recover from Brett's rough handling, Martin brought his open palm down on the table, interrupting Feathers in a fanciful but garbled series of compliments.

"That's enough, puppy," he blustered, ignoring Feathers's flush of anger and turning irascibly to Brett. "I demand one more chance to make good my losses." He jumped up and dragged his sister toward Brett. "I'm going to stake the last thing I have against my IOU's." Cries of protest and exclamations of disbelief erupted about him, but Martin kept his eyes glued to Brett's face.

"That's right," he stormed. "My sister against everything on that paper."

"Don't be a fool," Brett commanded, his voice rough and unsteady. "Nobody stakes his own kin in a card game."

"I *have* to. She's all I have," Martin declared, fixing Brett with a hawklike glare. "And by God, she's worth every guinea on the table, and then some. Look at her! Did you ever see anything to beat it?" He attempted to pull the cloak from Kate's shoulders, but her fingers clamped tightly over the folds of the flawlessly cut garment, and she turned to Edward with an imploring look.

"Thank you for your touching faith, my dear," he said, grinning ruefully, "but it's badly misplaced. I would strive to defend you with all my ability, but I'm persuaded you would do better to enlist Mr.

Westbrook's aid."

"She can keep the damned cloak," Martin cursed. "Brett's already seen her. You know she's better looking than the titled beauties you normally seduce. And you won't have to wait until midnight, or until her husband's out of town, either, for your little bit of fun." He leaned down the table and sank his voice into a conspiratorial whisper. "Wouldn't it be nice to have a warm little ladybird to cuddle up to whenever the mood strikes? She's a tasty morsel. Her temper's a bit sharp, but you ought to be able to handle that with some of your famous charm."

Brett was not accustomed to having his personal life discussed publicly, but to have his intimate affairs talked about in front of a gently bred female caused his temper to boil over.

"You contemptible swine," he rasped. "I'll oblige you with any wager you like, but I don't traffic in humans."

"The man's gone completely off his head," broke in Feathers, who had been making odd noises for several minutes. "I'm as fond of the game as any man alive, but I wouldn't wager my sister, even if I had one, which I don't, being an only child."

"I doubt there's any way to still his tongue, short of death," groaned Edward.

"It doesn't matter what you think, stripling," Martin roared. "I'm offering her to Brett, and he's honor-bound to accept any wager I propose."

"I cannot see how Brett can *in honor* accept your wager," Edward objected, clearing his throat. "Miss Vareyan may not be of any value to you, but she is a person, albeit a female, and should be treated with consideration. To drag her half naked about a castle and then offer her as a stake in a card game is behavior that would reflect poorly on us all."

"Westbrook's not afraid of what people might say about him," Martin exploded. "He's rich enough to thumb his nose at your whole bloody class."

"I'm nearly unmanned by your tribute, Martin," Brett snapped, "but I wish you wouldn't try to explain me to my friends." Martin flushed, but he held his gaze.

"You're nearly correct," Brett continued. "I'll accept almost any wager, but I'm not drunk enough, or heedless enough of society's customs, to toss the dice for your sister. Marry her off if you don't want her. With that face, you shouldn't have any trouble finding someone to take her off your hands. How about young Feathers here?"

Kate bit her lip to keep from speaking. How dare he talk about her like she was property to be disposed of at will. He was just as bad as Martin, a ruthless man used to having his own way and willing to walk over anybody to get it. She wouldn't be surprised if he had seduced half the women in London.

"You're so rich you can probably find half a dozen properties you didn't know you owned," Martin grumbled impatiently, "but Kate is all I have left. It's her against the whole estate. You can't refuse me."

Barnaby Rudge had sat quietly for the last while, but at those words, he turned and stared at Martin, his piglike eyes wide with the light of intense interest. "Estate?" he questioned.

"Shut up, Barnaby," Martin barked in warning. "This is none of your business." He glared so threateningly that the others thought he might attack his corpulent friend.

Unfazed by Martin's menace, Barnaby looked as though he was about to say something, but he apparently changed his mind and settled back in his chair. "Suit yourself," he muttered. "It's not my money."

"That's right," Martin snarled. "And Kate's not

your sister. If anybody else has a mouthful of high-flown words and mawkish sentiment, you can keep it to yourself. For the last time," he said, whirling about to face Brett once more, "are you going to accept my wager, or are you going to let these spineless ditch rats talk you into backing down?" Brett was silent.

"No doubt he's overcome by the eloquence with which you state your case," Edward purred, but Martin continued to watch Brett like a cat at a mousehole.

"Come on, don't keep me waiting all night," Martin erupted. "Dammit, you can't leave me like this. I *demand* satisfaction."

Brett turned his eyes from Kate; he was afraid if he continued to look at her, he would be willing to take any risk to get her in his possession. He told himself that one didn't gamble for human beings, that one person couldn't own another person, but after one glance at Kate, the primitive instinct to take what he wanted threatened to bury his carefully acquired veneer of refined behavior.

"Has it occurred to you that I might win this time as well?" Brett asked, hoping he could persuade Martin to withdraw his offer.

"I'm going to win," Martin screamed furiously. "I've *got* to win."

"Have you considered your sister's feelings?" Brett held up his hand to forestall Martin's explosive outburst. "I won't have it said I abducted anyone. I'd rather travel with fighting cocks than a female suffering from the vapors or fainting spells."

"She's my ward and she'll do as I say," Martin shouted, but Brett cut short his objection.

"How do you feel about being a wager in a game of high stakes, Miss Vareyan?" he asked in a voice not entirely free of mockery.

"Women have always been wagers in games of

'high stakes,' as you so carefully put it," she said, regarding him with scornful eyes. "Whenever a man takes a wife, her looks, breeding, dowry, family, and ability to breed heirs are all he considers. If the whole estate were my dowry and you were asking Martin for my hand in marriage, it wouldn't be any different, except that Martin seems to have lost his estate and I have no dowry."

Brett stared at her, the boredom and mockery gone from his glance and a questioning look filling his dark eyes, but Kate was staring at Martin. She knew she risked losing her reputation if she left Ryehill with Brett, but Martin hadn't allowed her outside the castle in four years; he could murder her and throw her body in the cellars and no one would know.

"As for my being a wager . . ." she resumed at last, "it might as well be now as another time. He's gambled away my dowry—do you know how unlikely it is that a penniless girl will receive an honorable offer of marriage?—and you see how he uses me." She massaged her bruised cheek. "In a few years I won't be pretty enough to attract a husband."

"Surely it's not that bad," Edward exclaimed, startled by the sadness in her voice.

"How can a man know what it's like to be a woman?" she demanded, turning on him with unexpected fury. "You come and go as you please and your honor isn't questioned, but I'm locked up like a prisoner, and there's nothing anyone can do about it, even if they wanted to." She started to cry and Feathers, startled out of his trance by her tears, offered her his handkerchief, but she drove him back to his seat with a gesture of furious rejection.

"You don't care about me," she shouted accusingly at all of them. "You're just embarrassed at being caught in such a disagreeable situation and hoping it will soon end." She buried her face in the cloak to hide her hot tears.

The truth of her words made Brett angrier still. Now, damn and blast, Edward and Feathers were looking to him to resolve this squalid little imbroglio. What in the world could he do with this girl? There was always the possibility he would lose the game, but that was no longer an acceptable solution. Kate was calmer now, but the tears still glistened on her lashes. By God, she was the most beautiful girl he'd ever seen. He could feel his pulses start to race and his desire rise just by looking at her. She had intelligence, beauty, and spirit. He turned abruptly to Martin.

"I'll accept your wager, but only on my terms."

"Any conditions you want," Martin panted.

"You haven't heard them yet," Brett replied with biting disdain. Ignoring Martin's eagerness, he paused to clear his head of the effects of the brandy. "If I win, everything goes to your sister. You'll leave this castle as soon as it can be arranged and have no claim on her."

"All right," Martin muttered impatiently. "Just get on with the game."

"I'm not finished," Brett continued. "I'm not betting the money, just the estate." Martin's eyes opened wider and his mouth worked nervously. "Is Rudge there your legal man?"

Martin nodded.

"Then remember what I say. I don't want any questions about it later. If Martin wins, he gets the estate free and clear, but the money on the table and the equivalent of one year's income goes to his sister as her dowry." Martin looked mutinous, but he nodded his acceptance.

"I'm leaving for Paris in a few days, but I'll have my lawyers set up banking arrangements and see that Miss Vareyan is settled in London and provided with a suitable companion. Finally, I'm not going to throw those accursed dice again. We're going to cut for the highest card. One card each. Whoever wins the cut, wins everything."

Martin regarded Brett steadfastly, his eyes glowing with hatred, but he'd gone so far he had no other choice but to continue. And his bitch of a sister was looking at Brett like he was an avenging knight! He'd settle with her later. She'd rot in hell before she handed over a single penny.

Brett seemed to divine his thoughts. "If you accept my conditions and don't carry them out, I'll personally rend you limb from limb."

"I said I would, goddamnit," Martin snarled. "Just get on with it."

"Here, I want your help," Brett said to Rudge. "Edward will shuffle the cards, but I want you to shuffle them again. Then Feathers can cut and stack. Is that satisfactory, Martin?"

"I can manage without your help, damn your eyes," Martin exploded, but the cards were prepared according to Brett's instructions and were soon stacked in a neat pile in front of Martin. He stared at them for a long while, then his hand slowly reached out to cover the cards; the room held its breath—Kate was almost sick with apprehension—as Martin's fingers moved nervously along the edge of the cards, stopping only to start again, afraid to make the choice on which so much depended. Then, in a moment of swift resolution, his fingers closed over the cards and he turned over the top half of the deck. Martin jumped to his feet with a shout of triumph; he had drawn the King of Hearts.

"What a singularly inappropriate card," Edward murmured, an unfamiliar tenor of urgency sounding in his customarily languid voice. "You're going to have to do better than that, old man."

"Be quiet," Brett snapped, his own nerves

stretched to breaking point. Kate's face was drained of color; anyone could see she was sure she would be left to her brother's questionable mercy, but after what Brett had seen tonight, there was no question of leaving her behind. Abruptly he reached out and turned over the top card. The Ace of Spades lay before him.

"Gad, you do have all the luck," Feathers marveled. Edward relaxed against the mantel and Kate, suddenly unable to support herself, slumped against a small table.

A roar exploded from Martin's throat as he lunged to his feet, upsetting the table and sending the brandy and glasses crashing to the floor. "You bewitched the cards," he screamed in a mad fury. "No man can have that much luck. You cheated me out of my estates, and now you want my sister to satisfy your filthy lusts. I won't let you get away with it! I won't . . ."

Brett came out of his seat with the speed of a striking cobra. He drew Martin bodily out of his chair and flung him across the table, striking his head on the black oak with a ringing crack that momentarily stunned him.

"I've listened to my last word from you tonight," Brett ground out from between clenched teeth. "*You* kept insisting that we raise the stakes, *you* made absurd bets all evening, and *you* demanded I accept your sister as a stake. Now instead of taking your losses like a man, you whine and accuse me of hellish connivance." Brett flung Martin from him as though ridding himself of something foul. "On your feet and face your sister. She's going to be mistress here now."

Feathers rushed up to Brett and clapped him on the back. "Well done. I say, well done." He beamed and turned to Kate who still leaned on the table.

"Who'd have thought this night would end with

31

you going to London? I've never been myself, but I know you'll get along famously."

"Do strive to contain your elation," Edward said, interrupting Feathers's effusion before Kate could faint. "I, too, am sure Miss Vareyan will become the toast of the *ton*, but at the moment she seems more in need of a good chair than vouchers for Almacks." He took Kate by the elbow and guided her to his own chair, then he turned to Brett, outwardly his usual urban self.

"That was a rather clever scheme, my friend, but the transfer of an estate to a young woman to whom you are not related or bound by any conventional tie is certain to give rise to considerable conjecture, the nature of which would be fatal to Miss Vareyan's reputation."

"The lawyers can transfer everything straight from Martin to his sister," Brett stated wearily, the strain of the tension and the long night beginning to show. "Right now I'm more concerned about the immediate future. I think it's best if we both escort Miss Vareyan to London, but she'll need some place to stay. My great-aunt Lindsay will take her for the season, especially once she gets a good look at her and knows she's an heiress, but she can't be seen like this." Kate cringed as he pointed a condemning finger at her huddled figure still wrapped in Edward's cloak. "She'll have to have some decent clothes and introductions to the right people. You're just the kind of dapper dog I need to take charge of things while I'm away."

"You're going a little too fast for me," Edward protested. "I hate to sound disobliging, even though I don't mind *being* disobliging in the least, but I've never acted the duenna for a young woman and I don't propose to begin now."

"You're all going too fast," announced Rudge's voice from the corner. "The money's not yours to give to anybody."

"What do you mean?" Brett demanded with a gathering frown. "Martin lost his whole estate. It's all there on these pieces of paper. It may not be stated in the legal language you prefer, but it's a binding debt nonetheless." Unaffected by Brett's disdain, Rudge's eyes searched out Martin as he backed away from the circle around Kate.

"I doubt Martin would have honored that debt, but in this case, he *can't* honor it. According to his father's will, Martin doesn't come into control of his estates until he's thirty-five, is married and the father of an heir, provides a tenth of his income or the revenue of two years for his sister's dowry, and his trustees feel he has become settled enough not to gamble away his inheritance the way he tried to do tonight. Until then, he may not sell any part of the estate, pledge any part of it, or legally raise funds against it. The only money he has in the world is the income paid to him each quarter, and that was gone before midnight. Everything else was a cheat." All eyes gradually turned to where Martin stood apart from the group; as usual it was Feathers who spoke first.

"The stinking swine!" he exclaimed. "When I think of how we gave in to him, letting him set up a lot of rules nobody liked, and all the time he was cheating every one of us. It doesn't seem possible."

"It does seem to bring the evening to an unnecessarily lurid conclusion, but somehow it fits with the rest of this hellish night," Edward said, meticulously straightening his waistcoat. His eyes searched out Martin, scorching him with contempt. "It hardly needs to be stated that you have placed yourself beneath reproach. I will leave as soon as my departure can be arranged and never set foot inside this house again. Until then, do not speak to me. Should you be so unwise as to address me in future,

33

I shall be obliged to cut you completely."

Edward broke off, certain he heard a sob from Kate, but when he turned around, she was sitting ramrod-straight in her chair, head held proudly erect, her face an impassive mask. What a magnificent creature, he thought. How *could* she be related to Martin?

Kate raised blank eyes to Brett's face. Her voice was tight and a trifle unsteady, but she resolutely forced the words from between her lips. "Thank you for your kind and thoughtful gesture. I had hoped I might somehow have enough money to live modestly, but if this can not be, I'll waste no time repining. I only want to know what you plan to do with me."

In that moment Brett would have gladly strangled Martin with his bare hands. He had planned it so either way the cards fell Kate would be free, but instead she had ended up on his hands. He might want her in his bed, but he didn't want to be responsible for her, and he certainly didn't know what to do with her. He had thrown his aunt Lindsay's name out as a gambit, but he wasn't at all sure she would take a debutante under her wing, no matter how rich, beautiful, and well-connected. He was damned sure she would slam the door in his face if he showed up with a penniless girl whose brother was a double-dealing skirter. God, what a tangle.

Brett's gaze encountered Kate's brilliant blue eyes so hopefully turned in his direction, and he cast all thoughts of Lady Lindsay from his mind. By God, she was a beauty, one to make a man's blood churn just to think about her. She was still wrapped in Edward's cloak, but it was impossible to look at her without imagining her lying naked in his arms. Desire instantly inflamed his senses, yet there was something more that compelled his interest. He

34

couldn't put his finger on it, but maybe that was why he had agreed to Martin's preposterous wager.

"How soon can you be ready to leave?" he demanded, throwing caution to the winds.

"Two hours." Brett pulled out his watch. "It ought to be light enough to travel by then. Make sure you're ready."

Kate started to leave, but turned back to Edward. "Thank you for your kindness," she said shyly, her unexpected gratitude causing Edward to shift his weight self-consciously. "I hope I may see you again under more pleasant circumstances, but if not, please know I'll never forget you." She hurried from the room leaving an awkward silence behind her.

Edward raised his eyes to Brett's face; neither man said a word, but their glances remained locked for some time before Edward spoke with jarring fierceness.

"You're a blind fool. She'll never have you on those terms."

Brett cursed.

Chapter 3

Brett pulled on his gloves with unnecessary violence as the first streaks of dawn showed through the trees; only Kate's absence prevented his departure. Edward and Peter waited with him, but Martin had closed himself up in the library with another bottle of brandy, and Brett hoped he would stay there. As Feathers had so succinctly put it, "You shouldn't have to speak to a cheater, but you can't ignore the damned fellow when you're his guest."

"I can and most certainly shall," Edward had declared quite positively, but Brett was inclined to agree with Feathers, and he began to tap his foot impatiently, wanting to be gone.

"Could you still your foot?" Edward complained with more than usual sharpness. "My much-abused head transforms each dulcet tone into a clap of thunder which threatens to deprive me of sight."

Brett complied with ill grace. His own head throbbed painfully, and his determination to leave at first light meant he would spend the greater part of the day in a swaying coach rather than a comfortable bed. He found himself trying not to blame Kate for his discomfort, not his usual response to a beautiful girl, but the contemplation of the pleasure her body could afford caused the blood to pound in his achingly sensitive temples and increase his agony twofold.

He couldn't see his way out of this tangle. Why hadn't he refused the bet, or given the money back to Martin? He might not care what people said about him, but Kate couldn't afford to ignore society's sanctions. He had always avoided marriage in favor of arrangements he could slip out of when he became bored, yet he had allowed himself to be bullied into taking charge of an unmarried female without so much as a maid to give her countenance. He was not sure of the rules governing the maintenance of a young lady, but he did know that turning her over to his lawyers while he was in Algeria would only postpone the difficulties and possibly make them even worse. Yet, every time he made up his mind to refuse to take her with him, the memory of Kate's body outlined under the nearly transparent gown would send a shiver of anticipation along his nerve endings. She was a worthy trophy and he could not let her slip through his fingers.

Kate's arrival interrupted Brett's fruitless daydreams. She wore a bonnet which was more useful than fashionable, a heavy blue wool cloak over a navy pelisse, a gray wool dress, gray kid boots buttoned high above the ankles, and mittens rather than a muff. Whether by necessity or design, her clothes appeared to be chosen for the express purpose of making her look like a dowd, yet she was the most beautiful creature Brett had ever set eyes on, and she drew his eyes like a magnet.

"I'm sorry if I've kept you waiting," she apologized, "but I couldn't find anyone to help with my valises. I had to leave one of them on the upper landing as it was."

"I'll get it for you," Feathers offered, his youthful gallantry filling the awkward pause.

"I'm sorry to put you to so much trouble," Kate told him thankfully, "but I couldn't carry both of them."

"No trouble at all," he smiled. "A lady should never be obliged to carry her own luggage."

"At least I'm not late," she said, turning to Brett,

"even if my valise is."

"Don't give it another thought."

"*You* certainly haven't," she said with pointed emphasis. Then as Brett's eyes narrowed in anger, she smiled sweetly. "If *gentlemen* can't carry luggage, how are we to get it to the coach? You can't mean to ask Mr. Feathers."

Edward's eyebrows rose questioningly, but Brett was thoroughly angry. "There's no need for either of us to carry luggage. My valet will see to it." Almost as if he had been waiting for a signal, Charles appeared at Brett's side.

"This valise and the one Mr. Feathers has gone to fetch are to be loaded with Miss Vareyan's trunk. We will leave as soon as they are secured."

Kate looked on enviously as Charles picked up the valise at her feet, relieved the just-reappearing Feathers of his burden, and quietly eased himself out the door without assistance or mishap. "It must be nice to have a well-trained servant to manage for you," she sighed.

"It ain't nice," Feathers stated in some surprise. "It's essential. My mother won't stir without at least six within the sound of her voice."

"We can't keep the horses standing," Brett said, anxious to be off; his proffered arm forced Kate to cut short her leavetakings.

Kate felt her own temper begin to rise, but she thanked both Edward and Peter and then surprised everyone by standing on her tiptoes and kissing each of them on the cheek. Feathers blushed from head to foot and began to stammer; Edward accepted his salute with his usual calm, but he startled Brett by bending over to plant a kiss on Kate's forehead.

"God be with you, my dear," he whispered softly.

Good Lord, Brett thought, *even Edward is acting like Sir Galahad. I'd better get her out of here before he demands to know my intentions.*

Unnoticed by anyone, Martin had watched the quartet from the library doorway, but when Kate turned to go, he stormed into the hall, a strange light in his eyes. "Are you so lost to all decency you would leave the house with that man?" he shouted in a menacing voice.

His words fanned the flame of Kate's already rising anger, and she hurled her reply in his face. "This show of outraged virtue suits you ill, dear brother. You lose me in a card game, yet you have the effrontery to ask if I'm going to leave with *that man!*" Kate paused for breath and then continued with increased vigor. "Yes, I'm leaving with *that man,* or any other man who offers. It's not proper and it's not the way I'd hoped it would be, but I'd crawl on my hands and knees rather than stay in this accursed place another day." She spun on her heel and strode through the open door.

Martin pushed past Brett, his face nearly purple with rage.

"Go with your whoreson and be branded a jade," he bellowed from the steps. "But understand me well. If you leave this house now, you'll never return."

Kate was in the act of climbing into the coach, but she paused and turned back to face her brother. "Nothing will ever induce me to return to this house while you live." She climbed into the coach and slammed the door behind her. Martin stormed back through the hall and closed the library door so hard the stag's horns mounted above it crashed to the floor.

"My, my, such a violent family," Edward purred.

"Quiet, you old fox," Brett admonished, a reluctant smile banishing his frown. "Try not to get yourself murdered while I'm gone. I don't know where I should turn for amusement. Do what you can to keep this business quiet," he said to Feathers. "I don't think Martin will talk, but he's too great a fool to know where his own best interests lie." He shook hands with both men and went quickly from the house.

Memories jostled each other in Kate's head as the coach sped down the lane, and a sense of loss settled over her. Ryehill was the home of her birth; she had grown to womanhood there and it represented a sense of belonging, a feeling of permanence. The world she was about to enter offered no such haven.

But Ryehill also held bitter memories, and more recently the twin specters of pain and fear. She was taking a desperate gamble, but it was with a sense of relief that she saw the castle towers disappear behind the trees. Now she could start anew. She didn't know what the next days would hold, but if this strange man were to be a part of them, she was sure they would hold adventure and excitement. After years of virtual imprisonment, she eagerly looked forward to both.

"I've been up all night and I'm extremely tired," Brett announced without preamble. "My coachman has instructions to change horses as often as needed and to provide you with food and refreshment. Is there anything you want before I go to sleep?" He stared wearily at Kate, his expression not encouraging.

"Not at the moment," she replied, pinpoints of anger showing in her eyes. Really, this man was abominably rude. "I promise not to wake you until the footpads are at the door."

"Not even then. There's a loaded pistol on the wall behind you."

"But I've hardly ever used firearms before," she said, startled.

"It's quite easy. You just point it and squeeze the trigger." Without another word, he drew the sheepskin rug over him and leaned back against the thick upholstering of the seats. Within seconds Kate could hear the soft sounds of his even breathing.

Conceited, thoughtless, and rude though he was, Kate couldn't stay angry with Brett. Handsome and virile when he was awake, his face assumed an almost cherubic beauty in slumber, an appearance she found incongruous with his brusque, unemotional character. His black hair rose in thick waves from a high, broad forehead, his thick brows and long black lashes giving his eyes an unusual prominence in his face. His nose was finely chiseled, and his lips full and firm. His skin was dark and closely shaved without the mask so common to men with heavy dark hair.

He had rescued her from Martin, and she would have felt drawn to him had he looked like a troll, but in her eyes he was Prince Charming, and he was even more handsome than in her dreams. She felt like a damsel in distress who had been rescued at the last minute by her knight in shining armor, but it would have been so much nicer if her knight errant had not fallen asleep the minute the rescue was over.

With a barely perceptible sigh, she shifted her gaze to the desolate and uninviting landscape. The sky was nearly clear of clouds, but a white haze hung in the air and the wind was sharp and bitter, sweeping up hills and down valleys with the swiftness of a diving hawk; it tore its way into the coach and forced Kate to burrow more deeply under her rug. There were no animals or birds to be seen and only an occasional sign of a cottage or a more substantial dwelling. The leafless trees, their naked silhouettes spread against the hostile sky, gave no promise of the spring to come, and the threat of a blizzard hung in the air.

Let it storm, she thought, trying to drive away the fear that threatened to weigh down her spirits. *Maybe we'll even get snowbound.* At least that would give her more time to figure out what to do with herself. She had no idea how to go about seeking a position. She didn't even know what kind of work she might do. Her mother had never taken the time to teach her how to manage a household, and her father thought it a waste of time to educate a girl. She would be lucky to be offered a position in a poor household, but even that would be preferable to becoming a ladies' maid.

The notion made her laugh. She had no idea what a ladies' maid did, at least not much of one. Her mother had spent her time in London, and Kate had never had a maid. She would probably be reduced to being a companion to some horrible old woman or scrubbing pots and pans in the kitchen.

Kate had some idea of what happened to unprotected girls, especially the pretty ones, and for a moment she wished herself safely back at Ryehill, but Martin's features swam before her eyes and any regrets over her hasty departure died. Becoming some man's mistress would be truly horrible, but if she were lucky she might be able to lay something aside for her future.

Her future! The only acceptable future for a girl like her was to marry a substantial gentleman, bear his children, and manage his household. Martin had seen to it she had no dowry, had met few eligible men, and now bore a dishonored name. No man in his right mind would marry her; not even her beauty could compensate for such grave shortcomings.

She fought against the tears welling up in her eyes, determined not to cry, certainly not in front of this brusque man who was so uninterested in her destiny that he had fallen asleep, but that only caused the tears to well up even faster until large drops streamed down her face like spring rain down a windowpane. She made no attempt to wipe them away, just closed her eyes and let them fall.

Brett changed his position, and for a moment Kate held her breath, unable to stop crying, but after a brief pause, she could hear his steady breathing once more. She was furious at herself for feeling embarrassed about crying in front of him and called herself some harsh names as she searched for a handkerchief. Brett would have one, she thought, but she would let the tearstains dry on her cheeks before she would ask him, even if he *had* been awake.

She finally found the lace-trimmed square and began to dab at her face. Why did women have to cry anyway? It never solved anything; it just made them look ridiculous and invariably made men angry. Why couldn't she curse and challenge people to fistfights and foolish duels? She was tired of being bound by an outmoded code of behavior.

She tidied her face and gave herself a mental shake. Feeling sorry for herself was not going to produce any answers. She knew she would have to discuss her plans with the sleeping hulk across from her, but she intended to have her thoughts in order before she did. She might as well be done with crying and start to rack her brain for ideas; it was obvious Brett wasn't going to do it for her.

She sniffed her annoyance. Brett Westbrook, the pride of English society, the darling of drawing rooms from London to Paris, lay slumped down in the corner of his coach looking very much like an ordinary man. Famed for his intrigues with titled women and feared for the haughty correctness of his polished manner, he now was sprawled over the seat, his face unshaved, his clothes rumpled, and his hair in disarray. She felt like laughing. He might be the most handsome man in the world—she had to admit she couldn't suppress a thrill of excitement at being with him—but she wasn't going to fall for a man who had already seduced half the women in London.

But immediately her attitude toward him softened. He *had* come to her rescue. She had been so shocked and upset when Martin dragged her into that room she hadn't felt the delicious tingle of pleasure she later experienced when she remembered how he knocked Martin down, the pleasure any woman feels when two men, *any* two men, fight over her. It made her feel beautiful in a way her mirror never could, and even the memory of the driving cloak held tightly around her nearly nude body could not rob the moment of its satisfaction.

A lock of Brett's hair fell across his forehead, and she had to resist an impulse to reach out and brush it back with her fingers. She trembled with excitement at the thought of actually *touching* him—the anticipation was delicious, but she was terrified of what would happen if he woke up. He was quiet now, but there was a kind of ferocious energy about him that frightened her a little, an energy that could reach out and ensnare anyone within its reach, and energy which could draw its victims into a maelstrom far beyond their understanding. Leaving Ryehill had already taken Kate beyond her experience, and she wanted to consider her next step carefully.

She scrutinized Brett more closely, admitted to a tug of attraction which seemed to grow stronger with every passing hour, and became aware of the feeling that with such a man at her side, things could never be very wrong. But almost at once she closed her eyes and laid her head back on the cushions trying to stave off the tears that threatened to overwhelm her once again. He was not her man, and he was not standing by her side.

Martin charged back into the library, his mind consumed with hatred for everyone who had helped bring about his disgrace. He ground his teeth in rage when he remembered Edward's snide and belittling remarks and how that damned puppy Feathers had turned on him in his own house; however, it was on Kate and Brett's shoulders that Martin placed the

44

blame for his whirlwind of troubles, and he intended to take his revenge in the most ruthless manner he could devise.

He could easily deal with Kate once he had her back at the castle. She was probably looking at Brett with sheep's eyes right now, thinking he would protect her. The slut! It would give him great pleasure to destroy that illusion.

He would have to kill Brett. He knew he couldn't do it in a fair fight, but he wasn't going to be held back by some outmoded code of chivalry; he would kill him if he had to stab him in the back.

But first he had to do something about Kate, and just getting her back wasn't enough; there must be some way to do it that would discredit Brett. In his frustration he uttered a loud oath, and his spaniel, once again lying near his chair and thinking he was talking to her, lifted her head. When Martin continued to pace, she settled her head back on her paws, but her eyes followed him as he moved erratically about the room.

By now Martin had drunk so much brandy his head felt like a lead weight and his thoughts refused to come into focus without a tremendous effort of will. He leaned his head against the cool marble of the fireplace hoping it would help to clear his mind. He stood quietly for so long the dog forsook her vigil and closed her eyes.

Suddenly Martin's head jerked upright, and his eyes focused intently as his mind worked frantically to grasp the elusive idea before it could slip away. Tenaciously he held on, becoming more and more alert as the plan took shape in his fevered brain.

"I've got the goddamned bastard at last!" Martin laughed wildly, and tossed off the last of the brandy. Now he could rest; there would be time enough later. In fact, it would be better if they were farther along the road, better still if they had spent the night at

45

some inn.

The spaniel had come to her feet at Martin's shout, teeth bared and hackles raised. She quieted down when she found no one else in the room but remained on the alert. Something in his laughter triggered a primitive instinct deep within her brain; there was danger in that room, an evil she could not trust. She left by the open window, and from that moment she would not come into his presence without uttering a low growl and removing herself to the farthest corner.

The afternoon sun scattered its last feeble rays across the barren fields and retired early to rest; by five o'clock a heavy twilight had fallen over the desolate countryside. The trees, some still stubbornly clinging to dried and useless leaves, grew closer to the road and branches brushed the side of the coach. To Kate, it seemed like a dark and endless tunnel to the ends of the earth, and unconsciously she drew her rug more closely about her. She withdrew her gaze from the window and lay back against the cushions, considerably comforted by the sight of Brett's broad shoulders so close by, even if he was sound sleep.

Abruptly the quiet of the wintry evening was rudely shattered by two pistol shots close to the coach. Kate sat up, staring with eyes starting from their sockets at four horsemen who appeared like magic from nowhere, their guns drawn and their horses in a lather. Before she could recover from her shock sufficiently to wake Brett, a hand was thrust through the window sending a shower of glass over the floor, and a gun pointed straight at Brett's head. Kate clamped her hand over her mouth to muffle a shriek.

The gun was held by a husky ruffian in a long, heavy coat, a dilapidated knit cap, and a stocking mask over his face. A second man, also with gun in hand, was at the other door. What did they want?

46

How could they get away? She supposed Brett had money, but Martin had never given her any, and if there were any family jewels, they had either been locked up by the trustees or sold for cash. All she had were some valueless beads and some mother-of-pearl earrings.

Brett continued to sleep, his rhythmic breathing never missing a beat. Provoking man! Just when she needed him most.

The man at the broken window spoke first. "We got us a looker this time, Sam. With a face like that, she ought to be dripping in sparklers." His eyes glowed in anticipation. "It's about time, too. Pickings haven't been too good lately."

"Shut up, Joe," Sam growled. "You talk too much. Just get on with it and don't forget the gentleman's strongbox. Sparklers are good in their own way, but nothing spends like yellow boys."

The man called Joe stuck his head in the window. "Don't you go getting upset, ma'am. We don't want to hurt you or your husband. Just give us your money and jewels and we'll let you go peaceable-like."

"Knock off the pretty speeches, Joe," Sam barked impatiently.

"You never did know how to treat a lady," Joe responded with a superior air.

An authoritative voice broke in on the flaring tempers. "You boys give over your arguing, or I'll take a pistol butt to the both of you."

"Hand over the valuables, ma'am," Joe said with none of his previous politeness. "We can't spend all day on this roadside."

If it had been up to Kate, she would have handed over any money Brett had in his pocket without even waking him. He was too rich to feel the loss of such a small sum.

"I know this will sound untruthful, but I don't have any money or jewels, or anything else of value. I'm a very poor woman. This gentleman is escorting me to London where I hope to find a position."

Kate had no difficulty reading the disbelief in their faces, and she struggled to overcome her revulsion at having to divulge her personal history to highwaymen. "You must believe me. Would I be dressed like this if I were rich?" She threw back her fur robe to show them her plain clothes and bare throat. "I'd give you anything I had rather than get myself shot."

Joe didn't know what to do next. He could see Kate wore no jewelry, and her clothes were certainly extremely plain. She didn't even have a maid. Yet she *was* riding in a luxurious coach, and the man was expensively clothed.

"They all say the same thing," Sam warned. "If she won't give over peaceably, we'll have her out of the coach and search her. We'll find her jewels if we have to strip every stitch off the both of them."

"Hurry it up back there," came the impatient voice. "Is the simple task of robbing a girl and a sleeping man too much for you?"

Kate turned white. "But I don't have any money, I tell you. Not even a shilling." She dug frantically under the sheepskin. "Here, search my reticule." She flung it through the broken window at Joe just as Sam leaned out of his saddle to open the other door.

Chapter 4

Things happened so quickly after that, Kate was never quite sure she remembered her part in the drama. Joe was caught off guard by the purse flung at him so unexpectedly, and he grabbed at it belatedly, trying to catch it before it could fall to the ground. His horse, startled by an object being thrown at its head, reared and shied to one side. For a few crucial seconds, Joe was fully occupied with trying to keep his grip on the purse, regain his balance, stay in the saddle, and calm his horse, time enough for Kate to snatch the loaded pistol from its place on the wall above her head and fire a shot straight into his chest. She cringed before Joe's look of startled surprise as he crumpled and fell heavily to the ground. His frightened horse wheeled and galloped off down the road.

In the same moment Kate threw her purse, Brett sprang to life. In a movement almost too rapid to be seen, he grasped the door with both hands and slammed it into Sam's skull with a loud crack. Almost as a reflex, Brett whipped a small pistol out of his coat pocket and placed a ball neatly between Sam's eyes. His horse followed Joe's down the road.

Stunned by the swift and unforeseen turn of events, the leader of the gang momentarily withdrew his attention from the box where the coachman and Charles sat under his harsh glare. Charles had been forced to throw his blunderbuss into the road, but he reached for a second gun hidden in the boot and blew the third thief out of his saddle. A fourth rogue holding the horses took to his heels before Charles had time to reload.

Almost as suddenly as it had started, it was over.

Kate had acted on impulse, and she blinked unbelievingly at the smoking pistol in her hands as the realization that she had killed a man flooded over her. She dropped the pistol like it was a coiled snake. It landed with a thud at her feet and she started to shake; she was too weak and dumbfounded to move.

"Very neatly done, Miss Vareyan." The sound of Brett's voice penetrated the layers of horror that hammered at Kate's consciousness, threatening to suffocate all reason. "I was particularly impressed by your quickness," he continued in a more friendly voice. "I didn't know how I was going to get one of those ruffians off guard long enough to put a bullet through the other. Throwing your purse in his face was about the neatest trick I've ever seen."

At last he seemed to realize Kate was in shock, he leaned across, took her hands in his, and held them tightly. "Easy, my girl. You've had a nasty jolt, but you'll get over it a lot quicker if you try not to think about it. We'll be stopping soon, and you'll feel much better once you've had a bit of rest and a good dinner."

Sympathy and a little understanding sounded in his voice, and Kate held tightly to his hands; the strength and warmth of his fingers comforted her. "I said I wouldn't wake you until the footpads were at the door," she managed to say with a tremulous smile.

"So you did, but I wasn't expecting you to keep your promise quite so strictly." He smiled at her for the first time, *truly* smiled at her, and Kate felt an overwhelming impulse to bury her face in his broad chest and deny the grim reality of what she had done. Instead, she struggled to pull herself together. He was a virtual stranger, and even though he did look like the answer to a maiden's prayers, it was unthinkable

50

that she should take such liberties with any man not related to her.

"I didn't mean to come apart like that. It's just that I've never shot a man before, much less *killed* one. I never held a pistol in my hands more than a couple of times in my life. I did it without thinking." She favored him with a grim smile. "It's going to take some getting used to."

Brett gave her fingers a tiny squeeze and released her hands. "Probably," he said, not unsympathetically, "but it'll be easier than being stripped naked in the middle of the road and raped by the whole damned gang. They're bound to have a hideout somewhere near here."

Kate's heart almost stopped beating. How could he talk about the possibility of her abduction as calmly as if he were discussing an invitation to a party? Didn't he have feelings? Didn't anything have the power to unnerve him? Just look at him now.

Brett had gotten out of the coach and was impassively inspecting the bodies of the slain men. He's not even upset, she thought, and there's blood everywhere. The sight was too much for her frayed nerves, and she quietly fainted, slumping back against the cushions.

Outside, Brett regarded the three bodies with disgust before directing his harsh glance toward his servants, a question in his cold eyes.

"I know what you're thinking, sir," Walker, the coachman, said to forestall Brett, "but those hedges were too close to the road. And Charles and me are cold and tired from being up here since morning." Brett's gaze did not relent. "It's more than a body can do to be wakeful all day with the cold freezing your wits. We should have stopped long ago, but Miss Vareyan wouldn't let us wake you."

"We'll talk about this later," was all Brett said. He picked up Kate's purse and started to climb back into the coach.

"What are we going to do with them bodies?" Walker asked. Brett paused with his foot on the bottom step.

"What do you propose I should do with them?" he asked ominously.

"I don't know," Walker responded, shaken but determined, "but we can't leave them lying in the road."

"Why not?"

"Someone might come on them unsuspecting," Walker explained. "Bound to give them a nasty shock."

"Do you think it would be better to put them in the coach next to Miss Vareyan or should we tie them on the roof with the trunks?" Brett asked. "Of course we could bury them by the roadside, but what shall we use for shovels? I packed for France, not America."

Walker realized the futility of the situation and gave up. "Where do you want to stop?" he asked.

"There's a village called Littledean about an hour from here. You can make arrangements to have the window repaired as soon as you see about fresh horses for tomorrow. Then you can report these bodies to the sheriff." Without a backward glance at the dead highwaymen, Brett climbed into the coach and closed the door.

He was brought up short by the sight of Kate slumped in the corner of her seat. He felt her pulse; it was strong and regular. His face relaxed, and he settled back in his own seat as the coach began to move again. The poor girl had endured a very trying day, and it might be best to leave her alone. She would come around soon enough on her own, and there was nothing to be gained by trying to wake her before they reached Littledean.

The sight of her lying there, crumpled up in the seat and looking utterly vulnerable, aroused his protective instincts, and he found himself fighting down an impulse to gather her into his arms and safeguard her until she woke. *You'd do better to keep a safe distance,* he told himself bluntly. *She's already thrown your plans into a turmoil; you can't afford to let her take up any more time if you're to be in France on schedule.*

Still, unable to help himself, Brett let his fingertips brush the back of her hand. He could manage a couple of days to see her settled in London. He knew he wouldn't be able to leave England unless he were certain she would be safe until his return.

Kate opened her eyes, but they would not focus and she couldn't remember where she was. She lay there, floating half in and half out of consciousness, enjoying the pleasant rocking sensation. She felt like a little girl again, being rocked to sleep on her old nanny's lap. She smiled and almost slid back into unconsciousness, but the movement of the coach was too erratic. Gradually she made out the shape of a person in the mist and heard a voice from far away calling her softly. She couldn't see the face, but she was sure it was her nanny calling her to come in from play. She tried to run, but she couldn't move. It took all her strength to call out; her voice sounded strange to her ears. The words echoed back at her, like they were being spoken into a long, narrow, empty room, but the sound didn't seem to come from her body.

Then she came suddenly awake and realized she was staring into the face of a man she had never seen before; a muffled scream escaped her and she sat up with a start. Brett was bending over her trying to wake her, his face so close she could feel his warm breath on her cheek.

He moved next to her, genuine concern in his face. "Are you all right? I thought you'd just fainted, but when you screamed, I wasn't sure. Are you sure there's nothing wrong?"

She tried to smile, and failing, shook her head instead.

"Okay, if you're sure," he said doubtfully, "but tell me if you begin to feel sick. I'm not much of a nurse, but between Charles and me, we can think of something."

Kate sat up. She removed her hands from his grasp and tried to tidy herself.

Brett laughed at this feminine trick. "You look fine. For a woman who's just shot a thief and recovered from a fainting spell, I'd say you looked marvelous."

Kate's eyes opened wide in alarm. "Shot a man? I didn't dream it then. It *really* happened!" She began to shake and lose her color. Brett took her hands again and she didn't protest this time.

"There's nothing to fear, either from the constabulary or from your conscience," he said. "It's not easy the first time you kill a man, but you shot him in self-defense, and I'm damned glad you did."

Kate could neither contain her horror at his words nor stem the rising tide of hysteria within her. "How can you *not* feel something? Even highwaymen are human." She lost the last shred of control over herself; tears streamed down her face and her voice escalated to a pitiful wail. "Are you human or the devil my brother said you were? How many men have you killed, or don't you know?"

Brett tried to talk to her, but the features of her exquisite face were distorted by shock and she didn't even seem to hear him; he chaffed her hands, but the wild look in her frightened eyes was not calmed; he took her by the arms and gently shook her, but her soft, pliable body had become rigid and it only served to increase her hysteria. Finally, Brett could think of nothing else to do, but still she seemed to be moving farther and farther beyond the grasp of reason. In desperation he dealt her a sharp slap across the face.

Kate stopped in midsentence, her hands flying to her cheeks in eye-popping amazement. Her disordered wits returned to normal and she turned blazing eyes on her attacker. "How *dare* you strike me!" she cried in a voice dripping with fury. "You're no better than Martin, knocking women around like the horses you ride, never once attempting to understand us or our fears."

Brett stared at her in burgeoning anger, but Kate was shocked by her outburst. She made a tremendous effort to pull herself together. When she continued, her voice was calmer, but it had lost none of its icy edge.

"I'm sorry I shouted at you, and I regret more than I can say that I fainted," she stated with rigid formality. "I can only blame it on the shock of knowing I had become a murderess." She sat bolt upright. "I'm better now, and I assure you I won't embarrass you again, but I would greatly appreciate it if you would not speak to me until we reach the inn."

Brett nearly lost his temper. Who did she think she was, this little nobody from the backwoods, to talk to him like he was a lackey?

"Rest easy," he said. "I am equally anxious to be spared the necessity of conversing with a virago who responds to courteous concern with ear-splitting wails. You know, you don't do much to raise a man's spirits. The sight of you tempts my senses almost beyond bearing, but your unreasonable temper slays all feeling of pleasure."

"It's a little hard to be grateful for a ringing blow across the face. Maybe with a little practice I can learn to smile and say thank you."

"I didn't slap you out of anger. I just didn't happen to have a pitcher of water handy."

"You must forgive me if I failed to distinguish between a slap given in anger and one meted out for my own good," she said scornfully. "There must be something in the nuance I missed."

"I promise to keep my hands off you for the remainder of the journey," Brett said, his response coming from between clenched teeth.

"I wish you would hurry up and find a place for us to stay," Kate replied, recovering as best she could from the harshness of his words. "I've been in this coach since seven o'clock this morning, and I'm tired and sore all over. I'm also hungry and I want to go to bed."

"We're going to stop in less than an hour. It's only a small inn, but you'll be well cared for. I'll see that your dinner is served in your room, but you're going to have to overcome your dislike of me sufficiently by tomorrow to discuss your future. I'm due in Paris in two days, and I have very little time to devote to resolution of your situation." He turned from her and stared into the gathering blackness outside.

Kate sat quietly in a chastened calm. She had had time to allay her fears and realize Brett had only been trying to help. In return, she had acted like a frenzied cat, clawing and biting. She swallowed her ire and made herself speak as calmly as she could. "I apologize for my rude outburst and spiteful remarks, but this whole thing has shaken me rather badly. I appreciate your concern, and I am indeed grateful for what you're doing on my behalf."

"I don't want your thanks," Brett growled, obviously not mollified.

"Well I *am* grateful, even if you are the rudest man on earth," she said with a spurt of temper. "I don't see why you should take pride in being so unfeeling, even if you are ten times as rich as anyone else in England."

"And you, my beautiful shrew, should have a care what you say before you become known as the most sharp-tongued female in all the kingdom."

For a moment, two pairs of blazing eyes locked and the space between them threatened to become incandescent. Kate was the first to lower her eyes and break the spell. She folded her hands in her lap and looked down. Neither spoke again for the remainder of the afternoon.

It was immediately apparent upon reaching Littledean that something out of the ordinary was happening. Fashionably dressed men strolled through the streets or stood in idle groups, while inns and taverns did a thriving business. Brett cursed when he recognized a dozen men before they had gone halfway through the village. How was he to keep Kate's presence a secret with so many of his acquaintants gathered in this out-of-the-way spot? Then he remembered the fight at a nearby farm and damned himself roundly for not stopping earlier. There probably wouldn't be a room at the Cock-in-the-Cradle, or anywhere else, for miles around, but it was too late to try to reach the post road. They pulled into the courtyard and his coachman gave a shout for the ulsters.

"Stay here and keep the blinds closed," Brett told Kate as he prepared to alight. "I'm going to see if I can find a room and get you inside without anyone being the wiser." He disappeared into the gathering dusk, and Kate huddled down in the corner to await his return.

Brett was tempted to enter through the kitchen, but he knew his disappearance from the courtyard would focus additional attention on his movements so he went through the front door and was hailed immediately.

"Westbrook! I thought you'd never get here," Stephen Wyndom shouted as he elbowed his way through the crowd. "I bet Hubart you'd never stay at

Ryehill above one day. Come join us. We have a table, and the ale's not bad." Brett liked Stephen, even if he was a little slow-witted, but he couldn't stand Hubart Sedley.

"Later," Brett said. "I've got to see about a room. I wasn't expecting to be met by half of London."

"There's not a bed within twenty miles of this place," Hubart assured him. "You'll probably have to sleep in your coach. You know," he said half to himself, "it must be damned boring in London this season if such an unimportant fight can draw half the blades in the city. Can't you drum up some excitement?"

"Not now. I've spent the whole day in my coach, and I shudder to think of spending the night there as well. What happened to your little widow? Did she give you the slip?"

Hubart favored him with a thin smile. "If you mean Mrs. Brightstone, she started to have expectations, and I had to give her up. I don't like clinging women. They remind me of my wife."

"You old devil," Stephen guffawed. "She gave *you* the shove. Probably wouldn't let you climb into her bed the first night. I've told you not to be so impatient. You lose more fillies than you catch that way."

Hubart embarked on an explanation of the intricacies of the chase, and Brett excused himself to go in search of the landlord. He found him serving up ale as fast as it came out of the barrel. The little man smiled broadly when he saw Brett, but his face fell ludicrously when he realized he must be in need of a room.

"Is there somewhere we can talk?" Brett asked as quietly as he could in the noise of the room. The landlord motioned one of the serving boys to take over and led Brett down a hall and into the still room.

"This is the most private place in the inn," he said as he closed the door behind him. "Nobody wants milk tonight." He laughed at his own joke, but smothered his mirth when Brett didn't join him. "I hope it's not a room you're wanting, Mr. Westbrook, because there's no way I can give you one, not even a closet."

"A room is exactly what I *must* have. Isn't there some way you can move one of these gentlemen in with someone else?"

"One won't do," Michael answered diffidently. "There's not a man here who isn't sharing his bed or sleeping on the sofa."

"I'm not interested in anybody else," Brett replied rather sharply. His temper was rising and his few shreds of politeness were about to evaporate. "Do what you must, but get me that room."

"But there *aren't* any rooms, not unless you drive on for ten, maybe twelve, miles."

"Damnation, man, I've been on the road since dawn. I'm liable to kill somebody if I have to spend another five minutes in that coach. I don't care how you do it or what it costs, just get me a room." He turned to leave but stopped dead in his tracks.

"Of course . . . why didn't I think of it before? We can use *your* room. I can sleep on the sofa and Walker and Charles can rack up in the stables."

"Have pity, for mercy's sake," the landlord pleaded. "You know I don't dare ask Mathilda to leave the inn, not with all those meals to fix and rooms to see after. She'll kill me."

"Your domestic difficulties are of no interest to me," Brett snapped.

"You don't have to live with her. Nothing goes right when she's angry. Besides, you can't sleep down here. The sofa is already taken, and the stable is full, too." He stopped suddenly and peered suspiciously at Brett. "If you're planning to sleep down here, who's going to sleep in the missus's bed?"

"I'm conveying a young lady to town," Brett dis-

59

closed. He hoped his formidable expression would keep the landlord from leaping to the wrong conclusion, but his hopes were in vain.

"This is a respectable house," Michael said, turning beet red. "I won't have your fancy woman in my inn, not if you have to sleep in the street. As for putting her in my wife's bed . . ." Words failed the little man.

"Do you think I'd bring my mistress to this godforsaken corner of England?" Brett demanded. "Or care who saw her if I did? This is a *lady*, and a damned good-looking one at that."

"Let me talk to Mathilda," the landlord said, his anger evaporating as suddenly as it had materialized. "It's got to be all right with her."

A few minutes later Brett heard a female voice rise above the clatter and continue to scale upward until the door burst open and Mathilda overflowed into the hall and set sail for the still room, brandishing a huge kitchen knife like it was no more dangerous than a wooden spoon.

"What do you mean barging in here with your foolish tales when I've got a house full of pesky men all wanting their supper at once? And where is this precious young *lady* you're so anxious about?" she demanded skeptically.

"In the coach," Brett answered. "I couldn't bring her inside without everybody seeing her." He was halfway down the hall before Mathilda could get off another barrage, and she surged after him with Michael right behind.

Brett didn't see Kate when he first opened the door. She had slipped down in the corner, nearly out of sight under the fur rug.

"Get out of my way, you overbearing man, and let me see for myself," Mathilda ordered, pushing Brett unceremoniously aside. At first sight, Kate's remarkable beauty convinced Mathilda that Brett was trying to pass off his mistress, but a closer look caused her to change her mind. There was nothing of the painted hussy in this pale face, and from the rigidity of her body, the set look in her face, and the pallor of her skin, it was clear she wasn't as brave as she pretended to be.

"I'm terribly sorry to impose upon you at such a busy time, but if you'll only give me a bed, I'll sleep with the serving girls if I have to," Kate pleaded, finishing up with a tiny hiccup that completely melted Mathilda's resistance.

"You poor lamb," Mathilda purred, "left out in this nasty coach without so much as a maid to keep you company. You should be ashamed of yourself, Mr. Westbrook, to treat a lady so shabby." Brett was too glad of Mathilda's change of heart to argue over the injustice of her accusation, but his expression was anything but happy.

"Michael," Mathilda trumpeted impatiently, "get my cloak, the one with the hood that's hanging in the passageway. And don't be all night about it," she added. "There's suppers to be cooked yet. You come with me, child," she said, helping Kate down from the coach. "I'll see you're put between warm sheets right away. These men are all alike, thinking only of themselves, while we poor females must look after ourselves and them, too." Michael knew Mathilda never meant half of what she said, but Brett muttered something under his breath about the murder of females being justifiable homicide.

"Don't you worry, miss. As soon as that man of mine gets back with my cloak, we can get you inside. Stand behind me. Won't nobody see a mere slip like you behind the likes of me." Her enormous body shook with mirth. "Though why men have to act like they've got lead in their britches just when you want them to step lively is something I'll never understand."

Michael came back with a cloak big enough to hide

six of Kate, and Mathilda bundled her up and hurried her inside, fussing and scolding the whole while. "Make sure nobody comes into this yard. Though I don't know what you can do about it if they do. Stands to reason you can't clap your hands over their eyes or talk them into not seeing what's right under their nose." Brett looked quizzically at Michael, but the landlord just shook his head. He knew when to heed Mathilda and when to say nothing.

Chapter 5

Despite Kate's assurances that she was quite able to take care of herself, Mathilda was still fussing over her when they reached the room. "You'll do no such thing," said Mathilda, scandalized. "Mr. Westbrook can bear you company until dinner. And it won't be long, either," she confided with a chuckle. "There's a fat old gentleman downstairs who's already had too many dinners. It won't do him any harm to wait a while for this one." She waddled out laughing merrily.

Now that she was no longer in danger of being left to starve or sleep in the coach, Kate's courage deserted her and she felt tired and extremely vulnerable. Her shoulders were no longer so square nor her back so straight. She looked very innocent, younger than her nineteen years, and Brett's irritation and impatience disappeared. Even after the trouble she had caused him, he found it impossible to deny his attraction to her. Her creamy skin invited his touch, the slim arch of her neck his caresses. He imagined kissing her full red lips until the cool creature lost her control and responded with an ardor Brett was positive waited beneath that glacial surface. No one who could be stirred to wrath as easily as she could was beyond the reach of sensual pleasure.

Kate looked up, and saw the way he was looking at her; she blushed red all over. With a stifled, "Oh!" she drew as far away from him as possible and clutched tightly at the huge cloak that still enveloped her.

Brett smiled in spite of himself. "Haven't you ever

had a man stare at you? I should have thought you had aroused quite a few animal passions in your brother's house."

Kate shook her head. "I never come downstairs when guests are present."

"Now you see why. Your effect at close range is such that I find it almost impossible to keep my hands off you." A hunted look flashed into her eyes. "Don't worry. I don't mean to give Mathilda an excuse to use that knife on me instead of the goose." Kate swallowed hard.

"I can't stay here anyway. Half the men downstairs know me. I want them to think I came alone, so I'll eat my dinner with them. You, however, are not to set foot outside this room. Ask Mathilda if you need anything."

Suddenly Kate was more frightened that he would leave than that he would stay. She couldn't understand the sudden reversal in her feelings, but she didn't have time to reason it out.

"Where will you go?" she stammered.

"To the coffee room. I'll see the fight and probably get back sometime after ten o'clock. Make sure your door is locked before you go to bed. I'll spend the night wherever I can."

Brett started to leave, but her deep-blue eyes continued to regard him so intently he hesitated. Once more the astonishing magnitude of her beauty swept over him, and he walked over to her. He stroked her soft cheek and traced the line of her jaw with his finger. Kate was rigid, but she didn't move away from him. "You've had a pretty terrible twenty-four hours," he said in a caressing voice, "but you don't have to be frightened now. You're safe as long as you're with me."

He walked briskly to the door, turned, and said in his usual curt voice, "Be sure to go to bed early. We have a lot to do tomorrow." Then he was gone.

Kate sat perfectly still trying to untangle the emotions churning within her. She was still weak from the exposure to his naked desire; she'd never had that effect on anyone before and it terrified her. Yet she was just as confused by the altered tone of his voice and the gentleness of his touch. Maybe he didn't dislike her so much after all.

She realized in amazement that she had responded to his kindness and had actually *wanted* him to touch her. It made her feel less alone in the world. He had a masterful way about him that gave her confidence he would take care of her. It wouldn't be difficult to learn to depend on a man like that. It might even be pleasant.

At the same time, an inner voice warned to her to proceed with caution. She knew very little about men, it forewarned, and nothing about such men as Brett Westbrook. It would be all too easy to read too much into his practiced chivalry, all too likely she would find herself developing a regard for someone who saw her as nothing more than a temporary responsibility. It would be much wiser to plan for a future that didn't include his broad shoulders and penetrating eyes. After all, she didn't really expect to see him again after they reached London.

On the other side of the door, Brett was breathing hard. This was going to be more difficult than he had thought. Didn't she know how desirable she was? You would think she had never met a flesh-and-blood man. If she didn't stop looking so deliciously fragile and helpless, she would soon discover how dangerous heated flesh could be. He would enjoy helping her discover the joys of lovemaking and generating in her a sensual excitement capable of matching his own.

You've got to stop this, he muttered savagely under his breath. *She's a lady, a delicately bred girl, definitely not the kind of female you think about that way unless you're also thinking of marriage. Touch her, and there's not a door in England that won't be slammed in your face. Abandon her to her fate, and the result will be nearly the same. The only way to avoid the inevitable consequences was to have never removed her from Ryehill in the first place, but it's too late to think of that now.*

He strode into the courtyard with a smothered oath. He needed some time to settle his emotions and let his blood cool before he could face the noisy camaraderie of the coffee room. He groaned as he thought of the evening ahead of him. He hoped Kate enjoyed hers more.

Brett stared impatiently into his brandy. The evening had been a complete bore and his patience was worn thin. After suffering through an amateurish fight, he had been forced to endure three interminable hours while his friends drowned their disappointment. Now, at last, the inn was quiet; he stood up, stretched his stiff limbs, and began to climb the stairs, leaving his brandy glass half full. He'd had more than enough brandy in the last two days.

Brett listened outside the door to Kate's room. There was no sound, so he eased the key into the lock and turned it carefully. The door swung open on soundless hinges, and he silently blessed Mathilda's careful housekeeping; Kate did not wake and he tiptoed in, breathing a sigh of relief as he locked the door behind him.

The small room was situated in the corner of the inn. Windows dominated two walls with several large pieces of furniture elbowing each other over the remaining space. The curtains were open and moonlight bathed the room in its pale glow, enabling Brett to see his own luggage where it rested on the floor next to a large chair. *This,* he thought gloomily, *will be my bed for the night;* it promised to be even more uncomfortable than the coach.

In the center of the room, and dominating the whole space, was a huge, uncurtained bed piled high with mattresses. In the middle, nearly lost among the pillows, Kate was fast asleep. The shock of coming upon her, vulnerable and at his mercy, caused Brett's body to tense with heat and hunger.

Her head rested on one hand, her golden hair spread over the pillow behind her like billowing clouds of spun gold; unusually dark lashes stood out against skin turned to alabaster by the moonlight's cool glow. The covers had slipped off her shoulders and he glimpsed the valley between her breasts through the unbuttoned front of her nightgown. He drank in her beauty as a man in the desert drinks spring water, in great gulps and without regard for the consequences.

He moved closer to the bed, staring as one hypnotized, as she turned from her side to her back offering him a full view of one young breast where the gown had fallen open. Brett's breath came hard and rough. He resisted the temptation to reach out and caress her face, touch the velvety skin, and run his fingers through her silky golden hair. With a strong effort of willpower, he turned back to his lonely chair.

For the first time in his life, a woman confused him, and that made him angry. He tried to ignore the conflict within himself, but he couldn't and he dropped into the chair, his mind prey to unpalatable thoughts. Damn! He felt more than naked desire for this girl. He had lusted after many women, but none had ever made him stand motionless, staring dumbly and drinking in the intoxicating feeling of her nearness. Never had he just wanted to hold her hand or simply enjoy the feel of her soft skin against the roughness of his own. And *never* had the appearance of helplessness made him want to enfold her in his arms and protect her from harm.

67

He pulled off his coat irritably. He was beginning to sound like those milky youths of his college days. He would do what had to be done to get her settled before he left for France, but that would be the end of it. Never before had he allowed desire to overrule his judgment, and he wasn't going to start now.

He took the time to hang his coat in the wardrobe among the less elegant garments of the landlord and his wife. He might have to spend the night in a chair, but he wasn't going to sleep in his coat. However, his tie and shirt were allowed to drop to the floor. After a struggle, he removed his boots and set them by the door. Then he rummaged in the bottom of the wardrobe until he found several thick blankets; the room was icy cold and he was going to wake up stiff and sore as it was.

Brett sank into the lumpy chair with a muffled groan and the expectation of a miserable night. He moved about trying to find a more comfortable position but soon came to the conclusion it was impossible. That was another thing. No woman had ever caused him to spend the night in a chair. And he was doing it voluntarily, too!

There was enough room in that big bed for four people. She'd never know he shared it with her. Wouldn't she be surprised to wake up and find his face on the pillow next to hers? It was liable to send her into hysterics or a dead faint. He wasn't sure which was more likely, but he didn't want to have to explain either to Mathilda.

Brett didn't know how long he slept before he was pulled from the depths of slumber by a soft moan. Even before his eyes could focus, he heard Kate thrashing around in the bed. The sounds increased in urgency, and as Brett fought to clear his mind of sleep, she suddenly cried out, "No! No! Oh, my God, no!"

Wide-awake now, Brett remembered the slumbering guests in the inn, all hungry for just such a scandal as finding him sharing a room with a gently bred female would create, and in an instant he had sprung to her side and clamped his hand over her mouth. Kate's brilliant blue eyes flew open, wide with fright, as she stared at him without recognition. She struggled frantically to break his hold, but he was much too strong.

"Kate! Kate!" he whispered as loud as he dared. "It's me, Brett. You're safe now. No one is going to harm you."

She still didn't know him, but at the use of her name, a puzzled look came over her lovely face. Then in sudden recognition she threw herself on him, wrapped her arms tightly around his neck, and sobbed into his shoulder. Worried that someone might hear her cries, Brett tried to soothe her nerves and calm her fears, but just as she would not be quieted when she shot the highwayman, so she failed to respond to his entreaties now. Soon at his wit's end to know how to muffle the sound of her crying, Brett kissed her full on the mouth, lightly at first and then with increasing intensity. His aroused senses, bursting from restraint, were urgent in their headlong rush to savor the delicious pleasures of the soft, supple warmth that had been just beyond their reach all day.

Brett laid a blazing trail of kisses from her lips to her eyes, over her ears, and down the fluted column of her throat to the beveled plane of her shoulders. He was intoxicated by the smell of her skin, and the sweet softness of her body caused the volcanic fires within him to blaze higher and higher. Oblivious to her resistance, he tore open the front of her gown and plunged his hand within to fondle the warm breast whose invitation he could not resist. Its soft and resilient fullness destroyed any remaining shred of control, and he lowered his head to savor its sweetness. Ignoring her shocked protests, his lips brazenly explored the softness until he became aware of a furious pounding on his head and a voice raised perilously close to a scream. Kate was furiously resisting the liberties he was taking with her body.

Kate had not been awake when Brett enfolded her in his arms. Feeling safe nestled next to him, she had clung blindly to her protector. She enjoyed the first tender kisses, but as they increased in intensity and wandered from her lips to her ears, she became uneasy and tried to push him away. Rather than let her go, Brett held her more tightly and pressed his scalding lips down her neck and along her shoulders. In the grip of fear, she struggled to break loose, but he continued to plant little circles of fire all over her flesh. The pinpoints of heat increased in intensity until her skin felt like it would burn up from the miniature cauldrons boiling below the surface.

To her utter amazement, Kate found her body responding to his touch. Little fingers of delicious warmth arched through her like forked lightning across the night sky. Shivers of excitement chased each other along her nerves, slowly at first, and then with mounting speed and increasing frequency until her entire being was alive and rebelling against her efforts to control it.

This rampaging fire threatened to consume her when Brett turned his attentions to her breasts. Struggling valiantly to keep from being swept away by the swift current of these unsuspected sensations, she pounded him over the head and shoulders with her fists, but it only seemed to increase his desire and the boldness of his attack.

"Stop," she demanded in a fierce whisper.

But Brett seemed not to hear her. His hands fondled a second breast and his lips sank lower until they found her nipple and started to nibble and caress until she feared she would faint from the intensity of

70

the wildly pleasurable sensations he had kindled in her body. She sank deeper and deeper into the warm, welcoming, engulfing embrace of the startlingly new sensations that threatened to wash away her resistance completely. With one final frenzied effort, Kate forced her mind back from the treason of her senses.

"In God's name, Brett, have pity," she cried, and kicked him in the groin.

With a howl of pain, Brett came crashing back to reality. The moment he released her, Kate scrambled as far away from him as she could and pulled the bedclothes tightly up under her chin. Her magnificent eyes watched him in fear and confusion; she didn't trust him anymore, and after what had just happened, she didn't trust herself, either. The two of them faced each other across the expanse of the bed like embattled wild animals.

Blazing passion still held Brett in its grasp, but the pain in his groin had broken the floodtide of its rise, and anger, a third violent emotion, penetrated his brain. Abruptly Brett tore his eyes off Kate's face and walked over to one of the windows. He threw it open and let a blast of frigid air cascade over him. The knifing cold of the winter night caused his teeth to chatter, and he trembled from the violent cooling of his passion. He felt like a dying man in the death-dealing grip of a fever.

But his growing anger caused him to forget his physical discomfort, and he rounded on Kate, his brow black with rage, but before either of them could speak, they heard footsteps coming quickly down the hall and a discreet but firm knock sounded on the door.

"Mr. Franks, is anything wrong?" a voice called, its quiet urgency laced with concern. "I heard the mistress and came as quickly as I could. Should I call Dr. Credlow?"

Damn the nosy wench, Brett swore to himself as he

spun around toward the closed door. She would ruin everything if he couldn't fob her off with some tale.

"Don't make a sound," he whispered fiercely to Kate who was still huddled under the covers. "I'll get rid of her." Kate just stared at him and clutched the covers more tightly than ever.

"It's all right, child," he said in a breathy whisper, trying to sound like a man waked out of a sound sleep. "The mistress just had a nightmare." His voice didn't sound like Michael's, but he hoped she would not be able to tell the difference through the door. "She's all right now. She's gone back to sleep." He had no idea if Mathilda suffered from nightmares, but he could think of nothing else.

"Are you sure there's nothing I can do?" the voice asked anxiously. "Would she like a glass of hot milk? Maybe a little whiskey to make her sleep better."

Persistent minx, Brett cursed. "No!" he said more emphatically. "She's asleep, and I don't mean to wake her. Now good night."

Brett waited anxiously. He heard the footsteps begin to retreat down the hall, pause, and then begin a slow, tentative return. He tensed and cursed under his breath; the footsteps paused once again, and then retreated, this time quickly, down the hall. Brett listened closely for the slightest sound, but when he heard nothing for several minutes, he let go of his breath and his body sagged against the door.

Kate was frozen in the same position, but as Brett moved away from the door, she immediately shrank from him, her eyes reflecting her alarm.

"You can rest easy," he said in something like his normal voice. "I have myself under control."

"That's what I thought before," she said a trifle breathlessly but with a resumption of her old spunk. Her response to his advances had stunned her, and she was more shaken than she wanted him to realize. The closeness of his handsome, virile body frightened

72

her, but it also filled her with an excitement as mysterious and disturbing as it was unanticipated. She needed to be able to calm her racing mind and consider the problem dispassionately, but Brett's proximity would not allow that.

Kate had never seen so much of a man's body at close range, and she had never seen *any* man with Brett's magnetic appeal. His shirt was open to the waist and his powerful chest, still heaving from unspent passion, was open to her wide-eyed view. His muscled calves, powerful thighs, and flat, taut abdomen all contributed to the impression of a sleek and hungry animal poised for the attack.

In spite of her chagrin, Kate could not tear her eyes off his mesmerizing torso any more than she could deny the surge of turbulent feelings springing up within her own body. She felt her nipples harden, and she blushed fiery red as she realized her traitorous body was crying out against the constraints of her mind.

Brett misunderstood her blush. "I would remove my inflamed body from your presence if there was anywhere I could go," he said with punctilious formality. "Unfortunately, the only piece of furniture in the inn not already in use is this miserable chair," he said, gesturing to the chair in the corner.

Kate crouched lower in her corner, and with his anger draining away, Brett found himself beginning to feel sorry for her. He had been her only protection, and now he had turned himself into the enemy. She must be feeling terribly frightened and utterly alone.

"You cried out and I tried to comfort you," he explained. "But I'm no different from any other man, and the excitement of holding you in my arms was more than I could stand." When she continued to stare at him in uncomprehending fear, he burst out in exasperation, "My God, girl, don't you ever look in a mirror?"

He stalked over to the dresser, picked up a small mirror, and thrust it in front of her. The undeniably lovely face of a young girl with wild, frightened eyes stared back at her. "Don't you know what a beautiful woman you are?" Brett thundered in her ears. "Every part of you cries out to be admired, touched, loved. Just being near you is enough to drive a man crazy. No wonder your brother kept you out of sight. He'd have had men climbing over the walls and in through the windows."

"I'm not blind, sir," Kate replied, a little frightened by the excessive energy of his outburst. "I realize I'm pretty . . ."

"Pretty!" Brett barked. "What bloodless turnip ever used such a paltry word to describe you? You're not pretty, my girl, you're absolutely stunning, and the mere sight of you sets my blood boiling. Pretty!" he repeated in disgust. "That sounds like the kind of stupid thing Martin would say."

Kate struggled to contain her pleasure and mask her confusion. "That may be, but no one ever became so overexcited by my beauty as you."

"That's only because they never saw you. To have you this close and not be able to touch is worse punishment than a whipping. Go back to sleep," he said, hoping to calm his own racing pulses. "It's past two o'clock already and the kitchen wakes up at a beastly hour." He settled into his chair, tucked the blanket up under his armpits so it wouldn't fall away during his slumbers, and leaned back closing his eyes. It would be some time before he got to sleep, but he was not going to let her guess that. He was not willing to admit to himself yet just how much she had disturbed him.

Kate stared resentfully at him but continued to sit up straight in her corner, her mind occupied with thoughts of what had almost happened. She was completely lacking in any practical knowledge of the feelings that could exist between a man and woman, but she knew enough to realize that what had occurred between her and Brett must have happened to many others. Yet how was she to know what was right and what was not? Her mother had never talked to her, certainly her aunt never had, and it would never have occurred to her father that a girl needed to be told anything. All she knew was what she could guess from the scraps of conversations she had overheard between Martin and Isabella, but she could not bring herself to take either of them as a model. Even though the thought of being alone in a strange city nearly frightened her to death, she desperately looked forward to meeting other girls of her own age in London.

After four years of virtual imprisonment, she was nearly starved for companionship. She needed someone to gossip with, someone with whom she could share confidences about men, clothes, and all those things girls enjoy talking about so much with other girls. But most of all she needed someone to talk to about the strange and unmanageable feelings that this man caused in her. They frightened and shocked her badly, but at the same time enthralled her.

London also meant parties, dresses, and lots and lots of people. She wanted to go to all the best parties, flirt with the most handsome men, dance every dance with a different partner, and stay up till dawn.

She dreamily imagined herself dancing with a handsome man under the moonlight, an orchestra playing softly in the distance, and the soft June breezes murmuring through the trees and mussing her hair. Her dress billowed behind her in weightless folds, her eyes sparkled, her hair was dressed with ribbons, and jewels beyond price lay on her white and heaving bosom. Her warm velvety skin glowed like living pearl in the moonlight. She sank even deeper into her pillows savoring the delicious sensations.

Mesmerized by her beauty, her partner held her tightly and whirled her round and round to the strains of the forbidden waltz. Shyly yet eagerly, she lifted her head and looked deep into his eyes, an enchanting smile playing across her inviting lips. As she stared ever deeper into his eyes, they danced faster and faster, and his eyes held hers in a hypnotic trance. It would have been impossible to look away even if she had wanted to. He held her so tightly she could hardly breathe. She could feel every inch of his body against her, her breasts pressed hard against his granite chest, his lean, muscled thigh against her leg. With a start, she realized his face was Brett's face, his magnificent body, too, and his great comforting strength.

He lowered his head slowly and his slightly parted lips met hers in a kiss of such shattering intensity she felt weak, barely able to stand on her own feet. His tongue raked her mouth and his hands played up and down her back creating patterns of dancing fire and making her body warm in response. As the kiss swelled in intensity she was overcome by its force, and a great lassitude came over her. She was unable to resist the force of his kiss, unable to separate herself from him. Kate smiled and snuggled further down in the bed. She drifted over the border into sleep on this feeling of disembodied passion.

Chapter 6

Both man and woman slipped into uneasy repose, victims of turbulent emotions heated to the point of eruption and then cooled with the agonizing abruptness of volcanic lava plunged into an arctic sea. Awake, they fought the passions that threatened to consume them, but in slumber, they succumbed to dreams of desire's torment.

Kate was the first to fall asleep and the first to cry out. Her lips formed Brett's name silently at first, but as her need became more urgent, a dry whisper of entreaty evolved. Her voice, reaching him through the mists of a deep sleep, seemed weak and far away. At first his mind tried to drive away her importuning cry, but it sounded again and again until an answering restlessness was ignited within him which threw off the armor of his exhaustion. He crossed the small space between them, and their bodies entwined like long-separated halves of a single whole.

Brett cradled Kate in his arms, infusing her with his heat; his lips found hers, and he kissed her with growing warmth until he had kindled an answering fire within her. Her supple form melted into his embrace and her lips clung hungrily to his.

His hands caressed her shoulders, the column of her throat, roamed freely over her smooth, soft skin until they found and uncovered her breasts, caressing and teasing them into hard peaks of desire. His hot, dry lips found them, too, and his scorching tongue traced little arabesques of scalding heat on her silky skin. His hands burned the surface of her body like branding irons claiming every part of her as his own.

By the time Brett came fully awake to what he was doing, his senses were inflamed beyond control. No hint of caution, no word of warning could have cooled the raging desire that consumed his being. His hands wandered over Kate's body until he drove her into full consciousness of her own desire and the flood of passion that was overwhelming her.

Her consciousness drugged by an equally insistent need, Kate woke to awareness more slowly than Brett. She tried to resist, even though her mind was surprised by the sweetness of this heady passion, but her body, glorying in its awakening, rushed joyfully toward its fate. The heat of Brett's manhood against her sensitive skin sent tendrils of flame and pleasure racing along her body. Unable to hold back any longer, Kate clung ever more tightly to Brett, pressing her body against his, pleading with him to become one with her.

Yet even though he was being driven by a need greater than any he had experienced before, Brett moved with caution and gentleness, heedful of her inexperience. It was this small remnant of control that alerted him to danger when he encountered the resistance of her maidenhead. The knowledge that Kate was a virgin and a lady pierced the cloak of desire that enveloped him, and he paused, irresolute, caught between a feeling that he must not proceed further and a raw need that demanded fulfillment. Something deep within him valiantly struggled to stem the onrushing tide of passion, some inner voice warned that he would forever regret this rash action, but Kate arched her body against his, uttering a groan of desire, and Brett was plunged headlong over the precipice of no return.

Still Brett refrained from joining his body to hers, letting his hands, mouth, tongue continue their feverish activity, working to propel Kate to a higher pitch of excitement, to a state of delirium where she would be almost unaware of pain. Finally, he entered her with a quick, knifelike thrust and she gasped with the double shock of pain and almost unbearable pleasure. Her ecstasy mounted quickly and she rose higher and higher to meet his pounding rhythm. She urged him on with a fury he never dreamed possible, demanding that he give her joy beyond her wildest expectations and igniting in him a similar desire to rise to his own pinnacle of triumph.

Brett fought to slow their feverish rush toward fulfillment, to prolong the exquisite pleasure found in the ever-expanding ripples of sensual delight, but Kate, unaware of the even greater bliss to be found in prolonging their union, drove him on with her body, demanding, beseeching him to release her from the almost unbearable torment that enslaved her. Finally, just as she thought she could stand no more, that she must lose consciousness from the jarring impact of this sweet agony, he released his passion within her and she felt that indescribable satisfaction of simultaneous release and fulfillment. Her whole body shuddered and grew rigid with pleasure as the waning pulses of his passion sent ripples of white-hot ecstasy through her. Slowly they relaxed and fell apart.

For long moments neither moved nor spoke. But as the euphoria of their pleasure subsided and the full realization of what had occurred began to sink in, Kate started to shake uncontrollably. She bit her lip hard and held her body rigid, but it was no use. Nothing could stop the onslaught of shock and mortification. The tears came first as glistening dewdrops on the ends of her lashes, then ran down her cheeks in ever increasing rivulets until her pillow became wet with her remorse. Brett attempted to comfort her, but she tore free of his embrace.

"Don't touch me," she hissed, her eyes bright with tears. She put her gown to rights and snatched up a heavy robe which she buttoned up to her chin.

"Keep your voice down," Brett whispered imperatively. "Someone might hear you."

"Do you think I care now? Can they ruin me any more than you already have?"

"No one ever needs to know what happened."

"You're worried about what somebody else might think, but I'm concerned with what *I* think, what *I* feel. I'm the one who has to hold up my head and pretend to be an honorable woman. I feel *unclean*."

"If no one knows, it won't be as bad."

"Do you honestly believe that?" Kate demanded, staring at him like he was some form of exotic beast. "Are you so utterly insensitive you can pretend nothing more has happened than a few moments of harmless pleasure? Tell me, conquering hero, how am I going to face an honest man, should one be so foolish as to ask for my hand? Do I smile prettily and say, 'I'll be delighted to accept your offer, kind sir, but I feel I must tell you there is a little something missing. Mr. Westbrook took it, but I won't mind if you don't.' Or should I accept gratefully and let him discover on our wedding night that I'm used goods parading as new cloth?"

Brett was stiff with anger, but he was also honest enough to admit the truth of what she said. "I can't alter what's happened, but I'm sure something can be done," he said with a half-goading tone.

"Something has already been done," Kate rasped. "You couldn't have destroyed me any more completely if you had stripped me of my pedigree and proved me of bastard birth. Go away!" she cried, some of the passion and anger wrung out of her voice. "Can't you see I'm crying, and I hate to cry in front of people I dislike." She buried her face in the pillows, and gave way to wracking sobs that shook her body from one end to the other.

Brett was trapped. He couldn't leave the room, but

his presence was doing nothing to help calm Kate down; in fact, it only caused her to cry harder. He couldn't even work off his own rage by hurling curses at the huddled figure in the bed. As much as he hated the appalling muddle, he was too honest to throw the blame on anyone but himself; still, that didn't prevent his being angry with Kate. Impotent fury boiled within him, but he could find no outlet other than rapid pacing about the small room, the sight of Kate's huddled figure a continual accusation which further exacerbated his raw nerves.

"You don't have to cringe in the corner like you're caged with a rabid beast. I promise I won't bother you again," he muttered angrily.

"You're just as lethal," Kate said, lifting her head from the pillow. "And you've given me sufficient proof of how to value your assurances of safety." She gave a sob and buried her face in her pillow once more.

"For God's sake, woman, you'd drive a saint to cursing with your incessant harping."

"Since we know you're no saint," Kate hiccupped, "I guess I'd better cover my ears before they're violated as well."

"By God, if I don't strangle you before the night's out . . . !"

"I wouldn't call upon God so often if I were you," Kate advised, not the least intimidated by his threats. "If He ever gets a good look at what He's created, He's likely to burn you to a cinder."

"You vixen!" Brett raged, giving free rein to his anger. "I ought to break your beautiful neck. It seems nothing else can still your spiteful tongue."

But somehow the tension was broken and both of them felt their anger begin to subside. "You're vile, loathsome, and you have no sense of shame," Kate said. "You've ruined me for a few moments of pleasure, and now you're threatening to break my neck if

81

I don't stop reminding you of it. No doubt you would enjoy ravishing me for the rest of the night, but I don't think I would like it. I don't see why you can't sleep somewhere else, but I'm too tired to argue with you. Just know that if you so much as come near me, I'll stab you with this nail file."

Shaking with rage, Brett opened his mouth to speak.

"And don't say another word," Kate ordered, forestalling him. She mounded up the pillows and settled back against them. "There's nothing more that *can* be said." Then she wrapped her robe more securely about her and held tightly to a long and very sharp nail file she had taken from the bedside table.

Though she would die before she admitted it to Brett, Kate knew she was as responsible as he for what had happened between them. It didn't matter that she had been half asleep or that he had refused to heed her pleas to release her, she was painfully aware she had responded to his every move, had even encouraged him to continue when he might have stopped. True, he was more experienced than she and should have been the one to hold back, but she had known the consequences of such an encounter and still she had begged him to continue. It mattered not that she had used no words; her body had spoken a language he could not misunderstand.

Why would she have done such a thing? She had admitted the attraction almost from the first, but that was no reason to throw herself at him in complete disregard of the consequences of such an action. And it wouldn't have made any difference if she had been in love with him; she was still unmarried and as such was ruined. She had left Ryehill with three advantages—beauty, birth, and virginity. Now she had thrown away the only one which could make the others worthless.

She made no move to try to sleep but stared vacantly before her seeing nothing but her own bleak thoughts.

Brett paced the room, glancing up at Kate every few turns; her eyes never once turned to his tall, athletic figure as it stalked the room, sending his muscles rippling in anger and frustration. The nail file remained tightly grasped in her right hand and the bedclothes held under her chin with her left.

Brett was preyed upon by so many conflicting emotions it took him close to the rest of the night to sort them out. He was not used to having accusations of guilt flung at him, and he was unaccustomed to any kind of self-chastisement, but his enormous wealth and undisciplined youth had not destroyed his innately fair and honest character. Even though his rage continued to feed on his sense of ill-treatment, it did not prevent him from admitting he had seriously compromised Kate's future and that it was up to him to make some kind of atonement. But the truth was bitter gall that kept his anger hot.

He was angry at her for showing him so irrefutably the injustice he had done her by making her the victim of his unbridled lust, regardless of her encouragement. Even though he had never given any thought to the plight of a gently born girl without money or the protection of a family, he knew he should have stopped himself before it was too late. Until tonight, he had confined his activities to mature women who were of the same mind as he and knew how to play the game according to the rules.

He was angry at her for having the temerity to throw his misdeeds in his face. He had done things he was not proud of before, but no one had faced him down or caused him to apologize. Yet this girl, with no one to support or protect her, had called him the worst names she knew, and he had practically admitted he deserved them.

He was angry because Kate wouldn't somehow

83

disappear and relieve him of the responsibility he had so thoughtlessly assumed and then made worse by his unbridled lusts. How in heaven's name was he going to find a situation for a penniless girl of extraordinary looks which wouldn't end up with her becoming someone's mistress? It was impossible to leave her unprotected; she'd be devoured by the town wolves in less than a fortnight.

He was angry because she had touched something within him no one else had even managed to find, something he had taken pains to hide. Now he knew he wouldn't be able to push her off on some distant relative, or leave her with a job-service bureau and forget about her. He wanted to know what was going to happen to her. And that wasn't all. In some as-yet-hazy way, he realized he wanted her to be accepted by her own class, not as an employee or mistress, but as an equal.

Finally, he was angry at her for disturbing the precision of his thoughts, for making him feel all these emotions. Never before had he bothered to concern himself with what other people wanted; he had certainly not sat for hours wracking his brains trying to come up with a solution to a problem that showed every indication of being insoluble.

He should have headed straight for France and left Edward to settle her in London. Then maybe he wouldn't have the nagging feeling he had behaved like a cad and it was his responsibility to compensate her for the consequences of his irresponsible folly. Something had to be done, but it might be weeks before he could find a permanent solution. He could hand the whole problem over to his lawyers, but he wanted to involve as few people as possible. Why had he accepted Martin's wager? One unthinkingly chivalrous act and look what it had gotten him into. It was beginning to seem like he would have to take her to France.

The pit of his stomach knotted and threatened to rise into his throat. He was horrified to discover he was pleasurably excited by the thought of keeping her with him. He cursed himself roundly. Lord, he was starting to act like a romantic fool. Nothing was more sure to jeopardize the success of his mission or make his work more nearly impossible than having a mettlesome girl on his hands with too much beauty for her own good and far too little sense about the world. If he wanted to spend all his time presiding over her entertainment and driving off seducers, then by all means he would take her along. He would have his hands full long before they reached Algiers.

Brett threw himself into the chair. He would drive himself to violence if he didn't stop thinking of Kate and her seductive allure. It was time he began to give some thought to his mission. The task before him was not an easy one. If he was to keep the dey of Algiers from provoking the French into invading his country, he would have to be a very clever and persuasive talker; the emissaries of el-Kader certainly would be, and they would have bribes to offer as well.

Brett's thoughts continued to revolve around Kate until the first rays of the morning sun came streaming through the bedroom windows.

The clatter from below proclaimed the house was up and readying for the new day. Brett woke feeling so bruised and sore he knew it would take several hours of heavy exercise to get over the effects of spending the night in that horrible chair. Kate still sat with the nail file in her hands, her eyes following him as he moved about the room. All the anger and fear had gone out of them, but they were wary and held an accusing glitter.

The memory of last night burst upon him in one devastating rush. Even though he had been half asleep, he knew he had enjoyed a sensual experience more glorious than any before. The memory of Kate's welcoming lips, her velvety skin, her enveloping warmth caused his hunger to rise up unappeased and his groin to tighten painfully. Cursing silently, Brett rose out of his chair, determined to leave the room as soon as possible. He knew if he did not remove himself from her presence quickly, he might be tempted to approach her again, and he dared not think of what she would do to him with that nail file.

Trying to ignore the tantalizing appeal of her loveliness, Brett poured some cold water into the basin and washed his face. He wondered if anyone would think to bring his shaving water or if he was going to have to get it himself; and his boots and coat needed serious attention before he could wear them again. His trunks hadn't been unstrapped the night before, but it was too much trouble to have them brought in just to look for a new coat. He would have to spend at least part of the morning in the same clothes. It would be a relief when he could return to his usual routine. He caught a glimpse of Kate's exquisite countenance in the mirror and realized that was a forlorn hope. Nothing in his life would ever be the same again. In less than twenty-four hours, she had smashed the tenor of his existence beyond repair.

"I'm going to be gone for most of the morning," he said, breaking the silence. "I don't know who's up yet, but no one ever lifts so much as a spoon around here without Mathilda's knowledge. She'll see to you when she gets here."

"Just go away," Kate said in a flat voice. "I can take care of myself. I always have." She seemed drained of all her vitality, but her eyes were still tightly focused on his every move. The bright light that burned in their azure depths showed that her unflagging spirit still burned brightly.

Brett busied himself with his shaving equipment.

86

He was in no mood to talk; besides, he didn't know what to say to her. If he had any sense at all he would pay as little attention to her as possible. Just the sight of her sitting huddled outside with the gold of the sun making her like something alive was enough to cause his passions to stir. He could almost feel her skin beneath his fingertips, smell the fragrance of her hair, taste the sweetness of her mouth, but he hadn't the least doubt she would use the nail file on him if he approached her again.

A vigorous knock was heard at the door and Mathilda's hearty voice easily penetrated the wood panels. "Are you up, Mr. Westbrook?" She waited a few seconds then tried the door; it was still locked. "Drat the man," they heard her say. "I'll bet the lazy boy is still asleep. And his shaving water getting stone-cold quick as a cat can lick her whiskers. I hope he doesn't think I'm going to stand out here until it pleases him to wake up."

Having delayed only as long as it took him to find his dressing gown and pull it over his bare torso, Brett opened the door.

"Humph! So you *are* up. Pity you couldn't say so," Mathilda grumbled and pushed past him into the room. "I hope you had a good night's rest, miss." Kate had pulled the covers almost up to her eyes at the sound of the first knock. The nail file was nowhere to be seen.

"I slept f-fine," she stammered, trying to avoid Mathilda's eyes.

"Let me take care of this man so I can get him out of the way, and then I'll help you get ready for breakfast. I've already got a girl grinding coffee beans and fixing to scramble eggs to go with some sausage and fresh-baked bread."

"I can't possibly eat that much," Kate said, feeling uncomfortable with so much attention. "Coffee and toast would be just fine."

"Humph!" Mathilda sniffed. "A young girl like you needs more than coffee and toast to keep the flesh on your bones. It's a right cold day, too, and you'll never be warm in that drafty coach without something to fill your stomach." She turned to Brett.

"You hurry up with your shaving while I see about your boots. You'd better give me your coat, too." Brett retrieved the garment from the wardrobe.

Mathilda looked put out. "What do you mean, putting that man's clothes up for him?" she scolded, turning to Kate. "We women are all alike, spoiling a man and making him think we're obliged to wait on him hand and foot. Let him hang up his own coat next time, or wear it like it is."

Kate couldn't repress a smile, but Brett wasn't amused. "Miss Vareyan was sound asleep when I came in," he informed Mathilda. "I may be spoiled, but I haven't yet been reduced to depending upon you or any other woman.

"Such indignation," Mathilda taunted, smiling wickedly. "I never knew a man to get the wind up if he wasn't guilty of something." She didn't notice Kate had turned ashen and had nearly slipped out of sight under the covers. Brett's face gave nothing away.

"Get out of here, you old termagant," he teased. "I'll be through shaving in ten minutes, and I expect you to be back with my coat and boots before the soap is off my face." He pushed her steadily toward the door. "And they'd better be spotless. Not a single speck or a wrinkle."

"If you're so particular, you can do them yourself, Mr. London dandy," she shot back at him. "You'll get what my girls can do and no more." She opened the door and was gone; Brett began choosing razors.

"It won't take me long to shave. I'll have my breakfast in the coffee room. I imagine everyone will try to make an early start. They ought to be gone before lunch." He finished shaving one side of his face and started on the other.

"It'll take most of the morning to fix the coach window. While that's being done, I'm going to take a ride to work out some of the stiffness. Just let Mathilda know if there's anything you want." He completed the last swipe with the razor and rinsed his face. As he patted his skin dry, Mathilda ambled in without knock or invitation. She grinned when she saw he hadn't yet put his razors away.

"I told you the service was quick. Good, too," she said as she handed him his boots. Brett packed his razors away, forced his feet into his boots, and quickly put on his shirt and tie.

"I always knew Michael kept you for something besides scorching the meat," Brett said, grinning provocatively as he let Mathilda help him into his coat. Mathilda let out a deep, rumbling laugh that set her rolls of fat to dipping and swaying like swells in a rough sea.

"If you aren't the worst! Get out of here before I empty that pitcher over your handsome head," she threatened.

"You probably would, too, if you weren't such a squatty thing," he shot back and quickly closed the door behind him as Mathilda aimed a coat hanger at his head. It struck the door and clattered harmlessly to the floor.

Brett's smile made him look indescribably handsome. Even though she told herself she didn't like or trust him and couldn't wait to be well beyond his reach, she couldn't repress the wistful desire to have him smile at her like that, at least once. She had always been attracted to him, even when he made her most angry, but now his smile made him seem human, almost friendly. Kate desperately wanted a friend, and she had the feeling that Brett could fill that position.

"Mercy on my soul, that man's a treat," Mathilda

said, laughing happily. "He's slippery as an eel and clever as an old cat, but for all that, he's as good as they come. Now what can I do for you, child? I know you don't have your maid with you so I'm going to tend to you myself."

"I don't need anything, really," Kate mumbled in a very small voice. "I never had a maid at home so I'm used to taking care of myself. There must be hundreds of things you need to do."

Mathilda smiled indulgently. "It's nothing my girls can't do by themselves, the silly giggling things. They'd roast a sausage on a spit if you didn't tell them different, but it'll do them good to have to manage alone." She moved briskly around the room, straightening the bureau and dresser tops behind Brett and tugging the chair cover back into its original position.

Kate stayed in the bed, clutching the covers tightly about her shoulders and trying to keep from shaking all over. She resolutely told herself she'd never be able to take care of herself if she couldn't keep her wits about her at times like this.

Mathilda set a match to the fire. "It's cold as a witch's breath this morning. I don't know why Mr. Westbrook never thought to light the fire, but this'll have the room toasty warm in a few minutes. You stay under those covers. There's no hurry to get up so you might as well stay in bed." She fluffed up two of the pillows and looked around the room. Everything seemed to be to her satisfaction, for she moved to the door. "I'll be bringing your breakfast up to you in about an hour. Is there anything you need before then?"

"I'd really like a cup of cocoa, if it's not too much trouble," Kate requested in an apologetic voice.

"None at all. I'll bring it up right away."

"And there's something else, too." Kate blushed fiery red. She tried to force her tongue to say the words, but they wouldn't come. Desperation gave her courage and loosened her tongue. "I need some new b-b-bedclothes." She turned redder still. "You see, it was my t-time of the m-m-month, and I'm afraid I b-b-bled on them. I'm sorry, but I didn't mean to ruin your lovely bed." Tears began to form on the tips of her eyelashes. "I'll wash them out for you."

Under her bossy exterior, Mathilda was a sentimental romantic, and the sight of tears in that exquisite girl's eyes melted her heart like butter on a griddle. "Don't worry, miss. A little blood won't worry me. And you won't be washing any sheets yourself neither. I'll throw them in the bottom of the pot and nobody'll be the wiser. Now you dry your eyes." She looked Kate full in the face. "With a face like yours, there's nothing in this world you can't have, so there's no call to be crying about something so silly."

Kate resisted a strong desire to throw herself on this huge, comforting woman and sob her heart out. Instead, she forced herself to smile and thank her for her compliments.

Mathilda brushed her thanks aside and waddled out to get the clean linens; she was back within minutes. "You put the old ones next to the door and I'll take them down when I bring up your breakfast." Her face softened into a motherly smile. "You have a nice morning in bed. I'll see that nobody bothers you." She went out and locked the door behind her.

Kate scrambled out of bed as soon as the door was shut; there was no sign now of fear or indecision. She searched her valise until she found a handkerchief. She dampened it in the bowl and carefully cleaned the blood from her thighs. She determinedly refused to think about how it got there. She just couldn't face that yet. When she finished, she threw the soiled cloth into the hottest part of the fire and kept moving it around with the poker until every bit of it had been turned to ashes.

Then she put on a fresh nightgown, and packed the

91

old one away. Though she didn't see any blood on it, it reminded her of the night before. She quickly stripped the bed, being very careful to fold up the bloodied sheet inside the unstained one, put them both by the door, and made up the bed with the fresh sheets. Then she fluffed the pillows and climbed back into bed. Now she could relax.

She lay there for a long time, thinking of everything that had happened to her since Martin had dragged her into the middle of his card game, and she was surprised at how many instances of Brett's kindness she could remember. It didn't do anything to alter the horror of the previous night, but she couldn't help but wonder what it would have been like to meet him under different circumstances. She was soon lost in a daydream of what might-have-been and was only shaken out of her trance by the sound of the key in the lock announcing the arrival of breakfast. Kate started to get up.

"You're going to have your breakfast in bed this morning," Mathilda announced. "I'm right sorry about your hot cocoa, but it went clean out of my head. I don't want you to think I'm like this all the time, forgetting orders and things, but I guess I got things on my mind I don't know about." She placed the tray on Kate's lap, and the delicious aroma of freshly brewed coffee assailed her. Suddenly Kate was enormously hungry, and the plate loaded with eggs, ham, sausage, bread and butter, and jam didn't seem like too much at all.

Mathilda watched her eat with satisfaction. "I'd have brought you more, but I was afraid a skinny little thing like you wasn't used to eating more than a bite." Kate didn't answer because her mouth was full. Mathilda smiled broadly. "You eat it all up. It'll put some flesh on those bones. You look like a starved wren. I've a mind to keep you here with me until I get you fattened up a bit."

Kate gulped down some coffee. "I'd grow out of my clothes in a week's time."

"You can always get more clothes." Mathilda picked up the sheets. "I'll be up to get the tray after a while. Lunch will be about twelve-thirty. Leastways it will if I can get those London gentlemen out of the house before then." *Poor little thing,* Mathilda thought as she closed the door behind her, *she's been through some sadness in her life. And her prettier than any picture you ever saw.* She sighed heavily and turned her mind to the more mundane business of the inn.

Chapter 7

Ten o'clock came and went and Brett still had not returned. Kate had finished her breakfast, repacked her valise, and put the room in such complete order that there was nothing to show it had been occupied.

Though the room was airy and bright with sunlight streaming in both windows, her lengthy confinement had become increasingly intolerable; her thoughts depressed her even further. She had never meant to become dependent on Brett, and after last night it was even more unthinkable she should do so, but no sooner had she reached the decision to never see him again then she was forced to admit the utter hopelessness of her situation. She had no fortune, no means of earning a living, and no one to turn to. She knew nothing of her father's family except that he had a younger brother, the trustee of their father's estate, whom Martin had cursed almost daily. Surely a man of his wealth, with a wife and servants to see to the running of his establishment, would not find it difficult to add one more person to his household. The more she thought about it, the more hopeful she became, and she sat down to think.

She couldn't remember where he lived, but she knew it was one of the fashionable streets in London because Martin had sneered that such a pinchpenny should live anywhere but among the bankers and merchants. She cudgeled her brains. Where *would* a member of her family live? But she didn't know anything about London—or her uncle.

Was he like Martin and her father? Would he have a genuine sympathy for her, or would he consider her a poor relation to be kept out of sight when guests were present? *Regents Square!* That was the street. She didn't know the number, but that would be easy enough to find once she reached London. All that mattered now was she had a refuge from Brett's charity and his lusts.

But she had to have money. She was sure the stage or the mail coach passed through the village, but how was she going to pay for her passage, food, and lodging until she could find her uncle? It was unthinkable that she should ask Brett to lend her money so she could run away from him. He probably wouldn't give it to her anyway, but every feeling revolted at the thought of being under further obligation to him in any case. Maybe she could ask Mathilda. She hated to return her kindness in such a manner, but she couldn't think of anyone else. If only Mr. Hunglesby or Mr. Feathers had been here, they would have helped her. *Her valise!*

"Brett left his winnings on the table, so I slipped them into your valise," Feathers had whispered in her ear as she kissed him good-bye. "Brett doesn't want the money, and Martin doesn't deserve it. Besides, he meant you to have it anyway."

Kate hesitated only a moment; even though he might have intended to do so, Brett had never actually given her the money. She would worry about that later. Either her uncle would pay it back or she could save it from her wages once she had a position, but somehow she would pay back every penny.

Next she had to settle on a course of action. She rejected the idea of hiring a private post chaise; it would be expensive and too conspicuous, and she doubted she could find one, or the post boys to drive it, in Littledean. Her only choice lay between the regular stage and the mail coach. Never having traveled on either, it was impossible to know which was better. Neither did she know when they ran, how to purchase a ticket, or where they picked up their passengers. Would Mathilda help her? She was sure Mathilda liked her, but she was also certain that in spite of the cheerful abuse she heaped on her husband, Mathilda firmly believed in the superiority of men, especially a man like Brett. She would have to be very careful. She wouldn't put it past Mathilda to tell Brett of her plans.

She settled down to await Mathilda's return. She was almost an hour late already. Surely she wouldn't be much longer.

"Lordy," Mathilda exclaimed as she came puffing into the room after what seemed like an interminable wait, "has this ever been a morning. Gentlemen as thick as flies on a carcass shouting like heathens, and every one of them wanting his breakfast at once, and half of them too hung over to know what they were served. You never heard such a racket, what with them all shouting at the same time, trying to get the boys to fetch up their curricles, or whatever they call those murderous contraptions they drive. And they call themselves Quality. Humph!" she snorted.

She looked around at the neat room and her eyes narrowed in surprised disapproval. "Well, I never," she exclaimed. "If more people left their rooms like you do, miss, running this inn would be a pleasure. But you had no call to do all this yourself. It's not proper for a lady."

"I wish I could do more," Kate countered with a grateful smile. "You've treated me better than my own mother, spoiling me with breakfast in bed and not getting upset when I took your bed and then ruined it. I'll never be able to repay your kindness." Her eyes were moist with emotion.

Mathilda sniffed and began rubbing her nose with the back of her hand. "Lawks, miss, you'll have me blushing and trembling like those silly gals in the kitchen if you keep talking that way. It wasn't much and I don't grudge it. You're too pretty to be cleaning rooms."

Kate laughed. "I never heard that pretty people made any less mess than ugly ones. Quite the opposite, I would imagine." Suddenly her mood sobered. "Mathilda, Mr. Westbrook promised my brother he would take me to London, but he has to be in France in a few days." She tried to avoid Mathilda's shrewd eyes. "It, uh . . . may be necessary for me to continue my journey alone." Kate kept twisting her handkerchief into knots, a move not lost on Mathilda. "Does the mail or the stage run through Littledean? How would I get a ticket, if I should need one?" she added hastily.

"I don't know your situation, miss," Mathilda said in a measured voice, "and I'm not asking you to tell me anything you don't want to, but you've got no call to take passage on the mail, much less that nasty stage. If Mr. Westbrook wants you to go to London, he'll take you himself or see you're sent proper in a post chaise with outriders. Mr. Westbrook gets a trifle preoccupied with his own doings sometimes, but I've never known him not

97

to do the proper thing. Now you stop worrying and let him take care of everything. What else do we put up with men for?"

"But I don't *want* to depend on him." Kate almost stamped her foot. "You see," she said, wringing her handkerchief again, "my brother virtually forced him to agree to escort me. He really didn't want to. Besides," she said, brightening with an idea, "I could hire one of the girls from the inn to go with me. That ought to make it perfectly respectable."

"That would make a difference," Mathilda admitted, "but I still don't like it. Those silly things wouldn't be any use to you except to act half-witted."

"I don't know that I shall need them in the end," Kate said as nonchalantly as she could, "but it would be nice to know I shouldn't be stranded here. It could be months before he returns."

"You can stay here until he comes back," exclaimed Mathilda, her face wreathed in a smile. "I don't know why I didn't think of it before. Then you'd have plenty of time to decide what to do." Kate tried to protest, but Mathilda had the bit between her teeth.

"You see, I don't have any children. It's just me and Michael here, and I'd love to have a pretty young thing like you to fuss over. You could stay here, quiet like, and not a bit of harm would come to you. We hardly ever have this much business. You'd be free to come and do just as you please." Delighted with her plan, Mathilda picked up the tray and headed for the door. "I'll talk to Mr. Westbrook as soon as he gets back."

Kate threw herself between Mathilda and the door. "You must tell me where I can buy a ticket," she pleaded. "I promise I won't do anything you or Mr. Westbrook won't like, but I can't just sit here and wait for him to make every decision for me."

Mathilda gave her a knowing look. "There's something you're not saying, but I'll tell you if you promise you won't do anything without talking it over with Mr. Westbrook first."

Kate nodded her agreement; she had lied so many times already, there was no reason to blink at one more.

"Not that it will do you any good because no self-respecting girl would even go near the Black Crow," Mathilda said, a look of stern disapproval on her face. "It's a low, dirty place on the other side of the village. They ought to change the route, but that's men all over for you. The stage is no better. It's just as likely to pick you up in front of the vicarage as on the lane leading to town, but it's a nasty contraption, filled with chickens and old men and smelling worse than a cow byre. You couldn't travel from here to Broxmore without getting sick to your stomach. But I'm going to talk Mr. Westbrook into letting you stay with me. Now move out of my way, young lady. I have more important things to do than stand around arguing with you over the mail coach." But she smiled broadly as she left, and Kate felt sure she entertained no suspicion Kate meant to be gone from the inn before noon.

Accepting the fact that no one was going to help her escape, Kate emptied both valises on the bed the minute the door closed behind Mathilda and started repacking them. She couldn't possibly carry both, not even just across the lawn, so she put everything she didn't expect to need during the

99

next few days into the large valise. Surely Mathilda would keep it for her until she could send for it.

She unwrapped Feathers's handkerchief; besides the money, it contained Martin's tie pin and ring as well as a few other personal items. She put the coins and notes into her purse and hastily put everything else back into the valise. She brushed aside the unpleasant feeling of being a thief; she couldn't afford the luxury of guilt now.

Kate dragged the larger valise to the corner and looked around the room, but she could find nothing else that needed attending to. With a fatalistic sigh, she set her small valise by the door and put on the heavy blue cloak, taking great care to pull the hood far down over her face. If she was careful not to look up, maybe no one would remember her. She opened the door and peeped out into the hall; the only sounds came from the kitchen below. She resisted the impulse to wait; if she was ever going to escape, she had to do it now. She plucked up her courage, picked up the valise, and stepped out into the hall.

The narrow passage ran along the back of the inn for its full length. Several doors opened onto it from one side while large windows overlooked the lawn behind the house on the other. The grounds included an orchard and an extensive garden. Kate knew the stables and kitchens were somewhere to the left, but all she could see to her right were the spreading limbs of several large yews. She strained her ears, but no sound disturbed the morning quiet. If she could just get to that side of the inn, maybe she could get to the lane without being seen.

Turning the corner, Kate came face-to-face with three doors; she had no idea where any of them led. The first door was locked; the second was also, but the faint sound of voices could be heard coming from behind the third. She paused, unsure of whether to proceed or turn back, but she had to go somewhere, and she couldn't wait around hoping everyone would leave the inn. To her relief the door was unlocked. She opened it carefully and found herself at the head of a narrow stair.

Kate made her way down very slowly, one step at a time, listening for voices or anyone coming along the hall behind her. When she reached the ground floor, she found the hall ran back along the rear of the house just like the upper hall.

The sound of male voices was clear now and quite near, so she started back down the hall hoping to find a door that led to the outside before she reached the kitchen; there was none, only more windows, one of which was open. Kate didn't hesitate. Without waiting to consider the alternatives, she dropped her valise out the window and then herself behind it. She landed awkwardly but unhurt. She brushed herself off, picked up her valise, and headed away from the inn as fast as she could.

She found herself in a wide lawn that merged about one hundred and fifty feet away with some grape arbors and fruit trees. A hedgerow and a low brick wall ran along the front of the yard to screen it from the road.

She scurried across the lawn. By the time she reached the cover of the grape arbor, she was out of breath from excitement and the weight of the valise. The hedge gave way to a high brick wall protecting the garden from marauding livestock and hungry little boys. Kate walked steadily forward, confident that before long she would come to a door in the wall. At the far end of the arbor, past the grapes and some espaliered pears, she found what she was looking for: she opened the unlocked door and found herself on a dirty lane in the full glare of sunlight. Behind her was the inn and its grounds; ahead lay the village. She pulled her hood low over her face and started forward.

Kate passed several cottages and shops, a blacksmith's forge, and at least one ale house before she reached a crossroads. Then she stopped to consider what to do next. She was out of breath and her shoulder ached from the weight of the valise. She looked up and down each street as well as she could, but she didn't see anything that looked like the Black Crow.

There were only one or two people in the streets, but others watched her from doorways and open windows. In a small village like this, everyone was known by sight, and a lone female on foot was bound to attract attention. She had to get off the street as soon as possible. "Young man," she said, addressing a small boy heading her way, "can you tell me where I might find the Black Crow?"

The child mumbled something she didn't understand, pointed in a direction farther along the street, then passed on without looking back. She smiled to herself; her fatal beauty obviously had no effect on seven-year-olds.

Kate picked up her valise and started to pick her way across the road. There had been no rain recently, but the lanes were badly cut up and liberally sprinkled with manure from the carriage traffic of the last two days. Kate's shoes weren't made for walking outdoors, certainly not through fouled streets, and even though she held her skirts up as best she could, she reached the other side in a less clean condition than when she began. She shook her skirts vigorously.

She came upon the Black Crow just around a turn in the street and was taken back to discover it was a small, mean building instead of a clean and respectable house like the Cock-in-the-Cradle. The paint was peeling and the yard unswept and littered with the droppings of assorted fowls that picked through its garbage for bits of food.

Kate was unnerved by its squalid appearance, but she hadn't come this far to allow her courage to fail now. The sounds of merriment coming through an open window gave her the pluck to enter.

The door opened into a dingy room containing several benches along the walls, two doorways, and a shallow stair. A small, battered table held what looked like a register and some other papers. Three men stood near one of the doors which appeared, from the noise one could hear through it, to lead to the taproom. Apparently some of the local inhabitants didn't believe in waiting until noon to slake their thirst.

Kate stood rooted to the spot. She had never been in a public room before and didn't know what to expect, but this was definitely not it. She had assumed it would be orderly and run by an elderly couple of unquestionable virtue. Instead, she found herself confronted by three ill-bred men who stared at her with open curiosity. One addressed her rudely in common accents.

"We don't have no work to give, and we don't let rooms to females that arrives on foot. State your business and be gone before you gives the

103

place a bad name." Anger momentarily overcame Kate's trepidation.

"It already looks like a barnyard. If you'd take the time to sweep your yard instead of abusing honest citizens, you might attract a better class of trade," she said scornfully. All three men gaped at Kate, and she pulled the hood a little further over her face, her courage waning as her flush of anger died. "Please tell me when the mail coach leaves for London. I wish to book a seat."

The man wearing an apron detached himself from the group. He was an ungainly individual with no neck and a torso that was much too large for the lower portion of his body. He examined her carefully, as though he were trying to decide what was hidden underneath that great blue cloak and hood. He appeared unwilling to provide the requested information.

"The mail does come by here, but not until late afternoon." He continued to inspect Kate so steadily her bones started to feel like rubber. "It don't get to London till after midnight though. Now what's a nice girl like you going to do all by yourself in London after midnight?" He tried to get a look at her face, but Kate turned her head away.

"That's no concern of yours," she said in what she hoped was a voice stern enough to stem his impertinence. "I shall be met when I arrive. All you need do is provide me with a ticket."

The man's smile showed several crooked teeth. "Spirited little wench, ain't you? Where'd you come from anyway? You didn't come on the mail yesterday. I'd swear to that. Don't tell me you're running out on one of them young swells staying at the Cock-in-the-Cradle?" He grinned widely. "Someone'll be hopping mad when he finds out you've skipped."

"Keep a civil tongue in your head, or I'll have the sheriff on you. I doubt it's the custom for innkeepers to insult citizens seeking to take care of their own business. How much is the ticket?"

The two men by the door snickered audibly, and the innkeeper turned surly. "I don't suppose you'd have two pound six about you, miss?" He clearly expected a negative response. "You can't expect 'em to let you ride free. Of course there's always the stage. It's cheaper, but it ain't so nice." Kate opened her valise and took out her purse.

"It would be foolish of me to inquire about a ticket when I didn't have the means to pay for it, wouldn't it?" she challenged, but the moment she opened her purse she knew she had made a mistake. She had thoughtlessly placed all the money in her purse, and even though the men could not tell how much she had, they could see she had much more than the necessary two and six. The eyes of the men by the door widened in surprise, but the innkeeper's narrowed and his manner changed abruptly.

"And of course you'll be wanting the use of a room to rest a bit and freshen up while you wait for the mail," he stated affably as Kate searched for some coins small enough to give him. "Or you can look at the shops if you like. I'd be happy to look after your bag for you."

Kate found the coins she wanted and handed them to him. "No, thank you," she said curtly. "I'll come back when the mail coach is ready to leave."

"But it'll be an awful long time, miss. You'll get tired of dragging that bag around with you. Perhaps you'd like to hire the parlor. You could take

105

off that old cloak and be comfortable, or even enjoy a bit of lunch in private."

Kate was tempted by the last offer. She was tired and heated from her exertions, but she didn't trust the man; the way his eyes were drawn to her purse made her feel unsafe. She thought of an inn she'd passed on her way. If she were going to hire a room, she'd rather go there. "I don't think I shall," she replied, trying to hide her distrust. "Just tell me when the coach will arrive, and I'll be back in time to meet it."

"I can't exactly do that, miss."

"Why can't you? You *do* have schedules, don't you?"

"Yes, but the mail don't always keep to a schedule."

"What do you mean?"

"Well, sometimes it's early and other times it's late. You can't never tell, but mostly it's early."

Kate knew nothing about coaches or their ability to keep to a schedule, but she guessed from the broad grins on the faces of the men at the door that the innkeeper wasn't telling her the truth. "What time do you *think* it will arrive if it's early?" she asked, trying to contain her rising exasperation.

"I can't rightly say." His glance had turned challenging and his attitude grew more menacing.

"You don't seem to be able to say much of anything for certain," she said, forcing a casualness into her voice she didn't feel. "How do your regular customers ever manage to know when to board?"

"We don't get much call to ride the mail. Too expensive."

"And those who can afford it, what do they

106

do?" she insisted.

"Mostly they stays here till it shows up. Now if you was to take a room, or even wait right here by the door out of the cold, you wouldn't have to worry about being on time. You'd be Johnny-on-the-spot whenever it showed up."

"I don't think I want to wait in this place," Kate said bluntly. Her gaze swept over the room in distaste. "It's dirty, you probably have bugs, and I don't trust you not to knock me over the head and take my purse the minute I'm not staring you straight in the eye." Rude horse laughs from the two by the door confirmed Kate's suspicions and threatened the innkeeper's hold on his temper.

Kate picked up her valise and turned to leave, but the innkeeper was between her and the door before she had taken two steps. "You really don't want to leave yet, miss. Why don't you have that nice lunch I offered you, or even a pot of hot coffee?" He moved to cut her off as she tried to go around him. "It's not safe out there. You never know who might sneak up behind you." There was no pleasantness in his smile.

"And deprive you of the privilege?" Kate taunted, persevering with her brave front. She was beginning to feel anxious to be out of this man's reach. "Thank you for your concern, but if you'll just step aside, I would like to leave. I'll wait for the coach outside where I'm convinced I'll feel more safe."

The man showed no signs of allowing her to pass. She looked for another way out, and realized with an unpleasant shock that the two men were no longer lounging against the door. They were standing close behind her, cutting off any possible avenue of retreat. "I asked you to step aside," she said, trying desperately to keep the fear out of her voice. "Now move out of my way before I give you cause to regret your insolence." Her heart was pounding so hard she could hardly hear her own voice. She had to clench her fists to keep her hands from shaking.

"I really can't let you do that, miss. There's no telling who you might meet out there," he said as he came a step closer. "And what's a poor little thing like you going to do without someone to look after her?"

"For the last time, get out of my way. If you come so much as one step closer, I'll scream so loud every person in the village will be in here within minutes."

"But what if they don't hear you?" he asked, and she saw that his hands were no longer at his side.

"They'll hear this," she shot back as she opened her purse and reached inside; however, almost immediately the movement was arrested and a look of relief flooded over her face. "Thank goodness you've come."

Chapter 8

The innkeeper never saw who hit him; he was spun around and a fist smashed into his face with such force he fell to the floor. The other men disappeared into the taproom, and Kate was left alone to face the full blast of Brett's fury.

"Only a simpleton would come to a place like this with a purse full of money. You could have been murdered." Brett was very angry and his voice was raised perilously close to a shout, but Kate thought she could hear a trace of anxiety in his anger.

"I can take care of myself," Kate flashed, but she couldn't keep the relief from her voice. "At least I knew what *his* intentions were from the beginning."

"I may have made love to you without your invitation, but I wouldn't hit you over the head for a few pieces of gold or leave your body in a ditch. Besides, you can't deny you responded to me," he countered, momentarily forgetting her attempt to escape.

Kate turned crimson at the memory of her body's betrayal, but she was determined Brett would not get the better of her this time; she ignored his remark, preferring to cross swords with him on more firm ground. "I came prepared," she said, opening her purse. "I took your pistol." She revealed Brett's small pearl-handled pistol. "It's loaded, too."

Brett broke into such an infectious laugh that

Kate's anger evaporated almost at once. "For a girl who's been virtually locked away in a castle all her life, you've certainly picked up some unexpected quirks," Brett said, recovering some of his gravity. "Brave but foolish—or are you determined to rid the world of all its thieves and blackguards?" Kate blanched at the reminder of the highwayman she had killed, but the worst of Brett's wrath was gone, and he spoke in a much kinder voice.

"I know I didn't treat you very well last night, but there's no need for you to take this kind of risk to get away from me. Give me your ticket. I'm going to see you safely to London myself." He tore up the ticket and scattered the pieces over the innkeeper. "Now let's go back. Mathilda's worried sick about you."

"He still has the money I gave him for the ticket," Kate told Brett as she knelt and began to ransack the innkeeper's pockets.

"My dear girl," Brett demurred, "certainly you can stand the loss of a few pounds."

"I borrowed this money. No," Kate corrected herself, "I *stole* it from you, and I'm not leaving until I get it back. At least I shall be spared the additional mortification of having to ask my uncle to repay you." Kate turned the innkeeper's pockets out, spilling all kinds of oddments onto the floor, but she couldn't find her two pounds six. "Would you turn him over for me?"

"Are you so desperate for a few coins?"

"Not desperate, determined. I refuse to be beholden to you for a single shilling," Kate declared pugnaciously. With one effortless thrust of his boot, Brett turned the innkeeper over on his back.

110

Kate found her money in the inside pocket and carefully counted out the exact amount. "Now we can go," she said, rising to her feet. She started to pick up her valise but stopped as a mischievous smile played across her lips. Drawing the great hood back so he could feel the full force of her magnificent eyes, Kate favored Brett with a brilliant smile. "Will you help me with my valise this time, or shall I be forced to walk through the streets carrying it myself?" She peeped guilelessly up at him from under fluttering eyelashes.

"Neither," Brett answered, his sense of humor warring with his sense of pride. "I'll have Michael send the boot boy back for it."

"No you won't," Kate snapped, her eyes now flashing brightly. "Everything I own of any value is in that valise. If the innkeeper is only half the rogue I think he is, there won't be anything left for the boy to bring back, *including* the valise. I'm taking it with me even if I have to drag it through the streets every step of the way." She snatched up the valise and stalked toward the door.

"Give me that damned bag," Brett growled, half angry and half appreciative of the way she'd trapped him. "I'm tempted to throw you *and* this benighted valise into the first river I come it." He snatched up the valise from where Kate had set it down, but Kate only favored him with a seraphic smile and preceded him out of the inn. "And when I do, I'm going to make sure you're securely bound to a sack full of stones," Brett announced to Kate's retreating back, a slow grin of appreciation spreading across his face. But they had not gone very far when Brett stopped a boy and paid

111

him to carry the valise the rest of the way. Kate was piqued, but wisely refused to comment.

Mathilda's anxiety was too great to allow her to wait inside the inn. As soon as she caught sight of the two of them coming up the lane, she surged forward, rejoicing and scolding, before Kate was within the sound of her voice. "The Lord be praised! I was so worried I didn't know what to do," she wheezed as she trotted toward them. "I just knew you were up to something terrible when you kept on about that nasty stage. It worried me so much I went back to the room to try and talk you into staying here. When I found you had gone, I nearly suffered a palsy stroke. It was all I could do to keep from letting out a screech."

"What she *did*," Brett interrupted, grinning at the woman, "was to fall on my neck the minute I stepped inside the door wailing that you'd run off and were certain to be found in a ditch with your head broken." Brett caught Mathilda in his powerful arms and held her helpless.

"Don't you dare mishandle me in a public lane, you wicked boy," she chuckled. "My reputation will be in shreds."

"You don't have a reputation to shred. Everyone knows you're a merciless tyrant who keeps her servants quaking with fear and her long-suffering husband under a cat's paw."

"Now you leave off your teasing, Mr. Westbrook," Mathilda said as she tried to right her apron and settle her cap on her head once more. "I'm sure I'm just as caring of my man as the next." She self-consciously picked some lint off her dress. "And if I do give him a hint every

112

now and then of how to go on, I'm sure it's only in the way of being a dutiful wife. As for those maids," she said, recovering energetically, "if I don't keep after them day and night, they'll lie abed till breakfast and never get the rooms straightened up before lunch."

Brett's eyes danced with merriment, and Kate thought how incredibly handsome he was when he was relaxed and happy. *I wish he would look at me like that* was the unbidden thought that flashed through her mind. Memories of the comforting strength of his arms caused a faint blush to warm her cheeks. She pulled herself up short recollecting he was a vile seducer and how she had hoped she would never have to see him again, but it was hard to remember when he smiled like that.

They had almost reached the door of the inn when a familiar voice hailed them from the lane. A racing curricle drew up abruptly, the horses practically coming to a stop on top of Kate, and she recognized young Peter Feathers.

"I've seen children handle a team better," Brett thundered, going to the heads of the plunging horses.

"Don't you try to drive that thing into my yard," Mathilda barked, no more tolerant of ineptitude than Brett. "I'll not have my gate knocked down."

Feathers's attempt to defend himself was ignored, and Brett handed the horses over to the ulsters while Mathilda pushed him toward the door.

"Never mind my driving," he said, giving up. "I came to warn you that Martin and the sheriff are coming after you. He means to have you arrested."

"What does he hope to gain by that?" Brett asked as the women stared at Feathers in unbelieving surprise. "How did you find out?"

"Overheard him last night. Should have known something was wrong at dinner, but after that brandy I had a devil of a head. Made all kinds of threats against you, but he was just too cheerful."

"Martin is always threatening to get even with somebody," Kate added.

"Went into the garden after dinner. Heard him talking in the library but didn't pay any attention until I heard Brett's name. Had to push through some monstrous big shrubs to get near a window. Your brother ought to trim those bushes, Miss Vareyan," Feathers said, momentarily losing the thread of his story. "Full of thorns."

"Will you get on with it," Brett exploded.

"Yes, well, I heard Martin say he wanted Brett thrown into jail. I was so shocked I peeped in, but the man he was talking to had his back to me. Martin said some pretty nasty things about the both of you."

"There's nothing unusual in that," Kate volunteered.

"I couldn't see the man's face when he finally turned around, those damned thorn bushes you know, but you can imagine my surprise when he spoke up and I recognized Frank Boyngton's voice."

"He's a fair man as far as his understanding goes," said Brett. "Surely he wasn't taken in by Martin's ravings."

"Not at first, but when the housekeeper told her

tale, he had no choice but to agree to come after you."

"But Isabella doesn't know anything," Kate stated, incensed. "She wasn't even up when I left."

"I don't know about that, but she said Brett had been paying you extravagant compliments and showering you with attention all week. Proper turned your head with his flattery. Talked you into going for an early-morning ride, and then abducted you. Martin said you were meaning to try for France before he could catch up with you."

Kate was too astounded to speak, but Mathilda did not suffer under the same handicap. "Well, I never! He ought to be clapped in irons for making up a story like that."

"Brett is the one likely to be clapped in irons unless he gets moving," Feathers observed.

"I won't let it happen," Kate stated indignantly. "I'll tell the sheriff how Martin drove me from the house."

"Unfortunately, your word won't carry any weight against Martin's. You're underage and he's your guardian," said Brett. "Just finding you here will be enough to convict me."

Kate turned white. "What can we do?"

"Michael and I will be glad to help if we can," Mathilda offered.

"Thank you, but I'd rather get through this without involving anyone else." He turned to Kate. "Are you willing to go to France with me?"

Kate struggled to calm her loudly beating heart. "We're not going to London?"

"We can't now. You won't be safe in England."

Kate's head reeled. There was too much to think about and no time to do it. She knew she should consider her future, where she could find employment, how she would live, whether she could survive without the support of her family, but all she could think of was the comfort of Brett's presence, all she could see was the irresistible appeal of his smile, and all she could feel was the touch of his lips on her skin. Faced with the decision to go with him regardless of the consequences or most likely never see him again, Kate did not hesitate.

"Yes," she heard herself say, and somehow both of them knew she had made a fateful decision. After this, everything would either be easier or impossible.

"You've got to be ready to leave within half an hour."

"I'm already packed," Kate said with a ghost of a smile. "I can leave right now."

"Don't worry," Brett reassured her with warmth in his voice. "I have no intention of letting Martin get his hands on you. Mathilda, tell Michael to see that my coach is ready immediately and that the rest of Kate's luggage is loaded. Now both of you go quickly."

"When did you leave?" he asked, turning back to Feathers. "Does anybody know where you've gone?"

"I told Martin I wanted to set out early for Newmarket."

"Then that's where you're going. Get back in your curricle and don't even change horses until you're at least ten miles from here. I don't want you involved in this, either."

Feathers tried to protest, but Brett was adamant. "You can get something to eat when you get back on the road. Make a big thing of changing horses, or anything else you wish, so the innkeeper will remember you." Brett called for the curricle and harried the ulsters so effectively Feathers was on his way in record time.

By then Brett's coach was ready. Mathilda hurried out with some bread and cheese, cold ham, and apples wrapped in a cloth. "You'll be getting hungry before you reach Dover," she said, carefully packing the food in the coach. "You can get something to drink when you change horses, but you won't be having time to wait for food." She moved without her usual cheerful animation. She looked tired and her body sagged as though it were weighted down with worry. "You won't let them hurt Miss Vareyan, will you?" she asked in an anxious voice. "The poor thing told me something about that brother of hers. You can't let him take her back to that castle. It's no more than a prison." Her distress was evident.

"I'll take very good care of her," Brett said, giving the older woman a pat on the arm. "I had hoped to take her to my aunt, but that's impossible now. I'll have to find some way of taking care of her in Paris until I get back from Africa."

"Mr. Westbrook, you wouldn't do anything against that poor child, would you?" Mathilda burst out, unable to contain her fear any longer but reluctant for once to speak plainly. "She's a good girl."

Brett didn't appreciate Mathilda's reading of his character, but neither did he pretend to misunderstand her. "You can put that worry out of your mind. She deserves only the best, and I'm going to see that she gets it." He spoke with such unex-

117

pected sincerity that Mathilda searched his face looking for a key to his thoughts. She could never say what she found there, but it did serve to ease her mind.

Kate emerged from the inn with Michael right behind her. "I'm sorry I'm so slow, but I didn't know Mrs. Franks was out here, and I couldn't leave without thanking her." She threw her arms around Mathilda and hugged her tightly.

Mathilda brushed large tears from her trembling cheeks. "You take care yourself, miss, and remember whenever you come back to England, that you can always find a home with us. It'd be a pleasure to have you." She pushed Kate toward the coach where Brett was waiting, then ran to Michael and threw her arms around his neck. She kissed him soundly on both cheeks causing the poor man to blush fiery red.

"If you don't hurry up, we'll still be standing here when Martin gallops into the yard," Brett said. Kate threw him a look of burning reproach but quickly climbed inside, spurning his help with an angry gesture. He ignored her pique and sprang up behind her.

As the coach pulled out of the yard and into the lane, Mathilda waved and smiled as merrily as her heavy heart would allow, but the moment it was out of sight, she buried her face in her husband's thin chest. "I just know some terrible sadness is going to happen to that poor little thing," she sobbed. "I just *know* it. And don't you think having Mr. Westbrook around will make everything safe," she said, lifting her tear-stained face and pointing an accusing finger at her husband. "That man is a wolf in sheep's clothing."

In later years, Kate could never remember much of their miserable race to the coast. They flew over the countryside and dashed through villages and towns, changing horses as often as needed and getting what little refreshment Brett allowed in those short intervals of relief from the constant rattle of the coach. Kate was too nervous to eat, but Brett twice had some of Mathilda's bread and cheese. At dusk he insisted she must eat something also. She gave in and took an apple, but as it was last fall's fruit and had begun to turn pithy, she was soon sorry she had agreed to eat anything at all.

"How much farther do we have to go?" Kate had asked that question so often Brett's response was rather curt.

"We're making good time and should be in Dover before nine o'clock, but we're not hurrying just to avoid Martin. If we can catch the evening tide, we can be in France in the morning and everything will be solved quickly and easily. If not, I'll be forced to find a place for you to stay tonight and another place to board tomorrow. As for Martin, I have no way of knowing where he is unless he should catch up with us." Brett then refused to answer any more questions or even carry on a normal conversation. That angered Kate, but she was becoming accustomed to his high-handed manner and she settled back to wait.

They pulled into Dover ten minutes before the hour, stopped briefly to notify the captain that a crew was wanted immediately, and then continued on past several large and small sailing craft. The docks were soon left behind and still the coach didn't slacken its pace. They were almost out of sight of the outlying cottages when, much to Kate's relief, the coach turned off the road and came to a halt before a large yacht at anchor in a secluded cove.

To Kate's apprehensive eyes, the yacht appeared far too small to carry anyone across so much water, but Brett obviously didn't share her doubts, and he eagerly climbed down from the coach. Kate tried to use his enthusiasm to bolster her own confidence, but she had never been on a ship and the gentle rise and fall of the swell was already making her feel queasy. She had a sinking feeling she was going to be seasick before they even left the dock.

As she watched her luggage being carried on board, the finality of what she was about to do swept over her and she felt alone and frightened. She was going to a foreign country with a man she knew almost nothing about. She had no say in what they did and no idea what was going to happen to her next. Even now Brett had gone off and left her to manage for herself. How could she place any dependence in a man who showed little concern for her person, feelings, and opinions?

Brett stalked down the ramp, startled to find Kate still in the coach. "We break our necks racing halfway across England to get to this damned yacht and now you sit gawking like you're afraid it'll gobble you up. Get on board, for God's sake. We didn't come this far to have your nervous apprehensions ruin everything at the last minute."

Brett had spoken to her in every tone of voice from kindness to fury, but she had never heard the harsh command of a leader who demanded instant obedience. She climbed down from the coach and hurried up the plank, all the while berating herself for obeying his orders so meekly. What he needed, she told herself under her breath, was someone who would refuse to be ordered about, who would stand up to him and give him back his own, but Kate knew she was not ready to be that person and hurried to get on board.

"The rocking shouldn't bother you too much if you don't think about it," Brett said, helping her up the ramp. "If it does, just think about what Martin would do if he finds you, and you're bound to feel better." He led her to a steep, cramped stair that descended to a dark and narrow hall off which several rooms were situated. "This is your cabin," he said, opening the second door. "It's small, but it has everything you need. You might prefer to come up on deck until we cast off. The moon is full and the sea is as calm as you'll ever see. But wrap up if you do. It's cold."

Kate didn't know what to make of a romantic invitation delivered in such a thoroughly unromantic manner, but she was too preoccupied by the rocking of the boat to bother with it. Her stomach was growing more uneasy all the time.

"What if I'm sick?" she asked.

"Sick?" Brett questioned. "Why should you be sick?"

"Seasick," she clarified. "This bobbing up and down is making me feel unwell."

Brett had never been seasick and had no understanding of anyone less hardy than himself. "If

121

you're on deck, you can hang your head over the rail, but down here you'd better keep a basin handy. The crew won't have time to clean up after you." He turned on his heel and left.

By now Kate was too used to his unsympathetic responses to waste time being angry even if she hadn't been so consumed with the feeling of nausea. She didn't even look to see that all her luggage was on board. If it was left behind, she would just have to do without it. She placed the basin on the floor by the bed and lay down. Maybe she'd feel better if she were still for a while.

The bed was narrow and short, but it was quite comfortable, and she found she did feel a little better when she didn't have to hold her head up. She was glad she had not eaten much; she hoped it would be harder to be sick on an empty stomach.

After several minutes, Kate felt well enough to try to go up on deck, but as soon as she sat up, her head began to swim. She lay back down until it stopped, then sat up more slowly. She still felt unsteady, but it wasn't as bad as before. She was determined to be on deck when they cast off if she had to hang over the rail from Dover to Calais. She'd show that heartless aristocrat she could handle the crossing as well as any man.

The cold sea air struck her an exhilarating blast full in the face and she staggered slightly. Brett immediately offered his assistance, and she gratefully relaxed against him as he steered her to a position on the rail near the bow. The sight of the open sea made her stomach start to heave again, and she grasped the rail with both hands. She decided if she had to be sick, she was going to be so all over Brett. It would serve him right for his lack of sympathy. Imagining his look of shock caused her to smile in spite of the feeling her insides were traveling in several different directions at once. However, on second thought she decided it might be wiser *not* to be sick over him. She wasn't at all sure he wouldn't throw her overboard.

When Martin learned Feathers had left Ryehill before dawn, he swore mightily and long. By the time Boyngton arrived, he had worked himself into such a towering rage that he was unable to exchange a civil greeting.

"That fool Feathers is off to warn them," he swore. "If you don't move your ass, we'll never catch the bastard before they reach France."

"I've known the boy since he was breeched," Frank said, dissatisfied with Martin's interpretation of Feathers's conduct. "He's a young waster, but it's not in his nature to aid in an abduction." Martin didn't bother to answer but drove his spurs into the flanks of his sidling mount and sped down the drive at a furious gallop.

They rode hard all day, never pausing to argue over which road to take. Martin insisted the couple was headed for the coast, and there was very little choice about which routes a coach could take to Dover. In spite of Martin's ill-tempered impatience, Boyngton stopped several times to inquire after Brett's coach. It was reported often enough to convince him Martin's guess had been correct.

They reached Dover, exhausted and dust-covered, soon after nine o'clock. Martin wanted to begin searching for the pair immediately, but Frank refused.

"I have no authority in this district," he told Martin. "I can't do anything until I contact the local officials."

"You're only trying to give that black-hearted devil time to make his escape," Martin exploded.

Frank controlled his temper and tried to explain to Martin why it was necessary for him to act in conjunction with the local constabulary, but Martin damned both Frank and the Dover police and galloped off into the night. He drove his exhausted horse from one end of the docks to the other, stopping everyone he met with a demand to be told where Brett's yacht was located. When they were unable to tell him, he struck one down with the butt of his pistol and tried to ride his horse over another. Finally, he found a sailor who told him of a big yacht at a cove on the outskirts of town. Martin nearly threw his horse to the ground as he jerked its head around and drove his spurs once more into its bloody sides. He knew the tide was already turning. Within minutes the yacht could be moving out to sea, and he was determined to find Brett before he could escape.

Kate and Brett were watching the night sky in companionable silence when Martin drove his staggering mount out of the clinging shadows. The ropes had been cast off and the sailors were pulling the landing steps aboard when Martin dismounted. With a superhuman effort, he made a frantic leap over the open water that separated the shore and the departing yacht and managed to get a grip on the rail. The crew was too shocked to do more than stare dumbly as Martin pulled himself aboard with a shout of triumph.

Brett's keen ears had caught the sound of an approaching horse, and he had leapt away from the rail before Martin exploded out of the night. Thrusting Kate into a doorway behind him, he moved to face Martin alone.

"You thought you'd get away from me when that worm Feathers came to warn you," Martin roared, "but I was too smart for you this time. I rode like the hounds of hell, and by damn I *got* you."

"Don't talk nonsense," Brett snapped. "Or am I to believe you're overcome with remorse and come to beg your sister's forgiveness?"

"I don't beg from anybody," Martin raged. "I've sworn out a warrant for your arrest on charges of abduction and kidnapping. Now that you've spent the night with the harlot, I can throw in rape as well. I'll see you in irons before dawn. You'll never be able to show your face in London again."

"No!" Kate croaked.

"Don't be such a fool," Brett ordered. "After abusing your sister in front of so many witnesses, you couldn't get a conviction with a jury of your own choosing."

"She's my ward, and as long as she's underage, anyone who takes her from my protection is a seducer and a thief." The force of Martin's emotion was so heavy that his voice cracked under the strain.

"That may be the law in England, but we've been drifting out to sea ever since you boarded,"

Brett drawled. "In a few minutes we'll be in open water and beyond the reach of your sheriff."

Tearing his gaze from Brett's contemptuous countenance, Martin's eyes searched the gathering night for the dock, his link with England and the force he was sure would destroy Brett Westbrook for him. He was stunned to see the shoreline had fallen well away from the sides of the yacht; they had reached the mouth of the cove where the placid water of the inlet gave way to the restless swells of the channel. Brett had slipped out of his grasp yet again.

The last tenuous thread of Martin's reason snapped and he could understand nothing beyond his consuming hatred for the laughing man before him. He drew his pistol and fired.

Chapter 9

When she saw him reach for his pistol Kate launched herself at Martin's arm with an ear-splitting scream, but she was too late. Her terrified eyes sought Brett, and she watched in helpless dismay as he sank to his knees, a dark patch of blood spreading over the front of his shirt.

Martin gave a shout and lurched forward, only to be brought to a wrenching halt at the sight of the small pistol in Brett's right hand. He heard the explosion and felt the bullet tear into his flesh as Brett slumped to the deck; Martin staggered and fell against the rail. He made a feeble attempt to stand, grabbing at the rail in his frantic efforts to keep his feet, but he stumbled and rolled over the low barrier. For a few heartbeats he hung suspended over the sea, his loosening grip that of a dying man.

Kate was too stunned to move. One sailor, transfixed by the violence of the scene which had unfolded so rapidly before his gaze, recovered his wits and rushed forward, but he was too late. A choking sound shook Martin's body, and losing his hold on the polished wood, he tumbled overboard. The dark waters engulfed his body and the sea gathered yet another soul to her watery bosom.

Kate's eyes remained on Martin as he hung poised above the rail, but the spell broke when he plummeted into the water, and she rushed to where Brett had fallen.

"He can't be dead," she muttered frantically.

"Please, God, not him, too." She pushed her small hand inside his coat. His heart was still beating, but the pulse was faint and irregular and he was bleeding heavily.

She struggled to stave off the panic threatening to paralyze her brain. *Think,* she ordered herself. *Don't sit here moaning and let him bleed to death. You've got to remember what they did when Martin's gamekeeper was shot. Gunshot wounds can't be but so different.*

Kate forced her mind back to a day nearly ten years ago. They had brought the gamekeeper in from the woods on a stretcher, but their main concern then had been only to stop the bleeding until the doctor could get there and not actually treat the wounds. Even now, Kate could clearly see the thick pads his wife had held firmly over the wound until the doctor arrived.

"Carry him to his cabin," she ordered the sailors who had gathered around. She then followed, giving orders to anyone within hearing distance to boil water, bring clean linen, prepare bandages, lay him down gently, strip him to the waist, and turn the ship around immediately and head back to Dover.

"How bad is he, miss?" the captain asked when they had laid him on the bed.

"I don't know. We've got to get him to a doctor at once. He's bleeding terribly."

"I'll do the best I can, but it takes about eight hours to make the crossing."

"I don't mean France," Kate said impatiently. "It shouldn't take more than twenty minutes to find a doctor in Dover."

"But we can't turn around, miss. We have to go with the tide."

"But you've *got* to turn around," Kate insisted. "He may be dying this very minute."

"Even if I could turn the ship around, I couldn't sail against the tide, miss, not to save all our lives. We'll be in France by morning, and I'll see you get to a doctor as soon as we land. But you're going to have to take care of him until then. We don't carry extra men on this crew, and none of them knows anything about taking care of sick people."

Kate was stunned. What was she going to do? She couldn't let him die.

"I can help, Miss Vareyan." For a moment Kate didn't recognize Brett's valet. "My name is Charles."

"Thank you," Kate said, recovering quickly and turning back to the captain, "but I'm going to need at least one other person to help me." He started to protest, but Kate cut him short.

"Don't tell me you can't spare anybody. *Find* someone. This man had better not die without you lifting a hand to save him."

Brett's wound was bleeding again. Kate grabbed his discarded shirt, folded it into a thick pad, and pressed it tightly against the wound. "Somebody open his baggage and get me some more shirts. No! Rip the sheets on his bed. Now!" she cried when no one moved. "I can't do everything myself with him bleeding so much." The blood had already soaked through the shirt. "Find me some handkerchiefs, lots of them," she ordered Charles. "I can use them as pads. I need lots of long strips," she told the two sailors who were speedily reducing the sheet to rags. "I've got to make a bandage that will hold until we land."

"I have some sticking plaster," the captain offered.

"Send it along with whoever is going to help me. You might as well get back to your station. If you can't get us back to England, at least make sure we don't end up in the North Sea."

The captain departed, grateful to escape the company of this imperious, sharp-tongued female. She was young and breathtakingly beautiful, but he would just as soon do battle with the Atlantic as spend the evening in the same room with her.

"Put four of those handkerchiefs together and hand them to me," Kate directed Charles. She exchanged the soaked shirt for the clean pad. "Now make up another and put it within reach. When you've finished tearing strips," she said to the sailors, "make a large, thick pad out of what's left. I've got to have a big one for the bandage. How am I going to clean the wound?" she asked Charles. "I don't dare take the pad away."

"I think the blood will clean it," he said.

"I hope you're right." Kate replaced the now-soaked pad with a new one, and was relieved to see the bleeding had slowed down. "If it will just stop until we can get him to a doctor, maybe he'll be all right."

As soon as the men finished with the sheet, Kate directed them to remove Brett's boots, but they fitted so tightly that Charles was forced to cut them off. Afterward the sailors departed, nearly colliding with a nervous young boy carrying an armload of lint, sticking plaster, and other materials.

"I'm Mark," he said nervously. "The captain sent me to help with Mr. Westbrook." He looked uncertainly at Kate. "Do you know anything about nursing? You look awfully young." He was embarrassed by his words as soon as they were out of his mouth, but he was even more distressed when Kate's shoulders slumped and she seemed ready to burst into tears. "I'm sorry," he apologized. "The captain swears he's going to cut my tongue out someday."

"But you're right. I don't know anything about nursing sick people," Kate said, recovering quickly, "but somebody has to take care of him."

"By the way, the captain says to tell you there's a squall coming up," Mark said. "Shouldn't be bad, but it might shake you up a bit. Anything you want me to do?" Kate refused to even let herself think about a storm.

"We've got to make a bandage tight enough to keep the pad from slipping and to keep enough pressure on the wound so it won't bleed," she said. "Help Charles hold him up so I can wrap these strips around him." It was impossible not to hurt Brett as she wound the bandage tightly around his chest and over his shoulder. The pad soon turned red, but when it turned brown, she knew the bleeding had stopped. She heaved a large sigh and offered up a silent prayer.

"I'm going to my cabin to change my clothes," Kate said, standing up. "Call me if there's any change."

When she came back, she had shed her cloak, brushed out her long golden hair, and put on a pale-blue gown of soft muslin which tied loosely under her bosom and allowed greater ease of movement. Charles admired her openly, but Mark was so startled by the vision, he jumped up from his chair stammering in confusion.

Kate couldn't help smiling. It was nice to know she was attractive, even to young boys, but she didn't have time for such vanities, she told herself, not with Brett so ill. The few minutes alone in her cabin had given her time to think and organize her thoughts.

"Charles, see if you can find a basin of water and a sponge. I'll need it in case Mr. Westbrook develops a fever. And I'll need another one for myself. If this boat pitches any harder, I'm going to be sick. Mark, ask the captain for a board so Mr.

Westbrook won't roll out of the bed. I'll never be able to hold him down. And stay close by in case we need you."

The boat was pitching more severely as it headed out to sea, and Kate began to feel decidedly unwell. She had gotten used to the gentle swells of the cove, but the waves were bigger in the channel. How could she take care of Brett if she was sick? She couldn't just leave him and go stick her head out the window. After all, he wouldn't be lying here with a bullet in his chest if it hadn't been for her brother.

Kate was conscience-stricken when she remembered Martin. Although she regretted his death, she had ceased to love him years ago. Still, she felt guilty that all she felt was relief that he was no longer a threat to her. There was nothing she could do to help him now, and if she saved Brett's life, she would have avoided one horrible consequence of his mad behavior.

Mark came back with the bedboard and fitted it into a groove already there for the purpose. "The captain says you're to tell me what you want to eat so the cook can fix your dinner before it gets too rough."

"I'd rather not eat anything if we're going to have a storm," Kate said, looking acutely ill at ease. "There's no point in putting food in my stomach if I'm going to turn around and throw it up."

"No, miss," Mark grinned. "I'll be just down the passageway when you need me."

She pulled a chair over to the bed. She hoped that once they reached France they'd be able to find a good nurse to take the responsibility of his recovery off her inexperienced shoulders. His extreme pallor worried her. Brett was naturally dark, but he looked so pale and drawn she was afraid he had

132

already lost too much blood. And he was bound to lose more when the bullet was taken out. His face looked so peaceful and relaxed, without the scowl of anger that usually marked his features, she wondered if he might not already be dead. But when she placed her ear close to his face, she could hear his rasping breath and feel the gentle warmth on her ear.

"Dear God, don't let him die," she implored. "Not away from his family. And not with Martin's bullet in him. I don't think I could bear that. Please let him get well so I can at least tell him how sorry I am."

Brett stirred, tried to turn over, but the pain tore an agonized moan from him and he fell back. Kate gently wiped the tiny beads of moisture from his forehead and tried to soothe him.

"You've got to lie still," she said softly. "If you toss and turn, the wound will start to bleed again, and you can't afford to lose any more blood."

He lay still, but, without warning, the boat lurched crazily and Kate's stomach leaped to her throat. A swift plunge to the bottom of a swell sent Brett crashing into the wall. "Charles, where are you?" she screamed. She tried to hold Brett still and cover her mouth at the same time. Charles burst into the room a step ahead of Mark, and the two of them held Brett on the bed as the boat bounced and dipped crazily. Kate dashed for the basin and was violently sick.

"Looks like we've got two patients on our hands," Mark observed. "But don't you worry, Miss Vareyan. We'll get you through this yet."

Kate retched again.

The next several hours were the worst she had ever lived through. All she could remember was the ceaseless tossing of the boat and retching long after there was anything left in her stomach. In between trips to the basin, she checked Brett's pulse and sponged his forehead; his skin was so hot it seemed to burn her fingers. Through her mind ran a constant litany: "We've got to get him to a doctor in time."

The sun rose from the frigid ocean, and with its emergence came the rebirth of hope. The sea had repented of her turbulence, but the air was thick with a cold, clammy mist that penetrated the cabin and compelled Kate to cover Brett with a blanket. The night's ordeal had convinced her they must find an inn the moment they landed. Brett couldn't possibly get well on this tossing boat.

The captain entered the cabin wearing a cheerful smile. "Morning, Miss Vareyan. Mark tells me you passed a bad night, but it looks like you held up right well."

"How I fared is of no consequence," Kate responded listlessly. "The only thing of importance is to get Mr. Westbrook to a doctor as soon as possible."

"That'll be in France in about a half hour. We're headed for a small village a little way down the coast. I've taken Mr. Westbrook across several times before, and he always uses the same place."

"You've got to take him to Calais," she objected. "He's got to have a doctor as soon as possible, and an inn where they can take care of him. How can I possibly find that in some out-of-the-way village?"

"We're too low on the coast now. I'm afraid it would be impossible to turn back to Calais without losing a lot of time."

Kate's endurance was at an end. She had spent the last two days in a coach and the last two nights

134

awake, all under circumstances utterly beyond her experience and at a tension level sufficient to unbalance even the most experienced woman of the world. Now this *captain*, who was responsible for the most harrowing night of her life, meant to abandon her in some tiny village; they probably didn't have a doctor or a nurse. She turned on him, her anger fueled by fear, anxiety, and exhaustion.

"You insensitive dolt. You've been at cross purposes with me ever since I got on this accursed boat. And now you calmly announce you're leaving me in some dinky little village just like Mr. Westbrook's life wasn't hanging by a thread and it didn't matter whether the local doctor could tell a man from a horse. You're cold-blooded, contemptible, and probably simple-minded as well. As soon as he's well, I'm going to have Mr. Westbrook see that you're never allowed to captain anything larger than a rowboat again."

"Now listen here, young woman, you can't talk to me like—"

Kate advanced upon him with upraised fists. "Get out of here," she hissed as he hurriedly backed away from her. "Set foot in this cabin again, and I'm liable to scratch your face to ribbons. If this man dies because of your callousness, I'll personally put a bullet between your eyes."

The captain was livid, but he left the room. He didn't know who this hair-raising female was, but she surely wasn't the common doxy he'd first thought. Only a real lady would look at him like he was vermin and throw him out of a cabin on his own ship. Still, he had to give her her due. If she stayed around to look after him, Mr. Westbrook was guaranteed attention worthy of a king.

He opened the door of the adjacent cabin. Charles was sitting in a chair sound asleep. He pounded on the door. "Miss Vareyan wants you. Mark, too. We're landing in half an hour, and I want you and everything you own off this ship immediately." Never again was he going to hire out to a gentleman, not even Mr. Westbrook. Most aristocrats were bad about paying late, but none had ever showed Kate's regal disregard for his position of command. His only consolation was that none of the crew had been present.

Minutes later, Charles and Mark entered the cabin to find Kate pacing the floor.

"Charles, do you speak French?"

"Yes."

"Thank God for that. How about you?" she said, looking at Mark.

"Pretty good, ma'am. I've been doing these crossings for more than five years and I've pretty near picked it up on my own."

"Wonderful. Now, do either of you know this village we're going to?"

"I do," Charles answered. "Mr. Westbrook has landed here several times."

"Then go to the best inn, hire enough rooms for all of us, and arrange for Mr. Westbrook's removal. Mark, I want you to find the doctor and take him to the inn immediately. There is a good doctor here, isn't there?"

"Yes, ma'am. There's a small English colony in the village. One of them used to be a big London doctor with a fancy practice, but he gave it up. Now he only works when he likes or if something interests him. I don't know if he'll come, but he's the best."

"Tell him we have a wounded man who's dying. Tell him anything you have to but bring him," Kate ordered. "Now, where is the inn and what is it like? Will the landlord help us? Can we hire the whole inn?"

Mark looked rather startled. "It's a small inn, but it's the only one in the village."

"It's called the Chére Madame," Charles informed her. "Mr. Westbrook has stayed there before, and the owner, one Madame Marcoule, knows him well. She's a peculiar old woman, but she took a liking to Mr. Westbrook the first time he stayed, and I know she'll do anything she can to help."

"Then you make all the arrangements. I'll stay with Mr. Westbrook." She turned to Mark. "Regardless of what the captain may say, I want you hanging over the rail ready to take off the minute we dock."

"I'm sure we can arrange for the captain to let him out of his duties," Charles said.

"Then you think more of the captain's Christian charity than I do," Kate stated waspishly. "Handle it anyway you think best, but the doctor must be notified as soon as possible."

Charles returned moments later to say the captain had released Mark and all his preparations were made.

"In that case, you can get Mr. Westbrook's things ready," Kate instructed. "I have to go to my cabin and pack, but I'll be back in a few minutes. I don't have much to do."

Kate was back in fifteen minutes. She had changed her gown, tied her cloak around her shoulders, and put on her boots and mittens. "My baggage is packed and ready to be unloaded. How are you doing here?"

"I'm finished," Charles said as he closed the last piece of luggage. "I'll need to arrange for porters because Mr. Westbrook has a great deal of luggage stored in the aft cabin. All of it has to be taken with him." He ignored her questioning look. "I'll

137

send someone to let you know when we're ready to take him to the inn. It shouldn't be long. And miss, on behalf of Mr. Westbrook's family, I want to thank you for what you've done for him."

Charles left the room before he could see the tears that sprang to Kate's eyes. She walked over to the chair beside the bed and sat down. Brett looked so pale. Surely he would die if they didn't get him to a doctor soon. The tears coursed down her cheeks, streaking them like windowpanes in a spring rain. She leaned forward and touched his cheek with her fingertips. After staring at him for a long while, she bent over and lightly kissed his hot, dry lips as tears from her cheeks dropped onto his.

"I'll see that you get well," she said fiercely. "I swear it before God and all the saints. And I'll find some way to take care of myself," she added more softly. "You'll never have to suffer because of me again." Her tears streamed down until his face had become as wet as her own.

A sudden onslaught of running feet claimed Kate's attention. The boat was docking and all hands were busy securing her moorings. In a little while she would be able to relinquish responsibility for Brett's care. Then she could go to London and her uncle Milford.

All during the years she had been kept in virtual seclusion, she had dreamed of going to London, of going to balls and parties, and meeting lots of new people. Now when there was no bar to the fulfillment of her dreams, she found it wasn't nearly as important as she had once thought, especially if one arrogant-but-ever-so-handsome man wasn't going to be there.

You've got to stop this foolish daydreaming, she

told herself. *He will get well and you will never see him again. You've got to think of your own life, your own future. Think of all the other men you'll meet in London. There ought to be dozens who are just as handsome as he, and they can't help but be more considerate and kind.*

She imagined herself admired and pursued by a crowd of handsome young men, all vying for the chance to place themselves and their considerable possessions at her feet. In her dreams she laughed a laugh so gay and smiled a smile so stunning they were sent into raptures and were made helpless before her.

But she refused them all easily, even joyfully, because she knew there was one who offered her a love that had nothing to do with jewels, fortunes, or professions of devotion uttered while kneeling at her feet. His was a love that would transcend time and space, that would enfold both of them in its all-encompassing warmth. His was a love that would make of her more than she already was, one that she returned with equal ardor.

A hush would fall over the room and the throng of admirers would fall back, first in surprise and then in recognition of the superiority of the one who came to claim her hand. She knew he was coming, she could sense his approach even before his form began to take shape through the mists. On and on he came, his tread firm and his purpose steady. As the mists began to thin, he stretched out his hand and Kate, her arms outflung, rushed to meet him.

She heard him calling her name, and as she covered the few feet still separating them, a cry tried to escape from her throat, a cry that would be his name. She reached out, she was almost there, but as she tried frantically to call out to him, the vision

139

vanished and Kate woke up with a start to the sound of vigorous knocks on the cabin door.

"Miss Vareyan! Is anything wrong?" Charles called anxiously. "The door is locked."

Kate shook her head to clear away the remaining wisps of her daydream and rose quickly to open the door, but her feet felt weighted and her mind somewhere outside reality.

Charles looked first at Kate and then at Brett. "I was worried something might have happened to you."

"I didn't feel safe with both of you gone," Kate explained, her momentary confusion gone. "I guess I dozed off." Charles looked at her closely, but he could see nothing wrong.

"I've talked with Madame Marcoule, and she's agreed to turn the whole inn over to us. She was going to ask her only boarder to leave, but he became so incensed over the idea of foreigners under the same roof that he left on his own."

"Where are the men?" Kate asked. Her immediate concern was to get Brett to the inn, not Madame Marcoule's boarders. "Are you sure they can get him up those stairs without jarring the wound?" Now she wished she had put Brett in the cabin on the main deck.

"I will keep a strict eye on them to make certain they are mindful of his wound," Charles assured her. The men arrived, and Charles piloted them through the difficult part of moving Brett out of the cabin and up the stairs. In spite of their care, however, they were unable to negotiate the stairs without putting stress on the wound, and Brett groaned aloud.

"Why is he groaning so?" Kate cried, unable to see what was happening. "You must be hurting him." Charles sighed with relief when they reached the deck. After the stairs, it was easy to convey Brett to the carriage even though Kate's fussing did more to hinder their efforts than the weight of the limp body, but it took both Charles and Kate to hold him on the seat as the carriage swiftly covered the short distance to the inn.

But when they reached the inn, Kate stared in openmouthed disbelief at the person who met them at the door. She was as fat as she was tall and dressed like a woman of thirty made up to look ten years younger. Her face was heavily rouged, her hair colored and crimped, and her lips lavishly covered in a gaudy shade of red. Her eyes were green and her lashes heavily blacked; her eyebrows had been ruthlessly plucked and a thin set penciled in above. Great gold loops hung from her ears, rings nearly covered her fingers, and an expensive-looking rope of pearls fell over her ample, tightly corseted bosom. She wore an emerald-green dress trimmed in gold-and-cream lace that was cut low even for evening wear. The whole startling phenomenon was balanced on a pair of flimsy shoes with heels so high she was forced to mince rather than walk.

Enough traces of her former looks remained to show that Valentine Marcoule must have been a beautiful woman in her youth. Though time had destroyed her figure and the perfection of her features, nothing had diminished her spirits and energy. Kate was shocked, affronted, and overwhelmed by her before she even stepped down from the carriage.

Chapter 10

"*Mon Dieu! Mon Dieu!* she cried. *"Il n'est pas mort?"* She switched abruptly to English. "Such a pallor. Careful, you fools. Do you want him to bleed on my carpets? Keep his head up and put him in the big room on the first floor. Valentine is too fat to be running up stairs to see if the doctor has killed him. *Sacrebleu!* Can you not get through a door without running into it? Must Valentine remove the side of the inn for such a clumsy as you?" The men redoubled their efforts under the lash of her tongue.

Valentine peered into the carriage and recoiled in horror. "Blessed holy virgin! The angel of death has come already!" She crossed herself twice, then in a complete aboutface, she fixed the startled Kate with a defiant stare. "You shall not have him." And with that strange pronouncement, she turned and hurried into the inn, her mincing step not slowing her down in the least.

"She doesn't really think you're the angel of death," Charles reassured a stunned Kate. "She's very excitable. Just forget she ever saw you. She will. I've taken the liberty of telling Valentine Mr. Westbrook was shot by a disgruntled loser in a card game. The French seem to accept these things. I also told her that one of Mr. Westbrook's young relatives was traveling with him to Paris."

"You've managed very well," Kate said with genuine appreciation. "Now if we can just find a nurse. I'll feel so much better once I know he's in competent hands."

"Maybe the doctor can recommend someone. If not, Valentine might be able to help."

Kate bridled at the mention of the woman's name, but they were entering the inn and able to hear Valentine hectoring the men as they put Brett to bed, so she swallowed her spleen rather than have her remarks overheard. However horrible that old woman might be, they needed her help.

"I want you to speak to Mark about working for Mr. Westbrook," Kate said. "If you're going to be acting as butler-valet as well as handling our arrangements, you'll be far too busy to run errands."

"Yes, miss, but I don't know what Mr. Westbrook is going to say when he recovers. He's not one to take kindly to anyone altering his arrangements."

"I'll think of something." She flashed one of her most captivating smiles. "I could always demote you."

"True." *Mr. Westbrook had better watch out if he wants to avoid parson's mousetrap this time,* Charles thought to himself. This was no ordinary girl.

Kate went straight to Brett's room to make sure he was comfortably settled. Valentine was hopping around the room fussing over everything and getting in everyone's way.

"Poor lamb. Such a handsome young man, and he is all bleeding and white." She rounded on Charles. "Is the one who did this terrible thing punished? Bah! They are like children, these bad-tempered ones, shooting at everyone when they get the insult. Your judges, they will hang him, *n'est-ce pas?*"

"He's dead, ma'am. Mr. Westbrook shot him."

"Magnifique! In my day men fought for the ladies only, and then never to the death."

"I thought you said she would understand," Kate whispered.

Charles merely shrugged as Valentine made a sign of the cross and bent over Brett peering into his face. *"Sacrebleu!* This doctor, he must come soon. He looks white as a virgin." She started to shake with laughter. "White as a virgin," she repeated and laughed even harder. Kate flushed deeply and remained rooted to the spot.

"Valentine," came an unexpected whisper, "remove your absurdly painted face, or I shall rise up and strangle you." Brett had spoken softly with closed eyes and barely moving lips.

"Nom de Dieu! Nom de Dieu! The dead speak!" Valentine shrieked like she had come face-to-face with the devil himself. "Blessed Virgin protect me," she pleaded, and fled from the room as fast as her feet could carry her.

Kate hurried to Brett's side, a bubble of merriment threatening to burst from her. She tried to contain it, but a chuckle escaped and it quickly turned into full-throated laughter. After the tension of the past two days, the relief of knowing Brett was conscious suddenly stripped away her ability to control her emotions. Tears poured down her cheeks and she laughed even harder. She started to straighten Brett's pillows and arrange his covers to hide her embarrassment.

"Let me alone," Brett grumbled. "Unless Charles has become less efficient than when I hired him, there's a doctor on his way here this very minute. By the time he's through cutting the bullet out, I should be unconscious again. Then you can fuss all you want, and I'll not stop you."

Kate felt his brow. "How do you feel? Are you in much pain?"

Brett opened his eyes. "I *had* thought you were an intelligent girl, but that question makes me wonder. My shoulder hurts like hell, I feel like someone's been driving a coach over me for days, and I still have to look forward to being mauled by some jackass and forced to swallow medicine that tastes like it was drained from a dunghill. And if that's not enough, he'll probably bleed me just to make sure I won't be strong enough to toss about in my sleep." He closed his eyes again. "Other than those trifling complaints, I feel rather well."

Kate straightened up. "You're the most ill-tempered man I've ever met. I've a good mind to let the doctor cut you to pieces."

Brett didn't open his eyes, but a faint smile played across his lips. "You can retire to your room and wring your hands. I'm sure Valentine will be glad to take your place. She's always had a soft spot for me."

Kate swelled with wrath. "How dare you prefer that painted witch to me. She's probably kept company with half the rakes and hellions in Paris."

"Nearly all of them. She ran the best whorehouse in France. Paris hasn't been the same since she retired."

Brett's words left Kate speechless, but before she could tell him how closely he resembled something found under a rock, the door opened a crack and the painted face in question peeped around the corner. The sound of laughter had convinced Valentine that whatever was wrong with Brett, at least he was not dead. Curiosity conquered fear, and when Valentine peeped in and saw Brett calmly talking to Kate, she surged into the room, wreathed in smiles and enjoying a hearty chuckle at her own expense.

"*Mauvais garçon*. You are not nice to shame me so before your friends. You know I have no courage and flee like the rabbit. What will they think of me?" She indicated Kate by a gesture of her hand. "That one, with the face of an angel, she thinks I

145

am nothing but an old *fille de joie*. She is wondering why you come to this house of an *entremetteuse?*" She looked at Kate again. "Because I love the naughty monsieur like an old cheese. *Hélas,* if I were but thirty years younger, even twenty, I would cut you out, *chérie.*" Kate blushed scarlet and directed a look of suppressed rage at Brett. Valentine only laughed.

"I know your story of the cousin going to stay with the aunt. Ha! Am I the complete fool? Am I blind? You can not fool old Valentine, but I will not give you away. You might be forty cousins, but you are crazy about him, too, and you can not wait to take him away from here. How you would love to see me dead, *n'est-ce pas?* Valentine understands the knife's edge of jealousy." She pantomimed a knife thrust to the throat in the best melodramatic style. *"La mort!"* she murmured and pretended to collapse. Suddenly her delighted giggles filled the room. Kate wished the earth would open up and swallow her. Her chagrin was almost past enduring.

Abruptly Valentine became serious and took Kate's face in her hands, scanning every feature with an experienced and critical eye. *"Oui,"* she sighed reluctantly, *"vous êtes très belle,* even more beautiful than I was. That is a great compliment because I was very beautiful. I had half of Paris at my feet and the other half at my throat." She chuckled again. "Valentine will tease you no more. I hear someone in the front hall. Maybe it is *le docteur.* I shall see." She paused at the door and turned back to Kate. "Do not worry," she said in a kind voice. "We will take very good care of monsieur, better than someplace where they do not love him."

Kate labored under the stress of so many conflicting emotions she was unable to think of any way to express the disarray that reigned in her mind. Brett watched her with a curious questioning glance.

Valentine returned almost immediately with Dr. Burton. He was a thin man of about seventy years, his aristocratic face deeply lined and his hair white and thin, but he moved with surprising vitality and his eyes were alive and intelligent. He went straight to the patient.

"Good work," he said when he saw the bandage. "It probably kept him from bleeding to death. Shame to have to cut it off." Brett was delighted to see Kate made uncomfortable by the doctor's praise.

"You women clear out and bring me a basin of hot water and a sponge," he said, taking out his scissors. "I have enough lint for one bandage, but you're going to need a lot more. Better set someone about it right away. You can stay," he said, pointing to Charles. "I'll need someone to help move him, and if that young man in the hall is still loitering about, send him in. He can be off to the chemist. Things are going to get worse before they get better."

Kate blanched. "I'd like to stay if I might," she said tremulously. "I'll try to keep out of the way."

"No." Dr. Burton was emphatic. "I won't have you fainting while I'm trying to get this bullet out."

Kate wanted to protest that she hadn't fainted when he was shot, that she had kept him alive through the night, but Valentine took her by the hand and led her to the door. "You can come back when I'm finished," the doctor relented. "He'll be cleaned up and easier on the eyes. I suggest you get settled while you've got the chance. He's going to need careful nursing during the next few days. That's when you can do the most for him." He turned back to his work, and Kate left with a sinking heart.

"Come along, *ma petite*. I will take you to your room. You put your things away, and I will make some of that tea you English like so much." She

147

made a face. "So sweet. Why do you not drink wine? Oh well, heaven can not be everywhere." On that philosophic note she preceded Kate to a door at the end of the passage which opened into a large, cheerful room.

"Tell me if you want anything more. Your breakfast will arrive as soon as my lazy girls get it ready," Valentine added. "And do not tell me you will eat nothing. You must eat while you have the time." She smiled kindly. "He will be fine, *ma chérie,* just fine." She went off to see about the tea and breakfast.

Kate picked up her valise and tossed it on the bed. It seemed she wasn't going to be allowed to do anything for Brett. They might, she thought petulantly, allow her to bring him his medicine if she were a good girl. She yanked the valise open and frowned as she laid out her clothes. Everything was badly wrinkled and would have to be ironed before she could wear it.

How dare that old crone say she was crazy about Brett. She was *concerned* about him naturally, but she'd rather be crazy about a goat than Brett Westbrook. He had taken her honor, and instead of making a decent show of regret, he'd said he'd like to do it again. Kate could not think of that night without blushing, and her cheeks glowed warm and pink with the memory of those passion-filled moments. Try as she might, she could not erase them from her memory any more than she could sustain her anger at Brett no matter how badly he had used her.

Now, after all his promises to take her to London, she was trapped in some obscure village on the northern coast of France. Well, running away from him should be easy this time because he was in no condition to come after her. It might take a little planning, but she could be halfway to London before they even missed her.

She couldn't understand why that thought should suddenly make her feel like crying. She had never been one to give way to tears, not even when Martin's persecution of her was at its worst. She was no match for him physically, but she certainly could use her tongue. Now her defenses were falling apart. Maybe it would be best for everyone if she went away. No one had time for a female who was constantly in tears over the cards Fate had dealt her. She winced at the allusion.

She sniffed out loud, but instead of breaking down completely, the sound of her own misery stiffened her resolve and she determined the situation would not defeat her. After she had eaten her breakfast and consulted with the doctor, she was going to sit down and not get up until she had come up with a definite plan. She was not going to allow Brett Westbrook, or capricious Fortune, to decide her future.

"*Voilà,*" Valentine announced, unceremoniously bursting into the room and banishing Kate's gloomy mood with abundant good cheer. "Do not say Valentine does not care for her guests," she said, setting down a -pot of steaming hot tea. "Do I give tea to anyone else? Yes, but not happily. Do I bring it myself? *Jamais!*" But then she infuriated Kate by opening her wardrobe and drawers so she could inspect the startled girl's clothes.

"You English do not know how to dress," Valentine declared, disgusted with what she found. "You do not cherish your clothes. To you they are just things to cover your nakedness. They should be like something alive, something that brings new life to you each time you wear them, something to make you feel like someone you have never been before. But these . . ." She made a gesture of contempt.

149

"They deserve to die."

"If I could dress you for one season, one month even, Paris would talk of you for years. But not in these rags! Bah!" She slammed the wardrobe shut. "They keep you warm, eh? They protect your modesty? So would a sack." Kate suffered an agony of embarrassment, but Valentine wasn't through yet.

"And the men, do they hover around you like butterflies at a flower?" She waited imperiously for an answer.

"I have never been to a city or attended any parties," Kate managed to mumble. "I made all my clothes, and for the last four years I've seen no man except my brother."

Valentine's mouth dropped open and her eyes threatened to pop out of her head. *"C'est vrai?* This is true? You do not tell Valentine the little fib?" Kate shook her head. *"Incroyable!* Can it be possible that even in a country so stupid as England such a thing can happen? *Ma pauvre petite.* I talk to Brett. He will take you to Paris, and Valentine will come to see he does not hide you away for himself." An irrepressible chuckle escaped her. "He is very naughty, that one. It would be too bad if he were to gobble you up."

"Ah," Valentine sighed in a suddenly altered voice, "to be young and in Paris in the spring is the greatest happiness one can know. The soul is born for the first time, and love lives as delicately as the fragrance of the blossoming cherries." Bit by bit, Valentine's animation was replaced by a look of quiet rapture.

"One morning you wake with a shiver of anticipation, a feeling that today something truly wonderful will happen. You float on the lightest of clouds until suddenly he is there. You know each other at once, and in that moment you experience complete happi-

150

ness. Love fills your heart and lifts you to heights you never dreamed possible until, like Icarus, you fall to earth charred by the heat of your passion. The pain of parting is very bitter, but in the winter of life you will recall the glorious spring of your awakening, and know you have been loved as few others have."

The gossamer threads of her memories tore silently, and Valentine smiled unhappily. "To grow old is a thing most sad, but it is better if the youth has not been wasted." Kate felt a sympathetic pang for this magnificent ruin.

"But enough of me," Valentine said briskly. "We must decide what to do about our Brett." Just then, one of the maids came to say the doctor wanted to talk to them.

"Tell him to come in here," Valentine commanded, fixing the maid with a remonstrating glare. "Mademoiselle is having her tea, and waiting most patiently for her breakfast."

The flustered maid stammered that it wasn't her fault, that the cook hadn't finished the breakfast, but Valentine drove her from the room with orders to deliver breakfast and the doctor without any more excuses.

"They can do nothing by themselves," she complained. "I work to train them, and then they run off and I am back where I started. It is enough to make me go back to Paris. At least there the girls come equipped for their work." Her eyes brimmed with merriment as she watched the blood rush to Kate's face. "All I had to do was stand at the door and collect the money."

Kate knew Valentine had said that just to make her blush. How could the old crone talk about being a madam as though it were nothing more than being an innkeeper? No matter how badly Valentine thought of them, no Englishman would have dared to mention the subject in the presence of a lady, much less joke about it. Kate choked back her chagrin, but before she could think of a reply, the maid returned with both the doctor and her breakfast.

Dr. Burton looked tired and worried. Valentine settled him into one of the deep chairs and Kate fixed him a cup of tea. He accepted it gratefully, but said nothing until the maid had finished laying breakfast and left the room.

"It's more serious than I thought." He grimaced. "Mr. Westbrook is a strong man, but he fainted when I cut the bullet out." He took another swallow from his cup and looked up, his wrinkles deepened by worry. "He lost a lot of blood last night. He lost still more today, and that'll make his recovery longer and more difficult, but he's basically a healthy man with a strong constitution. Normally I'd predict a rapid recovery, but the wound has become infected."

Kate felt stricken with guilt. She knew she should have tried to clean it.

"It's probably due to the long wait before the bullet could be removed. I've cleaned it as well as I can. It's probably just as well he's unconscious. Few men could stand the shock of brandy poured directly on raw flesh. My fear is he may develop gangrene. If he does, he will die."

Both women turned ashen.

"I've given him a draught to make him sleep for the rest of the day, and I'm leaving some more with you. Use it sparingly, but don't be afraid to give it to him. He must be kept as still as possible during the next few days. He needs absolute rest. Now, how do you intend to divide up the nursing?"

"We don't know anything about nursing," Kate said, thoroughly alarmed by his report. "I mean to hire a nurse. Isn't there someone you can recommend?"

"I will do what I can," Valentine interposed, "but I am not brave in the sick room."

"You'd fidget the man to death," the doctor declared fretfully.

Valentine swelled with indignation. "Valentine is not a *stupide*," she declared. "I can do this nursing. I just do not do it very well," she finished meekly.

"You may have to do it any way you can," the doctor replied. "Old Marie was the only good nurse we had, and she went to live with her son when her husband died. The midwife is awaiting a birth right now, and if you allow Brigette Faneuil in this room, I'll drop the case. She's a drunk, and filthy into the bargain."

"I've never nursed anyone before," Kate said, grimly acquiescing to the inevitable, "but I'll try if you will tell me exactly what I should do."

The doctor studied her briefly, taking notice of her intelligent eyes and determined jaw. "You'll do," he said brusquely. "Not that we appear to have much choice. I'll make some written notes in case of an emergency, but for the most part, I can tell you more easily than I can write it out."

"The first thing is to prepare a herb poultice to draw out the poisons. It must be changed at least three times a day. Be very careful to cleanse the wound with warm water laced with brandy, and be sure to use a fresh bandage. As few people as possible should touch the wound. It may need to be drained, but I'll take care of that."

"I hope he will stay quiet, but he already has a slight fever and I expect it will mount over the next few days. Try to keep plenty of liquids in him. You can bathe his face, or even his whole upper body, but the best thing you can do is keep him still. His body will do the fighting for you."

"The wound should be inspected regularly in case the infection gets worse. I'll come if I'm needed, but I'm too old to be running back and forth all day, and I'm not a nurse. Any questions?"

Valentine was so upset she could barely shake her head, but Kate had herself under control. She was scared, but now that she knew what to do, she was able to face it. Brett's only hope lay in her ability to accept these duties calmly and carry them out. She tried to smile, but her face felt wooden.

"I'll take the night hours, and Valentine and Charles can handle the day. That way you'll only have one of us to teach. Please be as specific as you can about what I'm to look for and what treatment to undertake. I'll do better if I know what I'm seeing, even if it's something dangerous." She stopped abruptly. "Please, Doctor, tell me how he *really* is. Will he get better? Will he live?" she asked in a hollow voice.

"With careful nursing and good luck, he will recover completely. A small scar where the bullet entered and a bigger one where I took it out ought to be the only signs he was ever injured. There may be some stiffness in the shoulder. The bullet nicked a bone and I removed some splinters, but it missed the lung. He's lucky to be alive at all, so maybe his luck will hold. We should know within forty-eight hours. I think we're going to come through all right. Just be calm and keep your wits about you and he'll have nursing that's as good as he could get from anybody else."

Kate was so grateful for his kind words that she felt like crying, but she told herself she had no time to waste on tears. Everyone was depending on her, and if she couldn't take a few kind words without her eyes filling, she'd never manage to keep her nerve if Brett got really ill.

"Do you know how to make a poultice?" Kate asked Valentine.

"Mais non! Never do I go into the kitchen. But the very fat Nancy can make one, and I will set the girls to making bandages. *Merde!* And I took such care to buy the very best. If I did not love Brett like my own brother, I would not turn my inn into a hospital with sheets being ripped to bits and poultices brewing in stew pots. Nothing like this ever happened to me in Paris, and there they shoot each other all the time."

"Quiet, you shameless hussy," commanded the doctor in not very stern reproof. "You know you love every bit of excitement your little heart can stand."

"Quelle horreur! You say such things about *ce chère* Valentine? *Bête noire!"*

Kate looked from one to the other expecting Valentine to throw something. But she just stood there, eyeing the doctor in a speculative fashion, and Kate decided if Valentine was an example of the average Frenchwoman, she would never understand them and the sooner she returned to England the better.

"I'll leave everything about the kitchen and household to you, Valentine. Charles can watch Brett while I sleep, but he must not leave the inn. Mark can run any errands required. Is there somewhere he can sleep?"

"Certainement. He can sleep in the room next door. Then he can hear Brett all the time."

"Good. Now I'm going to finish my breakfast. I've barely eaten for two days and I'm starving. I'm going to spend the morning with Brett then sleep all afternoon. You and Charles can divide up the time as best suits you. I'll take over after dinner."

"Could you come see Mr. Westbrook then, Dr. Burton? You can tell me how he's doing and what I have to do during the night. And please come as soon as you can in the morning. I'll probably be frantic by then, wondering if I've done the right things. Valentine, if Nancy would prepare that poultice now, maybe the doctor would show me how to apply it before he leaves."

The doctor had listened to Kate give her instructions in considerable admiration. It was obvious she was still scared, but she had conquered her fear and was already organizing those around her. He smiled warmly. "That'll be fine, miss. I'll be delighted to help if you'll allow me another cup of tea."

"The one with the angel face collects her wits quickly," Valentine observed, no less impressed than the doctor. "She will not let him die. Me? I go to the kitchen to dispute with Nancy. Bah! She is so fat she does not know if she walks on one foot or two. Poultices," she scowled. "Such nasty things. And to think I gave up Paris for this." She turned dejectedly toward the door. "Jacques would laugh to see me now. *Mon Dieu,* how he would laugh. Pagh!" she snorted, a martial light in her eye. "I will cut his throat, the little rat. No one laughs at Valentine." Her mincing steps became firm once more, and Valentine closed the door behind her and sailed down the passage to do battle with the mistress of the kitchens.

Chapter 11

An hour later Dr. Burton was gone. He had applied the poultice to the wound and bandaged it again, instructing Kate on how to keep it moist. She had had to fight down her nausea when she was confronted with the raw flesh oozing poisons, but knowing so much depended on her helped steady her nerves and calm her stomach, and she was able to listen to and remember most of what the doctor said. She tried to fix the smallest details in her mind so she could notice any change in Brett's condition. She didn't dare forget anything.

Nothing happened to disturb the remainder of her morning. She had lunch in her own room and lay down afterward. She expected to fall asleep right away, but instead found herself still tossing about half an hour later, haunted by the fear that Brett would die as a result of her ignorance and neglect.

She could see his face, so calm and peaceful yet so deathly pale, and she thought she wouldn't have minded his thoughtlessness if only he were well. She thought of his powerful chest hidden by bandages; now only the muscled arms were uncovered, the arms which had closed around her like bands of steel, crushing her to him while he bruised her mouth with passionate kisses. She could still feel his lips on her neck and ears, remember the touch of his hands on her body, recall the bliss of surrender to his assault and the fearful ecstasy of the pinnacle of their passion. Only now was she beginning to be able to admit to herself that she, too, had found pleasure in that night. She still blushed to think of her brazen entreaty, of her bold welcome, but she also knew that what she had experienced in his arms was something very rare that was given only to a special person.

A smile played across her lips and her body relaxed into the soft feather mattress. She remembered how incredibly handsome he looked when he was happy, the lithe grace of his trim body, and the seductive charm of his movements. It was unfortunate they were always at odds with each other. Maybe when he got well again they could try for a better understanding. True, he had treated her abominably and she could never trust him again, but she didn't really dislike him. Her plan to leave as soon as he could take care of himself was unchanged, but while he was desperately ill and dependent on her, she would stay.

Panic gripped her the moment the door closed behind the doctor, but she forced herself to settle back and take up one of the books she had borrowed from Valentine. Reading enabled her to keep a close watch on Brett and at the same time keep her fears at bay. Charles came in at eleven o'clock to help change the poultice. The wound was draining heavily and the flesh around it inflamed, but it did not look critical.

To Charles fell the unenviable task of telling Nancy that another poultice would be needed before morning. He was gone so long that Kate began to fear Nancy had refused point blank, but he finally returned saying the woman would make the poultice at three o clock.

"How did you manage it?"

"It was Valentine," Charles told her, unable to suppress a smile. "When I explained what I wanted, Nancy started shrieking in some kind of French I didn't understand. When I asked if she'd teach me how to make the poultice, she chased me out of the kitchen. I almost collided with Valentine who was standing in the doorway swathed in a voluminous nightgown, her hair twisted in little paper pigtails which stood out all over her head and her face smeared with a heavy cream. She rounded on Nancy, and somewhere in the middle of a fantastic exchange of Gallic curses, they arrived at the understanding that Nancy would make the poultice and Valentine would give her some piece of jewelry she's been mad to have for years."

"Couldn't you learn to make them anyway, just in case Nancy refuses again?" Kate asked, hoping the fight would smooth over. Brett needed the help of both women.

"Nancy won't let me anywhere near the kitchen. She only gave in because Valentine threatened to make them herself."

"You'd better get what rest you can," Kate said, refusing to waste her time worrying about Nancy until she had to. "I'll call you when it's morning." Charles went back to his room and Kate prepared to wait.

Brett became increasingly restless during the early morning hours, moaning and moving about in his bed. Kate sponged him constantly, but he continued to be hot and uncomfortable. The heavy drainage persisted and the wound seemed more raw and inflamed when Charles brought the poultice shortly after three o'clock. They gave him another dose of medicine, and for the rest of the night only his raspy breathing betrayed that all was not well.

Morning brought Dr. Burton, but no comfort.

"It's just as I expected. The wound is badly infected, but it's still draining so there's no need to open it up." Kate continued to sit with Brett after breakfast, but there was no lessening of the fever or his restlessness.

She was reluctant to leave him at lunchtime, but Valentine marched her off to her bedroom with orders to remain there until supper. Kate was certain she was too worried to fall asleep, but she had no sooner laid her head on the pillows when she sank into such a deep slumber she had to be roughly shaken to wake her up.

Brett was restless throughout the evening, and the wound continued to drain. Kate feared Nancy would refuse to get up in the middle of the night again, but Charles informed her that Nancy had agreed to make as many poultices as they needed. Everyone in the inn knew Brett was fighting for his life.

Kate increased Brett's medicine as he grew ever more restless, but it didn't seem to help. He was burning up with fever and she had to sponge him almost constantly. When they tried to give him another dose after changing his poultice, he wouldn't take it. He became steadily more uneasy, flinging himself about the bed. His fever continued to mount until his lips cracked and his breath came in dry rasps.

By five o'clock Kate could stand it no longer. She banged on the wall until she woke Charles.

"Send Mark for the doctor," she told him when he stumbled in, sleepy and half-dressed. "We've got to try to give him some medicine one more time. He's thrashing about so wildly he'll either injure himself or break the wound open." It took all their strength to hold Brett down long enough to pour the medicine down his throat. Even then, half of it ran down his chin or spilled over the bedclothes. It was the last of their supply and they would have to wait until morning to get more. Charles looked at the deathly pallor and the dryness of Brett's skin, and feared that death had already set its imprint upon him.

The drought only quieted Brett for a short time. He was fitful and fought Kate's efforts to keep him sponged. She sent Charles to the spring for cold water, but even that didn't seem to have any effect on his fever. And now he was also beginning to have difficulty breathing.

The doctor arrived about six o'clock and removed the bandages. The wound had turned ugly, but it was still draining. "I'm going to probe," he said tensely. "There must be a pocket of infection I can't see. If something doesn't break soon, we're going to lose him." He opened his bag and began to lay out his instruments. "I must have boiling water, two extra lamps, and someone to hold him down. I'm going to probe deep, and he may react violently."

Valentine, awakened by all the noise and movement, volunteered to bring the hot water, and Kate and Charles brought the lamps from their rooms. While the doctor positioned these to throw as much light as possible on the swollen flesh around the wound, Kate readied strips of lint for bandages. The doctor positioned Charles and Mark on either side of Brett's chest to keep him as still as possible.

Gently at first, he probed near the opening and then gradually moved farther into the wound. Brett lost color and twice jerked convulsively. Valentine returned with the water just as the doctor probed deeper with a firm thrust. Brett suddenly gave a convulsive leap that nearly hurtled Charles across the room; blood and puss spurted from the deep-seated infection and ran down his chest to foul his bedclothes.

"That's what I'd hoped to find," the doctor said, extracting a small piece of bone from the escaping poisons and holding it up to the light. "He'll be very sick for the next few days, but I don't think we have to worry about gangrene any longer."

He began the work of cleansing the wound. "You will have to continue the poultices for a while, but if no new infection sets in, you can probably stop them in a couple of days. What's most important now is to keep him quiet and the wound clean. His strength is completely gone."

"I blame myself for not opening the wound last evening. I should have realized the chance of a massive infection was too great to be ignored. I was misled by the wound's being open and draining." The old man looked tired and defeated. "It's a good thing I don't practice anymore. That kind of carelessness is unforgivable." He began to clean and pack his instruments.

No one spoke. Valentine remained motionless by the door, but Charles began to restore the bed to order and make Brett more comfortable. Already he was quieter. The doctor placed the last of his instruments carefully in the bag and closed it up. "I'll call again after lunch. Keep him cool and quiet. I'd like one of your boys to help me home, Valentine." She took his arm and helped him out to his carriage.

Charles finished straightening the room then looked at Kate. She was as white as a sheet and leaning against the wall for support.

"We're through the woods, Miss Vareyan. He's going to get well for sure now." He looked as though he wanted to say more but instead turned and left the room closing the door softly behind him.

The enormity of what had nearly happened left Kate feeling numb. Suddenly unable to stand unsupported, she staggered to her chair. Blindly she groped for Brett's hand and kissed his fingers fiercely again and again. Dry sobs threatened to choke her. Her eyes were blinded with tears and her heart was gripped by the horror of losing someone who had inexplicably become very necessary to her.

Over the next three days, Brett's fever gradually abated, his color grew stronger, and his breathing became less labored. The poultices were discontinued and the quantity of sheets consumed by the daily ritual of bandage-making was reduced to a number Valentine could contemplate without horror. Even though Brett had not yet regained consciousness, he had progressed so well that Dr. Burton thought it unnecessary for anyone to sit up with him all night, and a trestle bed was set up in his room so Charles could sleep close by.

On the fourth day the sun shone brightly, so following lunch, Kate put on her heavy cloak, tied an old bonnet under her chin, thrust her fingers into thin mittens, and went out for a walk. The wind was still cold, but after so many days in the sickroom, it felt good to be outside. She found a sunny corner in the garden next to some dead columbine vines and slowly walked back and forth.

Her thoughts were running more and more on what to do when Brett no longer needed her. She still had not been able to make up her mind when or by which means she should go to London. For some reason, she didn't want to leave him to the sole care of Charles and Valentine. It wasn't that

Charles was a servant and Valentine an innkeeper. What was she but a stranger forced upon him by a card game? No, there was some more subtle reason . . .

For seven days she had sat next to him, stared at him, watched over him; there was no part of his face she didn't know as well as her own. Illness had removed the harshness from his countenance, and it had become warm and endearing. Even though his face was covered with a week's growth of beard, he had found a way into her heart in his need that he never could have found while well and riding roughshod over everyone around him. A mirthless laugh escaped her. Need! He wouldn't need her or anybody else in a few weeks, and she was fooling herself if she thought he had any use for her other than the satisfaction of his boundless physical needs.

Kate knew she wasn't looking for a relationship based solely on physical gratification. She wanted a tenderness and thoughtfulness that Brett had never shown. True, he had exhibited some occasional concern, but it was perfunctory, something he did out of politeness. He had been reared a gentleman and knew how to treat a female of his class, but his concern was one of manner, not of the heart.

It hasn't been perfunctory all the time, some inner voice objected. Kate heard, wished it were true, but feared it would be wishful thinking to read more into his actions.

She admitted she was inexperienced with men, but surely a woman could tell when a man was interested in her in more than the ordinary way, and if this was the way Brett treated other women, she was surprised his face hadn't been scratched to ribbons before now.

Kate sighed heavily. From a heartless father to a

164

heartless brother to a heartless seducer! Why couldn't men see it was better to be loved by choice rather than by force? She wanted someone who would take the time to find the way to her heart, someone who would think of her first, want to please her, seek ways to give her pleasure.

Somewhere that man existed. In her heart she could feel he did. As in her daydreams, she felt he was near, only just beyond her reach and out of her sight. She reached out, almost able to touch him, knowing somehow he had finally come within her grasp.

Then suddenly she knew, knew with a certainty that sent her hopes plummeting to the earth. She loved Brett, and she loved him with an intensity that brooked no denial; she had loved him from the moment he sank to the deck of that yacht, felled by Martin's bullet. *I might as well die right now,* she thought, and sank to one of the benches placed about the garden to be used when the breezes were soft and the night air inviting. It was thus that Valentine saw her.

Even though she had lived by the world's remorseless code all her life, beneath her tough exterior and foolish facade, Valentine was a hopeless romantic. Yet she was a shrewd judge of people, and she had known almost as soon as she set eyes on Kate that she was in love with Brett. She had also guessed within minutes that Kate was no ordinary girl of easy virtue, that there was something more to this young woman than one saw in the little tarts of face and figure she had dealt with. By the end of the first day she knew Kate was not only hopelessly in love with Brett, but that she was as innocent and trusting as she was beautiful.

Valentine looked at Kate's slumped shoulders and hanging head and knew her moment of realization

165

had come at last. She walked across the dry grass of the small lawn. The girl must have heard her coming, for she looked up, her face tearless, her expression bleak, and her eyes filled with a pain more intense than anything Valentine had ever experienced. So great was the weight of grief she saw in Kate's face that Valentine's own romantic heart overflowed. Abruptly she sat down, threw her arms about Kate, and burst out crying as though the tragedy were her own.

If Kate was surprised at the older woman's actions, she showed no sign of it. She returned the embrace but remained rather stiff, and though her eyes swam with unshed tears, she did not cry. Valentine soon stopped sobbing and raised her brimming eyes to Kate's drawn face.

"To love but one man till the day you die is your fate," she said compassionately. "It will not be easy. From the depths of my heart I wish you happiness. There can be no greater joy, nor any greater sorrow." She enfolded Kate in another long embrace, but this time there were no tears, only an unspoken sharing.

"It is time to go in, *ma petite*. The wind grows cold, and we can not have you sick, too." She stood up and briskly shook out her crumpled skirts. "He would suffer greatly if you could not care for him. Neither Charles nor I have your touch." She linked their arms; unconsciously, she had admitted Kate into the chosen few permitted to see the real Valentine preserved behind the hard layer of her lacquered exterior.

Kate returned to Brett's room after dinner, still prey to the afternoon's dejection. Even though her eyes kept glancing in his direction to make sure he didn't need her, her mind still struggled to cope with the unwelcome knowledge she loved a man who cared nothing for her. She stared at the candle, idly wondering if the pain of a hand thrust into its flame would blot out the pain in her heart. Was there any way to ease the suffering, the overwhelming sense of loss?

The candle's flame seemed to hypnotize her and she did not see Brett's eyelids flicker and then open. The first thing he saw was her profile as she stared into the space before her, lost in her own thoughts.

At first she was only a hazy form to the left of a small point of light. With great concentration he slowly turned his head and forced his mind and eyes to focus on the mysterious being. As her shape became more clear, he wondered who she might be and why she was there, but when he did see her face he didn't know who she was. He closed his eyes and opened them again. She was still there, but her eyes were looking into his now, and a smile spread over her face wiping away the pain.

Brett searched his mind. Who was this magnificent creature and why was she here? Why was he lying in this bed unable to move? Something must have happened, but what? What had he been doing? Where was he going? Unable to come up with any answers, his brow furrowed in frustration. Then the vision spoke.

"You must not frown so," she said, a soft hand smoothing the wrinkles from his brow. "There's no need to worry. All you have to do is get plenty of rest and concentrate on getting well again." The hand went away and returned with something cool and refreshing. Brett closed his eyes. He was weary from the effort of trying to remember, and he floated back into his world of darkness. Later he would try to figure out what had happened to him.

For the moment, his mind was too weak to bear the weight of his thoughts.

Brett woke early the following morning. He felt much refreshed and his memory was restored. The same face he'd seen the night before was still at his side. "Do you ever rest?" he inquired, smiling at Kate in a way that made her heart throb in agony.

"Yes, often," she answered quietly, striving to keep the emotions churning within her breast from sounding in her voice. "I share the duties with Charles and Valentine." She smiled tightly. "To be sure Valentine finds it difficult to remain still for very long, but she tries to help."

"Do you mean Valentine of the Chère Madame? Is that where you've brought me?" Kate nodded and was pleased to see him smile. "I haven't seen that sinful old witch in ages." He tried to turn so he could face Kate where she sat, but his chest, arm, and shoulder were so heavily bandaged he couldn't move without sluing his whole body around. "I forgot. I was shot, wasn't I?"

"Yes," she answered, a feeling of guilt causing her to hang her head. "Martin shot you in the chest, but the bullet didn't hit anything vital. You're going to be well soon." She looked into his eyes and struggled to keep her composure. They were like deep pools, drawing her to them, entreating her to become lost in their depths, forswearing the world and its trammels. How could a face so dear be so far out of reach?

"And Martin?"

She tore her eyes away from those hypnotizing orbs. "You shot him." She swallowed hard. "He fell overboard and we never saw him again."

"Damnation!" he swore. "You might as well tell

me the whole story. I've got to hear it from somebody." He tried to move again, forgetting his wound, and grimaced in pain. "But then maybe there's no hurry. It looks like I'm going to be here for a while." He appeared to be in deep thought. "How long have I been here? I seem to remember waking a couple of times before."

"You were shot a week ago. We've been here for six days." She could understand his feeling of surprise, but the foulness of his curses brought a flush to her cheeks. Worn down by lack of sleep, continual worry, and a feeling of guilt, her temper rose quickly, and before she could stop to think, she blurted out, "I'm sorry you've been inconvenienced, but I couldn't arrange for you to get well any faster. If I'd known it was so important, I could have spoken to Martin and he might have shot you sooner. Maybe you should hand around a schedule of your engagements next time."

He blinked at her, bewildered by her sudden outburst, and immediately Kate was sorry. Her hand flew to her mouth, and she jumped up from her chair and stumbled over to the window, her finger between her teeth and wishing it had been her tongue before she spoke. Would she never learn to control her temper? Would she always speak in anger before she thought about the consequences?

"I'm sorry," she stammered. "That was rude and I don't know why I said it. I guess I'm a little tired."

Brett looked at her as closely as he could from his position. "Maybe you ought to take some of my medicine and lie down for a while," he suggested. He didn't understand what was bothering her, but he was feeling too awful to be able to cope with her problems now.

"I don't feel tired, I don't want to lie down, and

I certainly don't need any medicine to keep me calm," Kate replied promptly, turning around to face him. "You shouldn't have started cursing me. I've spent six days and nights in that chair laboring over those vile poultices, pouring medicine down your throat, and worrying myself sick wondering whether you'd get well or if your death would be on my conscience for the rest of my life. Then the first thing you do when you wake up is curse me." She turned her back on him again and busied herself straightening up the table next to her chair.

"I wasn't cursing you," he said in a tired voice, "rather the dilemma I find myself in because of this illness. I didn't mean to say anything to upset you, particularly not after you've worked so hard to save my life."

Kate sniffed, slightly mollified, but she didn't seem ready to forgive him.

Brett shook his head; she was going to be difficult, and he was too weak to think about it right now. He'd talk to Valentine later and see if she could explain this girl to him. There wasn't much about young girls Valentine didn't know.

For now, however, just looking at her was arousing his senses and he was in no condition to endure the frustration of teased and unfulfilled excitement. Even now he could feel his body tensing. He closed his eyes and forced himself to think about his wound. "I think I'll take a short nap. Wake me when it's time to eat."

Kate turned to face him, but he had thrown off his sheet and she was brought up short by the blatant signs of his arousal. *That man is worse than a mating bull,* she thought angrily. *All he has to do is clap his eyes on a female, and he's ready to devour her without a by-your-leave.*

"Lunch will be served in about an hour, but I

170

will not make up any part of the menu," she informed him and sailed out of the room.

Brett smiled dreamily. She was not only beautiful, but she had spirit, by God. And some day she would learn to be *proud* of what her beauty could do to a man, not frightened by their arousal or filled with prudish inhibitions. It would be a pleasure to teach her how to respond to a man, how to tease and tantalize, to drive him nearly insane before giving him pleasure beyond words. And he would teach her, that he swore, before either of them grew much older.

A satisfied smile spread across Brett's lips and he drifted off to sleep.

Chapter 12

Brett had company for lunch. Valentine announced she was tired of dining by herself while Kate ate in Brett's room, so a table was brought in and lunch was laid for three.

"You don't think I'm going to eat this slop, do you?" Brett complained, scowling at the chicken broth and barley water which constituted his lunch.

"You're going to eat what the doctor ordered," Kate stated firmly, "or I'll give you enough medicine to knock you out. Then I'll pour it down your throat." Valentine and Charles exchanged uneasy glances, but Brett simply looked amused and surprised them both by eating his unappetizing lunch without further argument. He then took a short nap and spent the rest of the afternoon closeted with Charles.

"What do they talk about for so long?" Valentine demanded of Kate for the twentieth time. "Young girls telling secrets are not so bad. They have been locked away for two hours, and still they do not finish."

"When we left Ryehill, Brett said he had to be in France in two days. That was seven days ago. Maybe something important has happened since then."

"What can he know when he has lain like the dead for five days?"

"He could have known something was *going* to happen without actually being there to see it."

"*Il est possible,*" Valentine admitted reluctantly, "but he should tell us, too. Here nothing ever hap-

172

pens. Even the tiniest bit of news would be better than to hear of Emilie Crecy's new baby or the progress of the wheat crop."

"That does sound a little dreary," Kate agreed, "but rather reassuring. Nothing *ordinary* has happened to me since I left Ryehill."

"And whose fault is that?"

"I don't know. Probably as much mine as Brett's, but he won't listen to anything I suggest. He's sure I'm utterly stupid and incapable of doing anything for myself. I feel like a prize to be handed out to some unlucky winner."

Valentine eyed her skeptically. "You *are* a great prize, you know." She laughed at the anger in Kate's eyes. *"Mon Dieu,* do not fight it so. Mind you, I was a great beauty. Still, I would give five years of my youth to look like you. Your features are perfection and still you are not insipid. There is life, color, and an energy in you that should not belong to anyone who is not French." She read the look of disbelief in Kate's eyes.

"Mother of God, girl. Do men not stare at you with their mouths open? And Brett, did he not make advances?" Kate blushed. "I thought so, the old *roué.*"

"Mr. Westbrook told me several times he found me attractive and that, uh . . . he had difficulty, uh . . . behaving himself."

"Humph! That Brett Westbrook ever behaved himself I do not believe, not since he was old enough to steal his first kiss *certainement.* That he would attack you is more likely. But what of other men? Do not hundreds of them sent you *billet-doux?"*

"I never had any beaux."

"C'est impossible!"

"Martin wouldn't take me anywhere. Those men

173

at his card party were the first I had seen in months. We didn't even have a stable boy. The youngest man-servant in the castle was old Ned, and he's a grand-father at the very least."

"But how do you live?"

"I found things to do."

"But not to have seen a young man in four years!" Valentine crossed herself. "What kind of man was *votre frère* to have done such a thing? There must be demons in his head."

"Martin hated me, and I grew to dislike him nearly as much. I kept to my room when he was home."

"Blessed Virgin, how it is possible to stay in one room and not lose the mind? *Pauvre enfant.* You have been cruelly used."

"I didn't like it much, but Martin was gone most of the time. The only person who bothered me then was the housekeeper."

"The housekeeper?"

"Martin's mistress. If he cared for anyone, it would have been Isabella."

"Il est un bête!" Valentine declared with feeling. "It must have been terrible."

"It *was* lonely. I couldn't even go to church. I read a lot until Martin sold the books."

"Quelle horreurs!" Valentine gasped. "Do the En-glish do this often?"

"I don't think so," Kate replied with a laugh. "There were never very many guests when I lived with my aunt, but she seemed to take pleasure in the visit and the visitors. I know I did. Even though most of them were older, I was always anxious to meet anyone new. Do you realize I've seen almost as many new faces in this last week as I've seen in my whole life?"

"Incroyable! I am surprised I do not cry just

174

thinking about it."

"Please don't," Kate begged. "I seem to be crying all the time, and if Brett finds out I've been making you cry as well, he's likely to wring my neck. I don't want to try his patience too far. He might leave me here, and I haven't a farthing to pay my passage back to England."

Valentine didn't want to add to Kate's discomfort, but she wanted to know more about her relationship with Brett. She was sure it was more than just a cousin being escorted to Paris. She doubted they were related at all. "Brett will not leave you here. He is taking you to Paris and the *vieille tante, n'est-ce pas?*"

Kate regretted her thoughtless words, especially since she wasn't prepared to tell anyone the whole truth. She had intended to ask Valentine to help her escape, but she still hadn't come up with a plan and she was unwilling to disclose her awkward situation before she had worked out exactly what she meant to do.

"Don't listen to me," Kate said, producing a facile laugh. "I'm so tired I'm saying foolish things. I don't know what changes this accident will make in Brett's plans, but I'm certain he will take me to Paris."

Before Valentine could pursue the subject further, Charles entered the parlor carrying several thick letters and wearing a heavy frown.

"Mr. Westbrook wants these posted right away," he said.

That broke up the conversation. Valentine went away to see about dinner, and Kate went to see how Brett had survived the session. She found him looking very tired and enduring a stern lecture from Dr. Burton with ill grace.

"Tried to do too much, didn't you?" the doctor chided. "First time you open your eyes and you

175

spend the whole day writing letters and arguing about knotty problems. Now you're weak as a babe and feverish besides. I never knew a young buck who had sense enough to lie back and let himself get well. You're always trying to rush things." He pulled the new dressings tight enough to make Brett wince. "You make sure he takes his medicine," he said to Kate. "At least he'll sleep through the night."

"I'd prefer not to be drugged," Brett said, trying to keep a rein on his temper.

"When I want your opinion, young man, I'll find a subject on which you're an expert. Medicine's my business, and I'm damned good at it. You'll swallow your usual dose, or I'll pour it down your throat."

"That's the second time today someone has threatened to use force on me," Brett said, grinding his teeth in fury. "No one has succeeded yet."

"But I have you at a disadvantage, don't I?" countered the doctor, undeterred by Brett's rudeness. "In a few days it'll be a different tale, but right now your strength would give out after a short struggle, so you might as well try and mend your temper. You won't get anywhere with me by being churlish, and I know Miss Vareyan's not afraid of you."

Kate's weak smile did nothing to lighten Brett's mood. He closed his mouth tightly and would say no more. The doctor filled the void with inconsequential chatter, and admonished Brett to "be less irascible. Tension retards the healing process."

Left alone, Kate and Brett glared at each other like two cats. What did she mean by staring at him as though he were a child to be reproved for bad behavior. He was unaccustomed to females who didn't defer to his wishes, and he was tired of putting up with this bumptious, mercurial girl. She'd been trouble from the first time he set eyes on her. The recollection of that evening launched a different train of thought in his mind, and in seconds the heat of his anger had turned to a very different kind of warmth. He remembered her in the candlelight, skin like ivory satin and hair of corn-silk gold, a generous mouth demanding to be crushed in a torrid kiss. His eyes traveled down the white column of her throat to the youthful thrust of her full breasts and he felt the heat begin to course through his veins.

He thought of a certain countess whose voluptuous body had provided him with many a pleasure-filled evening and wondered how he could ever have been attracted to such overripe beauty. He compared her lush charms to the slender, clean lines of Kate's body and discovered it was like comparing a brood-mare to a racing filly. There was lithe grace in Kate's movements, her flesh was firm and cleanly molded to her bones and she was filled with all the fire and determination of a young and vibrant animal lusting for life, willing to take it by the throat, willing to risk all to gain everything. That was his own attitude toward life, and to see it in a young and beautiful woman filled him with a passionate need to possess her, to claim her body *and* soul as his own.

Kate broke in on his pleasurable meanderings as though she had been reading his mind.

"Before your burgeoning lusts put you beyond the reach of rational conversation, I'd like to talk to you about my future." She fixed him with a baleful eye. "My honorable future!"

"Can't that wait a while?" Brett asked, reluctantly tearing his eyes from their contemplation of her body. "No one in England knows where you are, and no one here knows *who* you are."

"No, it can't wait. My prospects may already be ruined, but if there *is* something left to salvage, it will have to be done before anyone learns that it was I, and not some nameless trollop, who ran off to

177

France with you." She stifled a sob. "Or would you rather I ask Valentine to recommend me for a place in one of those *houses* I hear so much about? Surely I'm qualified now."

Brett was nearly exhausted, his temper had been sorely tried, and he was having to exert considerable effort to keep it under control. Unfortunately, he was not as mindful of what he said, and he uttered the first thought that came to his mind. "Oh for God's sake, don't start that again. I never heard anyone get so wrought up over a maidenhead."

Kate sucked in her breath in a harsh rasp. "You may have taken any number of maidenheads in your depraved career, but I had only one to lose," she exclaimed, her voice rising with each word. "Since you forced me to sacrifice it, it seems a small price to ask you to help me save my reputation. I imagine Valentine would have made you pay dearly if you had come to her. Or have you lost all interest in me now that I've been deflowered?"

Brett could have bitten his tongue, but he knew there was no use trying to explain to Kate just now. In her present mood, she was likely to take any apology as further proof of his depravity. Still, even though his mind was considerably irritated by Kate's prickly temper and his limbs ached from being over-tired, his body would not allow him to forget its consuming desire for her.

"You've got to be the most vexing female I've ever met, but all I have to do is look at you and it doesn't matter. Do you have any idea how maddening it is to have you so close and be unable to do more than turn my head in your direction? I would give a year's income to stop that scolding mouth with kisses, crush you in my arms, and make love to you all night long."

Kate flushed scarlet in spite of herself. "Can't you

178

ever think of anything besides your lusts? Has any woman ever been more to you than a passionate kiss and a tumble in the bed?"

"Not yet," he replied, and smiled so dazzlingly she thought her knees would give way.

Kate was speechless. How could he think she wanted nothing more out of life than to be mauled by someone like himself? It was beyond her comprehension. It ought to be beyond *anybody's* comprehension.

"I want more than that," she finally said. "I don't know how and I don't know where, but I'm going to get it. And you are going to help me." She turned on her heel and flung out of the room, slamming the door so hard Nancy heard it in the kitchen.

Brett swore at the closed door. What did she mean by saying he was going to help her? He wasn't about to be ruled by any woman, particularly not a girl who flounced out of rooms like a hoyden and was continually setting her mind in opposition to his. She was a tasty morsel, but there were other tidbits just as tempting to be had for less trouble.

But as the heat of his displeasure evaporated, he saw again that young and unspoiled body, her perfect face and figure, and the lithe, graceful movement that promised delights beyond those he had experienced that first night. The more he thought about her, the more he realized he wanted to keep her with him. He hesitated when he thought of the complications that would cause, but he was even more unwilling to contemplate being without her.

He might as well use the time while he was recovering and waiting for answers to his letters to get on better terms with her. He always preferred willing partners. The pleasure was much more intense when it was shared. He remembered her responses that night and his senses warmed again. Her body, willing even if her mind still held back, had awakened at his touch and made a stormy effort to match his own passion. He knew she was as yet unschooled in the pleasures of love, but when she had learned to revel in the mysteries and glory in the exultation of her senses, she would be a partner worthy of his skill. *Yes,* he thought, as he drifted off to sleep again, *I might as well try to make her like me more. While I'm tied to this bed, there's not much more I can do.*

All that evening and most of the next day Kate treated him with cool formality, but it was impossible for any woman to resist Brett when he exerted himself to be charming, and her feelings toward him started to soften before midafternoon. Brett didn't make the mistake of changing his attitude toward her; that would only have made her suspicious and even more distrustful, but he was careful not to make any remarks which might make her angry. He had reluctantly come to the conclusion that even though she had led a cloistered life, she had developed some pretty novel ideas about her own abilities and worth. The only thing she hadn't yet realized was the power of her beauty. Once she knew the full extent of that, Brett reflected grimly, he wouldn't be able to keep her to himself any longer; he determined right then he would not go to Paris.

Kate didn't unbend completely toward him or pretend she wasn't still extremely angry, but she did start to talk to him again. Once she tried to bring up the subject of her future, but he put her off.

"I'm waiting for answers to my letters. Once I have them, I'll be happy to help you go anywhere you want." Since he didn't bother to explain what kind of letters he had written and to whom they were addressed, she knew no more than before. She decided to forgo mentioning it again in the hopes of getting something definite out of him the next day, but she was doomed to disappointment. Brett spent most of the next day teaching her how to handle a pistol and a dagger.

"If you're going to go about shooting highwaymen, you should learn how to use a pistol correctly." Kate wasn't afraid of an unloaded pistol and she quickly mastered its handling. "I'll give you some ammunition as soon as we can get outside," Brett promised, "and then we'll see what you can do."

Kate was pleased with her progress, but was relieved to change to a dagger when all the possibilities of an unloaded pistol had been exhausted. It also postponed until another day the question of what Valentine and the villagers would say about a pistol being fired virtually at their back doors.

After spending the next morning in further practice with the pistol and dagger, Brett waited until after lunch to introduce Kate to the sword. She didn't care for it in the least, but Brett kept her at it because it prevented her from trying to reopen the discussion about her departure and also gave him a chance to tease her into a more amiable attitude toward him.

"Once you become more adept, you can carry a pistol in your muff and a dagger in your garter," Brett laughingly suggested.

"I'd prefer not to go about armed to the teeth," she replied, but Brett smiled at her in a way that brought the blood to her cheeks. "If you keep looking at me like that, I'll have to carry them to use on you," she threatened.

"The sword also?"

"I'm not good enough with that, but I could always plunge it into your heart while you slept," she added reflectively.

"You're a bloodthirsty wench. Didn't your mother tell you that proper girls don't think of such things?"

Kate's smile vanished. "What my mother taught me would probably shock you. It's something I'd rather forget."

Brett did his best to get her to explain that remark, but she refused to talk about her mother at all. Instead, she asked him to show her a particular pass with the sword again.

"Until I can get up from this bed, I'm going to have to enlist Charles's help. It's impossible to teach swordplay lying down, even if I do have half the pillows in the inn behind my back."

Their good understanding continued for two more days. They spent more time with the weapons, Charles even brought a dart board for her to use as a target with the dagger, and he taught her to play cards. She read to him occasionally, but that bored him and he fell asleep.

Valentine did her best to see they weren't disturbed. She never stayed more than a few minutes herself and always seemed to discover some urgent need for Charles whenever he joined them. Kate didn't realize they were being thrown together, but Brett did and wondered what Valentine was up to. He knew she was a shrewd observer who never missed anything for long, particularly if the intention was to keep it from her. She was up to some mischief, but there wasn't much he could do about it now. After all, he couldn't order her to stay in her room when it was her own inn.

The next day was particularly sunny and Dr. Burton agreed to let Brett spend some time in the garden if he would stay in his chair. "I don't want you walking unassisted, and you're not to stay out long. It could be fatal if you were to develop a chill. It's really too early to be getting up, but a little exercise and sunshine might do you good."

After lunch, therefore, Valentine ordered at least half the furniture in the inn carried out to the garden where they spent the next two hours luxuriating in the sun and trying to decide what to do with Kate's inheritance. Kate still thought of herself as penniless, so when Valentine asked what she was going to do with her castle, she was nonplussed.

"What castle are you talking about?" she asked in genuine bewilderment.

"Your home. You said you had no family. Did you not inherit?"

Kate looked dumbfounded. "I don't know. I mean, I *never* knew. No one ever said anything about it."

"It's yours," Brett said unexpectedly. "It's not entailed."

"How do you know?" she demanded, her voice sharp and metallic.

"Your brother's lawyer told us when he explained why Martin couldn't bet his estate."

"Bet what estate?" Valentine exclaimed, agog with curiosity. Brett didn't stop to explain.

"You're probably a very rich woman." He didn't sound the least bit pleased by the prospect. "I don't know why I didn't think to mention it before. I suppose my illness drove it out of my mind."

Valentine didn't understand half of what Brett was talking about, but she understood enough to know Kate was not the poor, dependent girl everyone thought her to be, and she could tell Brett didn't like the change. She would have been ready to bet her best necklace he wouldn't let her go, but if she had money in her own right, how was he going to stop her? She looked at the two young people, each lost in their own thoughts, and her heart chuckled with anticipation. There were going to be some fireworks before this day was out.

"If this castle is yours," Valentine said, merriment in her eyes, "you must chase away the old memories. Have you a moat and drawbridge?" Kate smiled and shook her head. "But surely you have a dungeon. You can bury the skeletons and paint it bright yellow." Gradually Kate responded to Valentine's efforts to make her laugh, and within minutes they were remaking torture chambers into wine cellars, using racks for quilting frames, branding irons to create needlepoint designs, and the iron manacles to hang up curing hams.

Brett was disgusted at the turn in the conversation and took no part in it, but he was no more pleased when Charles reported some letters had arrived for him, and he excused himself with visible reluctance. Oddly enough, the ladies found nothing seemed quite so funny after he'd gone, and they soon went inside.

Some very intensive thought took place in their three rooms that afternoon.

Valentine's mind was set on pure mischief; she had decided that Brett should marry Kate. The poor girl obviously adored him — she didn't have a single thought in her head that wasn't bound up in Brett — yet she wouldn't give in to him all the time. Valentine understood Brett well enough to know that part of the reason he held women in such contempt was that they had done exactly what he wanted all his life. Kate loved him completely and passionately, but she would fight him every step of the way before she would let him ignore her feelings and reject her judgment.

Brett wasn't used to *any* opposition, and Valentine positively burned to see him brought to his knees by a woman strong enough to give him back word for word and deed for deed. She felt sure Brett would never marry anyone who did not fight against his suffocating iron will. He might *think* he only wanted someone who would provide food for his lusts and satisfaction for his passions, but he would only bestow his name on a woman whose character he admired and whose strength he respected.

Valentine adored strong men and secretly wanted to be dominated herself, but she was a very forceful woman and had ultimately controlled the men who had loved her. Naturally it was too much for her self-control to stand by and see Brett escape without being brought to heel. She promised herself she would attend their wedding if she had to walk all the way to London.

Kate derived virtually no pleasure from her thoughts. She found it impossible to believe Ryehill was hers. She had never known who inherited after Martin, but she had never been given any reason to think it would be hers. Now she paced her room trying to ignore the nagging fear that some obscure cousin would materialize and snatch it from her before she learned if Martin had left her anything to inherit besides debts.

But she would have to wait until she got back to London and could see her uncle to answer that question. If it turned out there was something left after the debts had been paid, then all her problems would be solved. She didn't need much money; even a small amount would enable her to live quietly somewhere far away from the prying eyes of society. She had always known, though she hadn't admitted it to herself because of the terrible consequences, that the story of her leaving Ryehill would someday get out, maybe not now or all at one time, but once people learned she had gone with Brett unchaperoned, her reputation would be ruined and society would never accept her. If she had enough money to live, it wouldn't matter.

But that meant cutting herself off from Brett as well, and that was a prospect she couldn't face yet. Her love was too new and untasted, her youthful optimism too bountiful to accept the brutal finality of separation. Every time she saw his face, pictured his powerful body, remembered the wild passion of that first night, her hope was renewed that something would happen to bridge the gulf that separated them. The very thought of calling such a vibrant and sensual creature her husband started her senses racing and her whole body tingling.

But cooler and more objective thinking brought her up against the realities of the situation, and she spent the remainder of the afternoon in a despondent mood.

Chapter 13

Brett's thoughts were more clearly set out, but no less difficult to accept. The first letter came from the foreign minister's office and contained Brett's new instructions. Lord Thunderburke stated in no uncertain terms that it was "damned inconvenient of you to get yourself shot while you're working for the Foreign Office. You're supposed to be on your way to Paris and Rome, not lying up somewhere recuperating." The work of making new plans had clearly made serious inroads into his lordship's store of patience, and his instructions were succinct.

Brett was to proceed to Calais as soon as he got this letter. A ship was already waiting which would take him down the coasts of France and Spain, through the straits of Gibraltar, and then along the coast of North Africa to Algeria. When he arrived in Algiers, he would follow his previous instructions. The situation there was developing quickly and he was to proceed with caution and as much speed as possible.

Brett uttered several pithy oaths, but he had actually received the instructions he expected. Taking the nature and timing of his mission into consideration, there was really nothing else Lord Thunderburke could have done. Nevertheless, he cursed.

What was he to do about Kate? This business of inheriting Martin's estate had caught him off guard. Why hadn't he remembered it instead of accepting Kate's word for her poverty? Now that she had money and somewhere to go, he could not continue to put her off. She didn't have to depend on him any longer. If she got away from him this time, and he wouldn't put it past Valentine to help her, she would go straight to that cursed uncle and he might never get her back.

Brett pulled himself up with a mental jerk. He'd never acted like this over a woman before, and he didn't understand why he should be doing so now. He tried to tell himself it wasn't essential that she stay with him, that he'd get along without her just as he had gotten along without all the others, but he knew better. He didn't know what he wanted from her, but every time he remembered the taste of her sweet mouth or the feel of her wondrously soft skin, he suffered fresh agonies of desire. He could not lose her, and damn this wound for keeping him so helpless.

The second letter threw him into a towering rage. He had written Edward to ask if anyone knew what had happened at Ryehill, and now he wished he hadn't. After finishing the letter, Brett paused only long enough to crush the pages in his hand before delivering himself of some ripe curses; then he stalked to the door and shouted for Charles, all the while heaping curses on Martin, Boyngton, Sedley, and a nameless young man who Edward said had seen them in Dover and couldn't wait to tell anyone who would listen. It was clear that too many people knew too much about what happened at Ryehill for it to remain a secret much longer; however, he was the one who had made the mistake of accepting the bet and of leaving the castle with Kate. After that, everything else was inevitable.

"Somewhere in the village there's an English cleric by the name of Humphries," Brett barked as soon as Charles entered the room. "He's usually drunk before noon so you'll have to sober him up, but I want him here right after dinner. He's going to perform a marriage. Talk to Valentine. You'll find him a lot faster with her help."

"Y-your marriage, sir?" Charles stammered. He was an experienced servant and used to receiving unusual orders, but this time he was barely able to keep his eyes from starting from his head.

"Yes, my *marriage*. Charles Hunglesby has written me a damned impertinent letter, even for him. It seems Boynton talked too much and Sedley is nosing about as usual. The upshot is this whole mess is about to leak out, and he practically *ordered* me to marry Miss Vareyan to save her reputation. And not a word of concern for me, his friend of I don't know how many years. I'll kill Frank Boynton if I ever see him again."

"Does Miss Vareyan know?"

"No, and you'd better not get that priest here too early. I've got to have time to prepare her, and I'm not at all sure how she's going to take it."

Dinner that evening was a strain on everyone.

Brett was uncommunicative and returned clipped monosyllables to any remark addressed to him. He saw this marriage as a public admission of guilt and had to constantly curb an urge to lash out at Kate as the cause of his humiliation.

The more she thought about it, the less Kate wanted to return to Ryehill. After thinking that everything would be all right if she only had somewhere to go, she realized that even the ends of the earth wouldn't be far enough to escape from her love of Brett.

Valentine believed lovers had to suffer great misery before they could be happy, so she nearly laughed aloud when Kate snapped at Brett for one of his cutting remarks. She had refused to lift a finger to help Charles until he had told her the whole story, and now she couldn't resist the temptation to drive Brett hard. He was as thoughtless and selfish as he was handsome, and he deserved to be made miserable. Still, only a man of Brett's sensual appetites could appreciate a prize like Kate.

So Valentine chatted happily, answering her own questions and never waiting for Kate or Brett to respond. She was a naughty creature who loved to twitch others where it hurt. She always felt a little guilty afterward, but she could no more stop the devil in her from rearing its head than she could give up dying her hair.

After the dessert dishes had been taken away, Valentine and Kate rose to leave Brett with his brandy. It was the first evening they had eaten in the dining room and they were unsure whether to observe the formal custom or stick to their recent practice of talking long after the dishes had been removed.

"Don't go," Brett said, motioning them back to their seats with a frown. "I received some letters from London today, and I think we should discuss what to do about Kate." He kept playing with his brandy glass, reluctant to come to the point, and Valentine settled back to watch. The only way he could have gotten her out of the room would have been to push her out, and then she would have listened at the keyhole. Kate leaned forward expectantly, ready to listen to anything Brett suggested but determined to make up her own mind.

"You both know I was supposed to be in Paris over a week ago. Today I received new orders. I'm to leave as soon as I'm able to travel."

Kate's body stiffened and the color drained from her face. It had finally come; he was going to leave her.

"There's a ship waiting at Calais this very minute to take me to the Mediterranean. I leave at dawn tomorrow. I have lost a lot of time with this wound, and now I must move as quickly as possible."

Kate clenched her hands tightly in her lap to keep them from shaking. She had known it would happen and she'd been trying to prepare herself for it, but hearing it was a shock.

"I received a second letter from Edward," Brett said, turning to Kate, "and he tells me everyone knows I killed Martin. No one seems to know you were with me, but it's only a matter of time before someone finds out and your reputation will be lost forever. To prevent such an unfortunate situation, I'm offering to marry you. By the time we return from Africa, our marriage will no longer be news, and your uncle and I will be there to shield you from any persistently curious tongues."

Sacrebleu! Valentine cursed inwardly. *How could he have been so stupid as to propose in that insulting way.*

Kate listened to Edward's news with a sinking heart, but the moment Brett's proposal passed his lips, her eyes began to blaze. By the time he finished delivering himself of the infamous proposal, she wished she could die of mortification. He was the most incredibly blind and insensitive blockhead she had ever met, and she had to be an even greater fool to be in love with him.

She made a tremendous effort to control her voice before she spoke, but she was shaking and she didn't sound calm. "I appreciate your concern for my reputation," she managed to say from between clenched teeth, "but I'm afraid I must refuse your flattering offer."

Now the battle will start, Valentine thought gleefully.

"Didn't you hear what I said?" Brett demanded, regarding her impatiently but without surprise. "All London knows half the story, and any day now they may get the rest. Marrying me is the only hope you have."

Mother of God, Valentine thought, *I didn't think it was possible, but he's actually making things worse.*

Kate lost her temper. "My only *chance,*" she hissed in sulfurous choler, "was to have never met you in the first place. How dare you offer me marriage in such a degrading manner. I should have pushed you into the sea with Martin." The force of her anger was too great for her to remain seated and she stood up in her place, her blue eyes cutting through the air like swords of steel and her long tresses bouncing in her agitation.

"From the way you're carrying on, you'd think I'd asked you to become my mistress instead of my wife."

"If you had *asked* me, I might have agreed," Kate retorted, stunning both Brett and Valentine, "but I wouldn't marry you to save you from torture."

"Good God, girl, you act like the name of Westbrook belongs to some country bumpkin."

"The name may have been honorable when you took it, but it's become rather soiled since then."

Brett brought his good hand down on the table with a resounding crash. "We'll have no more of that unless you want to be whipped." His black eyes clouded and the lids rode low. He was making an extraordinary effort to control his temper, but he was rapidly losing the struggle. Like every man of ancient lineage, the defense of his name was an inbred instinct, and it was impossible for him to allow anyone to abuse his name and still hold up his head. His pride was embedded in the honor of his name, and on that foundation rested the essence of his being.

"Is it your normal procedure to whip females when they disagree with you?" Kate demanded.

"Much more, and you'll find out what I do to anyone who casts slurs on my family name."

"You misunderstand me," Kate purred. "I didn't cast slurs on your family, just on *you*."

Brett sprang up, but Kate skipped nimbly out of his reach. He knew he couldn't catch her, and would only make a fool of himself if he tried. "I have offered you the protection of my name," he said, drawing himself up stiffly, "and I still stand by that offer." He turned to Valentine. "See if you can talk some sense into her. She's clearly deranged," he said, and slammed out of the room.

"I won't marry you," Kate shouted after him. "Not if you begged on your knees." Her voice caught in a sob and she picked up a vase from the sideboard and threw it at the door. It shattered into a thousand pieces.

"To be sure, it was an ugly vase," Valentine commented cryptically. "I do not think I wanted it anymore, but calm yourself, *ma petite,* before you break anything more. I think I like everything else." She smiled, inviting Kate to resume her seat, but she had already begun to pace furiously up and down the room. She was tearing her handkerchief to bits and mumbling curses under her breath. Valentine watched in silence for a few minutes.

"Sooner or later you must sit down and face your problem with a calm mind."

"Why?" Kate demanded angrily. "Brett won't listen to anything I say."

"Not while you throw vases about the room."

Kate stopped pacing. "I'm sorry I broke your

vase, but I won't marry him and that's final," she almost wailed. "I'm rich enough to *buy* myself a husband. I can marry Charles, or even Mark. Surely either of them would be a better husband than that strutting bull."

"Sit down and do not try to show me how crude you can be," said Valentine said sternly. "I am much more vulgar than you can ever be, and I am not impressed by curses, flashing eyes, or a heaving bosom."

Kate dropped into the chair Brett had vacated without any lessening of her anger. However, a betraying tear welled up in her eye, moist and glistening, until it slipped over the lower lash and ran slowly down her cheek. She wiped it away with an angry swipe of her hand, but another welled up and then another until she could not stop herself from crying.

"Damn," she swore. "Damn! Damn! Damn! Why do I always cry? Every time that man starts to act like a Viking marauder, I cry like a weak-minded fool. Why can't I hit him in the face or scratch his eyes out?"

Valentine looked a little surprised. "So the beautiful kitten has claws. I did not think you could be so cruel."

"If the only men you had ever known were my father, my brother, and *that* monster of depravity, you wouldn't be able to think of any man without foaming at the mouth. As for my language, you forget I had Martin's curses as a constant example. If I'm driven much harder, you're likely to hear words that will shock you."

Valentine erupted into rich throaty chuckles. *"Mon petit chou,* do you think I am the infant, that I have not heard curses in French, German, English, Spanish, and Italian? And I remember a few Russians and Turks who became *très intéressant* when the wine was low in the glass. No, *mon enfant,* you cannot shock me. It is yourself you try to shock. You try to convince yourself you can protect you from the world, but Brett is right and you know it. *Encore,* there is no need to suffer needless disgrace, *particulièrement* when it is not your fault. You may be rich, but it will save your reputation not at all. *Cependent,* if you are Mrs. Westbrook, you must be respected and welcomed everywhere. Brett is a man most valuable. He will not be running all over the world to dusty kingdoms forever. When he takes his position in government, you will be at his side."

"And," she added in a softer voice, "he has a stronger feeling for you than you know. Do you think he would marry with you, no matter what the scandal, if he did not want to? *Sacrebleu,* he would turn his back on this *débâcle* and lift no finger to help you. In London, Paris, Rome, Vienna, he is chased all the time by the women, and still he does not ask one to marry with him."

Valentine broke into her rich chuckle again. "Every time he sees you, his blood it boils." Kate blushed and started to fiddle with the fringe off her shawl. "If it were not so *stupide,* it would be *très amusant* to watch the both of you pretend you do not love each other."

"I've admitted it to myself," Kate confessed, "but I won't marry him to satisfy his medieval sense of honor. I want him to marry me because he loves me, not to save my reputation. I want him to cherish me as a person, not as a body."

"But what a body."

"Please, not you too. I am a person, not a statue, and I have all the desires of any ordinary person to be loved for myself."

"*Hélas,* you must give up this trying to separate love of you from love of your body. No man can look at one and not think of the other. They are not made like that, and Brett is no different. But he has realized you have a mind and a personality to be reckoned with."

Resting her elbows on the table and her chin in her hands, Kate stared unseeing into the space before her, but her eyes gradually focused on the brandy decanter in front of her. The dark ruby liquid reflected occasional sparks of light as she moved her head from one side to the other. She picked up Brett's glass and held it up to the light. She studied the thick liquid, swirling it around in the glass to watch it cling to the sides in a thin film.

"I wonder what men find so wonderful about this stuff?" She sniffed the contents. The heady bouquet stung her nostrils. She snatched her head back and looked at it again. Then she put the glass to her lips and carefully sipped a small amount. The delightfully fruity taste pleased her tongue, but the liquid seemed to gather warmth as it slid down her throat. It hit her stomach like a small flame causing her eyes to open wide.

Valentine watched her with disapproval. It was all right for ladies to drink wine, but only men drank brandy. "Put that glass down and listen to me. Do not hide behind your foolish pride. It makes no sense. Marry Brett, even if you are so silly to think he does not love you now, and you can make him fall in love with you any time you want if you go about it the right way."

"Brett has never even pretended he cared for me," Kate said without taking her eyes off the brandy. "He's more worried about what people will say than he is about me." She continued to sip from the glass, each sip a little larger than the one before.

"Brett has never worried about what people will say of him. Hah! I laugh at such an idea. Many men do I know who are so impressed with themselves they can see nothing else, but Brett he is not one of these. He cares not one bit for anyone's approval."

But Kate was not listening to Valentine anymore. She had tired of the whole problem. No matter which way she turned, there seemed to be no solution; she wanted to crawl off somewhere and forget she had ever known Brett. A comforting glow was beginning to radiate from the pit of her stomach. She poured herself another glass of brandy and sipped it. Valentine advanced one argument after another as to why Kate would be making an enormous mistake if she did not marry Brett, but after a third glass of the fiery liquid had flowed down Kate's throat, she began to feel the detachment she longed for. The pain lessened and the importance of the moment vanished. *Nothing* was very important anymore. *Why didn't I ever know about brandy before,* she thought. *It's just like men to keep the best things to themselves.* But she knew about it now, and while Valentine continued to try to talk her into marrying Brett, she became quietly drunk.

Charles found Winifred Humphries trying to stretch a pint of cheap brandy by cutting it with water. He nearly fell on Charles's neck in thanksgiving when he was made to understand he would receive a substantial fee for performing a simple marriage ceremony.

Charles brought him back to the inn and was just pouring him a glass of ale when Brett flung through the door in a rage that came as close as anything could to driving all thought of drink from Winifred's mind. Winifred gaped at Brett with such trepidation Charles began to regret he had not taken him to the local tavern instead; Brett was scaring him in a way eternal hellfire never had.

Oblivious to the cleric's withering desire for complicity, Brett damned Kate to a hell reserved especially for short-sighted and obstinate females and went about his work.

"I suppose Charles has told you what is needed here," he barked, glaring fiercely at Winifred from under gathered brows. "This marriage has to take place tonight, but she's got some foolish notion it's not honorable, and now she's refusing to go through with it." His loud voice grated on Winifred's badly jarred nerves. "You're not to pay any attention to anything she says. She's going to marry me if I have to drag her to the altar. The menace in his voice startled Winifred into spilling some of his precious ale.

"Brett," Valentine hissed, sticking her head in the door, "I must talk to you."

"What is it?" he demanded.

"Kate."

"What has that obstinate female done now?"

"Not so loud," Valentine hissed. "Come out here and I will tell you."

"If she has run away again, I'll wring her neck!" Brett stormed as he stalked from the room.

Charles and Winifred, left to stare at each other in silence, listened intently. At first all that penetrated the heavy door was the sibilant sound of Valentine's urgent whispers, but abruptly Brett's voice cut her off with explosive force.

"May the vultures of hell tear you to pieces, along with every distiller of preach brandy in this benighted country," he raved. "I ought to choke you with the strings of your own nightcap."

"Save your curses for those who deserve them, or you can do your own dirty work," Valentine told him sharply. Brett's receding footsteps nearly drowned out her last words.

Winifred looked nervously about, hoping to find a way out, but Charles was standing next to the only door. He took a hasty swallow to fortify his nerves, waiting expectantly for Brett's return, but it was Valentine who opened the door a few minutes later and whispered to Charles in the same loud voice.

"Get the sot to the church. It is time for the ceremony."

Chapter 14

"I must protest this marriage . . ." Winifred began uncertainly, but Charles shoved him past Valentine.

"Wait until a difficulty arises before you decide to deal with it," he admonished. Winifred thought that was the best advice he'd heard in quite some time, so he righted his clothes and set off to the church fervently hoping no difficulties would arise. The thought of the ale he had drunk and the money he had been promised went a long way toward inducing him to ignore his nagging doubts.

But a difficulty did arise. Kate was drunk, so drunk Brett had to hold her tightly about the waist and lean her body against his own. Valentine tried to help, but she got in the way so often that Brett finally lost his temper.

"Leave her to me. I'd rather hold her myself than have to carry the both of you."

"*Bête!* You are ungrateful," Valentine said.

"I'd be a lot more grateful if you had had the good sense to put the brandy away before she passed out." Kate's head lolled forward, but occasionally she would raise it to mumble something no one could understand. Her hair fell over her face giving her the appearance of one demented, a feeling that was heightened when she croaked in a thick, raspy voice, "I won't marry the bloody seducer."

Winifred pulled his cloak more tightly about his ears trying to pretend he hadn't understood Kate's words, but she repeated them over and over again.

"Shut up," Brett snapped, losing his temper.

"There's no need to make the town a present of your history." After that, Winifred could no longer ignore his conscience. They had reached the church door, and he realized if he was ever to make a protest, it had to be now.

"Sir!" he said in a quavering voice, "I must insist that the young lady be allowed to recover herself. I cannot marry anyone who is drunk," he said with credible disapproval.

"Get inside, you piss-poor prelate," Brett roared with savage impatience. He handed Kate to Charles, threw open the church doors, and propelled Winifred inside. "Any more whining from you, and I'm liable to open your fat gut and take back my ale."

Incapable of further resistance, Winifred stumbled up the aisle to escape Brett's wrath. He managed to regain some of his composure in the familiar surroundings, but he started to shake again when confronted with Brett's murderous face. He fumbled with his books, unable to hold them still.

"Are you sure you can read the words?" Brett asked contemptuously.

"I have never failed to perform a service," Winifred said proudly.

"You must have failed at something or you wouldn't be leading this miserable existence," Brett observed cruelly as he turned away. Charles and Valentine dragged the stumbling Kate to the rail. "I'll have to hold her or she'll fall," Brett said irritably as he knelt at the rail, his arms tightly enfolding the lifeless girl, his blazing eyes compelling the cleric to proceed with all haste.

They got through the service even though some of Kate's lines had to be repeated several times before she could say them. The signing of the documents presented a further obstacle, but Charles distracted Winifred's attention while Valentine, holding Kate's

201

hand in hers, put her signature on them for her. This over, everyone breathed a sigh of relief

By the time they left the church, Brett had gotten over his anger at Kate's ill-timed experiment. He had been drunk too many times himself to begrudge her the same privilege. His hand at her waist kept coming into contact with her breasts and he lost interest in anything beyond the nearness of the body that had been teasing him almost beyond endurance for days. They were married now and all that he had longed for, all that had been forbidden this past week was about to be his.

He held her closer, savoring the anticipation of what was to come. He had relived the night at the Cock-in-the-Cradle many times during these last days as he watched her move about his room just out of reach. He had gone over every detail, drained each moment of every delicious sensation, all the while thinking how much more incredible it would have been if she had been awake enough to respond to him. He had tortured himself by watching her every move, knowing what her body looked like behind the clothes that obstructed his vision, remembering how it felt to hold her in his arms. Just looking at her caused his temperature to rise, a fact deplored by Dr. Burton. Brett could have told him it was not the fever of illness but rather of impatience to once again experience those elusive pleasures. Now Kate was his, *forever,* and his limbs trembled at the thought.

The cool air sobered Kate enough for her to realize she was no longer at the table but was being half-walked, half-carried through the streets. She muttered to herself all the way back to the inn, trying to figure out why she should be outside at this time of night. It seemed like a minor problem, but it was important to her to be able to grasp the reason.

She came to an abrupt stop in front of the inn.

"I know this place," she said in a bleary voice. "I have been here before." She shook off Brett's hold and embraced the doorframe with both hands. "I like it here. I want to stay."

Valentine was inclined to coax her to let go and ease her inside the inn, but Brett had other ideas. He broke her grip on the frame and propelled her through the door.

"Ladies don't ordinarily drink brandy," he said. "But if they do, they take care not to be seen embracing doorways."

But Kate felt the need to embrace *something,* so she flung her arms around Brett's neck.

"Now that's much better," he said and returned her hug with enthusiasm. His efforts to kiss her were thwarted by her inability to raise her head.

"You may be married," Valentine told him curtly, "but you will not misbehave on my doorstep. Take *la pauvre petite* to the parlor and walk her. I have a brew *extraordinaire* that will bring her around." She set off to the kitchen willing to do battle with Nancy to ensure that Kate was sober enough to remember her wedding night.

Brett tried to walk Kate, but after the ordeal of supporting her to and from the church, his wound was throbbing painfully and he was so weak he felt dizzy.

Fortunately Valentine soon returned with her suspicious brew. "Do not ask what it is," she said in answer to Brett's raised eyebrows. "It is very *désagréable,* but it will bring her around. Go see about your arrangements for tomorrow. I can handle her. Just set her down in that chair and lay her head back. Return in about an hour and maybe she will talk to you."

"It's not talk that I'm interested in," Brett said. It

203

was impossible to ignore the hungry look in his eye.

"That is more than you have now," Valentine said as she tried to settle Kate just to her liking. "I told one of the girls to pack Mrs. Westbrook's clothes, but maybe you should see for yourself. I have no idea what one needs for a sea voyage. Just to think about it gives me the *mal de tête*."

"Kate, too," Brett said absently as he headed toward his own room. Hearing Kate referred to as Mrs. Westbrook had taken him by surprise. His mother had died giving birth to his stillborn sister and the only woman he could picture with that name was his austere grandmother. It brought home to him with sledgehammer impact the fact that he had married a nineteen-year-old girl about whom he knew virtually nothing except that he was becoming unbearably impatient to take her to his bed. God, what a fool he had been.

He tried to imagine Kate as the mistress of his several houses with their enormous staffs, but all he could see was an innocent young girl with wide, clear blue eyes that were like an open invitation to love. They sparkled brilliantly when she was happy but glittered like blue diamonds when she became angry. He could almost taste her sweet lips returning his kisses.

In a trance, he reached out to free her hair. As it tumbled through the mists of his memory, his body quivered with a shiver of delight. The long, silky tresses, as pale as new corn silk, fell in abundance over her shoulders and down her back. She threw back her head revealing the white column of her throat resting on creamy shoulders with skin like satin. He could feel it under his fingertips, feel its warmth, feel it tingle from his touch.

As he mentally traced a line with his fingers down her throat, across the shoulder, and down the graceful line of her arms, his gaze fell forward to the dark cleft between the rising mounds of her breasts. His hands moved to the small of her back, lifting her up slowly and bringing his lips ever nearer to objects of his desire.

To touch them with his lips, to kiss and fondle their delectable tenderness, to take the ruby nipples into his mouth became the one thought burning through his consciousness. He was hot with churning passion and so uncomfortable he pulled at his tie to loosen it.

"Should I check with the maid before she finishes the packing?" Charles's matter-of-fact voice brutally interrupted Brett's enthralling daydream. He didn't answer, unwilling to let it go, but Charles's voice intruded again. "Is there anything in particular you would like me to tell her?"

Wrenched painfully back to reality, Brett swore. "I'll see to it myself," he growled in a hot and breathless voice. But Brett's steps did not go down the hall to Kate's room, and a few seconds later Charles heard the front door slam.

Kate was harder to revive than Valentine anticipated. She forced Kate to swallow every drop of the pungent liquid, but that failed to sober her and she went off to brew a stronger batch. Kate was sound asleep when she returned, and that annoyed Valentine so much that she almost left her to sleep it off. However, she relented and ruthlessly poured the second cup down her throat. This time Kate's eyelids began to flutter. Valentine pulled Kate to her feet and kept up a steady flow of heartening chatter, chiding the girl for being so silly as to get drunk on her wedding night and gently encouraging her to begin walking on her own.

Kate's befuddled wits recognized Brett's name, but she found it impossible to understand the rest of Valentine's conversation. The word "brandy" kept getting mixed up with a priest, but the part that made the least sense to her was the marriage Valentine kept talking about. Who had gotten married, and why should Kate be interested in them? She most certainly couldn't have anything to do with their wedding night, a subject that seemed to be of great concern to Valentine.

Kate started to frame a question, but then Valentine mentioned Brett's name and her heart lurched painfully. Brett couldn't have married someone else! She tried to grasp the thread of the conversation, but her head was aching so much she couldn't think. Now Valentine was mixing *her* name up with this unknown couple; her frustration made her angry enough to fight off the paralyzing effects of the brandy long enough to ask, *"Who* got married?"

"You did, *mon petit chou,"* Valentine crooned in a comforting voice, but her sharp old eyes were alert for signs of danger.

"Don't be silly," Kate giggled. "I don't even know the groom." *Oh my God,* Valentine thought, *she doesn't remember anything at all.*

"Do you remember going out a little while ago?" she asked. Kate shook her head. "Do you remember drinking Brett's brandy?" Kate didn't answer. "Can you remember dinner?"

Kate tried to concentrate. "I think so," she said, struggling to fight off her mental haze. "Brett was trying to make me do something that made me extremely angry, but I can't remember what it was." She had an uneasy feeling it was important. "What was it?" she asked, gazing empty-eyed at Valentine.

"He asked you to marry him. Do you remember?" Valentine asked, hoping Kate wouldn't recall the manner of his proposal.

Kate frowned with the effort to remember. "I think I do, but there was something else that got me so mad. Why did he do it, Valentine? I would give anything to marry him. I love him so much." Valentine almost cursed as Kate's eyes began to fill with tears. *You've got to think of something fast,* she told herself. *Brett will be back any minute expecting to see a smiling bride eager for her wedding night, and all I have to show him is a crying drunk with hair in her face.*

"*Bon Dieu,* were you angry when he said you must marry with him to save your reputation."

Kate's hiccups stopped. "I remember now." All desire to cry gone, she tossed her head in wrathful pride. "I wouldn't stoop to trap him into such a marriage."

Valentine steeled herself for the plunge. "You did marry him, *mon ange.* You have been Madame Westbrook for more than an hour now."

Kate's body became as rigid as if it had been turned to stone. Her brain fought for words, weapons to drive out the understanding of what she'd just heard. It couldn't be true. She didn't remember leaving the inn. Anyone could see she was still in the parlor. Maybe Valentine was teasing. That *must* be it, but Kate didn't think it was funny.

"You got drunk on brandy," Valentine told her, pointing to the empty bottle, "and we had to carry you to the church. Even now the maid packs for you. This is your wedding night, *ma chérie,* the most important night of your life. You must be ready when he comes."

Her last words were obliterated by a cry of anguish that rose from the depths of Kate's soul, soared until it became a bone-rattling scream, stayed suspended in space for several moments, then sub-

207

sided into a heart-rending sob. Kate collapsed into the middle of the floor, her dress and hair forming an arc around her crumpled form, her body rocking to and fro, and her arms clasped close to her bosom.

"My God, please let me die!" she wailed in anguish.

The door was nearly torn from its hinges as Brett, closely followed by Charles, burst into the room. "What's wrong?" Brett demanded, stunned at the sight of his wife sprawled on the floor. "She sounds like she's being torn apart." He turned to Valentine in frustrated impatience. "You didn't say anything stupid, did you?"

"No, but I did!" Kate moaned, her raised face distorted by grief. She was shaken to the very roots of her being by a sense of utter desolation at being robbed of the right to make the most important decision of her life. For the rest of her days, women would smile knowingly and whisper that she had taken shameless advantage of circumstances to catch the greatest matrimonial prize in England, that Kate Vareyan, a girl of no fortune beyond an old castle about to be sold for debts and a birth that was genteel only because it had no cause to be otherwise, was scorned by her peers.

She glowered at Brett. Being forced to marry him like this had robbed her of her only chance to prove she loved him. He would always remember he had been forced to marry her to save her reputation. Refusing to become his wife had been her only chance for true happiness.

"Don't sit there like a dog howling at the moon," Brett commanded. "You look disgraceful with your hair in your face and your dress dragging in the dust. Where's your pride?"

Kate would have thrown something dangerous at

him if she could have found anything, but all she had were her soft slippers, and they missed him. "My pride was stripped from me a short while back in the church when I was too drunk to do anything about it. Now I feel like howling at the moon. I feel disgraced and dirty. I feel like I've been violated, completely stripped of all decency and self-respect. I feel utterly and completely debased."

"I never heard such ravings in my life," Brett responded impatiently. "You act like I've committed a crime instead of doing what I could to protect you." Brett grabbed Kate's wrists and hauled her to her feet. "I'm out of patience with your tiresome predilection for seeing yourself as the mistreated innocent and me the ravishing savage. I don't relish the role of villain, particularly after I've gone so far as to take a bullet because of you."

"*Bête!*" Valentine interposed furiously. "That was not worthy of you."

Brett ignored her and turned to Kate. "When you left Ryehill, you placed your fate in my hands. Chance has done you better than I intended. It has given you a name, wealth, and position, and all you can do is sit on the floor wailing like a demented soul."

"You have never, from the first minute I set eyes on you, been able to see me as anything more than a body to incite your passions," Kate said with ice in her voice and fire in her eyes. "Not once have you stopped to think of what I might want, what might be best for me, or how your plans might hurt me, even if that hurt was only to my pride. You dismiss my ideas as female complaints and treat my anger as a childish tantrum. You see nothing but your self-consequence, your own important plans. No one is allowed to get in your way. They're either forced to mold themselves to your wishes or are brushed aside and dismissed as too stupid to bother with. You're arrogant, egotistical, and the most thoroughly selfish man I've ever met. Martin was not as bad as you."

"Little one," Valentine moaned in despair, "it is not fair to call Brett worse than a crazy."

Brett grabbed Kate by the shoulders and shook her violently, unconcerned that his powerful grip might hurt her. "If you had half the breeding and intelligence you think you have, you wouldn't disgrace yourself and my name by this shameless behavior."

"I'm sick to death of hearing about your name!" Kate shot back. She tried to escape, but she realized she could only get away if he allowed her to. That fanned her anger to a white heat. "Let me go," she hissed, and spat in his face.

Brett's reaction was swift and instinctive; he drew back his hand and brought it rushing down toward her cheek. But somewhere in the midst of his swing, Brett realized what he was doing and tried desperately to stop himself. Too late. The blow was only a tithe of what it might have been, but he had struck her nonetheless.

Kate withstood the diminished blow without swaying. "Just like Martin," she taunted him, her voice tight with rage. "Even the same cheek. Do they teach you that at school, or is it a natural instinct?" She threw back her head and swept the hair from her face, her eyes meeting his without flinching.

Brett had never struck a woman in anger, and he was momentarily stunned by what he had done, but under the cruel lash of Kate's tongue, his chagrin died and his anger flamed anew.

"You are the most poison-tongued female I've ever met. Every time I've tried to help, you've turned on me, accusing me of every vile purpose you can think of. You have the face of an angel and the body of a goddess, but you're certainly your brother's sister. Would to God he had killed me and spared me the agony of learning what a fool I've been!"

"*Nom de Dieu,* stop it!" Valentine screamed. "You are a *malédiction* and I am sorry I ever helped you to marry her." She folded Kate in her arms. "Oh, *mon pauvre petit chou,* he is a brute of the biggest, but he does not mean what he says. He has the *mauvais* temper." She was horrified at what they were saying to each other, but she was most shocked at Brett's striking Kate. In her mind, absolutely nothing could excuse striking a woman.

Kate pushed Valentine aside. She, too, was shocked at Brett's words, but anger insulated her from hurt. "Of course I won't pay him any attention," she said, steadying herself against the table. The brandy was still singing in her ears. "I don't want to ever set eyes on him again." She started toward the door, then turned slowly to face Brett. Some of the anger had gone out of her voice. "I will see you are released from this odious marriage. Maybe it can be annulled. If not, you can always divorce me."

Brett made a motion as though he would go toward her; she cringed involuntarily, and he froze in his tracks.

"I'm going to my room. Don't you so much as come near my door tonight," she warned, and disappeared down the hall. Brett started to follow her.

"Not now!" Valentine objected furiously, taking him by the arm. "After such a *débâcle,* all you can do is leave her alone. Maybe she will talk to you again if you give her time. If any man had ever spoken to me thus, I would have killed him!"

Brett turned his back on Valentine. The more he thought about Kate's words, the more his anger grew. He felt misjudged and cheated. He could have ignored her treatment at Martin's hands and left her at Ryehill; he need not have followed her to the Black Crow, he didn't have to take her to France with him, and most of all, he didn't have to face Martin's gun. He had done all of this and more, yet time and time again she turned on him like a mad dog. He hadn't meant to strike her. Yet even as he thought of her brutal words, her loveliness and soft, inviting curves teased his mind and began to sap the strength of his anger. The longing for her returned, and he could feel the tingling of his senses that was always started by the mere thought of her.

As quickly as Brett's wrath had been fanned into flame, his mood changed to one of contrition. "I won't let her have our marriage annulled," he said as he moved toward the door. "Get out of my way," he muttered when Valentine started to block his path. "I'm not going to hurt her. I can't let her go to sleep thinking I meant all those things."

"Be easy with her," Valentine counseled. "She drank so much her head will not be clear for hours yet."

"I'm not going to upset her. I just want to make sure she's all right." But his need of her would not lie still. Anger had aroused his every passion, and now desire ran headlong through his veins, the clarion call of unfulfilled yearning reaching to every part of his body. "Besides, she should be waiting for me. After all, the bridegroom expects to be invited to the marriage bed on his wedding night."

Valentine bit her tongue. They were married and she had no right to interfere, but she was concerned with what might happen if Brett's physical nature overpowered his momentary concern; knowing his character, she felt sure it would. Without a word she followed him into the hall.

Brett knocked on Kate's door. When he got no answer, he knocked again and called her name. Still she didn't answer. Piqued, he knocked hard enough to cause the door to rattle and grumble against him.

"Go away," she called.

Brett's anger, always simmering just below the surface, began to flare again. "Open this door," he growled. "I don't want to hurt you, but I'm your husband and I intend to come in."

"I won't open that door even if you stand there all night."

"Either you open it or I will. Valentine has extra keys for all the rooms."

"She won't give it to you."

"You forget you're my wife. By law it's my right to sleep in your bed. Surely your mother told you about your wedding night," he said with an anticipatory smile. The obsession had taken hold of him now and he would brook no refusal. Valentine waited uneasily.

"I won't open the door."

"Then I will."

"No!"

"Valentine, love, would you mind getting your extra key?" Brett teased. "Kate seems to have mislaid hers." He grinned broadly at his frowning hostess. "Don't be shy, Valentine, it's all right. We're married." He began to fiddle with the door, making sounds like he was trying to fit the key into the lock.

"I hope she hits you," Valentine hissed. "You deserve it."

There was a quick rustling movement from within, then Kate threw the door open and Brett found himself staring into the barrel end of a small pistol. It was loaded, cocked, and pointed at the exact spot between his eyes he had trained her to aim for. He instinctively jumped back.

213

"If you so much as touch this door again tonight, I'll shoot you," she threatened. She staggered, but caught her balance on the doorframe before she slammed the door in his face.

Brett recovered from his shock almost before the door had closed. "Then you'd better get ready to shoot," he stormed, "because I'm coming in, and I don't mean to shake hands good night." He threw himself against the door. It creaked, but held against him. An agonizing pain shot through his shoulder reminding him of his wound, but before Valentine could stop him, he slammed into the door once more. The lock broke amid the splintering of wood and the door swung wide open, slamming into the wall with a loud crash. Almost in the same instant Valentine heard the loud report of a pistol shot.

Chapter 15

Valentine screamed, expecting to see Brett's body crumple before her horrified eyes, but instead he remained standing, staring at the floor of Kate's room. Had the poor child shot herself! Terrified of what she might find, Valentine pushed Brett aside and rushed into the room.

Kate lay in a white, motionless heap by the bed, the smoking pistol under her right hand. Valentine flung herself forward with an anguished cry. "Holy Virgin, forgive us!" Her lamentations were so clamorous she didn't hear Brett speaking to her. He tried to raise her to her feet, but she fought him with fists and curses.

"May the demons of hell tear your soul to pieces!" she cursed.

Brett tried shaking her, but she continued to shout curses in his face. Swearing because of what he had to do, Brett slapped her sharply on each cheek.

Valentine stopped screaming then, but before her nails could find Brett's face to exact their vengeance, she heard him say, "Kate's all right. She just fainted." He pointed to a spot above the door. "Your wallpaper is the only casualty."

The rush of relief was so great Valentine nearly swooned. She sank down next to Kate and tried to cover her embarrassment by arranging Kate's clothes more modestly. "Don't bother," Brett said in a tired voice. "I'm going to put her to bed."

Valentine glared at him with hard, accusing eyes.

"For Chrissakes," he exploded. "You must not

think any more of me than she does. I'm not such a savage I'd rape her while she's out cold."

At this point, Valentine wasn't exactly sure what she did think he might do, but she moved aside.

Brett gathered Kate in his arms. The feel of her body against his skin and the scent of her perfume in his nostrils were almost too much for his weakened condition, and he hurried to lay her on the bed before he dropped her. He stood for several minutes, his gaze riveted to her bruised cheek, and silently castigated himself for his wretched temper. Why did it have to burst out of control every time something annoyed him? And why, of all people, did he have to hit Kate?

He seemed to have no self-control where she was concerned. Even now, when he knew he had behaved like a beast, he wanted her so badly he was shaking. He probably would have taken her, too, just like she was, even though her bruised lip was like a whip flaying his raw conscience, if he hadn't been certain she would never come to him as his wife if he took advantage of her tonight. It wouldn't be easy to calm his pounding pulses, but this was one battle he couldn't afford to lose.

It didn't do his temper any good to know that Valentine had sided with Kate. And Mark clearly worshiped her, too. "If she told him to jump in Nancy's stewpot and boil himself alive, the little fool would probably do it," Valentine had said in exasperation one morning. Even Charles's devotion to his master was suspect. Hell, Edward wasn't anywhere near Kate, yet not once had he expressed any interest in Brett's difficulties. In fact, he had advised him to not consider himself at all.

The most unnerving part was that the loyalty of all these people had belonged to him first. He knew that friendships altered with time, but not even a blind egotist could attribute such a wholesale defection to natural attrition. Besides, he was talking about less than a month, and half that time he had been too sick to do anything, right or wrong. What was it they saw in his treatment of Kate that he didn't see? What had he done, what was he *still* doing, that made them turn against him?

He shook off his reverie and began to undress Kate. He laughed, even though he didn't feel much like it. He had undressed many women in his time, but never one who lay in his arms like a deadweight. The others had been warm and coy, struggling just enough to keep his interest alive, but somehow managing to allow him to remove their clothes with a minimum of fuss. Kate did none of this. By the time he finally managed to get the gown over her head, he was so exasperated he threw it on the floor. She could do something about it tomorrow.

Brett carefully removed her chemise, the final bar to her privacy, and the youthful perfection of her body was laid bare to his heated gaze. He paused in wonder. He had never seen anything quite so lovely, so nearly perfect. He had intended to make sure she was comfortable and then pull the sheet over her, but he was drawn to her like a moth to a flame, and no thought of a sheet intruded to break the trance. Like the ancient mariners when they heard the song of the Sirens, he was helplessly in her thrall. He sank down beside her, touched her cheek with the tips of his fingers, traced the line of her jaw, caressed her shoulder, explored the ruby-capped mounds of her breasts. Her skin was invitingly soft, and his fingers continued their voyage down the tapering waist to the long, slim thigh; his eyes followed to the small shapely ankles and dainty feet. He snatched his hand back as if he had touched a red-hot iron, his senses reeling. He knew if he didn't get

217

out of the room at once his passions would overpower him, and he would take her despite his promises to Valentine and himself.

He lifted her head and spread her long silken tresses on the pillow. Then, before. he could give in to his throbbing need, he threw a sheet and two quilts over her and quickly left the room. He closed the door behind him and slumped against the wall like a winded fighter. Finally aware that his wound was causing him considerable pain, he opened his eyes and massaged the shoulder roughly.

"I think maybe a little pain is not a bad thing," Valentine stated unsympathetically. "It will give you something else to think about." She was standing in the doorway of his room looking at him with a measuring glance he found unfamiliar, uncomfortable, and unpleasant.

"You can relax your guard, you old alley cat," Brett snapped. "As you can see, I'm fully dressed and totally unsatisfied. I didn't know what to do about her night clothes so I put her to bed naked. I'll check on her later to see that she's still covered. I don't want her to catch cold." That sounded suspect, even to his ears.

Valentine continued to watch him with a calculating glance, but she evidently decided he meant what he said because she backed into his room, allowing him to enter.

"If you had stayed much longer, you might not have found it possible to leave," she said flatly. "I will stay in case you need *assistance*." Brett wasn't about to discuss his painfully throttled desire with Valentine or anyone else, so he changed the subject.

"Can you have somebody get Kate's things ready? We have to leave at daybreak. I'd like to leave some trunks here, too. Since I'm not going to Paris, I won't need so many clothes." He flashed the captivating smile that had melted so many female hearts. "There's no need for the wolf to dress in sheep's clothing in the desert. My only quarry is a warlike old man who won't care what I look like."

"Leave what you like. Kate, too, though I doubt she has anything to leave, poor girl. Now she is Madame Westbrook, you must buy her new things. She has nothing that is not *un disgrâce*."

"I'll see she's provided for," Brett promised stiffly.

"You go to bed. Valentine will check Kate," she said with a goading look as she moved to the door. "Tomorrow will be very busy, and I do not want you to have the bad dreams." She ducked the pillow he threw at her and skipped out the door.

Brett lay back on his bed, put his hands behind his head, and tried to relax. It was probably better he didn't see Kate again tonight. He felt calmer now, but the sight of her was certain to get him stirred up again. Just knowing she was naked under those covers was enough to set the fire raging in his veins again.

Forget tonight, he told himself. *It'll only make you more miserable. Tomorrow you'll be at sea with all the time in the world. Maybe we can start over.*

Somewhere in the distance Kate could hear a pounding like a pile-driver sinking timbers into the bowels of the earth. The concussions of sound came in a persistent rhythm, and the powerful, ringing blows hurt her head. She covered her ears and tried to run away, but her body was too heavy for her muscles to move. Her struggles only increased the ringing in her head, and she was forced to lie still to lessen the pain.

Gradually she became aware of a rocking motion, a slight but regular undulation that made her stomach feel uneasy. She tried to think why she should be rocking, but her mind was clogged with an enveloping mist. The more she tried to concentrate, the more everything moved beyond her grasp. And that awful pounding! Would it ever stop?

She opened her eyes, but the light coming from a small, round window stung her eyes like thousands of tiny sharp needles. That confused her even more. Why were the windows round? Why should her eyes hurt so? The spinning pinwheels and flashing lights gradually faded, and the objects around her came into a misty focus. She turned her head to one side, but everything more than a few feet away was lost in the haze. Kate struggled to sit up on one elbow and force her mind to concentrate in spite of the pain. She *had* to know where she was. Slowly the room came into focus, and a feeling of panic gripped her. She didn't recognize anything. Where was she? What was happening? What *had* happened to her?

She sat up abruptly and looked around for something familiar and reassuring, but a pain unlike anything she'd ever experienced seemed to split her head right down the middle and render her blind even though her eyes were still wide open. She fell back on her bed in agony, and after an exhausting struggle to keep from crying aloud in her misery, the throbbing subsided enough for her to open her eyes again.

The sheet had fallen off, and she realized with a jolt that she was completely naked. She yanked up the bedclothes to cover her bare breasts, shock and outrage momentarily overshadowing the pain in her head. She looked around once more and tried to remember where she was supposed to be. Why did this room seem alien and yet vaguely familiar? Surely she had never been here before. Bits of knowledge kept prodding her brain, trying to make themselves known, but the pounding in her head was driving away all memory. If it would just stop hurting for even a little while, maybe she could think. She lay back, closed her eyes, and tried to relax. Maybe, if she were absolutely still, the aching would lessen enough for her to remember how she got here.

After a while the pain did ease, and with its alleviation came a slow recollection of the events of the previous evening. Not everything at once, but enough to make her want to crawl into a corner and die.

The realization that she had married Brett came crashing in on her with awful force. In spite of all she had done, she had been forced to marry him against her will. This was undoubtedly their room on the ship that was taking him to Africa. That would explain the rocking motion and why she saw a man's coat over the chair. She felt some relief. At least she knew what was happening, but as the fact of her nakedness continued to burn its way into her consciousness, she lost any sense of relief and struggled to control her mounting anxiety. She remembered very little from last evening. Her last clear recollection was of drinking Brett's brandy, but she seemed to recall something about his forcing his way into her room.

She sat up and pounded her temples to jog her memory, but all she got was a terrible pain that crashed through her head and rendered her brain useless. She sank back on the pillows, and after a few minutes the pain subsided. She remembered screaming through a door that she would shoot him if he entered her room. Oh my God, she had opened the door and put the gun to his head! She could hear the shot in her mind, but no matter how much she cudgeled her brain, she couldn't remember what happened.

She couldn't face the thought of him being shot a second time by a member of the Vareyan family! Then she remembered his coat, it *must* be his coat, and some of her fears eased. They wouldn't be on the ship together if she had shot him, even if she had only wounded him.

Her thoughts kept returning to her nakedness. She didn't remember being put to bed or anything else until a few minutes ago. What had happened? Had he spent the night in her room? In her bed? She blushed. There was only one bed in her room at the inn and only one bed in this cabin. She didn't feel any different, but she felt sure *something* had happened. She couldn't imagine Brett making the least effort to control himself. Now that she was his wife there wasn't any reason to do so. She heard footsteps coming down the passageway outside the cabin door and quickly pulled the covers tightly over her rigid body.

"I'm glad to see you're awake." Brett greeted her cheerfully as he came in bearing a tray loaded with dishes. "I bet you have a king-size hangover." A wince of pain crossed Kate's face and Brett laughed. "I thought so. I can't imagine why a girl with no drinking experience would start with a whole bottle of brandy. You're lucky you can still see."

Kate relaxed slightly. "I've already been sufficiently punished for my folly. You needn't add your mite." She was *not* cheerful.

"I guess that was a little unfair," he said with a smile that Kate decided too closely resembled a smirk and set the tray down on the table beside her bed. "I thought you might need some breakfast. After last night, I was sure you would have a bear of a head." He put his hand under her chin and raised her face so he could look into her bloodshot eyes. "Poor girl, you really have shot the cat. I can see you're not used to spirits. I bet you've never had anything stronger than wine." Kate gave her head a tiny shake, but even that sent shock waves bouncing around the inside of her skull.

"Brandy is a hard way to begin," Brett said, not missing the grimace of pain. "Nothing is going to help much right now, but we've got to make a beginning somewhere, and food is a start."

Kate regarded the loaded tray with a skeptical eye. She didn't feel hungry, but she didn't think food could make her feel any worse. Brett brought a chair up next to the bed and sat down.

"I hope the maids got all your clothes packed before we left." There was a provocative smile in his eyes. "I would have asked Valentine to check, but I'm almost as familiar with a lady's wardrobe as she is." Kate blushed, and her grip on the bedclothes tightened. "You can let go of those sheets," he added with less warmth. "Not even I would attempt to make love to you while you're suffering from a hangover. Besides, there's plenty of time for that later."

Her stomach flipped over like a landed salmon, and her grasp on the covers tightened once more. She was thankful for his point of view but somehow didn't feel it stemmed from any consideration for her.

"The weather is perfect today," he said, changing the subject. "You should come up and have a look. I've never seen a more glorious day or a more magnificent view of the ocean.

Kate resisted the impulse to tell him that any view of the sea not seen from land would be unwelcome. She still remembered the rigors of her channel crossing, and the thought of spending several weeks at sea held no attraction for her. But she pushed those concerns aside. She needed all her energies to cope with

223

her throbbing head and to find out what had happened last night. She *had* to know, even though it probably didn't matter at this point.

"Thank you," she said, trying not to wince from the pain in her head, "but I couldn't possibly put anything in my mouth. My head feels like it's filled with huge spikes all pushing out against my skull. Every time I open my eyes I can hardly see for the shooting pains. Even that pair of pants over there is nearly lost in the blur."

Brett didn't misunderstand. He had planned to tease her a while, to let her think the worst, but her terrible misery aroused his sympathy. "Don't worry," he reassured her, "the pants belong to me, as do the coat, shoes, and everything else you see lying about. I'm not a tidy person, and I'm worse at sea. Usually Charles sees that I don't disgrace him, but my marriage has put the household arrangements momentarily out of order, and there's nobody to clean up behind me. Maybe you could take that on as one of your wifely duties. It would give you something to do."

Kate was suffering too acutely to reply, but she longed to hit him with something big and lethal. Why did she ever doubt he had taken advantage of her drunken stupor? It was just the kind of thing he would do. Look at him smiling at her, just like he loved her and was happy to have her for his wife. Cad! Bounder! She would love to scratch the smile off his face. That would teach him to look so unbearably handsome. Oh Lord, she sighed, it isn't fair. How could anyone so selfish look so devastatingly handsome? He was the answer to a woman's dream. But not hers. Her dream, yes, but not her answer.

"I know you're wondering what happened last night," Brett said abruptly. "You needn't pretend

otherwise. I can see it written all over your face."
Kate was sure even her toes blushed. "I didn't force
myself on you if that's what you're worried about. I
didn't even touch you. Fortunately for me, you
passed out just as you pointed that pistol at my
head. All you managed to shoot was Valentine's
wallpaper. I'm sure the Foreign Office is glad they
won't have to be told I've been shot a second time.
That kind of thing is hard on Lord Thunderburke's
indigestion."

"All the same, I was disappointed in your marks-
manship. I'd hoped you could hit something a little
more challenging than a wall. I think you ought to
apologize to Valentine," he went on as Kate grew
more and more embarrassed. "You ruined one of
her favorite patterns." He finally took pity on Kate's
chagrin. "I don't think she minded, though. She was
just glad to be able to put you to bed."

"But last night, here . . ." Kate managed to say
before her voice trailed off.

"You slept in the inn, not here. I never touched
you." Kate unconsciously relaxed her hold on the
bedclothes. "I would have had to do so over the
combined resistance of half the people in the inn.
You should be pleased to know Valentine guarded
you as jealously as she would her own daughter. She
hovered around like a pheasant hen with only one
chick. I wouldn't be surprised to find she slept in the
chair in your room, just in case I walked in my
sleep. And I suspect Charles slept with his door
open."

Kate couldn't think of anything to say, but her
eyes were misty. For the moment she didn't even feel
the throbbing in her head. The worst of her fears
had been removed, and relief flooded over her like
waves of the incoming tide.

"I brought you on board before the village woke

up. After all the trouble I had getting you undressed, I couldn't see putting your clothes back on and then having to put you to bed all over again, so I wrapped you up in the sheets and carried you over my shoulder." He gave a reckless laugh. "I hope no one saw you trailing bedsheets through the streets. The explanation would be beyond me, and poor Valentine's reputation would never recover.

"Now that ought to relieve your mind enough for you to eat . . . but drink this first." He handed her a glass with a dubious-looking liquid in it. "It's very nasty and you'll hate it, but it'll make you feel better." He held her chin and poured the liquid down her throat before she could protest. She choked and swallowed and choked again, but she got most of it down.

"I had to do that," he apologized. "If you had tasted it first, you would never have been able to swallow it." He poured out some coffee. "I know you'd prefer tea, but it wouldn't do you as much good. You can have some at lunch if you still want it. Eat up, and don't tell me you couldn't possibly swallow a bite," he said, seeing her prepare to make that very protest. "I'm an expert on getting over a hangover, and what I don't know, Charles does. After breakfast you can get dressed and we'll figure out what to do with the rest of the day. Now finish up every bite. If you offend the chef, there may not be any lunch or dinner for any of us."

"That's blackmail," Kate managed to say with a trace of a smile.

"Maybe, but it got a more favorable reaction than I did," he said unhappily, and got up. "I'm going to leave you alone now, but I'll be back before long. Charles is across the hall and the captain is in the next cabin, so there'll be someone to hear you if you should need anything before then." He looked at her, and a softer light came into his eyes. "I'm sorry I struck you. I tried to stop myself, but I couldn't."

"It wasn't all your fault," Kate said, somehow feeling relieved. "I said some rather awful things."

"We both made mistakes. Suppose we start over again. Do you think we can?" There was a tenor of anxiety in his voice that Kate couldn't miss. Could Valentine be right? Was it possible that he really did like her after all?

"We can try."

"Good. Now you just relax and don't worry about anything. Everything is going to be all right." He patted her hand reassuringly then left.

Kate collapsed on her pillows. She hardly knew what to make of Brett's apology. It must have been the first time in his life he'd apologized for anything, but she was certain he was sincere. In fact, he seemed altogether different this morning, and she was sure the brandy had nothing to do with this impression. There was a different *feeling* about the things he said and did. She couldn't forgive him for hitting her, but she had had no right to cast slurs on his family name. No man could be expected to tolerate that. Oh well, he had apologized, so maybe she should call it even and try to forget everything.

Though her mind was relieved on another score as well, she was greatly puzzled by Brett's restraint. Why hadn't he made love to her? She was mystified as to why he was so cheerful about everything. He didn't even seem to mind that Charles and Valentine seemed prepared to defend her. Kate wasn't sure she believed his reaction: he could just be trying to get her off her guard.

No, that was unfair. He was not above taking shameless advantage of her, but she had never known him to tell less than the absolute truth. And why was he so friendly? Not even when he was

227

teaching her to use the pistol had he been so genuinely relaxed and cheerful. He had never shown so much thought for her comfort, even to the point of forcing her to drink that awful medicine. He was right about one thing, though. If she had tasted it first, she would never have swallowed it. The memory of it still made her want to vomit.

Kate abandoned her thoughts. She could find no satisfactory answers and her head ached too much for futile pursuits. If she were truly on a ship bound for Africa, she would have plenty of time to look for answers to all her questions and solutions to all her problems. The smell of coffee and bacon was making it difficult to keep her mind on anything but food. Maybe that nasty potion really did work.

She sipped her coffee. It burned her lips, but it distracted her mind from the pain in her head. She continued to drink and let the scalding liquid scorch her lips and tongue while it relieved her parched throat. For the time being her mind was relieved of worry and she was beginning to take an interest in her situation. She looked around the cabin. It was spacious and much larger than the one she had occupied on the Channel crossing. Maybe this was a larger boat that wouldn't rock so much. She wasn't sure she could stand being seasick for several weeks. With everything else in her life going wrong, it might be better to jump in the ocean and drown.

Chapter 16

By the time Kate had finished her coffee, her outlook was more optimistic and her breakfast looked more appetizing. Maybe it was the sea air, it certainly *wasn't* the brandy, but she was hungry. She ate with a robust appetite, and when Brett returned nearly an hour later, there wasn't a crumb left on her plate.

She had also managed to find her clothes and get dressed. She would have gone without breakfast for the rest of her life rather than face him again nude under the bedclothes. Just knowing he had undressed her and carried her through the streets wrapped in nothing more than a bedsheet caused her to flush with mortification, but she was honest enough to admit she hadn't given him much choice. He probably could have found some other way if he'd tried, but knowing him, he had probably enjoyed it!

After the fuss he made over carrying her valise a few yards, she was surprised he hadn't dumped her on a vegetable cart and ordered Charles or Mark to carry her. Well, maybe not Mark. The poor boy would have walked the whole way with his eyes closed. Kate giggled just as Brett entered the cabin.

"I'm glad to see your spirits have improved. I knew you'd feel better once you got that drink in you. Now you won't mind facing a heaving deck and rolling seas."

Kate turned green. "I'd rather not," she said weakly.

"I couldn't resist," Brett said with another of his devastating smiles; his coal-black eyes looked more human than Kate could ever remember. "The captain says he's never seen the ocean so calm, so come up and enjoy it. Good weather never lasts long in the Atlantic." He took a shawl from one of the drawers of a large wardrobe and held it up for her. "I started to unpack for you," he said by way of explanation, "but decided you might prefer to put your own things away."

Kate couldn't think of a single word to say, and covered her confusion by accepting his help in placing the shawl over her shoulders. She gave it a final tug and moved out into the passageway. It was long and narrow with many doors opening from it, and as Kate climbed the narrow steps toward the welcoming sunlight, she wondered if every man on the ship slept within hearing distance of all that happened in her cabin.

Brett had not exaggerated. It was a magnificent day. The sky was a perfect robin's-egg blue from horizon to horizon with only a few wispy clouds to break the monotony of its endless expanse. They seemed immobile, blown into place by an unseen force but as carefully arranged as the beauty patches of a seventeenth-century courtesan. The sun's bright light caused her eyes to smart, but its penetrating warmth was a welcome counter to the chill in the air. A light breeze blew Kate's hair back from her face, and she wrapped the shawl more tightly around her shoulders as she faced into the wind, breathing deeply of the clean, invigorating sea air.

The water was a clear greenish-blue, and Kate watched fascinated as fish swam just below the surface. The ship seemed to be barely moving, but the white wake belied her speed. The huge, billowing sails were full, and she ran before the wind as easily and naturally as the great sea birds above floated on the ocean's updrafts. A dolphin broke the surface, playfully chasing a fish it didn't feel hungry enough to catch.

This was so different from her first experience when all she remembered was a black storm-tossed night filled with the spectre of Brett's wound and her illness; it was as though she was looking at the sea for the very first time. Brett was silent; he knew the Atlantic was showing her a false face, but there would be plenty of time later to warn her of storms which could toss a ship about like dry leaves in an autumn wind. For the time being, it was quite enough that she was enjoying herself.

He guided her around the deck pointing out things he thought she might find interesting, but Kate had no desire to learn anything about the workings of the ship or the tasks of its crew. She also disliked being near the rail and refused to get any closer than necessary. "I can enjoy the morning just as much from a chair as I can hanging over the edge," she retorted when he teased her about her fear.

Returning to the widest part of the deck, Kate settled back in a canvas chair and closed her eyes. The sea air was still cool, but the penetrating heat of the sun plus a heavy blanket provided by one of the sailors made it nearly too warm, and Kate began to feel almost languorous.

"It's still too cool to be really comfortable," Brett chatted companionably, "but it will get warmer as we head farther south. It can get quite hot in the Mediterranean in the summer, but we'll be there in May, before it gets too miserable."

A languid "hmm" was Kate's only comment. She felt so relaxed that she had almost forgotten her hangover. Her head still hurt when she tried to think, but it was much better than an hour earlier, and she gave herself over to the full enjoyment of the sun, the sea, the salt air, and the cool breezes.

The day passed pleasantly. After a light lunch, she was back on deck for a long nap, but when the sun began to sink into the far horizon, the deepening chill in the air woke her. For a moment no sound came to her ears and she could imagine she was the only person on earth, the sole witness to this magnificent panorama.

Dinner was a leisurely affair served in the captain's cabin. Even though it was their first day out of port, Kate could hardly believe the number and quality of the dishes spread before her.

"Where did you find a chef who can cook like this?" she asked in wonder.

The captain managed to stop staring at her long enough to reply somewhat incoherently, "Foreign office."

"This was Lord Thunderburke's personal touch," Brett explained. "Ill-prepared food gives him the melancholia, and he's certain everyone else suffers from the same annoyance."

Kate rose to her feet when the brandy was put on the table. The ship's officers begged her to remain, but Brett did not add his entreaty to theirs, so she declined their invitation with becoming grace and withdrew to her cabin.

The sound of the door closing behind her brought Kate face-to-face with what the evening held for her. All day long she had refused to think about it, but she was Brett's wife and she knew there was no way to avoid sharing her bed with him; not one soul would come to her aid now and

232

certainly not those officers with their bold and heated eyes.

She had avoided thinking of her forced marriage—the pain in her head wouldn't allow it and she felt too tired to tackle such a seemingly insurmountable problem—but she could no longer avoid the full significance of her spoken vows and she felt the familiar stirring of anger. Once again Brett had forced her to do something against her will, and once again she found herself helpless against him. Angrily she renewed her promise to find a way out of this fraudulent marriage the minute she got back to England. She was certain that once her uncle knew the circumstances, he would help her divorce Brett, or end the marriage in some less scandalous manner, but until then she had no choice. Like it or not, she must bow to the inevitable and accept her position as Brett's bride.

His *bride!* What she felt now was a mockery of everything a bride should feel for her husband. She didn't fear him or find his embraces distasteful, but she did not welcome his return to the cabin. Knowing what was before her, it was impossible for Kate to shut out memories of that night at the inn, but neither could she deny that she experienced a shiver of pleasurable anticipation. Once more she flushed with shame at the recollection of how her body's response to Brett had overruled all objections from her mind; she would never be able to erase from her memory the unexpected sensations that had enslaved her, body and soul, and made her, for a few minutes at least, Brett's willing and enthusiastic partner. Neither could she deny the feeling of pleasure and satisfaction that she had experienced before the enormity of what they had done banished all feeling except horror and rage. But most important of all, she could not forgive him for robbing her of what only she had the right to bestow.

She made up her mind that regardless of what she might have to deny herself, Brett would find no welcome in her arms; the laws of God and man might say that she owed him the duty of obedience, but he would get no more. *Obedience!* She had no intention of yielding anything more than her body to him, either now or in the future. She removed her gown and leisurely began to prepare for bed; she expected Brett to sit with the captain over their brandy for some time yet. The mere thought of brandy caused her to shudder.

She put on her nightgown and sat down to brush her hair, but she had not completed more than half a dozen strokes when Brett entered quietly. Surprised and somewhat fearful, her hand froze halfway down the length of her hair, then she quickly resumed her brushing in hopes Brett hadn't noticed her hesitation. She heard a click as he turned the key in the lock and her heart nearly stopped beating. Now there was no hope of escape. *You're a fool,* she told herself. *There never was.*

Brett came to stand behind her; without a word he took the brush from her hands and began to stroke her hair expertly. She could tell he had done this before. *He's probably brushed more hair than half the ladies' maids in London,* Kate thought to herself. There's no telling *what* this man has done.

Kate started to tie up her hair, but Brett pulled it loose again. "I don't want it in a knot. I want to be able to run my fingers through it," he said softly. For one moment she thought wildly of escape, of throwing herself on the captain's mercy or leaping into the sea, but she knew she was being foolish; she couldn't even get out of the cabin. She trembled inside. She could think of nothing to do, so she got up and walked over to the bed. "Which

234

side do you prefer?"

"It doesn't matter tonight," he said with a smile that made her eyes widen in alarm. She quickly threw off her robe, kicked off her slippers, and slid between the sheets. She lay rigid but less fearful than she had anticipated. She wasn't looking forward to the evening, but she was pleased to know she was no longer frightened.

Brett blew out all the lights except for the small lamp next to the bed, then in the soft glow of that single light he proceeded to undress, *completely.* He did so very slowly, methodically removing each piece of clothing and hanging or folding it up. Kate knew he was doing this intentionally to madden her, but she was fascinated nevertheless. She realized much to her surprise she had standards and expectations, and this man was not only meeting every one of them, he was exceeding them. She had already admitted he was the most handsome man she had ever seen. Even with his nearly perpetual frown, he was devastatingly good-looking. Any girl would think so. From the thick black hair to the penetrating black eyes set under equally thick black brows, from the straight nose to the full, generous lips, from the prominent line of the jaw to the jutting chin, his face was one to set a maiden's heart fluttering and to turn her dreams into a nightmare of hopeless longing.

But as he bent, twisted, and turned to complete his undressing, Kate became aware of his powerful physique, the heavily muscled shoulders, and the broad chest tapering quickly to a flat abdomen ribbed with muscle. His chest was covered with a thick short mat of curling black hair, but it did virtually nothing to hide the muscling of his torso.

Kate shivered and burrowed a little deeper into the covers; surely such a powerful body would crush her. Then he removed his pants and stood completely naked before her. She blushed from her toes to the top of her head, but she couldn't turn her head. His long, powerful legs rose straight and true to meet the rest of his body, but at that juncture, and thrusting out from a tangled mass of curly black hair, was his fully aroused manhood, frightfully enormous to Kate's untutored eyes. She knew a moment of terror.

Brett slid between the sheets and drew Kate to him. She was stiff and reluctant, but he was gentle, and under his easy persuasion, she began to relax. He let his fingers play over her face while his eyes examined every feature in detail. He drank in her beauty like cool spring water, sure he would never be able to satisfy his thirst. He kissed her eyes, nose, and lips, easily at first and then with growing passion. Kate continued to lie still under his caresses, but he showed no sign that it bothered him. The heat of his own passion made him less and less aware of her lack of response. He undid the buttons of her nightgown and fondled the column of her throat. Then his hands slowly sank until they met the nippled mound of her breasts. He cupped them in his hands and his lips played across her cheeks and down her throat until they, too, found her breasts. Tenderly he kissed each one and fondled it lovingly. Then ever so carefully he took one of the stiffening ruby nipples into his mouth and made love to it with his lips. Unable to remain still any longer under this merciless assault, Kate squirmed under him. When he attacked the second nipple and let his audacious hand play down her side and across her abdomen, all pretense of remaining coolly uninvolved fled.

Kate drew in her breath with a gasp, but Brett caused her further dismay by sliding the nightgown

236

slowly off her shoulders and under the whole length of her body until he dropped it to the floor. She was naked against him and could feel the burning heat of his body begin to flow into her own. His caressing lips and exploring hands were systematically working her into a frenzy. She had been determined to resist any advance, but Brett was moving deliberately, not rushing, and her own passion, stifled at first by fear and anger, began to free itself from all restrictions, and she could feel her body quiver with excitement.

Brett's lips and hands continued to roam over her body, caressing, tenderly kneading, stimulating her whole being. A low moan escaped her, and Brett's mouth immediately imprisoned hers in a searing kiss, his tongue raking her mouth and drawing out its sweetness in greedy kisses. Her lips felt bruised and sore, but she didn't shrink from him. One hand began its descent to her thighs and the entrance to her temple; shamelessly it brushed through the soft barrier and boldly entered where it had no right. Kate nearly sat straight up in bed, her body a welter of wildly confused sensations, her emotions a tangle of unresolved longing. All thought was suspended and her whole being was quickly infused with a whirling melee of desire that was increasingly impossible to resist.

Kate could feel the heat of Brett's engorged manhood pressing against her thigh as his hand continued to probe and rub and caress, drawing moan after pulsating moan from her throat. Before she knew what she was doing, she found herself beginning to move against him, fighting his command of her but encouraging his ultimate domination.

Brett entered her abruptly and drove deeper with each rapid thrust until Kate felt she would explode. She was moving with him now, slowly increasing the strength of her response until her body was flinging itself to meet his, demanding his strength, urging him to conquer and fulfill her.

Kate could feel the maelstrom spinning with ever-increasing speed until she felt as if every part of her body was being assaulted and bruised by its force. She tried to cry out, but Brett's mouth covered hers and her breaths were nearly strangled sobs as the tempo of her response rose to frantic heights.

Just when she thought she could stand no more, Brett gave an agonized moan and she felt his seed stream into her body. Simultaneously she felt her own body gather itself and pitch forward into an ecstasy of pleasure. She clung to Brett like a vine, striving to drain every ounce of loving from his body, then fell back exhausted.

They lay still for many minutes; the only sounds which came to Kate's ears were the creaking of the masts and their labored breathing. She found it difficult to realize that once again she had not only responded to Brett's advances but had enjoyed them. This time, however, she felt no shame or anger, only unbelieving wonder. Everything had happened so quickly that night in the inn, but tonight he had slowly and meticulously made love to every part of her body. Her hand brushed her mouth and she felt the soreness of her lips,. If this was what making love with Brett was really like, she'd spend all her time behind closed doors waiting for the bruises to go away just so he could make some more.

Her movement stirred Brett and his hands began to caress her body again, more gently this time. Kate couldn't believe he had the energy to begin again, but she soon discovered her mistake. He brought her back to a peak of excitement and expectation before he entered her again, but this time he moved more slowly and steadily, working to sense her pleasure and to build it to greater heights than ever. His hands gently caressed her body, methodically coaxing her to respond. His tongue snaked across her skin kindling little trails of fire and increasing her reaction tenfold. He continued to work within her, varying his rhythm and strokes until she felt waves of pleasure begin to wash over her, one after another, growing in strength and intensity. She struggled against him, demanding more, but he continued to move with maddening steadiness, stoking her fires until she felt scorched. Her body became a red-hot ball of flame and she thought she must faint. Only then did he change his rhythm, suddenly stroking sharply and quickly, and driving within her.

It was like an electric shock, and she nearly cried out from the intensity of her pleasure. He stifled her protest with a kiss and drove her relentlessly on. All at once she was gasping, fighting for breath, her entire body erupting with the force of her exploding sensations. Again she tried to cry out, and again he covered her mouth with his; with two final knifing thrusts, he drove her to an ecstasy of release and she experienced the inexpressible pleasure of final consummation. She fell away with a sigh.

He took her once more that night, against her protests, but to her ultimate delight and left her sore, bruised, and wondering if she would ever rise from the bed again. She felt like a hollow shell, with all the inner flesh burned away and just the dried husk remaining. She smiled, turned over, and fell into a deep sleep.

* * *

Kate knew it was late when she awoke because the sun was already high in the sky. She lay still, trying to remember as much of last night as she could. Once again she found it hard to accept her own response to Brett. In the privacy of her own mind she could confess she had enjoyed it, even reveled in it, but she would die rather than admit that to Brett. She had been half asleep at the Cock-in-the-Cradle and had never been sure of what she remembered, but she had been wide-awake last night and she could recall every passion-filled minute in detail. She could only wonder at herself, for she had never suspected the presence of such feelings within herself.

Kate raised her arms over her head to indulge in an expansive stretch. She had expected to enjoy it as she always did on cool mornings when she had slept well, but today it made her acutely aware of sore muscles and bruised flesh, and she frowned.

She got out of bed, bolted the door, and walked over to the long mirror on the back of the ward-robe door. She examined her face, but she could see no changes, no lines, no sign even of the bruised lips. She slipped her gown over her shoulders and dropped it to the floor. Carefully she studied herself in the morning light, turning first to one side and then to the other, minutely searching for something to show what she had experienced in Brett's arms.

The time of their first lovemaking, she had felt besmirched and dishonored, but now she felt transformed, like a butterfly which had emerged from her cocoon into the brilliant sunshine, and it was a little disappointing to find she didn't look any different. Rocking her body from side to side, she hugged herself in a spasm of delight. Now she was a woman and knew what it was to take a woman's pleasures. She had passed one of life's milestones and there was no going back.

Then she remembered that even though Brett was her husband, he had been forced on her as much by circumstances as by his own lusts, and she intended to leave him as soon as she could. She grew angry. That's not how it should have been, and it came close to destroying all her pleasure.

She shoved her thoughts aside and began to dress. She had enjoyed being on deck so much yesterday that she wanted to go up again. Then she remembered the cabins of the crew members that lined the passageway and she stopped in her tracks. Everyone must have known it was her wedding night, and she couldn't bear to be stared at with knowing smiles by every man she passed. It was too terrible to even contemplate. It might be better if she waited for Brett. Their curiosity couldn't last forever.

She went about her dressing without realizing she was spending a longer time than usual over her choices. She was displeased with everything in her closet; her clothes were drab and ugly. She didn't own a single dress that didn't make her look like a poor relation. As soon as they stopped at one of the coastal towns in France or Spain, or *someplace* civilized, she had to get some new clothes. If she was going to be forced to masquerade as Brett's wife, she refused to go about looking like a peasant girl. She threw the gown in her hands to the floor, but on further consideration picked it up again because she decided it was the least likely of all her garments to make her an object of ridicule. She finished dressing and studied herself critically in the mirror. The reflection wasn't what she would have liked, but she couldn't do any better now, so with a resigned shrug she sat down to wait for

Brett.

It didn't take her long to become extremely impatient. She was bored and there was nothing to do. In her haste to leave Ryehill, she had never considered the need for something to occupy her time. Kate had never liked needlework, but she would gladly have hemmed a dozen handkerchiefs just to fill the time.

The empty minutes continued to pile up. She searched the room for something to occupy her mind, but it had been swept clean before she and Brett boarded the ship.

She sat down again and tried to think of what to do about her future, a future that didn't include Brett, but the idea depressed her and she couldn't concentrate. She tried to decide what she would do or say the next time she was alone with him, but the memory of last night unsettled her so much she couldn't think at all. It probably wouldn't make any difference anyway. Brett had a way of expecting things to go the way he wanted them to, and from her limited experience, they usually did, despite any obstacle in his path. She sighed deeply once more and prepared to wait.

After one of the longest and most tedious hours she had ever endured, she heard a knock at the door and ran to throw it open. Only last-minute caution kept her from rushing out into the passageway to welcome Brett with open arms. "Who is it?" she called out, leaning her ear against the door.

"It's Charles, Mrs. Westbrook." Kate sighed with relief and unlocked the door. "Mr. Westbrook sent me to ask if you would like to eat lunch on deck. The weather's holding, and the sun is quite warm."

Kate would have eaten her lunch in the crow's nest just to get out of the room. She was sure she could endure the curious stares with Brett's support, but after a morning of being cooped up in the cabin, it was worth being stared at by any number of people just to be able to escape further confinement.

You're acting like a silly fool, she scolded herself. *You're a married woman traveling with her husband, and you've done absolutely nothing that all married women don't do. As a matter of fact, everybody expects you to sleep with Brett. They'd really stare if you didn't, so stop jumping at shadows and get up on deck and try to act like a sensible, normal married lady.* But even though she recognized the practical nature of that stern advice, she still had a nagging feeling she would have preferred to stay hidden forever.

Chapter 17

A small table already stood next to her deck chair. Brett had finished his lunch, but he gave orders that Kate should be served at once. He seemed completely at ease with her—it was as though last night never happened—but she was too self-conscious, too acutely aware of their recent intimacy, to meet his eyes; she busied herself getting settled into her chair and then lay back with her hands over her eyes pretending the sun was too strong for her to open them.

Brett filled the time with small talk, asking about her comfort and if there was anything he could do to make her trip more enjoyable. Kate remembered her hellish hours of boredom and forgot to be embarrassed.

"Yes, there *is* something you can do," she said, sitting up and facing Brett squarely. "I need something to do with my time. I spent an hour ransacking every crevice in that cabin trying to find a book or a game, *anything* to do. It nearly drove me crazy. There's not even a needle to mend a piece of torn lace."

"Do you *want* to mend torn lace?" Brett asked, nonplussed.

"Of course not, but I can't sit around for hours with nothing to do except doze in the sun. Besides, there's nobody to do it for me."

"I never thought about that," Brett conceded. He was never bored at sea.

"Neither did I," she admitted. "I didn't bring

anything from home, and no one packed the books I borrowed from Valentine. I'll go crazy if I don't find something to do. I might even be reduced to scrubbing the floors to keep my sanity."

"You'll do nothing of the sort," Brett snapped, quite unamused. "I'll speak to the captain. He's bound to have one or two books you can borrow, but I wouldn't expect too much. Everyone's busy when they're at sea, and they don't have much time for amusements. I'm sure we'll be stopping several times before we reach Gibraltar. We can look for something then."

Her eyes lighted up. "Can we go shopping?" she asked eagerly. "I need clothes, dresses, hats, just about everything you can think of."

"I'm afraid you won't find much you'll want to buy. The ports are small and not likely to have much that will interest you, but when we come back, I promise to mount a raid on the Paris dress shops they'll be talking about for years to come." In an effort to ease her disappointment, he added, "And we won't patronize any but the most expensive shops."

But Kate wasn't going to be talked down to. "I never imagined you wouldn't," she said with an impish grin. "You couldn't possibly let your wife be seen in the rags I have with me. Certainly not after the way you dress your mistresses." She almost laughed at his startled, disapproving frown. "You probably haven't noticed, but I don't have a single dress a parlor maid wouldn't be ashamed to wear. You should have heard some of the things Valentine had to say about them."

"You'll have closets full of gowns even Valentine will envy," Brett said, regaining his good humor. "And I'm going to give you a very special present for having to wait so long."

Kate's eyes grew huge and she gazed at him in surprise. "A present? You're going to give me a present?" Suddenly they filled with tears that ran down her cheeks. She tried to brush them away before Brett could see them, but she was too late.

"What's wrong?" he asked, puzzled.

"It's nothing," she said, turning her head away. But he took her chin in his hand and lifted her face until he could look into her eyes.

"Tell me the truth. Why did you cry?"

"I don't know why," she said, half angry at him for pressing for an explanation. "It's so stupid." She gave a loud, defiant sniff. "I haven't had a present in so long, I guess it was just too much of a surprise. I used to get them when I was little, but Mother always kept the nice things for herself. After she died, I didn't get anything at all. Martin never gave anyone presents."

Being an only child and raised in a household that centered entirely on himself, Brett had not been brought up to give much thought to the desires or happiness of others, but he had since learned enough about women to realize this was a nearly inhuman way to treat a young girl.

"Everyone should get lots of presents. When we get back to London and announce our marriage, I'm sure we'll get more than you ever thought possible. They'll keep coming for weeks until the house is full of them. You'll probably be so tired of writing notes you'll never want to see silver wrapping paper again."

"It can't possibly be that bad," she laughed with a watery chuckle.

"Worse! But you can always make Charles do the dirty work. He excels at keeping track of things."

"You know, you really are a terrible man."

"Maybe, but not so bad I'd make you wait until we get back to London for your present. As soon as we dock, we're going to turn the town inside out for something you'd like. Even a fishing village ought to have at least one decent shop."

Kate was delighted with the prospect of going shopping, but it made her uncomfortable to have him be so generous and thoughtful. He didn't know she wasn't going to go on being his wife after they reached England—she found it hard to remember it herself when he acted like this—but she wouldn't think of that yet. She knew she was being a coward, but the weather was divinely beautiful, she was hungry for her lunch, and Brett was striving to be a charming companion. For the moment at least, she was at peace. It couldn't last, it seemed nothing good ever did, but she wanted it to stay like this as long as possible.

The weeks that followed went quickly for Kate. The weather stayed clear and unseasonably warm, and she spent much of her time on deck enjoying the sun with Brett. He continued to demonstrate an interest in talking to her, amusing her, and discovering what pleased her. She began to look forward to these talks, and her feelings of anger toward him gradually disappeared. She started to think of him as a cheerful and relaxing force and began to look forward to being with him. She discovered he had a sense of humor and didn't mind being teased as long as she was careful. He refused to talk about himself or his family, but he seemed to take pleasure in satisfying her curiosity on many different subjects and would take great pains to be sure she understood his explanations.

In spite of her attempts to keep her feelings

under control, she felt her love for him growing day by day until it filled her with a perpetual warmth. She wondered that every man on the ship didn't take one look at her shining eyes and know she was more in love than ever. It was all she could do to contain it, to not break down and talk to Charles or Mark to relieve the pressure of keeping such a secret to herself. She would have given anything she owned for one hour with Valentine and a chance to say all the number of things bursting to be said.

She continued to keep her own counsel and to respond to Brett as normally as was possible for one in a state as near to heavenly bliss as a mere mortal could achieve, yet every day it became harder to hold to her resolution to leave Brett when they reached London. Her quandary grew deeper and deeper, but she cast it in the corner with all the other things she didn't want to think about just now. Her return was a long way off. Surely *something* would happen that might change things before then.

On cool, windy days she had access to the captain's books and quite a few games and puzzles. At first, she didn't know what to do with the last two, but Brett took her education in hand and soon she was fairly good at chess, quite capable of playing a decent hand of cards, and had waded through two books on ships and sailing. Brett also continued her training with the pistol, sword, and knife. One day she amused and cheered the sailors by putting a ball through the center of a playing card.

She didn't feel particularly comfortable with a knife, but she preferred throwing it to stabbing the target directly. No matter what they fixed up for a mark, it always made her think of human flesh, and that gave her a creepy feeling all over.

"Human flesh is what you're supposed to aim at," Brett said, impatient with her hesitation. "You're defending yourself against attack, remember? If you get squeamish over a little blood, you might as well give up altogether." But Kate continued to work on her toss and gradually improved her skill to the point the sailors began to take bets among themselves as to how close she could come to the target.

But none of them ever considered speaking to her unless it was necessary, or behaving with anything but the greatest respect in her presence. Brett kept a vigilant eye on the crew. One look at those black eyes and they knew he would kill anyone who dared to so much as lay a finger on his wife. They didn't need any hints from Charles or tales told by the captain to convince them of his ability to defend Kate's honor. They had watched him, too, as he showed her how to handle her weapons, and no one overlooked the fact that he *never* missed the center of his target with either pistol or knife. There was no reason to doubt his equal skill with a sword or cutlass.

Practice with swords was confined to their cabin. "It's too windy on deck, and the salt spray can cause you to lose your footing," Brett had told her, but the real reason was Kate had to gather her skirts tightly about her so they wouldn't get in the way of her movements. This provided a much-too-clear outline of her body for the crew's scrutiny, and Brett wouldn't allow that. Recently he had taken to having her wear pants. At first he had given her a pair of his own to wear, but they were much too long and too large. "You look like a kangaroo in its mother's pouch," he howled with laughter the first time he bullied her into putting them on.

Kate threw the pants at him. "Since you forced me to wear these indecent things," she scolded, "it's not fair to laugh at me." But that only caused him to laugh harder. "I hope you get a stomach-ache," she said spitefully.

The next day he handed her a pair of Mark's trousers, which fit her much better. She still felt like a shameless hussy whenever she put them on, but at least she didn't stumble over the rolled-up legs or have great bunches of material lumped at her waist. She took off her shoes and skipped around the cabin brandishing her sword at everything in her path, reveling in a freedom unknown to girls of her class. Her rearing had always been unconventional, but this latitude was now accompanied by the personal attention of a man and an active interest in her as an individual. It was a new and wonderful experience. She didn't know how to account for it, but she hoped it wouldn't end.

And why shouldn't she take advantage of it, she asked herself? Once they returned to England, it would all come to an end. She knew she would never find anything like it again. So she banished all caution and refused to look back, determined to extract every ounce of pleasure she could.

There was no need for them to experience the privation of ocean-going vessels that had to purchase everything they needed months ahead, and the ship put into port regularly to replenish its stores of food and water. No one was at war with England, and all the French, Spanish, and Portuguese ports were open to them. They never stayed for more than a few hours, but that was long enough for Kate to walk almost every street, staring in windows and peering into the recesses of shops for anything she might be able to use. She bought large numbers of French and Spanish books even though she could barely read the latter language. She had become an accomplished seamstress during the years she lived with Martin, and she purchased some exquisite embroidery as well as occasional laces, silks, and muslins.

After each stop she would retire to her cabin with her purchases and cover the floor with patterns and material. She enlisted the help of Mark and Charles, even Brett on occasion, begging and cajoling them until they agreed. She would cut, pin, and sew for hours on end until she emerged with a simple gown of fine craftsmanship. In this way she gradually built a wardrobe of suitable dresses trimmed with embroidered lace, velvet ribbon, and, once, even a small piece of fur. They were extremely flattering to her slim figure, and she received some nice compliments from Brett and the captain.

Though she still got angry whenever she remembered how she was forced to marry Brett, it had become important that he admire her. She didn't like to admit she now dressed to please him, but she never failed to look for the glint of appreciation in his eyes. Though she might deny it—indeed, she invariably did when he made her angry—she looked forward more eagerly each day to the nights spent in his arms. But it was not enough to know she pleased him in bed. She had come to look for, to expect, to *depend* on the look of appreciation in his eyes whenever she appeared on deck or at dinner. In pulling him away from whatever was occupying his mind at the moment, she felt she was increasing her hold over him; only belatedly did she realize she was increasing her dependence on him at the same time.

You're a giddy fool, she told herself severely. You swore that no man would ever own you, yet now you run about doing anything you can to make him smile at you. He doesn't have to *force* you to submit; you can't wait to do it yourself. But she never listened to herself any more. She knew her behavior would only intensify the heartbreak to come, but since it was going to come no matter what, she was determined to take every pleasure she could from the present.

One afternoon Kate lay dozing in the hot sun. Her eyes were half open, and through the glare she absently watched a sailor as he moved noiselessly along the deck. He was always looking out to the sea and she found his slow steady movement back and forth almost hypnotic. Lazily she followed the line of his gaze, but they had met very few ships of any kind on this trip, and she wasn't surprised when she saw nothing but sky and water. He called out something she didn't understand to a man in the crow's nest, and he called to someone on the other side of the ship, but his answer was lost in the breeze.

Kate opened her eyes and tried to rouse her dull brain. What were these men doing? At the beginning of the voyage she had been able to enjoy the deck in comparative privacy, but for the last several days, two men who did none of the usual work had been stationed on opposite sides of the ship. They appeared to spend all their time looking out to sea, occasionally using a telescope, but most often talking to the sailor in the crow's nest.

An uneasy question grew in her mind and nagged at her so insistently it destroyed her contentment. Finally she abandoned her chair and went in search of Brett.

"I'm sure it's just part of the routine," Brett answered, reluctant to admit there was anything unusual going on. "Maybe the captain is looking for a ship headed back to England. Whatever the reason, I'm sure it's nothing for you to worry about."

"Stop talking to me like I'm simple-minded," Kate replied irritably. "Those men haven't been there before—I know because I've been on deck every day—and they're not watching for an English ship. Whatever it is they're looking for, they mean to see it before it sees us. They're using telescopes." Brett realized Kate's suspicions had been thoroughly aroused and she would only become more upset if she weren't told.

"We're approaching Africa and some unfriendly waters," he explained. "The whole coast is under the nominal rule of the Turkish sultan, but in actuality it's controlled by the rulers of four countries. Below that, they break up according to tribes and ancient loyalties to carry on their ancient trades, one of which is piracy."

Kate's hands flew to her mouth. "Pirates!" she repeated in a horrified whisper. "But they won't attack us, will they, not a ship of the English government?" Her mind was filled with the gruesome tales she had heard of the torture and rapine practiced by pirates of the East.

"The captain says not. We're a large ship carrying no valuable cargo, so we have nothing to tempt them, but it's always best to take nothing for granted. We aren't armed for combat, and we have only two small guns for defense."

"But what about the Navy? You told me the British Navy patroled the Atlantic and the Mediterranean. Surely they wouldn't attack with them close by."

"The Navy does what it can," Brett assured her, "but they can't be everywhere, and some ships do get captured. But try not to let yourself worry. There is almost no chance they would be interested in us. We're too big to be a likely target. Most pirate ships are small, sorry little boats that have no size or guns. They depend on surprise, slipping up on their victims unawares and boarding them before they can run away or mount a defense. But our captain is alert. There'll be at least one guard on duty around the clock until we reach Algiers."

Kate's fears were not put to rest by Brett's glib reassurances. She suspected him of minimizing the danger to keep her from worrying, and from that moment her pleasure in the voyage was almost nonexistent. Still, when several days went by and no strange ships were sighted, Kate reluctantly admitted Brett must have been right, and she made up her mind to do what he said, to stop worrying and concentrate on enjoying the marvelous weather.

But that same afternoon, while she was practicing with her knife on the deck, a shout from the port guard brought the captain and Brett running to his position. Kate could see nothing at first, but finally she made out a tiny pinpoint on the horizon. She couldn't believe that anyone could tell what kind of ship it was, much less whether it flew a friendly flag or not, but the captain and Brett seemed to have no doubt.

"Get below deck," Brett ordered her abruptly after only a brief look. "And stay there until I send someone to tell you it's safe to come up again."

Kate went meekly because she realized there was little else she could do. If there was trouble, her presence on deck would just endanger others. Her porthole window was on the same side as the sighted vessel and she sat with her nose glued to the pane trying to see what a pirate ship actually looked like. As it grew closer, she strained her eyes to discover anything that would tell her if it was a friendly or dangerous ship. She was soon able to see the flag, but as she was unfamiliar with the flags of other countries, it didn't help her at all. She could tell that it had one gun, but it was a small ship and the men on deck gave no evidence of hostile behavior or of even being interested in their ship.

One of them, a short, stout little man, was standing at the bow of the craft and occasionally raised a spy glass to his eye to inspect them more closely as they passed. It swept back and forth over the ship, never pausing in its arcs. Then suddenly it did stop, and for one unnerving second Kate was certain the glass was aimed directly at her. She quickly drew her face away from the window, but she continued to watch the man. Even though the glass resumed its sweeping arcs and the man put it away altogether after a little while, Kate could not rid herself of the feeling she had been seen. However, the ship did not come any closer and soon passed off over the horizon.

"The ship has gone on by, but I want you to stay here until we're sure it hasn't turned around," Brett said when he came down a little while later. "It was a strange flag and they didn't return our salute. The captain feels sure it was just one of the many private ships that abound along the coast and it holds no threat to us. One of the most dangerous things we can do is to let them know we have a woman aboard." Kate drew in her breath sharply, but Brett smiled at her, and every thought of telling him she had her nose to the window left her head. His look melted her bones, and every time he smiled at her she was helpless for hours.

"One look at you and every pirate on the coast would be after us. I don't know what they would do with the men, but I'm sure you would be destined for one of the great auction centers in Africa, maybe even as far away as Damascus." Kate heard him in incredulous disbelief. "Do you realize the frenzy of excitement you would create? Half the potentates of the East would ransom their kingdoms to own a woman like you."

Kate could not believe her ears. "Do you mean they would put me in a *harem?*" she asked.

"Probably. You might become the wife of some rich lord or the favorite concubine of a powerful soldier, depending upon who had enough money to buy you, but it's most likely you'd end up as a favorite of some ruler."

Kate was immobilized by shock and disbelief.

"Whatever they might like to do, I would resist with my last drop of blood," Brett said, taking her hands in his and kissing her fingers lightly. "I have become very used to having you to myself, and I don't think I could give you up now."

But Kate was not listening to him. Several hours ago, even several minutes ago, his words would have been music to her ears, but her fears had moved her beyond the reach of caressing and flattering words. Her mind was racing with thoughts that only yesterday she would have dismissed as too fantastic to be given credence. A *harem!* A *concubine!* She wasn't sure she had ever actually believed such things existed. She had always accepted them as part of the colorful stories people told about foreign places to make them seem more exotic and exciting. Now she discovered they not only existed, but if the British Navy wasn't watchful, she might find herself in the ardent embraces of some olive-skinned Oriental potentate. Her mind refused to even begin to grapple with the situation.

The whole idea of being carried off into the desert by savages was too fantastic to be believed, but then two months ago she wouldn't have believed any of what had happened to her since. It was as though she had been living in a dream, and instead of waking up to find that everything was foolish phantoms, she was sinking deeper and deeper into the abyss of the phantasmagoric. She sought to drive off the curious lassitude that threatened to overcome her, sapping the strength from her limbs and depriving her mind of its ability to function.

She felt the warmth of Brett's lips on her fingers and the light pressure on her hands as he held them in his firm grasp. This at least was real, and she clung to him with a renewed sense of urgency. But if Brett's kisses were real, then so were his words, and the dangers around her must be real too, no matter how impossible that would have sounded just a few days ago. It would be better to die than to face such a future.

She made up her mind to carry her knife with her at all times. Maybe she'd keep her pistols loaded, too. She didn't know what good they would do, but they certainly wouldn't be any help lying unloaded in their cases.

"I'll send Charles for you when it's time for dinner," she finally heard Brett say. "I need to talk to the captain. We'll be approaching Gibraltar soon and we haven't made any plans for the landing." Kate couldn't understand why he was thinking about Gibraltar when there were pirates lurking all over the Mediterranean, but he put his arms around her and it didn't seem quite so important anymore.

"Don't worry," he whispered. "I'm not going to let anything happen to you. I've only just found you, and I mean to keep you with me forever, safe and sound." He kissed her lightly. "Now try to get some rest. You'll feel better if you can take a little nap."

Kate smiled up at him. "All right," she said. "I do feel a little tired."

"I'll make sure no one disturbs you."

"You're sure we're not going to be attacked?"

"Yes," he smiled at her, "I'm sure. Now lie down and try to put it all out of your mind. Think about Gibraltar instead."

"I'll try," she said. Brett kissed her lightly and left her to her thoughts.

Chapter 18

At dinner the captain made a few remarks about the incident and then dismissed it as unimportant. What did interest him was Brett's proposed expedition to Gibraltar. He was certain Kate would be anxious to see that recently acquired station.

"It will be no problem to stop for the day. And the commander of the garrison can probably tell Mr. Westbrook something of the latest happenings in the Mediterranean. Positioned as he is, he can hear quite a lot about the movements of the Turks and Africans up and down the coast." Even though Kate showed no more than a polite interest in seeing the famous station, he immediately made plans to stop.

"I'm sure I'll enjoy the excursion," she said, feeling she ought to show some appreciation for the captain's efforts to please her, but it was difficult to imagine why she should become excited about looking at a big rock. After all, the rock itself couldn't be interesting, and she could see more impressive vistas of the ocean from the ship.

The next day dawned clear and cool, perfect weather for the intended expedition. The commander welcomed them into his home and almost immediately sent them on their way before it became too hot. Kate agreed the views were magnificent, but having to walk so far took the edge off her pleasure. She didn't have proper shoes for the rough ground and her feet hurt. They were throbbing painfully by the time everyone returned for lunch. With the commander's wife's encouragement, Kate took off her shoes and soaked them in warm water before it was time to eat.

During lunch, Kate got her first real information about the nature of Brett's mission. Though she was unable to get a clear picture of the political ramifications from their random remarks, she did understand that Brett was supposed to somehow convince the dey of Algiers to stop harassing the French. The Foreign Office feared if the French put an army in Algeria, they would conquer it, and England was determined to keep France from increasing her colonial holdings. Losing the thread of conversation completely after that, Kate tried to talk to the commander's wife.

But Kate's life had been very isolated, and she soon found she didn't know any of the people the commander's wife knew, she had no knowledge of international events of the past few years, and she had never seen a play or been to a fashionable party. That effectively brought their conversation to an end.

It was with a sense of considerable relief that Kate rose from the table to return to the ship and her pistols. That was something she *did* know about, apparently more than was considered proper for a well-brought-up young lady. The commander's wife had made no attempt to conceal her scorn for a young woman, however beautiful, who showed so little knowledge and interest in London and English political life, and who had no accomplishments to compensate for this lack. In her mind, weapons were vulgar and no young lady of breeding would aspire to learn to use them, or be foolish enough to admit it if she did.

Kate was made to feel ashamed of her poor education for the first time in weeks, but she was also angry at the woman for being so insensitive as to expose her ignorance and openly condemn it. With a little adroitness she could have talked of virtually anything else and spared her guest embarrassment. *If I'm ever an important hostess,* Kate thought angrily, *I will make it a point to see all my guests feel appreciated.*

Kate returned to the ship with relief, and as they watched Gibraltar disappear in the distance, the sun turned the sky a fiery red with streaks of orange and purple running through it.

"It's much more beautiful when seen at a distance," Kate mused. "You'd never know it was just a hot rock that hurt your feet."

"I don't think you ought to tell the Foreign Office that," Brett said, chuckling at her prosaic point of view. "They like to think they got a little more for their money."

"I wouldn't dream of it. There are times when a little ignorance is a good thing. Which reminds me . . ." she said, making an abrupt change of subject, "there's one thing I'd like to be a lot less ignorant about, and that's what you're supposed to be doing on this mission of yours."

"I'll explain it after dinner if you're really interested," Brett offered. "At least I'll tell you as much as I'm allowed to tell anyone. Charles already has a general idea, but Mark knows less than you do. We can all gather in our cabin."

Kate had never been more anxious for a dinner to end. The captain kept droning on about first one thing and then another, and Brett did nothing to discourage him. Usually Kate laughed at his stories as much as anyone else, but tonight she was in no mood for amusing anecdotes. Her curiosity about Brett's mission was eating away at her composure even more than she had expected.

Kate had never forgotten Brett's remarks about her being sold into a harem, and when the commander talked of Turkish activity in the Mediterranean, Kate's interest was rekindled. Though she put less credence in the stories with each day they completed in safety, she wanted to know everything she could about the Turks. To her they seemed a nation of dangerous but terribly mysterious barbarians. She left the men to their brandy hoping Brett wouldn't linger, but she didn't expect him to hurry just because she was anxious to get started. Men never seemed to consider things like that, she thought to herself.

Mark arrived first, then Charles, and the three of them waited impatiently. Charles refused to tell her any of what he knew. "It's not my story, Mrs. Westbrook, and I know Mr. Westbrook would rather tell it from the beginning."

"That may be true," Kate remarked irritably, "but he seems in no hurry to get started." She paced the room, castigating the thoughtlessness of egotistical men in general and Brett in particular. When he finally did arrive, she pounced on him in such a fever of curiosity he burst out laughing.

"I didn't mean to keep you waiting, but I never thought you'd be so interested in dry political maneuvering."

"Not interested?" she echoed in amazement. "You drag me thousands of miles away from home, threaten me with pirates and sultan's harems, say you're going to leave me in a strange town where I don't know a soul and can't even ask for a glass of water, and you didn't think I'd be *interested?*"

"I'd never thought about it in quite that way," he admitted with a disarming smile. "Sit down and I'll tell you all I can, but I warn you, it's going to be less interesting than you think." He drew a chair forward for her and waited until she was comfortably seated before he began.

"My mission is easy to explain, but it may even now be too late. The commander at Gibraltar says the French already have a military force in Algeria, but he's not certain it's large enough to fight. If it is, and they have already engaged the dey's troops, we might as well turn around and go home."

"What are you supposed to do? Who is the dey?" Kate asked impatiently. "You're talking in riddles and telling me nothing."

"Let me back up a few years," Brett said. "At the first of the century almost all of North Africa was under the suzerainty of the Ottoman Turks, but the local rulers were to all intents and purposes independent. They engaged freely in piratical enterprises against the European commerce and made the coastal Mediterranean towns veritable slave emporia." He paused. Kate was listening with rapt interest to everything he said and Charles seemed duly attentive, but Mark showed no interest in the subject.

"Shortly after the Battle of Waterloo, the British fleet bombarded Algiers and forced the dey to put an end to Christian slavery. It wasn't much, but it was all we could do without bringing in an army and taking over the country. At the time, no one at the Foreign Office wanted to consider that, but things have changed since then."

"The French influence has continued to grow in Algeria. Just a few years ago there was an incident where the dey struck the French consul with a fly whisk. The dey has refused repeated French demands for satisfaction and continues to behave in an arbitrary and intransigent style. Now the Foreign Office is afraid France will use this diplomatic insult as an excuse to mount a full-scale invasion, defeat the dey, and take over the country themselves. The British government is opposed to any extension of French influence—we certainly don't want them establishing a colonial empire in Africa—and it's been the job of the British consul in Algiers to convince the dey to moderate his stance so as not to aggravate the French any further. If my information is correct, he's had only moderate success so far."

"But where do you come in?" Kate asked. She was impressed with all the talk of armies and governments, but she couldn't understand how any single person, even such a wonderful one as Brett, could affect the course of this imperial chess game. "Do they expect you to talk some sense into this dey? He doesn't sound smart enough to listen to good advice if he heard it."

"Make no mistake, Al Nasr is very crafty," Brett insisted, "but in this case he's made a slight miscalculation. He thinks that because Europe has never concerned herself with North Africa before, she won't do so now, but that's where he's wrong. Now that Napoleon is out of the way, everyone is looking to establish colonial empires, and Africa is the last unconquered continent. Al Nasr will soon discover to his great sorrow that his little spat with France is just the beginning. Europe will never ignore Africa again."

"But how are you supposed to convince this man to change his mind when the local consul can't?" Kate questioned.

"No one expects me to improve on the work of Kenneth Wiggins," Brett replied. "I've been given a more intriguing assignment. There is a maverick desert chieftain, one Abd el-Kader of Mascara, who is a wild card in this poker game. He's a powerful tribal leader, but he's not strong enough to stand up to the Turks or overthrow Al Nasr by himself. However, he's a wily fox and he's been busy flattering Al Nasr, trying to make the fool believe in his own self-importance. He hopes Al Nasr will provoke the French into sending in an army to depose him. Then he plans to take over as dey of Algeria without having done anything more strenuous than flatter one man.

"It's a very simple plan and everyone from London to Istanbul knows about it, yet it's just about to work. My job is to convince Abd el-Kader to withdraw his influence from Algiers and stay in Mascara. I'm supposed to make him understand that if the French do come to Algeria, he'll lose more than he'll gain. It's entirely possible they will depose him as well as Al Nasr."

Kate could not believe her ears. It was like something out of a fairy tale and each page was more incredible than the last. Until a few months ago, the most exciting thing that had happened in her life was one of Martin's trollops losing her way during a party and ending up in Kate's room; in the two months she'd known Brett, she had been gambled away in a drunken card game, endured a wild ride across half of England, been to sea twice, killed a man, become friends with a French madam, and been chased by highwaymen and Moroccan pirates. Now he was busy filling her future with harems, despotic deys, desert chieftains, and French armies just as casually as if they were people encountered on the street.

"But how are you going to be able to talk to them? They can't speak English, can they? Not out here in the desert?" It sounded childish even to her ears, but it was all her paralyzed mind could think to ask.

"No, they don't speak English, but I know a good bit of Arabic, and I'll have an interpreter along. I'll also see that one is assigned to you so you won't be totally dependent on Wiggins. He has his own duties to attend to, so we'll be on our own almost from the minute we arrive." All laughter faded from Brett's luminous black eyes.

"I don't know what kind of situation I'll have to face, but I'll have to go into the desert immediately to find el-Kader. He will have found some place not far from Algiers where his army can wait so he can move in quickly if the French leave. If there is any chance of making him see our position, I'll have to stay with him until he either agrees to help us or brings his forces into the city to take over. Either way, you may not see me for quite a while.

"It'll be your responsibility to see that Kate is safely established before you join me," Brett said, turning to Charles. "I don't know what kind of house Wiggins will be able to find for her, but I'm depending on you to see it's adequate for her protection.

"You must obey Charles in everything, my dear," he said, turning back to Kate. "You have no other choice." He brusquely cut short her strangled protest. "This is not a town where you can make mistakes with impunity. These people don't think like you do and they don't live like you do. Women are property to be used and disposed of at will. Foreign women are little better than slaves to be used for hard labor or sold to the highest bidder in the open market. There is no reasoning with them and no appeal from their system. If you were kidnapped, the whole force of the British empire might not be able to save you. The area these people control is so vast and insular it would probably be impossible for their own rulers to find out what had happened to you, even if they tried, which they most likely wouldn't. Now do you understand why you have to be so careful?" Kate nodded her head; her throat was too constricted for her to be able to answer him.

"You're not to be seen in public. If you have to leave the house, you must be completely veiled. If anyone gets a good look at your face, you won't be safe anywhere. Even your eyes are enough to arouse dangerous curiosity. I won't be there to protect you, so the fewer people who know of your existence the safer you'll be. The consulate is only a small one and we have no troops stationed here. If the local rulers decided not to help us, we will have to protect ourselves, and you can't depend too heavily on servants because their ultimate loyalties are not to us."

Kate didn't know what to say. It was too much; her mind couldn't accept it. It just didn't seem possible that only a few weeks ago she was living quietly at Ryehill hoping someday her prince would come. Her prince *had* come, but the world he was taking her to became more bizarre every day. Now he was about to run off into the desert and leave her at the mercy of a heathen town with no more than two servants and an aging consul to protect her. She didn't know whether to laugh, cry, or scream. The whole thing was too absurd. Surely she would wake up any minute and find herself in her own bed with old Ned shuffling in to warn her Isabella was in a temper and to stay clear of the kitchen unless she wanted to come face-to-face with the screeching harpy.

"I can't think," she finally said helplessly. "I can't make myself believe all this is really happening."

"It'll be easy enough once we land," Brett observed cryptically. "The country is poor, dirty, and disease-ridden. Algiers is hot, crowded, and stinking. The food is adequate, but it'll be strange, taste bad, and you'll have little choice."

"But this is horrible!" Kate gasped. "Why didn't you tell me this before you dragged me onto this boat? I would have stayed with Valentine until I turned gray rather than set one foot in this place."

"That's what I was afraid of," Brett confessed with his devastating smile. He pulled her into his arms and held her close despite her protests. "I couldn't bear the thought of being separated from you for months on end."

"That's not true and you know it," Kate contradicted, as she struggled unsuccessfully to escape his embrace. "You've just said you're going to leave me to the mercies of God-only-knows what kind of heathens the moment you set foot in this blighted country while you go traipsing over the sand dunes playing at God among the natives, and you want me to believe you can't bear to be separated from me? You're the most treacherous human being I've ever met, and I'll never understand how I could have been such a featherbrain as to run off with you. We'll be separated just as clearly as if I were still in France. And I'd be a lot safer with Valentine."

Charles unobtrusively shepherded Mark out of the cabin. "Sometimes I get so mad at you I could hit you," she said, pounding on his chest with her tiny fists. The only response she got was a great gust of laughter as he captured her hands in his. "But you're so mean you won't even let me do that."

"I'd much rather spend the time kissing you," he said, and smothered her in his embrace.

"But that won't solve anything," she added rather

breathlessly when she finally managed to tear herself away from his iron grip.

"I know, but I enjoy it so much more," he said, and engulfed her again. She abandoned her resistance and returned his embrace with equal ardor.

During the next few days, Brett answered an endless stream of questions. Kate's interest grew as her fear of the unknown receded, and Brett soon reached the conclusion that if Kate were given a little time to grow accustomed to the exotic lands he found so exciting, she would make a worthy, even challenging, companion. Her limited knowledge was apparent in the naiveté of some of her questions, but her interests were seemingly boundless and her mind capable of digesting large amounts of new material. Brett found himself enjoying their discussions, so much so that he began to regret he had not told her about it sooner.

In fact, Kate's mind was so caught up with the new experiences in store for her she failed to notice several small boats hovering in the distance. But Brett and the captain didn't miss them. At first they thought they were ordinary ships going in the same direction—the Mediterranean was much smaller than the Atlantic and ships of all kinds were more frequent—but over a period of several days they seemed to remain about the same distance from the ship and the spyglass convinced Brett they were the same ships. For some reason they were being followed, but the boats showed no sign of wishing to approach them.

Brett and the captain discussed the escort each evening after Kate had left them, but they could come up with no satisfactory explanation. They could be fishing boats, they certainly weren't large enough to haul a profitable cargo, but Brett couldn't imagine how they could have anything to do with his trip to Algeria. Pirate ships struck quickly to catch their prey off guard and then disappear before they could be chased down by bigger and faster ships.

Unable to explain their presence, he kept on the alert and spent a lot of time on deck watching them. He asked the captain to be prepared in case there was an attack, but the ship was not armed for attack and there was little to be got ready. They were known to be a diplomatic mission and the captain said he expected an uneventful trip.

Then one day out of Algiers, the boats vanished as suddenly as they had appeared. Brett could not rid himself of the uneasy feeling they weren't really gone, but the captain was convinced there had never been any danger and jokingly referred to them at dinner that evening.

"You can't imagine how relieved First Mate Thompson was to find those little boats gone this morning," he said with a self-satisfied smile. "I believe he was beginning to develop a phobia about them." He was watching to see how Kate would react to his startling news and failed to notice Brett was frowning, very angry at him for bringing up the subject.

"What boats are you talking about?" Kate questioned, suddenly alert.

"Just some small boats we've been watching for the last several days." He chuckled. "Thompson would have it they were pirate ships, but they were too small to do anything more than yap at our heels."

The word "pirate" caused Kate to lose all interest in her food. She laid her fork down and swallowed convulsively. "We're being followed by pirates?" she

270

asked as calmly as she could.

"No," Brett interrupted, throwing the captain a furious glance. "We saw a few small craft, but they never came near the ship. Anyway, they're gone now." He spoke in a flat voice, hoping to imply the subject was of little importance, but it was easy to see Kate's fears had not been banished.

She looked from him to the captain. "How can you be sure they're gone? They could be hiding. What were they doing here?"

"It was probably a group of fishing boats following a school of fish," Brett explained. "It's easier to handle some of the large nets when they work together. Anything of this kind excites the curiosity of the crew, and after such a long, uneventful trip, their imaginations sometimes run away with them."

"Are you sure they were just looking for fish?" Kate persisted in a voice that was still unsteady. Damn that fool of a captain, thought Brett. Now she's really upset.

"No, I can't be sure of anything," he returned noncommittally. "They never came close enough to see their flag, but they were too small and too few in number to pose a threat." The captain attempted to apologize for upsetting Kate, but Brett changed the subject adroitly and saw to it that the conversation stayed on other topics for the rest of the evening.

But Kate didn't forget. Brett might pooh-pooh the possibility they were being pursued by pirate ships, but she couldn't. The idea she might be sold into a harem had taken a strong hold on her mind and she couldn't shake it. It was still uppermost in her thoughts when she returned to her cabin. She sat down on the edge of the bed and lectured herself sternly, taking herself to task particularly for acting like the kind of silly, whining female she

271

most deplored. *Nothing unusual has happened,* she told herself. *Everything lurid and frightening is only in your imagination. All that has actually taken place is that you and Brett have enjoyed an idyllic trip and have gotten along much better than you ever thought possible. So stop looking for trouble,* she added as a clincher.

Everything had turned out so well that she sometimes forgot to add "but I'll leave him when I get back to England" to the end of her thoughts about the future. His thoughtfulness and attention still surprised her. She couldn't understand why he had changed so much, but she reveled in it. He still forgot her presence at times and habitually threw commands at her as though she were a servant, but she had gradually become less sensitive to his rough manners and he had become less abrasive.

She found herself wishing this trip could go on forever. Once they landed, she would never again have him so completely to herself and she was afraid everything would change. He might not *want* to stay with her once other pressures and interests started to take up his time, and she couldn't bear that. She didn't really care about learning to use a pistol and she positively disliked the knife and sword, but she was so hopelessly in love with him she would have agreed to wear medieval armor and carry a lance if it would have kept him by her side.

She finished her preparations for bed and crawled between the sheets. Tonight, as on every night for several weeks past, she waited for him with pleasurable anticipation, wanting his fiery lovemaking and ready to respond with a heat of her own. Brett had brought her along carefully, slowly expanding her knowledge of the excitement physical love had to offer. For her, the trip had been one of constant surprise at the incredible

272

pleasures to be found in the arms of the man she loved. Just thinking about him sent tiny tingles of excitement through her body, and she snuggled down a little further into the cool sheets.

Chapter 19

Brett was furious with the captain for mentioning the boats to Kate. He *hoped* they were merely fishing boats or a convoy of small cargo ships, but since every theory was only conjecture, it was pointless to say anything to her. Still, he couldn't shake the gut feeling they constituted a danger. He had no real reason for his belief, but knew that it was unusual for fishing boats to work together for so long. The natives were well known for their constant bickering, and he couldn't think of anything more certain to start them fighting than the division of a cargo.

The captain had not earned Brett's respect. Maybe the last-minute change of plans hadn't given the Foreign Office time to find anyone more competent — he was merely a pleasant man who told amusing stories — but Brett decided he would hire his own crew, one he felt he could depend on, if he chose to return to England by sea. True, no one had expected him to bring his wife on board and that had changed what he looked for in a crew, but then lots of things had happened recently he hadn't expected.

He had entertained no thoughts of marriage when he met Kate, yet with every passing day she became more necessary to his comfort, and he no longer even considered the possibility of living without her. At first he had been so bowled over by her beauty, so caught up by the stormy passions she aroused in him every time he set eyes on her, he didn't stop to ask himself what he was doing or why. Even now, after weeks of what could pass for quiet married life, his quickening pulses still tended to block out all thoughts of anything but the immediate present.

For the life of him he couldn't figure out what it was Kate had in such abundance that every other female lacked. Never before had he confined himself to a single woman for very long, yet no matter how many hours he spent with Kate, he never grew bored with her company. He was teaching her to handle a man's weapons because it amused him and because it was a useful skill to have, not because they had nothing else to do. He enjoyed each day's practice and was filled with pride when she put a bullet through the center of the target without flinching at the loud report of the pistol. Yet if he roared with laughter when she berated herself mercilessly for a missed shot, she always took it in good part.

His respect for her was growing with each passing day. She had unsuspected reserves of strength. She had taken command during his illness with calm determination and cool-headed intelligence. She didn't panic when she was frightened or didn't understand things; she didn't shrink from unpleasant tasks or offer excuses for failure. When she needed to know how to perform a task, she set out to master the required skills and didn't forget anything of what she learned.

Even though he had decided to take her to Africa without consulting her wishes, knowing all the while she suffered from seasickness, she had settled into the routine of the ship easily and adjusted her life to fit his without a word of complaint. Her presence never seemed to cause extra work, but she would lend a hand when she could. She was

275

friendly to a fault with the crew but never gave them reason to treat her with anything but the utmost respect.

Brett's presence alone would have been enough to ensure her preferential treatment. He was a man who inspired other men with confidence in his leadership and a belief in his ability to handle difficult situations. But at the same time it was easy to believe there was a black streak in his character. It wasn't something you could explain or even point to, but one look at those coal-black eyes flashing with anger and his bulging muscles taut with scarcely restrained fury and no one could doubt a demon lay just beneath the polished surface.

"The way you watch over your wife, one would think you'd kill anyone who touched her," the captain had once remarked with a nervous laugh.

The pleasant smile had faded from Brett's face and his tightened mouth betrayed just how little he liked the idea. His reply was a succinct "I would," but the captain felt eternity lay in those words for anyone foolish enough to approach his divinely beautiful wife, and he changed the subject to something less likely to arouse the animosity of a man he didn't entirely trust.

Brett entered the cabin on silent feet even though he knew Kate would be waiting for him. The room was in shadows and the light of the single lamp burning by the bedside seemed to flow toward Kate, framing her face against the darkness of the cabin like a Rembrandt painting. Brett was drawn irresistibly toward her, wondering all over again how anyone could be so lovely. He still found it hard to believe she was really his, that she wouldn't suddenly vanish from the pillow without a trace.

He moved to the bed and sank down beside her. He liked to look at her at any time, but he particularly loved to see her as she was now, in the half light with her face framed by the gold of her cascading hair. His hand reached out and his fingers caressed her cheeks, marveling anew at the velvety softness of her skin. He looked deep into sea-blue eyes that gazed at him with a look of deep contentment and he felt himself falling further and further under their spell, almost suffocating in their enveloping depths. Then suddenly he was snatched from his reverie by an unexpected revelation that whiplashed his mind, ricocheted down his body, and landed in his stomach with the force of a hammerblow: he was in love with this girl.

He was shocked and stunned to the very foundations of his being. Here, nestled within his arms, lay the only thing in the world that mattered to him. All the things that used to mean so much could never offer him half as much pleasure as one simple smile from this lovely, courageous, girl.

She looked at him as though she, too, had found the object of her dreams. If that could only be true, he reflected, but how could she love him after all that had passed between them? How could *any* woman love a man who had done only a tithe of what he had done to Kate? He felt a sick sensation in the pit of his stomach, a feeling of hopeless despair. In that moment, he would have traded everything he owned for a chance to start over again. He had never tried to make himself acceptable to her, not even after they were married; he had run roughshod over her from the moment they met. If she hated him forever, he would only have himself to blame.

The sound of Kate's voice penetrated the barricade of his unwelcome thoughts. She had been talking to him for some time, and he hadn't heard a thing she had said until the word "love" erupted from her conversation to scatter his gloomy thoughts.

"What did you say?" he asked suddenly. "I didn't catch the first part," he confessed.

Kate laughed softly. "How like you not to pay the least attention when I'm talking. I should be used to it by now, but I hope you'll want to hear what I have to say this time. I've wanted to tell you for a long time, but I've never had the courage. I was afraid, I'm not entirely sure of what, but I guess I didn't want to leave myself open to be hurt again. After my father and brother, I found it difficult to trust any man. I kept it to myself, not telling anyone, not even Valentine until after she guessed."

"You were afraid of me?" he asked, surprised. "Why?"

"How can you ask me that?" she demanded, amused in spite of herself. "You were mean, rude, cruel, and I was sure I would hate you with my dying breath. For weeks I planned and plotted to get to London once you were well. I knew Martin had forced me on you, and I couldn't believe you wouldn't get rid of me as soon as you could. Gradually I realized I was less afraid of you than I was of the future without you. It was then I realized I didn't want to escape, that I wanted to stay with you, but I was afraid you wouldn't want me."

Brett tried to speak, but Kate put her fingers over his lips.

"Let me finish. Since we've been on this ship there has been a difference in you, from the very first morning when I woke up with that awful hangover. You've made me feel wanted, important,

278

as though I were something valuable and precious in a way that had nothing to do with my looks or whether I could hit those stupid targets. I felt it was *me* you cared about, and I just wanted to curl up in the crook of your arm and never leave. Most important, I wasn't afraid of you any longer.

"I don't know what the future holds for us, or if we have a future—I have a great fear it won't be what I want it to be—but these have been the most wonderful days of my life. I never dreamed I could be so happy."

Brett held tightly to Kate and buried his face in her hair. For the first time in his life, he was content to be near a woman without devouring her like a raging fire consuming dry tinder. He tried to speak, but he had trouble swallowing and his throat wouldn't let the words out.

"Our idyll is about to come to an end," Kate continued. "The captain told me this would be our last night at sea. Once we land, all manner of things will intrude, and we'll never be together like this again, just the two of us, without anyone or anything from the outside world to come between us. This could even be our last night together for a long time so there's something I want to tell you, something I *must* tell you.

"I love you. I have loved you ever since you were so sick, probably even before that. It doesn't matter when it started, just that it did." His grip on her tightened until it hurt. "I hadn't meant to tell you this. I was going to keep it to myself and then disappear to a little cottage where I could hide from you and the rest of the world, but I *had* to tell you. I hope it doesn't make you angry. I know I often put you into a towering rage, but I promise I won't say anything about it again." She took his face in her hands and looked into the depths of the

279

black pools that were his eyes. "I love you with all my heart," she whispered. "And I will always love you as long as I live." She kissed him lightly on the lips with a tenderness he found more overpowering than the fierceness of her passion.

Brett gently forced Kate to lie back on her pillow. He propped himself up on one elbow and with his other arm steadied himself across her body. He looked at her lovingly and then kissed her very tenderly. Their lips clung to each other in a long embrace that lacked the fire of their other kisses but promised instead a warmth and permanence that no passage of time could diminish.

"I love you, too," he said, tearing himself from her warm embrace. "I didn't know it until tonight when I looked at you lying on the pillow with your hair all around you and your eyes staring so steadfastly into mine. At last I understood why I have been so determined to hold on to you from the very first. I never did want to let you go. Even when I couldn't think because my head ached from brandy or my brains were turned to mush by the coach ride, I rejected every plan that meant giving you up. Edward told me I fell in love with you at first sight. I begin to think he may have been right."

Kate made an ineffectual attempt to wipe away the tears that were coursing down her cheeks.

"But what I felt for you then was nothing compared to what I've learned to feel for you since. You struggled so hard to keep me alive, fought to keep your independence and honor, and never asked for anyone's pity. Yet after I forced you into this marriage, you still had the courage to laugh, eat at the same table without hating me, even aim your pistol without making me its target. I felt your anger melt and drain away, but I never thought it would turn to love. I didn't even know I wanted it to become love until I came through that door tonight."

His infectious chuckle rumbled from deep in his chest. "All I had in mind was a lusty romp in bed. I am aroused by the very sight of you, but then you know that. I thought I knew everything there was to know about love, but I feel like I'm just starting to learn, that all I've experienced before had nothing to do with what I feel for you now." He wiped away some of her tears. "I have to thank you for that, but I'm even more grateful for your presence. I know now that to grow old wrapped in the warmth of your love will be worth the loss of youth."

Brett enfolded Kate in his embrace and she clung fiercely to him, hardly able to believe he loved her as much as she loved him, hardly daring to allow herself to be convinced by the words she had heard with her own ears. His lips descended upon her mouth, greedily taking kiss after sweet kiss, yet waiting for her to join as an equal participant in this act of adoration. His lips parted and his tongue touched hers, seeking, tasting, probing, inviting, wanting. Kate's arms tightened around his neck as his lips planted kisses on her neck and cheeks, tickled and teased her lashes on their way to plant a tiny kiss on the tip of her nose. His fingers moved through her silken hair like a comb, making her skin tingle and her body tense with expectation. Yet Brett's kisses continued to linger on her lips, straying only occasionally to tease and torment her ear.

Kate pressed herself against the length of him, reveling in the feel of his hard, heated body against her soft flesh, wanting his strength to satisfy her desire. Her breasts were pressed tightly against his chest, her legs, trembling and rigid, entwined with his.

Brett paused only long enough for them to slip out of their clothes before his insatiable lips again sought her mouth, traveled over the exquisitely sensitive skin of her neck and shoulders and down the length of her arm. Cradling her hand in his, Brett kissed each finger, turned it over to plant several kisses in her palm before doing the same with the other hand. Then, placing her palms against the soft mat of black hair on his chest, he allowed his lips to sink to the excruciatingly tender tip of her breast. Kate gasped for breath as his tongue gently laved her inflamed nipple until her whole body squirmed and her other breast cried out for identical attention. She arched against him, brought her knees up on either side of his body as though to draw him within her, but his hands could not be deflected from their caressing of each breast nor his lips from the impassioned attention to each nipple.

Kate moved more strongly against him, but still his attention was not diverted to the part of her anatomy which was torturing her with spasms of intense yearning. First one hand and then the other roamed over the skin of each leg, covering it with goosebumps of desire, setting her on fire with an urgent need, but he continued to slowly feed the fire in her body until Kate was sure she would perish in the flames.

But when his hands did seek out the sweet agony between her thighs, their lovemaking took on a new and unreal quality. There was no rush, no urgency, no violent surges. Despite the convulsive shudders that periodically shook her body for its whole length, Brett continued to carefully tend the fires of his passion, inviting her to join him in a union which aimed toward the future, not just the pleasure of the moment. Gradually the desperate need for release left Kate and she felt herself being wound tighter and tighter, lifted higher and higher, until the admission of Brett's driving heat deep into her hot, moist flesh became a continuation of the surging ecstasy.

He moved in her with a delicate restraint which served to excite her in a way she had never experienced before. Instead of consuming her, fiercely demanding satisfaction of her, it seemed to invite her very being to become a part of his fulfillment, and Kate's heart was filled with such an overwhelming sense of love she feared she might break into tears. She clung to him, longing to feel as one, to move as one, to *be* as one in this consummate expression of their love.

With all the intensity but lacking the frenzy of previous nights, they rose smoothly to a passionate conclusion. Their bodies tensed, arched, and became rigid as the final release erupted from deep inside them, but there was an extra dimension of satisfaction, a kind of fulfillment that had not been there before. It was as if they had only been friends before, partners in a voyage of pleasure. Now they were truly united and every part of their being rejoiced in their newly achieved completeness.

Kate was jerked awake by the sound of a bell ringing wildly in the crisp cool of the hour just before daybreak. She turned frightened eyes to Brett, but before her lips could form words to ask the questions in her mind, he was out of bed and staring through the porthole for the cause of the alarm. There was nothing, however, to be seen in the expanse of blue sea except tiny, whitecapped

283

waves dancing about under the encouragement of the last breath of the night breeze. In the distance, a bare tracing of coastline lifted itself above the horizon, giving support to the captain's promise that they would be in Algiers before noon.

"That's a general alarm," Brett said as he left the window and jumped into his clothes with none of his usual regard for neatness and elegance. "We're either under attack or threatened by some kind of danger. Stay in the cabin and lock the door. No matter what happens, don't open it for anyone but me. *No one,* do you hear? I'll send Mark to stay with you if I can, but we may need him." He jammed his feet into his boots and grabbed his sword and a large knife he had been using only the day before for target practice. "I'll be back as soon as I can."

"No," Kate cried. Her stunned immobility ended, she bounded out of the bed and clung to Brett. "Don't leave me alone." For a brief moment Brett's eyes softened as he enveloped Kate in a short embrace.

"I don't think there's any immediate danger, but I've got to know what's happening. I'll only be gone a few minutes." Kate's grip on him slackened and she watched with fearful eyes as he backed away from her and went through the door.

For a brief moment she stood still, listening to the hysterical ringing of the bell and the pounding of running feet as the crew prepared to meet this unexpected danger. What could it be, she thought? We can't be sinking. Could the French Navy have mistaken them for an enemy ship? She hadn't heard any gunfire.

Then she remembered the group of small boats, and cold fear clutched her heart. Could they really be pirates? Could that absurd nightmare really come true? She wanted to reject the idea as too ridiculous to even consider, but she had a horrible feeling it *was* true. Somehow she *knew* that somewhere out there a pirate ship was coming after her. She knew it just as surely as she knew she would take her own life before she would let herself be despoiled.

Kate dressed quickly in her ugliest dress—a high-necked gown of dark apricot with long sleeves and a full skirt trimmed with lace and ruched at the sleeves. She hid her hair under an oversize cap and slipped her feet into a pair of light slippers. As she looked around trying to decide what to do next, Brett threw open the door.

Kate's heart sank when her eyes flew to his face. For a second he stood framed in the doorway, his skin ashen and his eyes wide with a fear she knew was not for himself. He stumbled into the room and enfolded Kate roughly in his arms.

"There's a large ship bearing down on us from the rear. It'll be upon us within half an hour." He took her face into his hands, and she could see his eyes were moist with unshed tears. "The captain is certain it's the flag ship of a bandit called Raisuli, the most feared pirate in the Mediterranean." He paused to clear his throat. "His usual practice is to sell his captives at the slave markets of Damascus."

Kate felt her knees start to give way. "Do you mean me?" she asked, petrified of the answer she knew he must give. "*I* will be sold as a slave?"

"You'd be a bigger prize than all the rest of us put together." He took her by the hands and pulled her down on the bed. His voice was steady, but the pallor of his skin betrayed his dread. "He has a very large force, and there's no chance we can drive them off. He'll probably try to capture us with as few injuries as possible—unmarked slaves bring higher prices—and that just might give us a chance to escape. We're already within sight of the coast. If we can find some way to prolong the fight, maybe someone will come to our rescue."

"What are our chances?" Kate asked.

"Not very good. If I didn't know better, I'd swear he was after you."

"But how could he know I'm here?"

"That's just it, he can't. We haven't stopped anywhere since Gibraltar. I just don't understand why he's taking such a big risk for a handful of men who aren't good for more than a few years of hard labor," he wondered more to himself than to Kate. "I'm going to put you in one of those unoccupied cabins on deck. If they search the ship, maybe they won't look too closely at a storage room. Whatever happens, I want you to bar the door and not come out. Even if he takes us, you may still get away."

"I couldn't leave you," Kate cried. "Not to be carried off to some terrible place and made to work until you die."

"Listen to me," Brett snarled; fear for her made his voice harsh and he shook her with a sudden and fearful rage until she feared her neck would snap. "It's quite possible they'll negotiate for my release, but if they even suspect we have a female on board, they'll take this ship apart plank by plank. My God, Kate, don't you understand what will happen to you if they find you? The very *best* would be for them to sell you for a slave or concubine. That way there would be a small chance you might find someone who would care for you. Otherwise your life would be a living hell, continuing until you lost your mind or cut your own throat."

Kate was limp with fear; her face was white and words wouldn't form in her throat. All she could do was stare at Brett in disbelief. A loud explosion from somewhere overhead surprised a scream out of her and she flung herself at Brett expecting to see hordes of savages burst through the door at any second.

"Blast the fools!" Brett cursed. "Don't they know those guns can't be of any use? Let's get out of here while we still can." Brett hurried Kate toward the door, but she suddenly turned back.

"Wait a minute," she said, going over to the bureau.

"What are you doing?" Brett demanded. "We've got to get on deck before they get close enough to see us."

Kate pulled open the drawer and took out her pistols and knife. "After all the time I spent practicing, I'm not going to leave these behind."

"Don't use them unless you have to." He didn't have the heart to explain to her why no weapon would be of any use in her hands. "Once they know where you are, all of our weapons won't be able to hold them off."

But Kate clutched her weapons tightly as he hurried her along the passageway and out into the morning light. The sun was just coming up over the horizon and the cloudless sky promised another beautiful, clear day. "Keep down," Brett said as they moved to the right side of the deck. "They can't see anything on this side yet. Raisuli is approaching from behind, the only direction these useless guns can't defend. This man, if he *is* Raisuli, leaves nothing to chance. He even knows where the guns are placed." He pointed to one of the guns as they passed. "Some fool had both of them mounted on the bow where the deck cabins block the line of sight to the rear.

Brett unlocked the door of one of the cabins and thrust Kate in before him. The jumble of trunks,

287

crates, and furniture made the room look like a warehouse. "I've told Charles to pack up everything you own and write Wiggins's name on all the trunk labels. If we can just convince them there is no woman on board, maybe they won't search too carefully. I still don't understand why he's attacking this ship for just a few dozen men." Brett didn't really expect an answer. He was thinking out loud, trying to explain away the sickening feeling that weighed more and more heavily in his stomach. No matter what the cost, they must not find Kate.

Mark suddenly rushed into the cabin. His frightened eyes frantically searched the room for some kind of refuge. "I've got to talk to the captain," Brett said to Kate. "It can't be too long before we make contact. Remember, don't open this door until you hear my voice, not under any circumstances, do you understand?"

Kate nodded dumbly.

"Mark . . ." He addressed the nearly witless boy sharply to get his attention. "You're to stay with Mrs. Westbrook. I'm making you responsible for her safety. Lock the door behind me and push that wardrobe, or anything else you can move, against it. But no matter what, don't leave her." Mark nodded his agreement with every word Brett spoke, but his eyes showed no understanding.

I hope he can think, Brett said to himself, *but I can't wait to find out.*

Abruptly Brett swept Kate into his arms, and kissed her with ruthless energy before burying his face in her hair. His throat was too constricted with emotion to speak, and they clung to each other, knowing these could be their last moments together, that the love they gave to each other in these precious seconds might have to last them for the rest of their lives; all the while they refused to

288

let go of a dream they had only begun to savor.

"I love you," Kate managed to whisper, her lips so close they brushed against his ear. "If this is the only way I could have had these last weeks, then I don't regret it."

Brett's body was convulsed with a wracking sob, and his arms closed around her with suffocating strength. Then suddenly the door was open and he was gone.

Kate was too stunned to move right away, but Mark ran to the door and locked it with fumbling fingers. He tried to push the huge wardrobe over to the door, but it wouldn't move. Kate gathered her wits and tried to help him, but it still wouldn't budge. "It must be bolted to the floor," she said in frustration. A brief inspection showed that all the furniture was bolted into place so it wouldn't slide about during a storm. *But we're being attacked by pirates, not a storm,* Kate thought irrationally.

"Did you bring a pistol?" she asked Mark, trying to use her brain rather than her emotions. He shook his head. *He is so frightened he's useless,* she thought. If any thinking had to be done, she was going to have to be the one to do it. "Do you have any weapons?"

"A knife," he said through chattering teeth. "I'm not any good with a sword, and the captain would never let any of us keep pistols. We didn't need them on the channel crossing." He continued to stare at Kate with dilated eyes, making her feel guilty for having taken him from a safe job and put him in the way of real danger.

"Put that chair against the door. Wedge it under the handle. I have to get my pistols ready. If they break in, move out of the way quickly. I'm going to shoot anyone who comes through that door. Do you understand?" Mark nodded his head, but Kate

289

doubted he understood more than one word in three.

Kate gave her pistols a final check, then hitching up her skirt before Mark's fascinated eye, she strapped the knife to her thigh the way Brett had taught her. She didn't know if she'd be able to use it, but she wanted every possible chance to fight for her freedom. Finally she picked up the tiny pistol Brett kept in his drawer. She carefully loaded it and slipped it into the bosom of her dress. *If all else fails,* the thought with a heavy heart, *this will be for me.* She glanced around the room to see if there was anything more she could do. "Are you ready, Mark?"

He nodded assent, but his eyes still showed little comprehension.

She tried not to think of Brett, tried not to think of what would happen if he wasn't the first person to come through the door. Her fear for his safety was desperate, but she couldn't allow it to take hold of her mind or she would become just as useless as Mark. She didn't know what she would be able to do, but she must be alert to any opportunity, no matter how small. They *had* to come through this; her mind simply would not accept any other outcome.

She picked up her pistols and turned to face the door.

Chapter 20

The captain said that any possible threat had ended with the disappearance of the small boats, and he had reduced the night watch to a single sailor. The pirate ship had surprised the seaman by coming up quickly out of the night just as the first light from the sun began to melt away the black of the night sky, and he had not seen it bearing down on them until it was too late to have any hope of outrunning it.

Within seconds of hearing the alarm, the deck was filled with half-dressed men rushing about in bewildered response to the call. The captain, who alone seemed to be in control of himself, shouted orders to man the rudder and hoist the sails. The crew had only enough men to put the ship under full sail; if they followed the captain's orders, there would be none left to defend it.

It took no more than one look for Brett to know there was no time to raise sails or alter their course. The pirates would be alongside before half the rigging was in place. In a short and savage exchange of words, he tried to convince the captain to abandon the idea of running away from the pirates and to organize the men to defend this ship instead. The captain turned his back on him, and Brett whipped him around. "Hell and damnation, man! Can't you see there's no use in raising the sails? There isn't time for anything but a desperate defense."

"Get out of my way," ordered the captain, furious that anyone should question his orders. "I'll have you removed from the deck if you don't go back to your cabin and stay there." He turned and started shouting at the sailors who had stopped to listen to Brett's argument, mixing his orders with pithy curses.

Looking back at the rapidly approaching ship, Brett realized it would be alongside in fifteen minutes and they still hadn't made any attempt to organize a defense. Once again he tried to get the captain's attention, but the furious man tried to push him from the upper deck. Brett took the butt end of his pistol and brought it down with brutal force on the base of the man's skull, and the captain dropped to the deck like a deadweight. The first mate stared openmouthed at Brett, undecided as to what to do.

Brett turned on him like a whirlwind. "Can you get this damned crew out of the rigging and organized to fight off these bloody devils?"

The man came to life. "Yes, sir!" he replied, and with a few concise commands ordered the men out of the rigging and began to position them to get the greatest advantage from their numbers. Brett raced below deck and broke the lock on the munitions closet, but there was little to be found beyond a few pistols, several kinds of old swords, and some ancient knives.

"Good Lord," Brett exclaimed in disbelief, "doesn't anyone in this tub know about the invention of gun powder? This looks like the hole of a Viking ship." No one dared answer him. "You might as well pass these things out anyway. If worse comes to worst, we can always *throw* them at the bastards when they try to board." He left in disgust with sinking spirits. There was even less chance now of his being able to protect Kate; their only hope was that the pirates would never find her.

By the time he returned to the deck, the pirate ship was closing in quickly, its crew gathered along the rail ready to board as soon as they came alongside. The motley band was at least three times their number and heavily armed. They were a ragged group, all dressed differently and wearing bits and pieces of clothing they had taken from previous captives. They were in a cheerful mood, joking and laughing among themselves as they pointed to the ship and its crew. Brett delivered himself of some rather ripe curses that caused one young sailor to stare in awe.

As the ships drew closer together, a hairy man of medium height and rotund shape came to the side of the pirate ship and called out, "Surrender now and no one will be hurt."

Brett looked questioningly at the first mate, but he was too nonplussed by the unexpected command uttered in excellent English to be able to reply. The call came again the same as before. "Surrender now and no one will be hurt."

"Better to fight now than later," Brett muttered as he studied the ship and its crew, trying to determine a possible line of defense. "Tell the men to wait until the ship comes alongside before they attack," he said, turning to the first mate. "Then when they try to cross from one ship to the other, push as many of them as we can into the water. Maybe we can reduce their numbers enough to give us a chance to hold them off until help comes."

"What help? From where?" the first mate asked, unable to believe they might be rescued but willing to grasp at any hope however slight.

"One of those ships riding at anchor in the harbor at Algiers," Brett said, pointing to the masts of several large ships in the distance. "It's the only way. These men are ruthless and battle-hardened. It'll be impossible for us to drive them off by ourselves." The first mate's fleeting hope died, but he moved quickly among the men giving them last-minute instructions and encouragement.

When the ships were only yards apart, the hairy man pointed to the few sailors and howled in derision. "You have no chance," he sneered. "My men can take you without working up a sweat." He received no answer. "Don't be foolish," he growled, irritated by their silence. "We only want the girl. Let me have her and you can all go unharmed."

Brett's body stiffened. How did they know about Kate? Were they just guessing? He looked at the cold, piglike eyes of the swarthy leader and knew he was not a man to go anywhere without a purpose. Somehow he *knew* she was there, but was it idle conversation or sold information that had found its way to his ear? *What does it matter,* Brett thought? *It won't change what's going to happen in the next hour.* A feeling of desperation threatened to overwhelm him, but he fought it off. As long as they were free, there was still the chance of escape; they would never get Kate as long as there was breath in his body.

"If we have to take her by force, I'll sell every one of you to the Turks," the fat man yelled with rising anger. "No woman is worth that." The crew stirred restlessly; despite their chivalry and their fear of Brett, it was hard not to think of themselves first.

"You can't pretend you don't have a woman on board," Raisuli screamed, for it *was* the feared pirate himself, "and a fine-looking one at that. Yukor has the best eyes in all of Morocco and he spotted her at your porthole. He had his fishing fleet fol-

294

low you until I could get here. He's promised me she is more beautiful than any woman we have ever captured before. You can't expect me to overlook a prize like that, not a poor man like me." Raisuli chuckled.

The first mate involuntarily looked at Brett and then turned quickly away. But despair showed in Brett's face for only a brief moment, to be replaced by a fierce hatred for the laughing barbarian across the water and a muttered vow to kill him rather than let him get his hands on Kate.

"Fools! What's wrong with you?" Raisuli shouted, angry again. "Are you going to let your Christian chivalry send you to hell? Give me the woman and save yourselves. You can always find another." But the moment of indecision was gone and the crew settled in, prepared to do battle. "So be it," Raisuli shouted. "Not even Allah can save you now."

He turned to his men and shouted some staccato-like orders in Arabic. When he was satisfied that everything was ready for the attack, he turned back toward the ship.

"Be careful you don't cut them up too much. Damaged goods don't sell well. Dead ones not at all." He appeared to be talking to his own men, but he aimed the words at his intended victims, hoping to demoralize them before the fight began. He laughed raucously and pointed his sword at Brett. "Take good care of the big one. Even without the girl, I can get enough for him from some sugar planter to pay for the whole trip. Each bruise is worth fifty florins." He threw back his head and howled with laughter. Some of his crew joined him as he moved about the deck making ribald jokes which the men enjoyed.

"I don't understand Arabic," the unnerved first

mate stammered.

"He's promising them rewards if they capture us without skin wounds," translated Brett, who understood only too well. "He's a cunning villain and will kill a man without a qualm, but this may be enough to make the difference. Tell the men to save their shot until the last when it may count for something. There's no sense in getting ourselves killed unnecessarily." Again the first mate moved among his men, but the two ships came together before he had completed his circuit, and the air was filled with the pirates' bloodcurdling screams as they leaped from their ship.

Some of the pirates, overly anxious to win the rewards, leaped too soon and fell into the water on their own, but the first wave was repulsed and sent splashing into the cold sea. To the surprise of everyone, Raisuli only laughed and mocked his men in the water. "Will you let a few soft Christians make fools of you? How can you go home to your women with your pride floating in the sea?"

A few more of his men were unceremoniously thrown into the water, but once the ships locked it was impossible to hold them off any longer. The pirates boarded in force, and within minutes the deck was covered with struggling men. Using their old and unfamiliar weapons bravely, the crew fought desperately to drive them back, but the pirates were secure in the superiority of their numbers and weapons, and they fought steadily to bring the ship under control.

Charles fought valorously, but he was unused to such efforts and was soon sent sprawling by a blow from a big hairy fist. The first mate followed right behind him. The captain regained consciousness sufficiently to see what was happening and decided to stay right where he was.

In the midst of the seething, struggling mass of humanity, Brett fought like a man possessed. Raisuli knew he was the prize of the lot and kept an eye on him.

"Go easy with him, Asra. We don't want any bloody wounds," he called to one muscular individual closing in on him. But Brett deflected the blow and sent the man reeling toward the rail with a cut tendon. Raisuli's eyes glistened in admiration as he landed on the deck with a flourish.

"What a pirate he would make!" Raisuli taunted his men as he took up a position on the bow where he could direct the battle. "He fights like the devil himself. Maybe the woman belongs to him." He watched Brett cut down another of his men. "These Christians are so selfish with their women. They do not like to share."

It wasn't long before Brett was the only man left fighting; the crew were either unconscious or held prisoner.

"Women!" Raisuli spat in disgust as he continued to taunt his men with Brett's superiority. "You are no more than beardless boys before this raging bull. Three of you go after him, and yet he cuts you down one by one. Can none of you tame him for me?" Raisuli's taunts infuriated his men, but fewer and fewer of them were willing to risk Brett's sword. Brett fought tirelessly, with his back to the row of deck cabins, and one after another of the men who faced him fell away until at last Raisuli's good humor turned sour.

"Fools!" he screamed. "If I do not stop him, he will defeat all of you one by one." Uttering a string of blasphemous curses, he climbed onto the roof of the cabins and moved with catlike tread until he was directly behind Brett. Waiting only until Brett moved forward to press the attack against a much-

297

scarred foe, he jumped noiselessly down to the deck; a sixth sense warned Brett of danger, but he was too late to dodge the blow from the hilt of Raisuli's sword that sent him crumpling to the deck.

"This man is worth a dozen of you," Raisuli said, waving his sword at his pirates. "With him at my side, I could rule the whole Mediterranean. It is too bad he is a Christian dog."

Raisuli strode the deck of the captured ship like a king. He was a mean and petty man of small stature and only moderate physical strength, but he had a cruel and cunning mind that had earned him unquestioned command over his ignorant and ragged forces. He got a feeling of cruel satisfaction from humiliating his captives when they were defenseless and likely to beg for mercy, and he inspected the men with slow and deliberate malice. Grinning expectantly at one hugely muscled sailor, he said, "Hmm, if I have you castrated, you'll make a perfect eunuch." The man nearly fainted as the pirate crew jeered its ribald enjoyment.

Next he approached a handsome young man with a smooth chin and a clear skin. He had him roughly stripped and as the poor unfortunate flushed crimson, Raisuli leaned forward and whispered loudly in his ear, "I know a grand Turk who would pay a king's ransom to have you in his bed." He screeched with laughter when the man blanched and struggled vainly to free himself.

He nudged Brett's inert form with his booted foot. "This is the prize of the lot." He pulled Brett's head up by the hair and then let it drop back to the deck with a thump. "With a physique like that, he won't die of the heat or overwork. He'll be worth his weight in gold to some planter, or the planter's wife." He howled with laughter once more.

Abruptly his humor changed and he became anxious to finish his work. "Search every corner of this ship," he shouted to his men. "I want the girl found at once." He paced the deck impatiently while his men fanned out to ransack the ship from one end to the other.

As his impatient strides brought him near where the captain still lay, the man opened his eyes and spoke softly in Arabic. "Did the dey send you? Did he give you my money?"

Raisuli froze, his attention riveted but his gaze still straight ahead. "I do not work for anyone," he hissed.

"I sent a message from Gibraltar to warn the dey about the man."

"I do not come for a man. It is the woman I seek."

"Forget her. The man is the one who will ruin the dey's plans."

"So you are playing at the traitor," Raisuli sneered, his cold, hard gaze suddenly turned squarely on the captain. "I do not talk to a dog like you." A vicious kick to the unfortunate man's head broke his neck. "Now you have no need of your money."

Raisuli turned back to his men, his temper worse and his mood blacker because they had failed to turn up any sign of the girl.

"There's no trace of a woman," one man reported. "Not even a dress or a comb."

Raisuli boiled with impotent fury. "Damn Yukor's eyes. If that fat pig has sent me on a fool's errand, I'll spill his guts and leave them for the buzzards." He turned to Brett, but neither he nor the first mate showed any signs of life. "Search again. I want every inch of this ship turned inside out, including these cabins."

"One of them is locked, but the others contain nothing but trunks and crates being shipped to the British consul in Algiers."

"Break everything open. The girl could be hiding anywhere, even in a trunk."

Brett regained consciousness in time to see one of Raisuli's men throw his considerable bulk against the door to Kate's cabin, and fear for Kate drove him to superhuman effort. Throwing off the two men that held him, Brett struggled to his feet and plowed his way through half of Raisuli's force before anyone could stop him. Of the two men who first attempted to seize him, one fell back with a broken collarbone and the other a smashed nose. Brett was almost buried by the bodies of his attackers before he could be brought down.

"What's wrong with you?" Raisuli screamed at his struggling men. "Are you weak virgins that it takes six of you to hold one man?" Under the scorn of their leader, the pirates finally managed to pin Brett to the deck. "Knock him out before he overpowers you again. He's better than I thought," Raisuli mused as Brett slumped to the deck again. "Someone will pay dearly for him."

He looked at the locked door then back at Brett's inert form. "So the little bird thinks to escape from me by locking a flimsy door," he said, amused. "Break it down. She must be in there."

A sail boom was found and they fragmented the door on the first try. "Bring her out," Raisuli shouted. One of the men put his hand through the splintered hole in the door and fumbled with the knob before he was able to unlock the door. It swung inward on its own, and he stepped forward. The moment his foot lifted from the floor, the onlookers were dumbfounded to hear the loud report of a pistol and see the man drop. There was a bullet hole neatly centered in his chest.

The stunned silence was broken by Raisuli's loud voice shouting more Arabic curses. "Drag the Christian whore out by the hair. If she is not as beautiful as Yukor says, I'll blind the lying beggar."

Suddenly the fear-crazed Mark launched himself from the dark shadows of the cabin and threw himself at Raisuli. Thinking it was Mark who had fired the shot, Raisuli drew his sword and severed the unfortunate boy's head from his body with one powerful swipe. The air was rent by a scream. A pirate stepped across the bodies to reach the girl he assumed was now alone and defenseless; again the sound of a pistol exploded from inside the room and a man fell dead.

Raisuli lost all control of himself. Screaming filthy abuse, he unexpectedly grabbed Brett by the hair and pulled him to where Kate could see him through the open door. She stood by the bed, two pistols in her hands. For a second, Raisuli paused in stunned surprise as he realized that it was this young girl who was responsible for shooting two men as neatly as any he'd ever seen in his life; but in spite of his stunned surprise, he was murderously angry at the loss of his men.

"Come out of there," he ordered. When Kate remained motionless, he called out again. "Didn't you hear me, you infidel she-wolf? I'll have this man cut into little pieces before your eyes." As an afterthought, he added, "You can leave your pistols behind."

Kate dropped the useless pistols to the floor, and as though propelled by an unseen force, she began to move toward the door. But she stopped at the doorway, unable to force herself to walk over the jumble of bodies lying in her path. Raisuli motioned to some of his men, and the bodies were pulled from the doorway and callously shoved overboard.

"Now let's have a look at you." Raisuli could see no more than Kate's outline in the dark cabin until she stepped into the early-morning sunlight; then a single glance at the unbelievable beauty of this girl sent a shock of pure surprise racing through his body and flamed his animal passions to such a consuming heat he forgot his surroundings, the crew, the ships, even that he intended to sell her for a fortune. Blood thundered in his veins, and lust blocked out everything except his desire to take his pleasure of this gift from Allah. He didn't care if she lost half her value; he might even keep her for himself. She was the most beautiful thing he'd ever seen. With something like this waiting at home, he wouldn't mind longer stays on land. He was getting too old to be roaming the sea all the time anyway. A quiet little village, a cool house with this girl to warm his body and satisfy his loins, and life would be sweet indeed.

He swaggered up to Kate and took her chin roughly in his grasp. "Yukor did not lie. You are worthy of the great sultan himself."

Kate's frightened eyes never left Raisuli's face, but her whole mind was on Brett. He looked so lifeless. If she could only have touched him to make sure he was still breathing.

Raisuli turned her face from one side to the other. He spun her around in front of him noticing how the high breasts thrusting out against the fabric of the dress further accentuated the slimness of the waist. He reached out to catch his fingers in the neck of her dress and rip it away so he could study her charms unhindered, but Kate drew back with a tiny gasp of fright.

Anger and lust warred in his breast; lust won, and he erupted with hoarse, heated laughter that sent terror racing through every part of Kate's body. She prayed for strength, knowing she had to wait; she must do nothing to antagonize him while he held Brett's life in his grasp. He grabbed her roughly and took her into his arms. The ugliness of the man and the stench of his unkempt body were too much for Kate and she fainted, slithering to the deck at his feet.

Raisuli spat out another oath. He couldn't decide whether to take her like she was, or wait until she regained consciousness. Her face, so angelically fair, and the sensual allure of her creamy skin fanned his appetite and he couldn't wait. He picked her up and was nearly driven crazy by the warmth of her young body in his arms, the fresh smell of her skin that filled his nostrils. Blind to all danger, he couldn't control himself; he had to have this girl. He didn't care if he lost a fortune on the auction block. He'd never get another chance at such a prize as this and the temptation was too much for him to withstand. He signaled two men to guard the door as he started to drag her toward the cabin she had just left.

Kate had only pretended to faint, but when she found herself pressed to Raisuli's odorous body with his foul breath in her face, she nearly fainted in truth. Keeping her arms clasped close to her side, she fumbled with her right hand under the ample folds of her dress until her agitated fingers closed around the hilt of the dagger she had hidden. Her body was suddenly infused with energy, and as Raisuli started to carry her through the doorway, she struggled to regain her feet.

Electrified by her sudden awakening, Raisuli hungrily fastened his lips to hers and pressed her body against his inflamed loins. With one rough hand he fumbled with the buttons as he tried to get inside the bodice of her dress.

Fighting waves of nausea, Kate gathered all her strength and tore loose from his grasp. Raisuli's anger flamed to a dangerous heat, but before the first word could pass his lips, Kate snatched the dagger from its hiding place. In one desperate lunge, it flashed through the air and sank deep into his throat, parting flesh from flesh and tearing through tissue and sinew. The razor-sharp blade severed Raisuli's jugular just above the collarbone and his life's blood spilled over Kate and the deck in huge rhythmic spurts. An expression of bemused questioning covered Raisuli's face; he staggered back two steps and slowly sank to the deck where he lay at her feet as the last feeble tremors of life left his body.

Stunned by her own deed, Kate dropped the knife with a clatter as she stumbled back from the bleeding corpse.

For a moment everyone stared in shocked disbelief at the gruesome and unexpected death of the pirate leader at the hands of this frail girl; in the next instant, everything was pandemonium. Sailors who had minutes before given themselves up for dead grabbed any weapon they could see, even the pirate's own weapons held momentarily in slack hands, and sprang at their enemies. The ruffians came to life, too, but without their leader they were disoriented and their efforts to recapture the ship were soon in confusion.

Then a piercing cry of warning cut through the noise of the conflict.

Chapter 21

The pirates who fell into the water had climbed aboard their own ship by the sea ladders placed there for that very purpose and were following the progress of the battle on the captured ship with real, if dampened, enthusiasm. The unexpected turn of events caused them to forget their usual caution, and unnoticed by any of them, the ships were drifting rapidly toward the coast and a French man-of-war that was racing toward them under full sail. The single pirate's frenzied cry of alarm caught the attention of his mates, and their eyes turned in the direction of his shaking finger. It was their united cry that finally penetrated the confusion and clamor of battle and caused the combatants to pause. The approach of the French ship and the sight of their fellows preparing to leave them behind filled the pirates with panic and they scrambled to regain their own ship as quickly as possible, even abandoning their victims in the act of aiming a blow. For them, capture meant certain death.

In the wild melee, the pirate who had directed the search for Kate suddenly swept her up over his shoulder and dashed for his ship. Charles had partially regained his senses by now, and he made a valiant attempt to intercept him, but the man grabbed one of the ropes which had been used to tie the ships together and swung across the water, safely out of Charles's grasp. Ruthlessly tossed over the man's shoulder like a sack of corn, Kate was held virtually upside-down, and the small pistol she had hidden in her dress clattered to the deck of the pirate ship as her captor landed with a thud. Now she was defenseless against whatever awaited her.

Leaving their tardy and wounded mates to fend for themselves, the pirates cut the last of the ropes holding the two ships together and made a desperate attempt to turn their vessel around before the French warship could overhaul them. The last pirates left on board either jumped into the sea or were run through by a crew who had been revived and heartened by the sight of the fleeing pirates, as well as spurred on to one final effort by the shame of knowing they had failed to save Kate.

The commander of the French ship called to them as he passed to ask if they needed help.

"No," the first mate, now in command of the ship, called back, "but I have an Englishman here I need to turn over to you." But first he wanted the pirates captured. He glanced again at the body of the captain and a frown furrowed his brow. Why had he been killed? Why had he been talking to Raisuli? There was some mystery about this whole thing and he wanted it cleared up. He owed that to his crew.

"There's a second ship on the way," the French commander called back as the two ships quickly separated. "Hand him over to them. I'm going after the pirates."

The first mate went among the men checking on the wounded. It seemed a miracle that the captain and young Mark were the only casualties suffered in the attack. There were many cracked heads and some rather nasty flesh wounds, but the pirates' greed for marketable slaves had prevented them from doing any real harm to the crew. So, bruised and battered, they were able to return to the task of sailing their ship. The new commander decided he would not stop at Algiers but instead go on to Tripoli. Someone had betrayed the Englishman, and he had the feeling neither he nor his crew would be welcome in Algiers just now.

Unaware they were about to be given over to the French, Charles cut Brett's bonds. Mercifully, Brett was still unconscious, but nothing was going to help once he learned what had happened to Kate. In a way it would have been easier if he'd been killed instead of Mark. Charles had been in Brett's service for eight years and he had not foreseen, and still could hardly believe, that Brett would fall so deeply in love, but there was one thing he had learned about him: Brett could not accept failure or defeat. How was he going to live with her loss? How was he going to live with his failure to protect her? Most important of all, how was he going to live knowing she probably wasn't dead?

Charles had no answers, and he knew Brett wouldn't have any, either. It might have been more merciful if she had let him die on the yacht.

Algiers was a towering formation of dazzling whitewashed buildings dominating a snug harbor. The white cubes of the older section of the city piled up the hillside, nestling under the canons of the Ottomans and the green flag of Islam. In the labyrinths of the Medina, where overhanging eaves allowed only a slit of the vivid blue sky to be seen, Spanish, Italian, Berber, English, Greek, and Arab merchants congregated to do business. Commercial ships from every nation anchored in the azure waters of the bay and were boarded and left by way of small boats rowed between the shore and the ships.

It was some time before the French ship bearing Brett returned to port, where it was met by a large and curious crowd. A rumor had raced through the town that a ship had been set upon by pirates within sight of land earlier that morning. The mention of pirates sent a thrill of fear and excitement through a population accustomed to such things; they were anxious to see any man or ship who could fight off Raisuli. They gathered along the waterfront and the streets, their long robes merging into a single mass of off-white, while their colorful turbans dotted the whole like sugared fruits on Christmas baking. Here and there a veiled face denoted the presence of a woman, but their numbers were few.

There were only two piers of the most rudimentary kind in the busy port. As soon as the ship was tied up and a gangplank laid down, a smartly dressed man of medium height and slight build climbed down from a closed carriage and walked up the gangplank. He spoke briefly to the seaman in charge before he was escorted to the cabin of the ship's captain. It was quite some time later before he knocked at the door of Brett's cabin.

Charles opened the door with his usual cheerful demeanor despite a bandage that covered a third of his head and face. Brett, disdaining bandages, lay on his side on his cot to avoid putting pressure on two enormous knots that had formed at the base of his skull. His hands and feet were encircled by iron manacles which were firmly anchored to the wall.

"I'm Kenneth Wiggins, the English consul in Algeria," the man said, introducing himself. "I'm afraid your welcome to Algiers has been rather rude," he purred in a quiet, cultivated voice which seemed incapable of rising to anger, or any other form of passion.

Brett suddenly sat up in the bed, and despite the excruciating pain at the back of his eyes, his eager gaze fixed itself upon Wiggins. "Did they capture them?" he demanded abruptly.

"I beg your pardon?" Wiggins said, appalled by Brett's deathlike appearance.

"The pirates," Brett repeated. "Did they catch them?"

"I do not know. They haven't yet returned. I am sorry it should have to be a French ship that rescued you, but as you know, we have no regular Navy here. We could see your ship from the roof of the consulate, but there was nothing we could do. Not even one of our ships could have reached you in time."

"You've got to find out for me. I've got to know."

"Certainly," Wiggins replied, still rather cool. "But surely you can wait for their return. There is no great hurry."

"My wife was on that damned boat, man!" Brett shouted at him with savage anger. "They took my *wife!*"

"Oh, I see," Wiggins mumbled, his pale skin turning a pasty white. "That does put a rather different light on the situation." He paused for a moment, deep in thought, and then redirected his gaze to Brett. "I was not informed you were bringing a wife. I was told you were unmarried."

"We were married in France, just before I left. We didn't want to be separated so soon."

"Understandable, but rather unwise," Wiggins replied. "This is no place for a young woman."

"I know that," Brett shouted. "Don't you think I've cursed my selfishness every minute I've been awake? Just get me out of here," he said, jangling

309

the chains that held him. "I can't do a thing as long as I'm anchored to the walls of this bloody ship."

"I'm not sure I can do that at least not just yet."

"What do you mean?" Brett demanded.

"It seems the man who took over your ship gave the French captain a rather prejudicial account of your purpose in coming to Algiers. So prejudicial, in fact, he has decided to wait until he can consult his government before deciding whether to let you go."

"This is intolerable. They have no right," Brett raged.

"You also seem to have aggravated an already difficult situation by attacking the captain when he would not give you command of his ship," Wiggins continued as imperturbably as ever.

"I only wanted to follow Kate before their ship was out of sight," Brett raged, straining against the chains.

"Surely you could have tried talking to the captain before you struck him?"

"I did, but the bloody fool kept on coming up with objections, and there wasn't time to convince him. With two ships, we could have caught them for sure."

"Possibly, but you can't expect a Frenchman to allow his ship to be taken away from him, especially when the person doing the taking is an Englishman."

"I can see you're well suited to be a diplomat," Brett remarked scornfully. "You're the kind who would stand around talking policy while cutthroats burned, pillaged, and raped their way through every village in the county."

"We can't all be men of action," Wiggins purred softly, his detached gaze showing no hint of emotion. "Besides, someone has to save you intrepid warriors from the consequences of your ill-judged deeds."

"Talk if you must, but get me out of here now," Brett shouted. "Every hour lost gives those damned heathens a better chance to hide."

"I will do what I can as expeditiously as possible," Wiggins said, rising to his feet, "but I fear it will take some little time. As for the pirates, unless the French ship has kept them from going ashore, they will disappear into the countryside and our next step will be to discover where they have taken your wife. That will take even longer."

"But you can't let them keep her, man. She's an English citizen, just like you."

"If she were the queen herself, I couldn't do any more than I'm doing now," Wiggins informed him. "I have my sources, but out here everything takes time. Forgive me for asking, but is your wife pretty?"

"She's beautiful!" Brett thundered. "The most beautiful woman you'll ever see."

"Then things aren't quite so desperate after all."

"How can you say that? She's alone with those savages somewhere in the desert."

"If she is young and lovely, she is too valuable to be harmed. She is also worth too much to be sold anywhere except in one of the major slave markets, so we have time. If she is as beautiful as you say, then we have even more time. They will try to interest one of the sultan's agents in bidding for her."

"You've got to find her," Brett said, his voice suddenly more pleading than demanding. "She killed three men. They may want revenge."

"She killed three men!" Wiggins echoed, his voice losing its calm control. "How can this be?"

"She shot two of the pirates and severed Raisuli's

jugular with a single knife thrust," Brett said, unable to keep the pride from his voice.

"Raisuli!" Wiggins repeated, his voice rising yet another octave. "Are you trying to make me believe your *wife* has killed the most feared pirate in the Mediterranean?"

"You can ask anybody on the ship," Charles said, speaking for the first time. "They all saw it."

"Your ship did not stop here," Wiggins said, recovering some of his control. "The French captain doesn't know where they were headed."

"Then someone did sell information about us," Brett said, black fury working in his face.

"Most probably. Any kind of information can be bought for a price, but that need not concern us any longer. I will see what can be done about your release. I'll also set inquiries in motion to discover where they have taken your wife and what they plan to do with her. Until then, you really can do nothing, even if you were free, so lie back and do strive to contain your temper in the presence of your captors. You do neither your cause nor ours any good by such intemperate behavior."

"The bloodless turnip," Brett hissed after Wiggins had departed. "I have no doubt he was glad to leave his wife in England. He'd probably have apoplexy if she ever bared her breasts to him."

But Brett soon forgot Wiggins. Kate's whereabouts and safety were the only thoughts occupying his mind. Ever since he had awakened to find himself chained to the wall, he had gone over the battle step by step, from the time the warning bell rang until he was knocked out the second time, searching for something he could have done differently, some way he had failed, but he couldn't think of what they could have done to defeat the pirates. They were lucky to have gotten off so easily, and they would all be headed for some slave market if the French ships had not come to their rescue. But it was hard to be thankful for the French intervention when it was the French commander who had refused to go after Kate and who now kept Brett from following.

He tried hard to believe Wiggins's assurances of Kate's safety, and he succeeded most of the time, but then he would remember her great beauty and worry would nearly drive him crazy. He didn't know Raisuli had tried to rape her—Charles had decided there was nothing to be gained by telling him—so he was able to believe Wiggins knew what was likely to happen because he knew the people and their habits. It was fear that had driven him to try to take over the French ship, it was fear that caused him to strain against the chains until his skin was broken and bleeding, and it was fear that made him feel physically ill when he thought of what could happen to Kate. He had to believe she was safe. Otherwise—well, he couldn't face the otherwise.

He closed his eyes and lay back, but he couldn't rest. He was bombarded by memories of mornings when he would wake and be awed by Kate's glorious beauty as though he were seeing it for the first time, of afternoons when they played together like lifelong friends, of evenings when they battled over cards or shared thoughts on any number of subjects, or of nights in her arms when he felt like he never wanted the dawn to come. Over and over he could see the love in her eyes, feel her soft skin, smell her hair and skin, taste her lips, hear her voice as she called out his name, and the thought that he might never experience any of these again was cruel torture.

But it was the feeling of helplessness that was

the hardest of all on his temper. Never before had he been a prisoner, and only common sense kept him from senselessly struggling against the chains that bound him. His proud spirit rebelled at the knowledge someone had dared to confine him, and it was all he could do to keep from swearing vengeance on the French captain even though he knew he would have been just as helpless had he been free. Wiggins was right, however little Brett wanted to admit it; if the French ship did not capture them before they reached land, they would be gone beyond recall, vanished into the innumerable towns and villages from whence they and their kind continued to spring every year. To have gone charging into the countryside would have endangered his life and Kate's, as well as doomed any hope he had of accomplishing his mission. His mind told him there was nothing he could do now, that the best course was to wait for the French ship to return and for Wiggins to learn what he could. But then he would think of Kate, remember some little quirk, some little thing she did, something she said, the way she would laugh when she hit the center of the target, the way she would scatter the cards all over the room when he beat her, and the pain would be so great he was certain he would die if he didn't get up and do something.

He lay back and tried to clear his mind of everything except his mission. True, there was nothing he could do about that, either, but at least it didn't make him feel like his insides were being pulled out by hot pincers.

Kate awoke to strange surroundings for the third consecutive day, but she sensed at once she was in a very different place this time. Even before she opened her eyes she could tell it was quiet, cool, and that she was sleeping on a soft, luxurious bed. After the terrors and discomforts of the last two days, that in itself was reassuring. It meant she was someplace where she was valued higher than by the unwashed man who had taken her off the ship.

She opened her eyes and looked around. She was in a small but luxuriously furnished room. Gleaming brocade covered walls of veined marble, while carpets were piled two and three thick over the floor. She lay on a raised podium mounded high with fluffy mattresses and pillows; its sides were covered in bright tiles framed with strips of cedar and held in place with silver nails. A bowl of fruit sat on a low onyx table; Kate took a date and ate it hungrily. She had been offered plenty of food since they had taken her from the ship, but she didn't always know what it was and often the smell alone was enough to make her stomach rebel. Here at last was something she recognized and could enjoy.

Once the edge was off her hunger, Kate began to be curious about her surroundings, but the only door to her chamber was locked. Clearly, she was no closer to being free than she had been before.

For the one hundredth time, her thoughts went back to Brett. She couldn't forget how he looked when she last saw him, pale and sprawled over the deck. Was he badly hurt? Was he still alive? She dared not allow her mind to dwell on that last question. He *had* to be alive. Otherwise there would be no point in living. She had been nothing but bad luck for him ever since he tried to help her. Maybe he was better off without her. Maybe he wouldn't want to see her again after this. Her dreary thoughts were interrupted by the sound of a key in the lock and the door was opened by an enormous black man who looked as fierce as the pirate who had abducted her. Kate gasped and drew back, but immediately a tiny woman of many years ducked under his arm and entered bearing an armload of clothes.

"You may go, Bismillah." She spoke to the huge eunuch in Arabic, but turned and addressed Kate in English. "I see you are as beautiful as they said."

"You speak English?" Kate gasped.

"I *am* English," the girl replied. "My name was Susan, but I am now called Olema. I have been here many years."

"But how did you get here? How did *I* get here?"

"You came in the night, on a litter carried between two asses. I came out many years ago to marry a cousin, but our ship was captured off Corsica and I was sold. I have been here ever since. All in all, it is probably a better life. I must work hard, but I am cared for and I live comfortably."

"But where am I?" Kate asked.

"You are in Algiers. This is the palace of the dey."

A thrill of relief coursed through Kate. "But why was I brought here? Who brought me? Are they going to let me see my husband? Are they going to free me?"

"I have the answer to none of those questions," Olema replied with no indication that she was interested in Kate's past or her future. "I have been instructed to prepare you for an audience with the dey. That is why I am here."

"But you must help me."

"I shall. I have brought you clothes, and soon Bismillah will return with water to bathe you and scented oils to rub over your body."

"I mean you must help me to get out of here,

316

find my husband."

"There is no escape from the dey's palace," Olema said, her voice still flat and disinterested. "It is best that you put it out of your mind. You are to make preparations to see the dey."

"But I want to go to my husband," Kate insisted. "He's here in Algiers, I know he is. He landed several days ago when the pirates took me from the ship. Surely that's the reason the dey has brought me here."

"I do not know what the dey will do with you. That is not my place," Olema said. "My duty is to prepare you for your visit to the dey's apartments, and that is what I shall do." So saying, she began to spread out the various garments she had over her arm. Kate had never seen anything like them and didn't have any idea how they should be worn, but she could tell from the material that they were too sheer to cover much of her body unless she was going to wear several layers of them all at once. Bismillah, accompanied by several other slaves who entered bearing trays of food, beakers of water, a basin, slippers, and several things Kate never seen before, returned with the bath oils.

"Now you must allow me to bathe you," Olema said when they had withdrawn. "The dey does not like for people to have an odor." Kate allowed herself to be undressed. After three days in her clothes, she was too glad to be rid of the hateful apricot dress to feel immodest. It was a wonderful luxury to have herself gently bathed in warm, scented water in the comfort of her chamber. There was even a small brazier to take the chill out of the air. It was a far cry from hot water carried up to a copper tub in her icy bedchamber at Ryehill.

"Tell me something about the dey," she asked after Olema's gentle rubbing had rid her body of

317

some of its tension. "Where am I?"

"You're in the harem," Olema answered without slowing her work.

"I'm *where?*" demanded Kate with a near shriek.

"The harem," Olema repeated. "It is where all the women of the palace live. It is the only place we are allowed."

So Brett had not been exaggerating after all. She *was* in a harem, and she had no idea when or how she was going to get out.

"But who are the women who live here?" Kate asked, unable to suppress her curiosity.

"They are many people—the dey's mother, his wives, and their households. Then there are the concubines and their attendants. Finally, there are the eunuchs who are responsible for the harem."

"How many people is that?"

"I don't know. Certainly several hundred altogether."

"And they all belong to the dey?"

"The dey is a very rich man. He has many wives."

"Do they know I am here?"

"The wives? Not yet, maybe, but they will know soon. The concubines knew as soon as you were brought in last night. Your arrival caused quite a disturbance. There are not many comings and goings here, and everyone gossips about everything."

"What are your usual duties?" Kate asked Olema.

"I used to serve the old dey's sister. She died last summer and I have been with the dey's mother, but she has her own household and does not need me. I am now your servant."

"But I'm not staying here. I'm sure the dey will send for my husband as soon as I explain to him what happened."

"No one ever leaves the harem," Olema stated with finality.

"But I must. I mean, I will," Kate insisted. And she continued to do so while Olema dressed her in the traditional costume of the harem, which left little of her charms unrevealed. Her hair was pulled back from her face and hung loosely down her back. She wore a sheer top over a halter that supported rather than covered her breasts, and pair of loose pants that left her stomach and ankles exposed. The velvet slippers on her feet did nothing to make her feel properly dressed.

"I can't go anywhere looking like this," Kate protested. "I'd be more modestly attired in my chemise."

"Come. It is time to leave." Her protest had no effect on Olema, and Kate soon found herself in an immense sitting room as long and as wide as a cathedral. Its vaulted ceiling was a fresco of woven cedar strips; a marble fountain gave the air its freshness and serenity, cascading water falling from one basin to another its soft music. The room was crowded with dozens of women clad in equally scanty raiment. Talking energetically as they ate and reclined on podiums shaped like long sofas, they fell silent when Kate entered. If the looks they directed toward her were any indication, they didn't like the way she looked, either.

"They do not like you," Olema explained. "You are more beautiful than any of them, and each is afraid you will take her place in the dey's affections."

"Tell them I don't want to displace anybody, that I don't want any affections beyond those of my husband, and that I don't even know the dey."

"It is not what you say that matters," Olema informed her bluntly. "It is what the dey says, and he has called for you first on this day, even before his wives. Even more portentous, it is a rule that the dey does not see any woman before evening. An exception is made only for his mother. He has called for you to join him at breakfast." Kate felt a chill of apprehension. She didn't know what all this meant, but if she were to judge from the looks around her, it didn't bode well. They passed out of the large chamber, crossed an open court, passed through a small garden, then through a larger one, then entered still another garden which led to a much larger building. As they moved along the paths, they passed a tiny woman with glistening black hair and hard eyes who glared at Kate with undisguised fury.

"Who is that?" Kate asked. "Why does she stare at me so?"

"That is Nuzhat al-Zaman, the dey's first wife. Her son is the heir. She fears you because you are much more beautiful than she ever was."

"But why, if *she* is the dey's wife?"

"Your hair is white. That alone would make you one to be hated. These men, both the Turks and the Africans, prize women of white hair." Kate was silent, but she noted that of the gazes she encountered, only the slaves were curious; the others seemed angry. It was almost a relief when they arrived at the dey's compound. They were ushered in by two black Nubian eunuchs who were even larger than the ones she had seen in the harem.

Kate came to a halt just inside the door, unsure of what was expected of one upon meeting a dey. She was even more bewildered when she saw a slim, handsome, and relatively young man reclining on a bed piled high with cushions directing a penetrating gaze in her direction.

Chapter 22

"Come closer," he said, his English excellent but heavily accented. "I did not expect Raisuli to bequeath me such a fine treasure."

"You paid Raisuli to steal me?" Kate said before she could think whether that was a wise question.

"No," the dey replied, beckoning her to move closer still. "I have never known Raisuli to do anything except what he wanted, whether he was paid or not. No, it seems it was your knife that destined you to end up in my possession."

"P-possession?" Kate stammered.

"Perhaps that was the wrong word," the dey corrected himself, inviting her to be seated on a cushion near him. "Shall we say 'in my care', instead?"

"Please, I want to see my husband. He's an Englishman. His name is—"

"I know who your husband is, and I know his name," the dey stated, his smile a little strained. "I also know what he came here to do, and that does not make him my friend."

"I don't really know what he's supposed to do, but I'm sure he doesn't *want* to do anything you would dislike," Kate stammered wildly, trying to think of something to say that would not anger this cold-eyed man. "He only does what his government wants."

"And I do only what I want," the dey murmured. "I am the government in Algeria, you see." Kate did see, and it frightened her half to death.

"How did I get here? How did you know I was

on the ship?"

"I knew of your husband, but I knew nothing of you. That was a pleasant surprise." Kate didn't think he looked particularly pleased. "You see, your captain warned me your English husband was coming here to interfere with my plans."

"The captain?" Kate squeaked, unbelieving. "He wouldn't do anything like that. He is an Englishman."

"It is not a nice thing to betray one's own country, even for money, but your captain did so. I am very sorry Raisuli killed him. He has been very helpful."

"Raisuli killed him?"

"You did not know?" Kate shook her head. "Ah well, it is done with now. How you came to be here is much more interesting."

"I was carried off by a foul brute," Kate asserted, remembering the rough man who had locked her in a cabin and then thrown her across a horse the moment they landed. Her body still ached from that terrible ride to the squalid village where she had spent her first night.

"I do not know what your *brute* intended to do with you, but that is no longer a concern. He was a Moroccan peasant. They are less than camel dung." The dey spat out a grape seed. "He was also stupid not to know beauty such as yours cannot go unremarked anywhere, especially in a country like Algeria. One of my representatives tried to bargain for you. Unfortunately, the man would not cooperate. He will not go to sea again." Kate was appalled at the dey's complete indifference to death. "I think my servant meant you to become a concubine in my harem, but by the time you arrived last night, the news of your husband's loss had spread through all of Algiers, and no one had any doubt as to who you were."

"Then you don't want me for your harem?"

"What I want is not a matter to be taken into consideration, at least not yet," the dey said, his eyes as unblinking as a dead fish. "However, if your husband does not value you as he should, perhaps I may reconsider."

"He wants me back," Kate announced, desperately hoping Brett's love for her was stronger than his desire to find Abd el-Kader.

"This may surprise you, but I hope he does, quite as much as you do."

"Why?" Kate didn't trust the dey at all.

"I hope we may be able to strike a bargain?"

"What kind of bargain?" Kate asked, but she knew already.

"He was about to do something I would not like. If I were to keep you for my harem, that would be something *he* would not like. Why should both of us be unhappy when it would be so easy for each of us to be well pleased with the other?"

"You're holding me as a kind of ransom so Brett won't talk to el-Kader?"

"That's not exactly the way I had it planned."

"You mean you won't give me back?"

"Certainly I will give you back to your husband. I keep my promises, but not for a mere pledge not to seek out el-Kader. I think it would be more prudent to keep you with me until your husband has quit the country, maybe even left the Mediterranean, before I returned you to him."

Kate's heart sank. "He'll never do that. It would humiliate him too deeply. He may agree to your requirements if they are reasonable, but he won't work against his country, not even to save his wife or himself. He will *never* compromise his honor. He couldn't go back to England if he did."

323

"I see." The dey paused. "I must think about this further. It would be foolish to offer conditions which are impossible for him to accept. How fortunate that you are here to consult with me. You can guide me, help me decide just how far I can press him." His words made Kate feel like a traitor.

"I will call for you again as soon as I have taken council with my ministers." He clapped his hands and the two enormous eunuchs swung open the door to reveal Olema waiting for Kate just outside. "Treat her well, and provide her with anything she needs for her comfort," he commanded, then turned away in dismissal.

Kate hurried from the chamber wondering what this cold-blooded man was going to think of next. She knew Brett's love for her was strong, but she also knew his sense of honor was at least as strong, and was of much longer standing. She prayed the dey would not demand so much of Brett he couldn't accept it, but she had a feeling deep in her heart the dey understood nothing of the honor that operated in Brett or anyone else in England. She didn't want to spend the rest of her life in a harem, and she didn't want to *ever* be forced to endure the embraces of that cold, conscienceless despot, but it looked as though her chances of seeing Brett again were growing dimmer.

Behind the closed doors, the dey leaned back on his pillows, the lingering excitement from Kate's presence amiably teasing his senses. He found himself wondering if it would be possible to keep her for himself and at the same time induce Brett to stay out of his affairs. Maybe he would wait to let the Englishman know he had his wife. There was always a chance the French would keep him, or send him to England themselves, or that he would go on his own. If any of these occurrences materialized, there would be no need for anyone to know he had the white-haired woman. He would have achieved his objective without using her as a pawn. And he could think of several other ways he would very much like to use her.

Wiggins studied the French commander with a frosty eye. "It should not be necessary for us to even hold this conversation. Our envoy was handed over to you during an act of war, as it were, for his safety. Holding him in confinement, and most particularly in chains, can be viewed as a breach of diplomatic ethics."

"France does not appreciate what he was to do here."

"Neither do I appreciate what *you* do here," Wiggins replied with a hauteur the Frenchman could not equal, "but I do not hold you in chains."

"That you *cannot* do," the French commander replied, indignant at the thought, but feeling a little superior as well. "You do not have the means."

"In diplomatic circles it is not, and never has been, the practice for *strong* nations to hold the ambassadors of *weaker* nations under restraint." Wiggins spoke as though he were addressing a particularly slow student, which infuriated the Frenchman. "If that were the case, England would hold all of France's emissaries in fetters." The Frenchman seethed with fury, but there was no denying that England ruled the seas.

"Do you propose to take him from me by force?"

"As you've so acutely observed, I do not have the means. However," Wiggins continued, wiping a smile of satisfaction off the commander's face, "my government may see a precedent for future behavior in this single act. It is quite possible they may wish to make an issue of it. I do not say they *will*—one can never speak for one's government in every instance—but would you wish to be the cause of an international incident? Do you consider your actions to have been so well thought out that your government would stand behind you?"

The French commander had put Brett in chains because it was the only way he could control him; he had kept him there because it was convenient and would annoy the British, but he had no wish to attract the attention of his superiors. The reason he was in this hellhole now was that he was in disfavor with the government at present.

"I see no reason why a single man should be the cause of so much trouble," the Frenchman said at last. "After all, what can one Englishman do?"

"I agree with your first statement. As to the second, perhaps a perusal of history would enlighten you," Wiggins said, rising to his feet. "We dine at eight o'clock at the consulate. I should hate for Mr. Westbrook to be late for his dinner."

Brett managed to stand still long enough for Charles to help him into his coat, but he was bursting with eagerness to see Wiggins. The French commander had released him just hours earlier, and he had come straight to the consulate intending to corner Wiggins and demand he begin an immediate search for Kate. Instead he'd been handed a message saying Wiggins wouldn't be back until dinner but that he hoped to have some news of his wife's fate by then.

Even though he knew there was nothing he could do until morning, Brett strained at the bit to do

326

something immediately. It had been three days since Kate was captured, and thoughts of what had happened to her, what *might* be happening to her now, kept needling him, accusing him, destroying his peace and his control over his temper. He had told Kate they would be helpless if she were captured, but he had never realized the full weight of his words until she had disappeared and he found himself powerless to do anything, unable to even make up his mind where was the best place to begin. In England, the government could have been called upon to deploy the combined expertise of all its separate departments to hunt down and punish her captors. Here, the government was more likely to reward the villains and take a share of the profits.

"While I'm at dinner, see if you can learn anything from the natives who work in the consulate," Brett told Charles. "Make it clear I'll pay generously for any information they can give us, even if it's only a rumor."

"And after that?"

"I'll be able to tell you more after I've talked with Wiggins and whoever this man is he's invited to dinner."

Brett found no one in the salon when they came down, and he cursed vigorously. Three days of waiting while he lay flat on his back had exhausted his patience and his Christian charity. He craved something to do, someone to fight, or an arduous physical task to accomplish, anything but this infernal waiting. He felt so utterly useless, so frustrated and helpless, that he had the urge to run into the street and beat the first man he saw into a bloody pulp. But before desperation could cause him to turn his back on Wiggins and take the whole thing into his own hands, the consul walked into the room as imperturbable as ever.

"Thank you for arranging for my release," Brett said, struggling to control his impatience and his dislike of a man who seemed to think his wife's disappearance was of no more importance than dinner. "It's galling to have to be grateful for such a damnable mess."

"Put it down to overreaching ambition," Wiggins replied. "The commander hoped to restore himself to favor by detaining you. I merely pointed out the possibility he had made a miscalculation."

"And . . ?" Brett asked encouragingly.

"I implied our government might take his action as a sign of future policy and feel required to express their disapproval."

"And his government would undoubtedly sacrifice him rather than back him up with ships."

"I said I thought it the more probable course of events."

"Even though you know the French government is just looking for an excuse to bring their troops into Algiers and that England has no intention of fighting over Algeria?"

"If his superiors have not seen fit to inform him of the current opinion in government circles, then I see no reason why I should do it for them."

"I can see why you've been so successful," Brett said, his admiration genuine. "I'm surprised they haven't called you back to England."

"I can't stand the climate," Wiggins replied in clipped tones.

"Who is this man you've invited to meet me?" Brett asked abruptly. He was all out of patience with polite conversation.

"Someone I hope might be able to help us discover the whereabouts of your wife. I have set inquiries of my own afoot, but to no avail. It is possible this man can succeed where I have failed. He may also agree to help you recover her, but it will be up to you to convince him it would be to his advantage to help you."

"What is his name?"

"Ibrahin. He is the second son of Mohammed Ali, governor of Egypt. He is a relatively young man, but it is a sign of the respect in which he is held that his father has sent him here alone. This is one of the most sensitive spots in Africa and one that needs expert watching. In thirty years, Mohammed has raised himself from a tobacco merchant to ruler of Egypt, as well as the Sudan and Crete. He does not often make a mistake in the people he appoints to act for him."

"I can find Kate myself," Brett said, realizing all the time it was wounded pride speaking and not his common sense. "Why should I ask for his help?"

"Because he has the best network of spies in all of North Africa. There is nothing that happens along the Mediterranean coast he doesn't know or can't find out. If anyone can find your wife quickly, it is he. If there is anyone who would know how to go about arranging her return, it is he also."

"I'm not going to haggle with anyone where my wife's safety is concerned. I'll buy her back. I'll send agents to every auction within a thousand miles if necessary. Cost is not an object."

"You will of course do what you think best," Wiggins stated with prim indifference, "but I would strongly recommend that you talk to Ibrahin first."

"What can I offer a man such as this to cause him to help me?"

"He would be better able to answer that question than I, but I imagine he would appreciate anything you can do to help him toward his goal."

"And what is that? Or does he have several?"

"He would of course have several, but I think his primary objective in Algeria is to bring the country under the influence of his father. He is always looking for opportunities to weaken the Turkish sultan."

"How does he plan to do that?"

"Probably by any one of several ways. Mohammed has never been known to be hampered by a lack of choices."

"And you think he will help me?"

"I hope he will. Unless the dey decides to find her for us, Ibrahin is your best hope."

"And you don't think the dey will help?"

"What do you think?"

"If he knows why I'm in the country, he would do anything in his power to stop me."

"He knows." Brett felt the muscles at the back of his neck tighten. He had to keep the nightmarish images of what might be happening to Kate from his mind; he couldn't think at all if he didn't.

"I am not yet sure of the source of his information, but I know he was informed of your coming and the nature of your mission before you arrived."

"Then if he knows where Kate is, he's likely to use her to force me to go back to England."

"If he can get her into his possession, that is what I think he will do."

"You're not sure he has her?"

"The dey's influence does not extend very far from Algiers, and thus he is not feared by those on the fringes of his power or those in neighboring countries. Raisuli operated out of Morocco, and they don't particularly care what the dey thinks. On the other hand," Wiggins continued, looking at his nails, "the dey is not above sending agents into

Morocco, Tunisia, and Libya as well, with orders to kill for what they want. For your sake, I hope he does know where your wife is to be found. She will be far safer in his hands." There was a brief pause before Wiggins spoke again. "When Ibrahin arrives, let me do the talking. I suspect you lack the temperament to handle him properly."

Neither man spoke for a while. Concern for the safety and whereabouts of Kate was in both their minds, but in very different degrees. Brett had almost forgotten about trying to find el-Kader, and if he had been told he could only save Kate at the expense of his mission, he would have declared for Kate without a second's pause. He worked for the Foreign Office because he enjoyed it, but he would have handed all of Africa over to the French before he would have let anyone harm a single hair on Kate's head. Had it concerned the safety of England, it might have been different, but this was Africa and there was no doubt in his mind.

Wiggins did not share his point of view. He had never met Kate; he didn't love her and he wasn't dazzled by her beauty. She was just an Englishwoman who had gotten in the way of his work, and he was anxious to get rid of her so he could go on about his business. The fact that getting rid of her meant rescuing her was not the issue—but rather, her presence in the midst of his work—and any suitable plan that would remove her was acceptable to him. Naturally, he wouldn't do anything that might harm her, but her safety was not his primary consideration. She should have stayed in England. She had no business out here, and her husband knew it if she didn't.

Their silent ruminations were interrupted by the entrance of one of the most handsome—and shortest—men Brett had ever met. He was a Turk, but he had abandoned the traditional Turkish garb except for the fez. He was dressed in a blaze of French regimentals, the smartest-looking uniform in Europe, but even they could not conceal the fact that his powerful shoulders and torso were more fitted for a man nearly twice his size. His skin was a very light olive and the characteristic features of the eastern face were muted by a generous infusion of European blood. One look at his soft brown eyes and Brett was tempted to spurn his help before it was even offered. He felt an immediate antipathy for this man; he didn't trust him, either.

Wiggins walked forward to greet his guest. "I was afraid you had decided not to come," he announced rather bluntly.

"Why should I not come to dine with the English consul?"

"I imagine you could find a reason if you wanted."

Ibrahin's face was flooded by a brilliant smile. "But of course I come. I am told you have a wonderful chef." Wiggins did not appear to be particularly pleased with the compliment.

"Let me introduce you to my guest," he said, turning to Brett. "This is Mr. Westbrook, a special envoy from our office in London."

"Your *confrère,* so to speak?" Ibrahin asked, turning to Brett.

"You might say so," Brett said, "but actually my work is of neither the importance nor the magnitude of Mr. Wiggins's responsibilities."

"In other words, you should not tar him with the same brush you may have already used on me," Wiggins said, his chilly reserve divesting his words of any possible humorous interpretation. "Shall we go in?" He indicated his guests were to precede him into the dining room.

Conversation was general while the meal was served and eaten, but after the servants had placed liqueurs on the table and withdrawn, Wiggins promptly turned to the situation at hand.

"We find ourselves faced with a rather unusual difficulty and we hoped you might be able to advise us on how to handle it," he said, ignoring Ibrahin's broad smile which clearly said, *aha, I knew you wanted something.* "As you undoubtedly already know, Mr. Westbrook's ship was attacked by Raisuli three days ago as it was coming into Algiers."

"Yes, I heard. I also heard the ship did not land but sailed on to Tripoli."

"As usual, your information is better than mine," Wiggins said with tight smile. "We did not know her destination, but that is of no interest to us, at least not at the moment."

"You are not interested that it was the captain of your own ship who told the dey you were coming?"

"The captain is dead," Brett interrupted, unable to endure the polite exchange any longer. "Those cutthroats have my wife."

Ibrahin turned his bland gaze on Brett. "Your wife? Is she pretty?"

"She's *beautiful!*" Brett exploded, "and I'm going to find her if I have to tear down every building in this country stick by stick."

"You English are so fiery. You think because you want something, you will have it. Yet you do not even know where to look or how to begin. So you have come to Ibrahin to find her for you." He spoke with irritating slowness, his smile a mask which could have concealed half the evil in the world.

"No, by God . . ." Brett half shouted, rising furiously in his seat.

"We hoped you might be willing to help us," Wiggins interrupted, in much the same bland, uninflected voice Ibrahin used. "For a consideration, of course."

"And what might that be?"

"Influence. You have come to Algiers because you want something."

Brett had to bite his tongue to keep from speaking as the two men stared silently at each other. If this was the kind of diplomacy Wiggins had to conduct, he was glad he was not a diplomat. Ibrahin's insolent, sneering manner put his teeth on edge and it was only by reminding himself over and over that Kate's life might depend on this man's help that he was able to keep from springing to his feet and choking the life out of him. He had never met anyone he had disliked and distrusted more on first glance. If Abd el-Kader was like this, he might as well turn around and go back to London.

"First, I think we must find where she is. Could you give me a description?" he asked Brett.

Brett wondered how anyone could describe with words all the things that were Kate. You needed eyes to see her beauty, a nose to smell the freshness of her hair, a tongue to taste the sweetness of her mouth, hands to feel the texture of her skin, ears to hear the music in her laugh, but most of all you needed a bottomless heart to hold all the love she poured out so unselfishly. A lifetime would not be enough to encompass what she was and he was being asked to do it in a few words.

"She's of average height, but very slim," Brett said curtly. "She has blue eyes, long blond hair, and is extremely beautiful. If anyone has seen her, they will not have forgotten."

"You sound as though you want her back very

much," Ibrahin said, letting a little surprise show. "Is it necessary to go to such trouble for one woman? You can find another."

"She is my *wife*," Brett almost shouted.

"I have six wives," Ibrahin stated nonchalantly. "I will probably have many more."

"I have only one and I don't want another."

"You English are so stubborn." Ibrahin sighed with another of his irritatingly, superior smiles, "but I think I will help you. The dey is waiting for el-Kader, el-Kader is waiting for the French, and the French are waiting for both of them. Until somebody does something, I have nothing to keep me interested. You should stay here. Do nothing. I will let you know when I have found her."

"I can't just sit around waiting. I want to help."

"I have ears planted all over Africa. I know if a mouse crosses the street. You wait. I will tell you when she is found."

"I will mount my own investigation," Brett insisted stubbornly. "There must be more than one way to gather information."

"You may do as you please, but if you interfere I shall not lift a finger to help. You English always rush about. You talk, you threaten, you are so *noisy*. I, however, know how to wait and listen, to appear uninterested in the very thing I must know. Stay here, or you may never find your wife."

"If I can't help find my own wife, am I allowed to do what the Foreign Office sent me out here to do?" Brett asked furiously, seething with inward rage because he knew Ibrahin could serve Kate better at this moment than he could.

"By all means, but do not leave Algiers just now. Who knows when I may have news for you."

"I couldn't find any news of Mrs. Westbrook," Charles told Brett the next afternoon. "I don't think anybody here knows anything."

"Did you offer to pay them?"

"Yes, but they had nothing to sell."

"I didn't do any better. Whenever I ask, they just look at me like they didn't know what I was talking about."

"Do you think they know but are afraid to say?"

"I don't know. I was sure I would, but I just don't know."

"I have found her," Ibrahin announced proudly as he entered in the middle of dinner the following evening. "Even though you and your man have been stirring the waters with your silly questions and even sillier bribes, I have already found her."

"Where is she?" Brett demanded, relief, hope, joy, and at least a dozen other emotions making him feel weak. "Take me to her at once."

"I cannot," Ibrahin declared. "In fact, if you do not leave Algiers immediately, you may never see her again."

Chapter 23

"What are you talking about?" Brett demanded, anger instantly overpowering all other emotion. "I mean to see Kate before I do anything else." Ibrahin turned to Wiggins in mute appeal.

"Sit down, Mr. Westbrook. Ibrahin will tell us what he has to say in his own time." Wiggins rang for a servant. "Would you join us for dinner, or would you prefer something to drink."

"I think I will have a little of that delicious liqueur I had last time. What was it again?"

"Drambuie."

"I must remember. I think my father would like it also."

"To hell with your liqueur," Brett exploded. "Tell me what you're talking about before I choke it out of you. Where is Kate and why can't I see her?"

"You English, always so impatient. I think I must tell you the whole story quickly." He settled himself into a chair. "Your pirates could not outrun the French ship, so they came ashore at a little village west of Algiers where they scattered into the hills. The villagers hid them for a price, whether it was money or fear I cannot say, but they could not hide your wife. You spoke truly. Everywhere she goes she is remembered. Before she had been there an hour, rumors of her beauty had spread halfway to Algiers."

"I don't want to know where she *was*," Brett thundered. "Tell me where she *is*."

"The pirates made a mistake in not getting out of Algeria before they stopped running," Ibrahin continued, ignoring Brett's interruption. "Some men in the pay of the dey heard of her and became very interested when they learned the story of her capture. It seems your arrival was expected in many circles. Someone has been very indiscreet." Brett ground his teeth with impatience.

"I am told they tried to talk this pirate into exchanging your wife for a considerable sum of money, but he thought he could get more for her in Damascus, so he headed for Tripoli. Unfortunately, he had waited too late. They found him next day with his throat cut. In the end he didn't get any money at all."

"Where is my wife, you chattering fool?" Brett demanded, his patience completely at an end.

"In the dey's palace, comfortably lodged in the harem."

Brett sprang to his feet and headed for the door.

"Where are you going?" Ibrahin asked, his voice never rising above a moderate level.

"The dey's palace," Brett called back over his shoulder. "I'll have her out of there inside an hour."

"You won't find her."

"Then I'll throttle the dey until he tells me where she is."

"Touch that man, if you make it that far, and all you will find is her body."

Brett stopped in his tracks. After a moment's frozen silence, he turned around.

"The dey thinks he has gotten what he wants from you already," Ibrahin explained. "You have not convinced el-Kader to abandon him—you have not even attempted to find him—and thus you

338

have lost your only bargaining advantage. Your consul has no Army, no ships, and the dey does not want your country's goodwill. On the other hand, he has your wife, and I am told that every time he sees her, he becomes more anxious to keep her for himself."

"So that's what you meant by leaving town. If I don't find el-Kader, the dey will have no need to let me see her again."

"See, you can think when you do not let your emotions overcome your intelligence. That is why it is good to have many wives."

"I will leave as soon as possible," Brett said, turning to Wiggins. "Tonight if I can. Do you know where el-Kader is waiting?" he asked Ibrahin.

"Of course. It is no secret that he waits at the palm oasis. With a good camel, you can be there before dawn. I will have one of my men guide you." Brett stared at Ibrahin expectantly. "You must be careful when you travel at night. Many things can happen then that would not happen in the day."

"And what do you expect me to do in return for your help?" Brett knew he should be thanking Ibrahin, but the words would not pass his lips.

"Just what you are about to do now. I do not want the French in Algeria any more than your Mr. Wiggins does. I prefer to see the dey and el-Kader snapping at each other like hungry foxes. After el-Kader has been sent back to Mascara to lick his wounds, the dey will need someone to support him in his stand against the sultan. Who better than my father, who has already defied the sultan and won.

"I'm grateful to you for finding my wife," Brett managed to say after some struggle, "but I won't plead your case with el-Kader."

"There is no need. Your country's objectives will serve me just as well."

"Then if you both will excuse me, I have some preparations to make. When can I expect your guide?"

"He is here now." Brett looked surprised. "I knew you would want to go tonight," Ibrahin explained with a deprecatory tone.

For the first time, Brett smiled. He just might be able to like this man after all.

Three days had passed since Kate had been brought to the harem, and she felt more miserable and disheartened with each passing hour. Everything possible had been done for her comfort, even to allowing Olema to scour Algiers for food more to her liking, but she was still despondent. She missed Brett and worried about what he was doing to try to find her. She knew he was strong-willed and stubborn and inclined to think he could get what he wanted by running over anyone who stood in his way, but Kate hadn't been in the harem for more than a few hours before she knew this was one time Brett wasn't going to get his way so easily. She couldn't go ten feet out of her little room without running into some huge man who blocked her way. There might be a way out of the palace itself, but she didn't think she could ever find her way out of the harem. It was enormous and she was never permitted to leave the small court where she was lodged.

The dey had sent for her at least once a day. The second time she had been summoned, she was anxious to go to him, hoping he might have a message from Brett, sure at least he wanted to talk about how far he could expect Brett to go to ransom her. Instead, he had spent the whole time asking about her trip, her life in England, and what she thought of his harem. Since her only thoughts about the harem were centered on leaving it, she had turned him off with empty words, yet she doubted he was fooled.

He had continued to call for her, and the feeling was growing in the harem that he was no longer anxious to exchange her for Brett's return to England. He refused to talk about it when she asked, and his eyes watched her more intently. Too, she had been sent some exceptionally luxurious clothes on the second day and ordered to wear them when she visited the dey. This hadn't seemed particularly important to her, but it had to Anis al-Jalis.

The concubines had not been friendly to Kate at first, but they were apparently used to having new members join their ranks on a regular basis and before twenty-four hours had lapsed, they were indifferent to her presence. The same could not be said of the dey's wives. Kate didn't know how many wives he had — they had separate houses in the compound and their own staff to see to them and their children — but two of them, Anis al-Jalis and Nuzhat al-Zaman, were familiar to her by now and she dreaded seeing them. Nuzhat was probably close to thirty-five and well beyond any years of beauty she might have had, but what Nuzhat al-Zaman lacked in youth and beauty, she made up for in hate; Kate was almost afraid to eat or sleep for fear she would be poisoned or stabbed to death.

Anis was barely older than Kate and still enjoyed the remarkable beauty which flowers so early in eastern women. She was the dey's favorite, and Kate could see why. She was very small, almost tiny, with well-rounded curves and almond-shaped eyes of jet black that gleamed as brightly as her equally dark hair. She glared at Kate when she saw her, but Kate had seen her smile on several occasions and the girl was enchanting. It was no wonder the dey called for her so often. That was all the more reason why Kate was stunned when she found herself summoned to Anis's house.

"Go to her," Olema counseled. "Anis al-Jalis is angry that you are here, but she will not harm you."

"But Nuzhat al-Zaman would?"

"Nuzhat al-Zaman will allow no one to threaten her position."

Anis's house was as beautifully appointed as its mistress. "Who sent you here?" she demanded the moment Kate was seated. "Why do you come? The dey does not need more wives. You have not been bought with money from the harem treasury."

"I don't know who brought me here," Kate said, feeling ill at ease before the accusing glare of those angry black eyes. "I'm being held for ransom, as a threat to keep my husband from doing something the dey doesn't like."

"You have a husband! You are not a virgin?" Anis exclaimed, her attitude shifting instantly. "Does he know you are here? Will he come for you?"

"I don't know if he knows. I don't know if he'll come," Kate admitted, unable to keep the tears from welling up in her eyes. "The dey refuses to tell me what is happening. I would escape if I could, but I can't even find my way out of this court. Will you help me?"

"There is no escape from the harem," Anis al-Jalis said unequivocally. "If you are being held as a ransom, you may be allowed to go, but the rest of us will never leave."

"Do you want to stay here?" Kate asked. "Don't you want to leave?"

"Why?" Anis al-Jalis asked. "Where else could I live as I do? I am the dey's favorite. He will do almost anything to please me."

"But there are so many other women here? Aren't you jealous?"

"Only of you. All men have many wives. I am only afraid to lose my position in the court. I know that time will fade my beauty, but nothing can stand against such beauty as yours. I fear the dey is even now falling under your spell. If you do not leave the harem soon, it will not matter that you have a husband."

"Please," Kate begged, "you must help me escape. I'll do anything, pay you anything, but I've got to find my husband."

"There is no escape unless the dey wills it," Anis replied firmly. "But I will tell Nuzhat al-Zaman and the others. Maybe we can encourage the dey to send for your husband."

"I'll never be able to thank you."

"Just getting rid of you will be reward enough," Anis answered candidly. "None of us feel our positions are safe with you around."

At first the noise was barely audible in the dey's apartments, but it quickly grew in volume until the men listening to the dey found themselves straining their ears in an effort to discover what could be the cause of such an unprecedented commotion. Suddenly there was a shout, then a chorus of shouts, followed by the running of many feet. Before the astonished ministers of the dey could come to their feet, the door to his chamber burst open, and Brett, literally dragging two armed guards along with him, burst into the dey's domain. His ministers rose to their feet, staring with open mouths; the security of the palace was thought to be impenetrable.

"Where is my wife?" Brett demanded, now literally surrounded by guards. "Where are you hiding her?" Only surprise, his great strength, and an exact knowledge of how to reach the dey's apartments had enabled Brett to get this far into the palace.

It was clear from his calm manner that the dey had a good idea who this intruder might be. He signaled his guards to release Brett.

"I do not know who you are and therefore cannot possibly know the whereabouts of your wife," he answered coldly, but no one believed him. If it had been true, Brett would have been dead with at least a dozen swords through his body.

"I'm Brett Westbrook, and you know where Kate is because she's right here in the palace."

"There are too many individuals in my palace for me to know the identity and whereabouts of every one of them, but I have not had cause to order any female, English I presume, to be brought here."

"You're not going to get around me like that," Brett shouted. "I know she's here, whether you yourself had her brought here or not, and I mean to have her."

"Did your estimable consul accompany you here?" the dey inquired blandly.

"No. The dullard can't be made to stir himself for any reason not his own."

344

"How unfortunate. But why don't you sit down. We can't go on talking like this."

"I don't want to sit. I just want my wife."

"And *I* want you to have your wife, but I'm afraid there are matters here that must be sifted."

"Get rid of these," Brett said, indicating the guards. The dey waved them away, and pretending to be slightly mollified, Brett took a seat. "How about them?" he asked, indicating the two officials.

"They are my ministers. They will need to be here if I am to help you. Now, tell me what your wife looks like and how you happened to misplace her."

"The whole of Algiers knows what happened and what she looks like," Brett said impatiently. "Stick your head out the window and ask the water carrier."

"Well, perhaps I have heard *something* about her, but I will need to know more if I am to help you look for her."

"Your agents have her," Brett said accusingly. "They killed the man who took her off the ship and brought her here. She is in the palace this very minute."

"As I have said," the dey repeated, his calm unruffled, his smile immobile, "the palace contains many people not known to me personally. I will have a search begun and I will inform you immediately of the results. However, I can not encourage you to hope she is hidden within these walls. My agents do not spend all their time working for me. If, as you say, they have bought her from this man . . ."

"Took her," Brett corrected him. "They killed him."

". . . it is possible they have other plans for

her." He indicated that the interview was over. "I will make the promised inquiries . . ."

"I said I mean to have her, and by God I'll turn this palace inside out if I have to, but I *will* have her."

"And how do you propose to do that?" the dey inquired. "I admit you have surprised my guards once and managed to force your way in here, but you cannot expect to use the same ruse again. Besides, anyone trying to get into the harem will be killed."

"I will return, and I will not be alone."

"Ah, yes. Your consul, Wiggins."

"No. El-Kader!" The dey's body stiffened, but his expression remained one of tolerant amusement.

"And what have you to do with that desert rat?"

"He wants to get rid of you, and he doesn't care if he kills you or the French depose you. He's promised to bring his troops into Algiers if you don't hand over my wife."

"And what could you offer el-Kader to commit him to such a foolish course of action?"

"Guns," Brett replied bluntly. "I'm an extremely wealthy man. I can't give him an army, but I can supply him with enough guns to drive you into the sea." The dey's expression didn't change, but it didn't have to. The faces of his ministers were a parody of shock and fear, and Brett knew he had hit home.

"I would hate to see you put to such expense," the dey said smoothly, but his color was pasty. "As I promised, I will have a search made of my household to see if your wife is truly here. The minute I find her, if I *do* find her, you will be notified."

346

"I want to search myself. I do not trust you," Brett said, hoping to put still more pressure on the dey.

"My dear man," the dey said, his smile distinctly forced, "I cannot allow anyone in my harem. *No one,* not even my most trusted ministers, could venture in there and come out alive."

"Then how will I know you are not hiding her?"

"I have many wives and concubines of my own," the dey stated with cold pride, "and I can have more any time I wish. I do not need to put up with el-Kader's hordes rampaging about Algiers just to add a white-haired Englishwoman to my harem."

"Then you *have* seen my wife."

"No, but I know of her," the dey said irritably. "Everyone who has seen her talks of nothing else."

"Then you will find her?"

"I will *look.* If she is here, she will be found."

"I will come back tomorrow," Brett said.

"As you will. Now leave me. I have important work to do. And please do not seek to stir up more trouble. It is all too easy for people to disappear forever during a raid of the kind el Kader favors. It would be distressing if your wife were to be one of the misplaced persons."

"If anything happens to Kate, you won't live to see your wives ever again," Brett swore. The dey was confident that Brett would never surprise his guards again, but he came to the conclusion it might not be a bad idea to increase the guard.

"He swallowed the bait," Brett said to Ibrahin and Wiggins as soon as he returned to the consulate. "His spies will have told him I've been with el-Kader and he's moving his men closer to Algiers."

"Your plan has worked well," Ibrahin said, complimenting him. "What is it you have in mind to do next?"

"I told him I was coming back tomorrow. When I do, I want you, Charles, and Wiggins to go with me."

"Wiggins, yes, me possibly, but why your servant?"

"You and Charles will be disguised as my wife's attendants. Someone must make sure she gets out of the harem and that no guards come back with her." Ibrahin didn't look entirely pleased. "Wouldn't you like to see the inside of the dey's harem?" Ibrahin's eyes shone with amusement.

"Yes," Ibrahin said. "I think I would enjoy to go with you."

"Now all you have to do is make sure your part of the plans works."

"Do not worry. It will. I think I would not like to miss this."

Kate was despondent. Even though Anis al-Jalis was almost friendly now, and Nuzhat al-Zaman and the other wives had ceased to frown so fiercely, she still felt lonely and threatened. She had heard nothing of Brett, and the dey refused to even talk about him anymore. By now she was certain he would not let her go. He hadn't said so, but she could see it in his eyes. They became more possessive each time she visited his apartments. Even while she slept, she could almost feel his eyes on her, boring through her clothes to the soft skin underneath. It made her feel uncomfortable; it also made her feel unsafe. She had seen enough of the dey to suspect that no kind of duplicity was beyond him. She wouldn't put it past him to deny any knowledge of her, to say she had been killed, that the pirate ship had gone down at sea with all hands, *anything* to achieve his own ends.

Kate thought desperately of escape. Even though she knew anything could happen to her on the outside — she could even be captured again! — she couldn't remain here. Somehow, she had to convince Olema to get a message to Brett. Once he knew she was in the dey's palace, Kate didn't believe he would wait even one hour before he would try to secure her release. She *knew* he would come after her; the problem was to find a way to let him know where she was being held. Olema's entrance interrupted her thoughts.

"Anis al-Jalis would like for you to join her in the garden," Olema announced.

"I've got to talk to you first."

"You must go to the garden at once. You can't keep one of the royal wives waiting."

"But I must talk to you about getting a message to my husband."

"Don't. Even the walls have ears here. Never speak to me of escape or sending messages. Even if I just listen to you, it could mean my death." Olema turned to leave, and Kate had no alternative but to follow her.

Anis al-Jalis sat in one of several small courtyards within the extensive gardens that surrounded her house. "I love sitting here in the spring when the bulbs are in bloom," she said of the tulips that bloomed in profusion around the tiny courtyard. "You should have seen it earlier when the crocus and cyclamen were in bloom. It was really lovely."

"I'm certain it was," Kate said, too disheartened

by Olema's outright refusal to even consider helping her to be interested in flowers of any kind. "They are beautiful in England, too, especially the daffodils."

"Let me show you my favorite tulips," Anis said, rising. "I just got them last year." The two of them walked over to a corner where dozens of pink tulips with lacy edges bloomed against the wall of Anis's house. "They even have a nice fragrance," Anis said, kneeling to smell the delicate flowers. Kate knelt also, but she could detect no scent from the flowers.

"Do not move or make a sound," Anis said in an urgent undervoice. "I have something of importance to tell you, but we must whisper. I have received a message from outside the palace that your husband knows where you are and will come to take you away soon. Shh" Anis hissed imperatively. "You must not move, or we shall all be discovered and die."

Kate's first impulse when she heard the news was to shout with joy, and only Anis's urgent command kept her from leaping to her feet. Her heart beat so ecstatically she could hardly think. Brett knew where she was! Brett was coming! She no longer had to shiver before the dey's cold eyes, have nightmares about his embraces. Soon she would be in Brett's arms, and Kate swore that once there she would never leave them again.

"My servants will make sure no one comes close enough to hear us, but keep moving and do not talk unless we are kneeling. The eunuchs can read your lips." The women moved to another spot in the garden and knelt again. "I do not know when he will come, but you are to be called for by your ladies." Kate looked sharply at Anis, but did not speak. "As soon as they come

350

for you, we are to make a disturbance in the harem, one such that all the guards will be drawn away from the dey." They moved to another group of flowers.

"How did you hear of this?" Kate asked as she inhaled the heavy fragrance of a spray of deep yellow flowers. "How can you be certain this is not a trick?"

"I have relatives in Algiers who depend upon my generosity. They would not lie to me for fear it would stop. Shh! Here comes one of the guards." The women continued to move from one clump of flowers to another, alternately sniffing their fragrance and talking about their beauty.

"The dey wants to see you in his apartments at once," the huge black man said to Kate. "I am to take you now."

"I need to go back to my chamber. I can't go to the dey dressed like this." She glanced helplessly at Anis, but she shook her head indicating that she didn't know what the summons could be about.

"The dey said you were not to wait for anything. I am to bring you at once."

It was not a long walk from the harem to the dey's apartments, but Kate felt it was every bit as far as it was to England. She was plagued by worry every step of the way that something had happened to Brett or that somehow his plan had been discovered. She hoped her face did not show how frightened she was, but she was certain the dey would know something was afoot.

"Come in," the dey said, inviting her to make herself comfortable. Kate, settling herself on a cushion as far away from him as she dared, felt as though metal bands were tightening around her chest, making it impossible for her to breathe.

"It seems your husband is ready to bargain for you, and I thought you might help me decide just how far he would be willing to go for you." Kate's muscles relaxed and she took a deep, slow breath. Brett was all right and the dey did not know of their plan. She was worried about what he had in mind, but for the moment that was enough. She would deal with everything else as it came.

"I'm sure he knows what you want of him," Kate said, trying hard to keep her voice steady. "You might wait for him to make an offer. Then you will know how much room you have to bargain."

"That is an excellent suggestion," the dey said, his hard eyes watching Kate more keenly, his wintry gaze as repellent as ever. "In fact, it is such an excellent suggestion, I begin to wonder if there may not be something behind it I do not see."

"But there isn't," Kate insisted, alarmed. "I haven't been married very long and I know almost nothing about his mission, so I don't know what he will do. I really don't." Kate could tell from the dey's expression that he did not believe her. She redoubled her effort to convince him.

"I don't care about el-Kader or the French or Algeria, I just want to go home. But I know if you push him too far, he won't budge and then something awful will happen. He has a terrible temper and he's likely to do the most unsuspected things."

"I know."

"What do you mean, *you know?*"

"I should have listened to you in the beginning."

"Why? What happened?"

"He has already gone to el-Kader and talked

him into threatening to bring his troops stamped-
ing into Algiers. Then he had the impudence to
break into my palace to tell me about it."

"Brett was here? Why didn't you tell me? Why
didn't you let me see him?"

"I must admit he caught me by surprise, and I
was not prepared to deal with him. He is to return soon, and now that I have talked with you, I
feel we may be able to deal better together. He
must give me certain assurances, but I am anxious for an agreement. It is not just you and
your husband who will suffer if we fail to come
to an agreement."

"And if you don't get them?" Kate's knees felt
weak.

"I would prefer not to think of that just now.
For the moment you may rejoice that your husband has come to seek your release and that I
feel I know him well enough to hope we can
reach an agreement that will satisfy us both."

"When will he come?"

"I really cannot say."

"Will it be soon?"

"I think within the next few days." Kate tried
to hide her disappointment. "I will let you know
when he arrives. I imagine he will be unwilling to
make any promises until he can see for himself
you are unharmed."

Chapter 24

Kate returned to the harem, her thoughts in a muddle. Brett was coming for her, and the dey had promised to let her see him. It was wonderful news, yet she felt unaccountably ill at ease. Why? If there was something wrong, she couldn't put her finger on it. She didn't trust the dey, but she was also certain Brett would never leave the palace without learning whether she was alive and within its walls. Once he knew where to find her, she was sure he wouldn't leave without her.

Then why was she so uneasy? Could it be the message Anis had received? What did that have to do with Brett's coming for her? Surely it was not from Brett. Wiggins couldn't know Anis's relatives and Brett certainly wouldn't.

Her eyes swept over the hundred or so women in the room. She had no friends among the concubines, no one she could trust, but if there was to be an uproar loud enough to draw all the guards away from their posts, then they would have to be part of it. In fact, because of their numbers, they would have to take the largest part in the disturbance. Kate paused by a fountain, trailing her fingers through the cool water, and studied the women as unobtrusively as possible.

All of them appeared to be quite young, many of them even younger than Kate, and all were attractive in some way. A few had classical beauty, but most had flaws of face, figure, and probably personality, but there was something about each of them, if nothing more than animal magnetism, that drew the eye. Kate had seen some dance while others sang or played instruments. They were all trained in the ways of love, costumed to arouse the senses, and taught to move and speak with sensual grace. Yet now, with no one but women of their own age for company, they were acting much like young women acted anywhere, all talking at once, laughing in high-pitched squeals, and moving about the room with boundless energy. How different from the manner they would assume if called to visit the dey.

What did any of these women care about Kate? Why should they risk their positions in the harem, possibly their lives, for a stranger? Surely there would be more additions to the harem in the coming months and at least one of them would be certain to have blond hair. She found it very difficult to understand, even after Olema and Anis had both explained it to her very carefully, why these girls were happy to be in the dey's harem, how for them it was the pinnacle of achievement. They understood their position and they accepted the addition of new girls as naturally as they accepted the fact that they would be called to the dey no more than two or three times a year unless they were lucky enough to become one of his favorites. Most of them would never visit him at all, and only two or three of them would be elevated to the status of wife.

Anis and Nuzhat, on the other hand, did have a position to protect, but again, they had so much more to lose than gain by helping Kate. Nuzhat was the mother of the heir and thus one of the most powerful women in the harem. Even though she was too old to be called to the dey's bed—she seemed to have accepted being replaced by Anis without any of the anger she leveled at Kate—she would always have a close relationship with the dey, and one day she would be the mother of the ruler. Why should it matter to her whether the dey's bed was occupied more often by Anis or Kate?

Anis had nothing to fear from Kate but pride of position. She was just as lovely as Kate and could expect to remain the dey's favorite, or at least one of his favorites, for a long while yet. Could she fear that if Kate took over her position, she would never conceive a child and would lose her standing in the harem as well as in the dey's affections? Kate saw Olema approaching and decided to abandon her thoughts for the present. She would seek out Anis as soon as she could and try to learn more from her, but for now she could find no answers to her questions.

"Neither of you is to utter a sound or do anything to draw attention to yourselves until we have Kate safely outside the palace. He's going to be suspicious enough about my wife having a female servant as tall as Charles." Brett was explaining his plans for the evening to Wiggins, Ibrahin, and Charles. "Wiggins, I'm depending on you to help me keep the dey's attention off Ibrahin and Charles. I'll be as argumentative as I can. I want you to support my demands and at the same time position yourself between them and the dey. The less he sees of them the less suspicious he's going to be."

"How do you propose to get us into the harem?" Ibrahin asked. "As anxious as I am to restore your wife to you, I also want to see how the dey's women compare to my father's."

"The problem that concerns me the most is getting Kate out," Brett stated impatiently. "I'll refuse to even begin talking about a compromise until I can see for myself she's all right."

"Do you think the dey will agree?"

"I am sure he will expect Mr. Westbrook to demand some confirmation of his wife's well-being," Wiggins said. "What better proof can he offer than Mrs. Westbrook herself?"

"I'm still worried," Brett continued. "I don't think he means to let me take Kate away with us. I suspect he's going to want me to leave before he releases her, have her sent to England after me, or something like that. Whatever he does, I imagine he's going to want to keep us apart. The more distance he can keep between us, the less likely I am to do anything to thwart him. It's crucial that we keep his attention off you two, that you do nothing to make him suspicious. Everything must happen too quickly for him to be able to figure it out."

Brett was referring to Charles and Ibrahin, each dressed in a long robe that covered everything from their necks to the tips of their sandals. Each also had a headdress equipped with a veil that covered their face leaving only their eyes exposed. Ibrahin's short stature made it comparatively easy to disguise him; his muscular development could be disguised as plumpness, but it was his extraordinary eyes which made him convincing as a female. If the dey *did* become curious about Kate's two servants, Brett hoped it would be Ibrahin's eyes rather than Charles's height that attracted his attention. Charles was short for a man, but he made a tall woman and only his thinness made it possible for him to pass as a female.

"If everything goes according to plan, the only guards we'll have to overpower will be the dey's personal bodyguard," Brett explained.

"They are especially chosen for their strength and loyalty," Wiggins pointed out.

"Nevertheless, if we can't get them out of the room, we must overpower them. And it has to be done before the dey can escape or call for help. The disturbance in the harem will only hold them for a short time and it won't pull all the guards away from the palace. If we don't succeed, you will have to escape with Kate from the harem itself."

"It cannot be done," Ibrahin stated emphatically, "not unless you plan to have el-Kader and his horde pounding on the front door."

"I've convinced el-Kader it's in his best interest to withdraw from Algiers and let the dey make his own mistakes. He's convinced the dey will provoke the French into attacking and that he'll then be able to take over the city."

"The dey does not know this?"

"Not from me, and el-Kader wants him to think he still has his support so he will go on harassing the French into bringing in their army."

"You managed things well," Ibrahin stated in admiration. "You should have come earlier, without your wife, and we could have arranged the whole matter between us."

"I doubt my government would have approved such a collaboration," Wiggins demurred. "If they don't want the French to take over Algeria, I doubt they would see Egypt as an acceptable substitute."

"Not take over," Ibrahin said, much in the manner of a French aristocrat refusing an inferior wine. "It is much too expensive to conquer a country. It takes guns and men and camels, and the peasants are the ones who lose the most. It is better to *influence* them. You have much the same results and it costs very little money."

"Your tactics may be the envy of the diplomatic

world, but they have nothing to do with this situation," Brett stated brusquely.

"They are brilliant, but I will listen to you," Ibrahin said. "For an Englishman, especially one who is in love with his wife, you do quite well. I applaud you."

"Save your congratulations until we're out of this mess with a whole skin," Brett retorted irritably. "There are so many things that can go wrong."

"There is always much that can go wrong. That is why it is necessary to have men of brains and courage. You are one, so am I, and I have discovered that, though he looks like a sleepy camel, your Mr. Wiggins is a very clever man also."

"Good. We'll need every bit of cleverness we can muster before this evening is out."

"I am eager to see this wife for whom you are ready to tackle all of Algiers. I would bring her out by myself if necessary. And let me tell you, there is no woman in Egypt for whom I would do such a thing."

"There is no woman in the-world like Kate," Brett said. He thought of what failure tonight would mean to her, and his heart nearly stopped beating. Was he doing the best thing in trying to steal her from the dey rather than accept his terms and hope he would return her as he promised? That was the very issue Brett had wrestled with ever since he learned Kate was in the dey's palace. If she had still been with the pirate or a slave seller, he would happily have killed the pirate or paid the ransom, but the dey was another matter entirely and Brett did not trust him. He was thankful he had decided to break into the palace. It had given him a chance to measure the dey before the confrontation, given him time to weigh his tactics against the mettle of the protagonist he faced.

It hadn't taken long to convince Brett that if he didn't rescue Kate himself, he would never see her again. Whatever the risk, he was certain the dey would not give her up for anything short of an invasion by el-Kader's plunder-hungry troops.

Brett had never been one to be assailed by self-doubt, but he had been forced to wait for a long time and he had had time to question every part of his strategy over and over. Yet, every time he went over his reasoning, or his scheme, he came up with the same decision. This was the only way. It had to work.

Kate was invited to dine with Anis, and she followed the footsteps of Anis's servant as she guided Kate through the multitude of courts, gardens, and colonnaded walkways to Anis's quarters. She couldn't help but notice the loveliness of the grounds as she followed the servant from the building where the concubines were kept to the part of the compound reserved for the dey's wives. The gardens of the harem were extensive and meticulously maintained—care of them was one of the few activities the women were allowed to participate in—and each woman who was given a space of her own tried to outdo the other. Under any other circumstances Kate would have been overwhelmed by its beauty and hesitant to rush away without enjoying it to the fullest, but now it represented an artificial world, a world of idle wealth and useless captivity in the midst of grinding poverty, and she could hardly wait to escape. Even more important to her, it represented the bars of a gilded cage that kept her from the arms of the man she loved.

Kate could remember complaining bitterly that

she was in prison when Martin confined her to the castle, but at Ryehill there was always the possibility of escape, and there were limitless opportunities once she was outside. Now she realized how deceptive a real prison could be. It was impossible to escape from the harem, no one ever had, but even if they could reach the outside, escape would only mean poverty, similar incarceration in the home of another and less wealthy man, or certain death if the agents of the dey ever found them. More important, these beautiful women, precious flowers of the eastern world, were imprisoned more securely than she had ever been because they had imprisoned themselves.

For the first time, Anis greeted Kate with a friendly smile. "Come inside. We will dine at once. The food is already laid out so we can serve ourselves. My servants are loyal, but it is better that no one hears our words. Everyone can be made to talk if the pain is great enough." Kate was led to a large room in the middle of the house with no windows and only two doors.

"Do you have more to tell me?"

"Eat," Anis said. "It is best that we do not talk now." Kate wasn't hungry even though it was clear Anis, or one of her servants, had taken the trouble to talk to Olema and discover the foods she liked. They ate and talked of their lives before they came to Algeria until an old female servant entered through the second door, whispered something to Anis in a language Kate didn't recognize, and departed once again.

"It is arranged," Anis said abruptly. "I did not want to speak of it again until everyone had agreed to do their part."

"What is arranged, and who has arranged it?" Kate asked. "I know it's not my husband. How do

I know it's not a trick to catch us both?"

"I told you I had relatives in Algiers," Anis began. "That is true but is misleading. I do not come from Africa, but from a very poor country to the west of Constantinople. Many people leave to seek a better life elsewhere, and long ago a cousin of my father went to Egypt. He was an ambitious man who dared to test the might of the great sultan himself, and today he is governor of Egypt. His son is in Algiers. It is from him that I received the message and am told what to do."

"But why should they want to help us?" Kate asked, more confused than ever. "I don't even know anyone from Egypt."

"I do not know, but Ibrahin would do nothing that would harm the position of dey, and along with him, myself. At the same time, Ibrahin will do nothing that does not further his own interests, so it must be that he and your husband want the same thing."

"How can I be sure?"

"Ibrahin would not go to all this trouble for nothing," Anis answered a little impatiently. "It can be too dangerous for everyone if things go wrong."

"But why should you take such a risk? And everyone else? You could all die."

"We would not die," Anis said, but she refused to meet Kate's eyes.

"There is another reason, isn't there?"

Anis nodded.

"Please tell me."

"There is a story told to every little girl," Anis began reluctantly, "of a woman with white hair who came to the harem of the great sultan many generations ago. She was exceedingly beautiful, just as you are, and the sultan became so bewitched he vowed he would do anything to please her. She was very jealous, very wicked, and she forced the sultan to exile his wives and strangle all his concubines so that she would be the only one left. Everyone in the harem knows how the dey looks at you, how he has not been pleased with anyone sent to his bed since you arrived, and they fear it will happen again."

"But you can't think I would do anything like that, even if I wanted to stay." Kate was stunned to find Anis's eyes offered no friendliness.

"Maybe I do not believe you would do such a thing, but it is still best that you go."

Kate wasn't entirely convinced Anis was telling the truth, but there didn't seem to be any point in trying to change her mind. For whatever reason, some kind of plan had been set in motion and she was being forced to go along with it.

"You must be ready to leave the palace the minute the dey sends for you," Anis continued. "You must have a veil with you at all times. There can be no waiting. The timing must be exact."

"I have no preparations to make. I can leave at any moment," Kate said.

The excruciatingly slow plop-plop of Wiggins's tread was like acid on Brett's nerves; he wanted to pick Wiggins up and hurl him forward through the dark and opulent halls they traversed on their way to the apartment of the dey. He wanted to walk quickly, to burst through every door, to run until his breath rasped painfully in his chest, because each step brought him closer to Kate. But Charles and Ibrahin couldn't walk any faster. Ibrahin had conceived the clever notion of outfitting them with peasant's clogs and they minced along like the daintiest of women.

The guards were different from those of his previous visit—he wondered if the others had been put to death for their failure to protect the dey—yet there was no difficulty in gaining entrance to the palace. Evidently everyone knew Wiggins and didn't suspect him of being dangerous. Every guard they passed looked at him with curiosity, but evidently he was expected and they allowed him to enter.

The dey was without his ministers when they entered his audience chamber. Two large Nubians stood guard inside his door and two more without. *I've got to eliminate at least two of them if we are going to have any chance at all,* Brett thought as he eyed the tall, heavily muscled men. *With the dey on their side, they outnumber us and they have better weapons.*

"You don't trust me very much, do you?" Brett said, with just enough mockery in his voice to prick the dey's pride. "I'm flattered you think me dangerous enough to warrant four of your best guards. There was only one before."

"Two of them are from the harem. However, after your previous visit, I did think it wise to employ an extra one today. Won't you be seated." His eyes moved to Charles and Ibrahin, but he made no comment. Brett and Wiggins settled down on cushions, and Charles and Ibrahin arranged themselves so that Brett and Wiggins blocked the dey's view of them.

"You will be pleased to learn that my agents have found your wife and that she is at this very moment resting within the harem."

"I want to see her," Brett said, starting up impetuously.

"All in good time," the dey replied in a conciliatory voice. "We have certain things to discuss first."

"I won't discuss anything until I've seen my wife," Brett announced. "I've got to know she's all right, that your men haven't mistreated her."

"We only mistreat our enemies," the dey replied haughtily, "and we do not make war on women."

"Nevertheless, I won't enter into any agreements or even discuss terms until she's in my arms and can assure me with her own voice you haven't mistreated her. If anybody has harmed her, I'll personally break their neck."

"I think it would be wise to allow him to see his wife," Wiggins suggested diplomatically. "He will undoubtedly be able to listen to your offer more favorably if his worries are removed. It is also possible the presence of his wife might influence him to see your position more readily." The dey pondered Wiggins's suggestion a moment.

"I forget that you English take only one wife. I have often wondered why Europeans attach such importance to a mere woman. However, we are not here to discuss Europe or its customs, only to establish an agreement between ourselves. I will send for her."

"She will need her women." Ibrahin and Charles got to their feet.

"I see you have a native servant?" the dey observed. "The one with the beautiful almond eyes."

"Neither my wife nor her maid knows anything of the language or customs of Algeria. It was necessary to provide her with a servant who could act as an intermediary, especially as I had to leave them and go into the desert," Brett added, his meaning obvious.

"I do not think it will be necessary to do that again."

"I'll have to wait to find out," Brett replied.

"The other woman is quite tall," the dey remarked, changing the subject. "Were you anticipating trouble, or can you not protect your own wife?"

Brett ignored the slur. "The woman is a Scot. They make excellent servants, but they grow too big sometimes. I'll keep her here if you're afraid she might overpower your guards."

"I have no such worry," the dey responded angrily. "One of my guards could handle a dozen such women." He rapped out an order in Arabic and the two Nubians summoned the guards outside the door.

"Tell your women to take their time. I want them to make sure your wife is properly prepared to receive her husband. We have many things to discuss before their return."

Brett breathed an inward sigh of relief. He had accomplished the first and most crucial part of the plan, getting Kate out of the harem and the guards away from the door. Now if Ibrahin's people could draw the others away, even if it were only for a few minutes, and Ibrahin and Charles could eliminate the two guards before they returned, they would be able to bring it off.

"Now to business," the dey said.

"I want my wife to leave the palace with me," Brett announced.

"I think we should talk about el-Kader before we make any arrangements for your wife's departure," the dey objected. "After all, that is why we are here. Otherwise, I could just have sent your wife to the British consulate the moment she was found."

"That would have been the best thing to do," Wiggins said, intervening. "My government would have thought well of you."

"But I'm not interested in what your government thinks of me," the dey replied. "I am only interested in my position."

"Then you'd be well advised to listen to my government," Brett said sharply, "before your miscalculations cost you your throne."

The dey's eyes hardened. "I do not need the eyes of an Englishman to see what happens in my country," he stated curtly. "I would rather seek the advice of my wives."

"They couldn't do any worse than you have," Brett said, speaking before Wiggins could offer a more temperate reply. "You insulted the French ambassador and taunted their government. That was the action of a fool."

"It is never wise to offend one stronger than you," Wiggins explained.

"Your next mistake was to think the French weren't interested in Africa. They are, and they'd like nothing better than to use your behavior as an excuse to bring an army in here. Your third miscalculation was to think you could use a victory over the French to gain ascendancy over the rest of the North African countries. You won't get a victory, and not one of the rulers, from Mohammed Ali to the Sultan of Morocco, wants to have you as an overlord instead of Turkey."

"You think the sultan and el-Kader will help you, but the sultan is too weak and too interested in his harem, and el-Kader is only interested in taking your throne for himself," Wiggins explained. "There is still time to apologize to the French and defuse the incident."

The dey's olive skin had turned nearly white with rage, but he curbed his fury and replied in a low voice, "And how do the desires of your government contribute toward my well-being?"

"We do not want the French in Africa," Wiggins replied. "They have a regrettable tendency to want to settle in for a long stay, and they tend to make rather a mess of things. Too, whenever they overcome a foe, regardless of how small or ineffectual"—the dey swelled with fury at the aspersion against his country—"they start thinking all over again they ought to be the rulers of Europe as well. Convincing them otherwise has been a tiresome necessity for England off and on for some five or six hundred years. So much better for everyone if we could destroy their delusions before they flower."

"I have convinced el-Kader it's better for both of you if he takes his troops and retires to Mascara," Brett added. "That way he's no threat to you."

"But suppose I *want* his support?'

"As long as it is not against the French, we have no objection. We would prefer you remain on your throne."

"You have no idea how grateful I am to you and your country."

"We know exactly how you feel," Brett said with brutal frankness, "but you should be thankful to us. We saved your neck."

"And you expect me to hand over your wife, along with my most profound thanks, for this?" he demanded angrily.

"You said you didn't want el-Kader's troops in Algiers. I even got him to move them farther away."

"I did not want you to *interfere* at all," the dey rasped. "I do not want you making plans for my country." The faint sound of raised voices could be heard in the distance, but it was too soft and too indistinct for Brett to know whether it was coming from the harem or elsewhere in the city.

"Give me my wife, and I promise never to set foot in Algeria again."

"I shall send her to you, but not now," the dey replied. "I do not trust you not to turn around and talk el-Kader into changing his mind. I will not send her to you until you are on a ship headed for your country."

"And I don't trust you, either. I won't leave this palace without her." Though the disturbance was growing louder, it did not seem to have attracted the attention of the dey.

"Maybe we can look at this a little more calmly," Wiggins intervened. "It is possible I may be able to offer some assurances that would allow one or the other of you to moderate your position."

"I do not see any reason to alter my stance," the dey stated unyieldingly. "Mr. Westbrook has come to my country and interfered in my affairs. It is therefore necessary for him, *not myself,* to demonstrate his good intentions by making the first move to conciliate."

"I have already done that by—" The door burst open and Kate catapulted into the room.

"Brett!" she cried, and covering the distance between them, she threw herself into his arms, laughing with tears running down her face. Brett had barely made it to his feet before Kate's body struck him full force, but he enfolded her in his arms, kissing her feverishly.

For the moment the dey and their precarious plan of escape were forgotten, and he gloried in the feel of her warm, supple body in his arms. For nearly a week he had gone to bed each night dreaming of her, feeling as though he could reach out and touch her, teased and tantalized by the memory of nights when they lost themselves in each other only to emerge at dawn more deeply in love than before. Heretofore he had never been denied anything he wanted, and knowing she was beyond his reach was agony to his soul as well as his pride. It had taken all his restraint to keep to the plans he and Ibrahin had worked out. Now, with the sounds of the growing disturbance in his ears, it was necessary to restrain himself one last time from doing the one thing he most wanted to do.

"Are you all right?" he asked, holding Kate at arm's length so he could look at her. "Did they treat you well?"

"Everything has been wonderful since they took me from the pirates. I've been here so long I have become friends with half the women in the harem."

Brett threw the dey a menacing look, but he merely shrugged.

"I even had my own room and servants to wait on me."

There was a sudden surge in the noise that made it clear the disturbance was coming from within the palace. The dey looked to the door for the two guards who had escorted Charles and Ibrahin to the harem, but they had not returned with Kate.

"Kamil, what is this disturbance?"

The guard spoken to stepped out into the passage. "It comes from the harem, my lord."

The dey's eyes cut to Kate. "What do you know of this?" he demanded suspiciously.

"Nothing. There was no one about when I left. In fact, now that you mention it, I haven't seen the women for quite some time."

"Where are the guards who accompanied your servants?"

"They left us when they heard the first scream."

"What scream? Why did you not tell me of this?"

"I couldn't think of anything but reaching my husband. I probably wouldn't have noticed if they'd all screamed at once." Right then it seemed that they did.

"Kamil," the dey ordered, "summon the guards and find out what is happening. If this is el-Kader's doing," he said, returning his furious gaze to Brett, "neither of you will leave this palace alive."

In a few seconds of inattention, the dey had allowed himself to approach within arm's length of Brett. At the very second when Kamil left and the second guard was occupied with closing the door behind him, Brett leaped upon the dey, forced one arm behind him, and pointed a dagger at his throat. In the same instant, Ibrahin threw up his robe and struck the Nubian a near-crippling blow from behind without ever lifting the veil from his face.

The dey didn't struggle or even seem surprised at the sudden turn of events, but his eyes were ablaze with rage. "You have some remarkably accomplished women in your service," he remarked with admirable fortitude. "What do you mean to do with me now?"

"Merely invite you to dinner at the consulate," Wiggins answered while helping Kate cover her face with her veil. "We have a lot to talk about."

"Do you really expect to escape from the palace alive?"

"If we don't, you won't, either," Brett answered.

Chapter 25

"There are still many guards."

"Then you'll have to tell them to let us pass," Brett said, forcing the dey toward the door. "Your dinner grows cold, so let's hurry."

"And if I do not?"

"You have two alternatives. You can choose to lead us out of here and enjoy an excellent dinner as Wiggins's guest or we can leave your body in the streets to become dinner for the wild dogs."

"You have an extremely unpleasant way of putting things," the dey replied, but he moved toward the door without further resistance.

There were no guards outside the dey's apartments and Brett hurried him along the way they had come. Wiggins walked on the dey's other side—his steps were surprisingly quick this time—and Kate followed, flanked on either side by Charles and Ibrahin, all three with their veils securely in place.

"I assume the disturbance in my harem was no accident."

"Any man who surrounds himself with two hundred jealous women instead of one loyal wife must expect such outbreaks from time to time," Brett said with a humorless smile. "Women are not as fond of sharing their favors as men."

They entered a colonnaded courtyard and could see two guards straight ahead. Brett moved closer to the dey and increased the pressure of the knife point in his side. "Tell them what you will," he hissed in a fierce undertone, "but get us out of here without raising any suspicions."

The dey appeared to be having some difficulty keeping his temper under control, but he had no desire to embarrass himself before his own men. He also had no doubt Brett would kill him the instant a wrong word came out of his mouth.

"I have been invited to dine with the English consul," the dey stated as he paused before the guards. "See if you can help quell that disturbance." He nodded his head in the direction of the noise still coming from inside. "I do not wish to hear it when I return."

They passed three more guards, but the dey directed the attention of all of them to the noise from within and walked quietly between Brett and Wiggins until they reached the street.

"Surely this is far enough," he said when they were safely outside. "Let us make an end of this extremely foolish game."

"But I do wish to invite you to dinner," Wiggins said, pausing to allow the dey to climb into the waiting carriage before him. "There is a great deal more to the situation than we have yet had an opportunity to discuss."

It took some time and considerable jostling before all six people could squeeze into the carriage, but they were in at last and the driver hurried them on their way. The short trip was made in virtual silence.

"I want to introduce you to my wife's attendants," Brett said with a grin as they gathered in the hall of the consulate. "The tall, thin Scot is my valet, and I think you already know the one with the almond eyes." Charles disappeared immediately, but Ibrahin removed his veil and head covering.

"I should have known you were in this somehow," the dey exploded at Ibrahin, intense hatred flaming in his eyes. "I should have known the English could never penetrate my palace guard, but I did not think you would join with foreign devils to destroy one of your own brothers."

"Someday you will be pleased—obviously this is *not* the day!—that I have interfered," Ibrahin predicted, not the least annoyed by the dey's violent animosity. "Our goals may not be precisely the same, but at least we agree you should remain on your own throne."

"I do not need your help to keep what is mine," the dey snapped furiously.

"That is what you say now, but I wonder would your story be the same if you were to find yourself deposed?"

"We dine in an hour," Wiggins intervened smoothly. "Allow me to suggest that everyone retire to his room to change. I was sure you would wish to join us, Mr. Ibrahin, so I have had a room prepared. I also have a room and attendants ready to serve you," Wiggins said, turning back to the dey. "Additionally, I have caused a message to be sent to the palace requesting your guard to come for you at midnight. Until then you are my guest. You have only to ask, and my staff and I will do everything we can to see that your every wish is gratified."

The dey gave Wiggins a look almost as hate-filled as the one he directed to Ibrahin before turning to follow the servant waiting to take him to his chamber.

"You must not delay any longer," Wiggins said, turning to Brett. "I am not at all sure the message I sent will prevent the dey's personal guard from coming here as soon as they realize he is not in the palace. If you are gone, he will have nothing to gain by exposing the ruse which brought him here. Mr. Ibrahin's presence is a kind of guarantee that he will pretend this was his idea. However, your presence, and that of your wife, would probably be too much of a temptation, and he might decide that embarrassment would be a small price to pay for your capture."

"Where can we go?" Kate asked, fear of recapture doubly bitter after the brief moments of freedom.

"We're leaving Algeria tonight," Brett told her. "There's a ship waiting for us in the harbor right now. If we leave immediately, we can be on board before the dey comes down to dinner. Thank you for your help," Brett said, turning to Ibrahin. "I wasn't very nice to you at first, but I admit I might never have found my wife without your help."

"It is a pleasure to serve one of such supreme loveliness," Ibrahin said, shifting his gaze to Kate. "To have an opportunity to gaze on such beauty is not a thing which happens often in a man's lifetime. In my country, we would keep such a treasure far from the sight of other men's eyes. Her beauty would cause great jealousy."

"It has already been the source of quite enough difficulties," Wiggins observed as he herded Brett and Kate toward the door. "Be gone before you cause any more."

"Thank you both," Kate said. "Please come visit us when you're in London, Mr. Wiggins. And Mr. Ibrahin, if you ever decide to come to England, we would love for you to be our guest."

"I would be honored," Ibrahin said, "but now I feel I should add my pleas to those of Wiggins and urge you to make haste. The time is shorter than you think."

Brett and Kate ran from the building and

climbed into the waiting carriage. It started forward without waiting for a command from Brett. It was the time of evening when everyone was home eating; the streets were empty, and the carriage made the trip in only a few minutes.

They sat in silence, their arms around each other, their hearts so full neither knew how to put their feelings into words. No beginning would have been able to tell what it meant to be together again, and no conclusion could have more than hinted at the joy with which they faced the future. So they sat quietly, Kate within the circle of Brett's arms, and let the concreteness of their physical touching speak for them in those all-too-brief minutes before they reached the bay.

Brett and Kate climbed down and hurried to where Charles was already waiting with a boat to take them out to the ship.

"Which one is ours?" Kate asked, looking around at the harbor full of vessels.

"That one, the one with its sails up," Brett pointed out. "It's already moving. We're going to have to row like hell to catch it."

The four rowers dipped their oars into the water and the boat leapt forward. The breeze was coming in from the sea, and Kate turned her face full into it. A bubble of laughter escaped her and she self-consciously clamped down on it. But it would not be quieted. The bubble grew and grew until it erupted from her in a cascade of mirth.

"What are you laughing about?" Brett asked, smiling in spite of himself. "We've had a very close escape. In fact, we're not entirely clear yet, and you're laughing like it was all a game."

"How can you *not* laugh at this absurd situation?" Kate said, struggling to control her hilarity sufficiently to be able to talk. "Do you realize if I were to go about regaling people with the story of these last incredible days, there probably isn't a single person in England who would believe a word of it? I'd either be locked up for a madwoman or accused of being queer in the head and avoided by everyone except very small children and mental deficients for the rest of my life." Another peal of laughter soared into the night. "And to think I used to sit at Ryehill longing for adventure, complaining that nothing ever happened to me. After this, I'll be more than content to manage the house, look after my babies, and never set foot beyond my own front gate. And the first person to mention ships, harems, deys, or Algeria will be treated to a good bout of hysterics."

"You know you'll do nothing of the sort," Brett said, settling down next to Kate and putting his arms around her once again. "You've handled every crisis like a born vagabond. I never knew anyone who could get a grip on unfamiliar situations as fast as you. In a few weeks, I bet you'll be bored to death and straining at the bit to see what Ibrahin's country is like."

"Then I'll write and ask him to send me a painting," Kate insisted stubbornly. "I am quite serious when I say I never want to leave England again."

"Not even to go to Paris?"

"No, not even to go to Paris, especially if I have to cross the Channel in a storm. I was never so sick, or scared, in my life. You can invite Valentine to visit us, and we can go shopping in London. She complained the whole time that nothing exciting ever happened to her anymore."

"Can you imagine what people would say if they came to see us and encountered Valentine?"

Kate's expression changed to one of unholy glee. "Do you think we could? It would be a marvelous joke. I can hardly wait to see their faces."

"It's tempting, but we'd be ostracized by the ton for the rest of our lives." They were nearing the ship and suddenly Kate's mood turned serious.

"I don't know anything about the ton or London or running a big house. I don't know anything about anything. If that horrid woman on Gibraltar looked down her nose at me because of my ignorance, what will your friends do?"

"Be too stunned by your beauty to say a word."

"Be sensible," she said irritably. "Women don't react the same way as men to another woman. They're more likely to become jealous and start looking for faults."

"You'll do just fine. I've never known anyone like you for landing on their feet."

"I know I can learn eventually, but I may have made too many mistakes by then, and I do want you to be proud of me." Kate stopped, her expression one of sudden realization. "That's not true. I always meant to leave you when we got back to London. I never thought about what it would be like to be your wife."

"What do you mean, leave me?" Brett demanded.

"You didn't marry me because you wanted to, and anyway that was before you decided you loved me. I never *wanted* to leave, only I couldn't live with you, loving you as I did, and knowing all the while you didn't love me."

"You don't ever have to doubt that again," Brett assured her. "I've known you for only a short time and yet I can't imagine how I ever lived without you. It seems like you've always been part of my life." They had reached the ship and Brett and Charles helped Kate up the ropes as the men in the boat held on to the ladder so they could keep up with the moving ship. When they were on board at last, they turned back to look at the lights of Algiers against the night sky.

"You know, it would be easy, standing here like this, to believe I imagined the whole thing," Kate said. Brett wrapped his arms around her to keep her warm.

"Holding you in my arms reminds me it was all so very real," Brett whispered, and Kate snuggled deeper into his embrace.

"That's almost harder to believe. It seems like just yesterday I was sure I would die at Ryehill, still an old maid."

"It was only last week I was still thinking I would spend the rest of my life going from one woman to another, never finding real love, never thinking I even wanted to find it."

"Promise me it won't change when we get back to London?"

"What won't change?"

"Us. That we won't let people and houses and the Foreign Office and I don't know what else come between us. I felt it coming when we approached Algiers, and I'm sure it will come again when we reach London."

"Kate, nothing is going to change my love for you. It's a part of my thinking. It's the way I *am*. Nothing can alter that, but in the course of everyday life, things will get in our way. We won't ever have a time like we do now where we have nothing to do but love each other. But that's as it should be. Love is a part of life, not life itself."

"But I don't want our love to ever be any less than it is right now. I couldn't bear it if you started acting like Martin and your guests and horses and gambling came before anything else."

"I'll never be like Martin, and our love will never

be less than it is now. It will grow to become a part of everything we do. We can share every part of our lives, our children, our work, our pleasure, *especially* our pleasure," he whispered provocatively as he nibbled her ear. "And it will grow for the giving."

"Promise?"

"I promise."

Kate leaned back against Brett once again, lost in thought. Abruptly she turned and looked up at Brett. "Are you hungry?"

"I'm hungry for you."

"I'm talking about food?"

"You're the only food I need."

"That's really quite romantic, but it's an extremely silly thing to say. A few days of that diet and you'd be as weak as a woman."

"I'd still be strong enough to handle you," Brett said, sweeping Kate off her feet and heading toward their cabin.

"That's just like a man, always assuming a woman wants something just because *he* wants it."

"Don't you want to make love to me?" Brett asked, pausing uncertainly as he closed the door.

"Of course I do. But I wouldn't have taken half as long to get around to it."

Brett attacked Kate with a ferocious growl that made her giggle with delight.

"You know, you're not too bad once you get started, but I wonder if I shouldn't have stayed with the dey a little longer. Then I would have had someone to compare you to."

"You shameless hussy," Brett growled, and attacked her again. "You've been talking to Valentine too much."

"You can't pretend you've never made love to another woman. It's not fair for men to have all the fun."

"I've made love to only one woman in my whole life—you." Kate saw the changed look in Brett's eyes and swallowed her protest. "What I did with those other women has nothing to do with what I've come to know in your arms. I would never have believed it could be so different, but it was as though I, too, was making love for the first time. Before, I was only concerned with satisfying my physical needs, whereas now, all of me yearns for fulfillment. And it's you, too. It's both of us bound up in something bigger than we could ever be by ourselves. Do you remember when I said love was only a part of life?" Kate nodded. "Well, making love to you is only part of loving you. Love just *is* all the time. That's something I never knew. It's something no one but you could have taught me."

Kate buried herself in his embrace, too shaken to speak. Maybe tomorrow she could put into words some of what she had learned from him, share some of the secrets of her heart, but for now, being in his arms was all she could stand. Her heart would burst if she were given any more.

Author's Note

In 1827, the dey of Algeria slapped the French consul at Algiers in the face with a fly whisk. After the dey had ignored repeated demands for satisfaction, the French sent an expeditionary force to Algiers in 1830 and took the city after a short campaign. They deposed the dey and occupied a few of the towns, but they were unsure of their ultimate objectives in Algeria and did not immediately penetrate into the interior of the country.

Beginning in 1832, Abd el-Kader of Mascara, proclaimed dey of Algeria by the native chiefs, began a series of wars against the French which lasted until 1847 when he was finally captured and sent to France. He was released in 1852 by Napoleon III and died at Damascus in 1883. It was during these wars that France extended her control into the interior and established a government which lasted until Algeria won her independence in 1962.

Mohammed Ali, a tobacco merchant from the town of Kavalla in present-day Greece, went to Egypt in 1799 and rose to become governor of that country in 1805. His descendants through his son Ibrahin ruled Egypt until King Farouk I was deposed in 1952.

Though I have woven the story around facts and have used the actual names of three historical characters, their words, actions, descriptions, and motivations are purely the product of my imagination.